Praise f

"A roller coaster of a ride from the get-go!"

~*InD'tale Magazine*

"Cleverly plotted with strong characterization and a tantalizing sexual undercurrent. The author has worked hard to offer the reader a fantasy world to get lost in; a world of blood lust and dark, complex characters – oh, and a little wine too!"

~*A Wishing Shelf Book Review*

"*Dark Wine at the Grave* reveals an authentic emotional acuity amidst a secluded vampire community. Written with insight and brimming with mystery, each story has captivated my imagination. *Grave* is my new favorite."

~Sharon Bonin-Pratt's *Ink Flare*

Also by Jenna Barwin

The Hill Vampire Series

DARK WINE AT DAWN (BOOK 9)

DARK WINE AT HALLOWEEN (BOOK 8)

DARK WINE AT THE GRAVE (BOOK 7)

DARK WINE AT DISASTER (BOOK 6)

DARK WINE AT THE CIRCUS (BOOK 5)

DARK WINE AT DEATH (BOOK 4)

DARK WINE AT DUSK (BOOK 3)

DARK WINE AT SUNRISE (BOOK 2)

DARK WINE AT MIDNIGHT (BOOK 1)

DARK WINE AT THE GRAVE

A Hill Vampire Novel
Book 7

Jenna Barwin

Hidden Depths Publishing

Dark Wine at the Grave by Jenna Barwin
Copyright © 2022 by Jenna Barwin. All Rights Reserved

This book or any portion of it may not be reproduced in any form or by any means, or used in any manner whatsoever, without the express written permission of the publisher or author except for the use of brief quotations in a book review.

This is a work of fiction. Names, characters, businesses, public entities, products, places, events and incidents are either the products of the author's imagination or used in a fictitious manner. Any resemblance to actual persons, living or dead, businesses, public entities, locales, or actual events is purely coincidental. Any trademarks, service marks, product names, or named features are assumed to be the property of their respective owners, and are used only for reference. Opinions of the characters are not necessarily those of the author.

Printed in the United States of America
First printing & ebook edition, 2022

Hidden Depths Publishing
Dana Point, California
www.hiddendepthspublishing.com

Cover design: Covers by Christian (Christian Bentulan)
Images used under license from Shutterstock.com and Stock.adobe.com
Cover art is for illustrative purposes only and any person depicted in the cover is a model or artist's creation.

Editing team: Katrina Diaz-Arnold, Refine Editing, LLC; Trenda K. Lundin, It's Your Story Content Editing; Arran McNicol, Editing720.

Library of Congress Control Number: 2022904078

eBook ISBN 978-1-952755-07-1
Print 978-1-952755-08-8

1) Paranormal Romance 2) Urban Fantasy Romance 3) Vampire Romance 4) Vampire Mystery 5) Vampire Suspense 6) Paranormal Romantic Suspense 7) Romantic Fantasy

v1.1

JOIN JENNA'S VIP READERS

Want to know about new releases, and receive special announcements, exclusive excerpts, and other FREE fun stuff? Join Jenna's VIP Readers and receive Jenna Barwin's newsletter by subscribing online at:

https://jennabarwin.com/jenna-barwins-newsletter/

You can also find Jenna Barwin on Facebook, TikTok, Twitter, and Instagram: @JennaBarwin

Email: https://jennabarwin.com/contact

DARK WINE
AT THE
GRAVE

A character in this story struggles briefly with thoughts of suicide.
If you or anyone you know is struggling with thoughts of suicide,
please call your local suicide prevention lifeline,
or if in the United States,
the National Suicide Prevention Lifeline: 800-273-8255

Chapter 1

MAGNIFICENT

Rancho Bautista del Murciélago—Early October

Enrique Bautista Vasquez, also known as Henry Bautista, and more recently as Enrique Vasquez, leaned against the doorframe, watching his fiancée as she moved around the bedroom. Her long, wavy hair—the color of dark chocolate—was tied back in an intricate braid. He could imagine running his hands through it to unwind the strands as he pressed her onto the bed.

"I will miss you while you're gone," he said.

Cerissa looked up from the small suitcase she'd been packing, her stunning emerald eyes meeting his. "I'll miss you too, Quique, but I'll only be gone one night."

"I know."

She stuffed the last of her toiletries into the bag. "Did I tell you my itinerary? I've been so frenzied..."

The corners of his lips twitched. Even though she'd already emailed him the details, he was willing to indulge her just to have an excuse to be in the room with her. "Why don't you tell me again?"

"I leave tomorrow with Christine and Karen. We're spending the night in Los Angeles to make sure Christine arrives on time at the outpatient surgical center the next morning. It's an early procedure. Then Karen and I will wait at the hospital and drive her back to the Hill afterward."

Cerissa bounced around the room, grabbing clothes to pack, her nervous energy over the trip filtering through the crystal and flooding him with the same emotion. In one of her rushed passes, her delicious scent reached his nose—a light touch of Chanel No. 5 and her own unique, earthy musk.

His fangs responded to the enticing combination. "What time will you return?"

"Depends upon traffic." She stopped in front of him for a quick kiss without giving him an opportunity to deepen the embrace. "The surgical center expects to release Christine around four in the afternoon, so we might not arrive home until early evening. And it was kind of you to suggest she stay in the pool house while she recovers."

Before Cerissa scurried away to resume packing, he caressed her cheek, letting his fingers linger on her jaw. "It's the least we could do. Besides, Christine should become accustomed to staying there. Once she is satisfied with the results of her surgery, I can turn her."

He inhaled deeply and let out a slow breath. The idea of being a maker still struck him as strange, notwithstanding his body's strong desire to create a child.

Despite the North American treaty's prohibition on creating new vampires, the community could do so to replace those who had been killed, keeping the population stable. And the town council had chosen Christine Dunne to fill one of those open slots.

He'd agreed to be Christine's maker partly because Sierra Escondida needed another attorney—Christine had done an outstanding job for the Hill when the Mordida Water Company tried to steal the town's water—and partly because he'd been suffering from fang fever, the intense physical drive to spawn a vampire child.

He sighed. Making a child was a big decision and an even bigger responsibility, one he wasn't entirely sure he wanted, despite what the council and his body demanded. Christine's surgery and recovery period would give him time to settle into the reality of his decision and get to know her better before embarking on a lifetime commitment.

Just thinking the words *lifetime commitment* caused him to cringe.

Was he really ready to be a father?

Cerissa bit her lip as she considered the contents of her suitcase, pulling his attention back to her. The trip she packed for would benefit his future child. At close to sixty years old, Christine had decided to freshen up her body before becoming a vampire. For the rest of her immortal life, she would look the way she did on the day she died. So she decided to undergo a mini-facelift and liposuction first.

Henry understood. She wanted to be at her best before the turn. The lawyer exercised regularly, keeping her underlying muscle structure toned. Nothing could be done about her graying hair, but she'd told him she liked her hair color, which got her the respect she deserved after long years practicing the law.

Except her long years as an attorney wouldn't matter in Sierra Escondida. She would go to the bottom rung of the seniority ladder once turned. In the Hill's vampire hierarchy, age and experience when turned didn't accord her any greater rank. A fledgling was a fledgling and had no status in the community.

But as she aged as a vampire, she'd learn the trick of changing her appearance. He could make himself look older; she'd have to master the reverse, transforming herself to look younger. While drinking extra mortal blood energized the change, the process required more power than a fledgling had.

He had restrained himself from bombarding Christine with all these details. She'd find out soon enough when he began her training prior to the turn.

Cerissa paused in her packing and looked over at him, one eyebrow raised. His mixed emotions must have slipped through the crystal. He gave a slight bow in her direction. "I am not sure I'm ready to be a maker."

"Quit worrying. You'll be a great parent."

Arguing the point wouldn't persuade her. When it came to his abilities, his lovely mate sometimes wore blinders.

So he changed the topic. "Even though it's for a good cause, I do not like the thought of you being gone."

"Oh pooh." She wrinkled her nose at him. "It's only for one night."

Cerissa folded her jeans into precise thirds, followed by the perfect rectangle she made of her shirt before folding the fabric in half. Funny, considering she frequently accused him of being a neat freak. And yet watching her pack made him conclude the same moniker applied to her.

He didn't often have the opportunity to watch her at work, and her hands drew his focus now. Graceful and efficient, her fingers were neither too long nor too short, but the perfect length for her body. Her engagement ring adorned her left hand and shone magnificently, a beacon to everyone, telling them her heart belonged to him, and only him.

"You and Rolf probably have plans to play video games all night," Cerissa said with a smirk. "That or some equally frivolous pastime."

"A poker game at his house is planned. After all, since we began dating, this is the first time both you and Karen will be gone at the same time."

"I'm happy to learn you're making productive use of your free time. Try not to lose too much money."

He flinched inside. Money remained a touchy subject for him. After the damage the earthquake caused to the winery he and Rolf owned, his cash flow had been tight. In response to her teasing, he moved quickly, pulling her into his arms. "No lip from you, woman."

She snorted a laugh. "Nice impression of Rolf."

"But Rolf cannot do this." He slanted his lips over hers, taking full advantage when hers parted on a moan.

But he couldn't contain her energy for long. With a twist, she escaped from his arms.

"You are feeling high-spirited tonight," he said as she slipped away and opened a drawer in the dresser. "Did you accomplish a breakthrough in the lab?"

"Not yet." She moved back to the four-poster bed, adding a few underthings to the bag. "I'm still trying to figure out why Rolf needs adrenaline-enhanced blood, although his moods seem to have stabilized now that he has a regular supply. And I still have more tests to run on the modified vampire genome."

Using tissue saved from the vampire prototype the Lux had created millennia ago, Cerissa had performed gene surgery, altered the original genome to withstand daylight. An amazing development, but Henry wasn't volunteering for any experimentation. She'd explained the risks attendant to gene surgery—including the possibility of death or deformity. Going out in the sun wasn't important enough to him to gamble his life on with a perilous procedure. He was more than happy to allow someone else to eventually play the guinea pig.

She and her cousin, Ari, were also experimenting with an integrated circuit microprocessor, which they referred to as a crystal. In theory, this new crystal would be worn on a metal wristband and bend daylight away from the wearer. So far, the prototypes had failed, but they now had a team of Lux engineers working on the design. Agathe, the head of the Alatus Lux, had authorized the project, although if Henry understood correctly, Agathe had labeled the research "top secret." No one outside of Cerissa and Ari's team could be told about it except for himself. Cerissa had already explained it to Henry before Agathe made the rule, so he remained the only outsider in the know.

Cerissa folded the suitcase closed and zipped the heavy nylon fabric shut. "I'm glad things have calmed down. No stress for a while would be nice."

He wholeheartedly agreed. With the water rights trial behind them, the harvest had gone well, taking another worry off his shoulders.

They had employed a combination of mechanical harvesters and vampire pickers in the end. He felt sorry for the mortal men and women they usually hired to pick the crops. They lost work because of the mechanical harvesters, but Vasquez Müller Winery had no choice this season. As it turned out, a general shortage of workers at the time meant the solution he devised not only saved the winery money—it saved the harvest.

He and Rolf had gleaned their own fields over the course of a few nights, *whooshing* through the rows on foot, filling giant baskets. The larger fields further up the valley made use of the machines. And most community members offered to help, grateful for all he and Rolf had done to fix the water situation.

Rushing past him, Cerissa then returned from the bathroom with a thin cosmetics bag she slipped into an outer compartment of her luggage, and looked around. "I think that's it."

He closed in on her, hooking an arm around her back and looping the other arm under her knees, lifting her. "Speaking of stress reduction, I have found that feeling competent is always helpful in improving my mood."

"And what are you feeling competent about lately?"

"Well…" He pushed her bag to the floor, tossed her onto the bed, and leapt onto the other side. "I have become quite competent at pleasing you in bed."

"'Competent' is not the word I would use, Quique." The corners of her mouth quirked up. "I'm thinking 'magnificent' might apply."

"*Mi amor*," he said, slowly unbuttoning her shirt, "I can only hope to rise to your kind words."

Chapter 2

RECOVERY

Los Angeles General Hospital Outpatient Surgical Center—Two days later

Fighting traffic to get to the hospital proved challenging. Cerissa white-knuckled the ride while Karen navigated the morning rush hour, blowing through yellow lights and tailgating the cars in front of them. They had to arrive two hours before the surgery was scheduled to give the hospital enough time to process the paperwork and allow the nurses to prep Christine.

They barely reported to the front desk on time. Feeling a little buzzed with adrenaline, Cerissa quickly hugged Christine goodbye, wished her a quick and painless surgery, and then settled in the waiting room with Karen.

Finally, at eleven o'clock in the morning, the nurse told them Christine's surgery had begun, so Cerissa suggested an early lunch in the hospital café.

After they finished eating, Karen took out a gloss wand from her designer bag and applied the tip to her lips. "I can't wait to see how she looks. A little nip and tuck, subtly done, can take ten years off."

"I'm glad the idea occurred to her. It might help her adjust to the prospect of living forever."

Karen pressed her lips together to evenly distribute the peach color and dropped the wand back in her purse. "Rolf mentioned that some vampires have trouble mentally accepting the transition. She's smart to think it through and take her time."

Cerissa nodded, but in truth, the speed with which Christine had scheduled the surgery on the heels of the council's vote impressed her. The whole process felt like a whirlwind. "I'm still surprised by how fast the council agreed to give her one of the open spots."

"Same here, though I'm not surprised how over-the-top Zeke made the ritual bite." Karen rolled her eyes.

Since Christine had never been a vampire's mate, the council suggested she experience having a vampire feed on her. They wanted her to have firsthand involvement in a bite from the mortal side of things—and not solely when Henry turned her. Henry had agreed to be her maker but refused to take part in the ritual bite, a decision Cerissa wholeheartedly endorsed.

Zeke Cannon volunteered instead.

On the appointed night, everyone gathered to watch. Christine stood by the audience podium in the council chambers wearing a low-cut blouse, one she didn't mind getting blood on. When Zeke stalked through the double doors, he entered slowly, locking eyes with Christine from across the room.

The attorney had already proven she could withstand a vampire's mesmerizing abilities. At Cerissa's suggestion, Christine didn't resist Zeke, so she would have the visceral experience of being put under a vampire's spell, and stood there, held in place by Zeke's gaze.

He tossed aside his black cowboy hat, which Cerissa caught before it hit the floor, and then stopped in front of Christine. Brushing his fingers over her cheek, he tilted her head to one side, wrapped his arms around her, and, embracing her tightly, slowly lowered his mouth to the rapidly pulsing vein in her neck.

Every vampire in the room seemed frozen in place, their hungry eyes locked on the scene, clearly envious of Zeke. Other than their mate's blood, the Hill forbade feeding on mortals within a hundred miles of the town. The only blood from strangers they received came in a bag—stale donor blood.

At least, that was all they had thus far. After Cerissa built her biotech research facility and began producing enough clone blood to distribute across the community, they'd have another option.

Cerissa could tell when Zeke's fangs hit their mark. Christine let out a little moan, and Zeke's pupils expanded until his eyes were almost solid black and glazed over.

Quite a long time passed while he drank—enough that Cerissa grew concerned. When he finally finished, he licked Christine's neck until the small punctures stopped bleeding, and then took a vial from his jeans pocket. Only the blood of another vampire could heal the bite. He unscrewed the cap, struck his tongue in, and then, with a flick, spread the healing blood across the wounds, which closed over.

Zeke returned the capped vial to his pocket, swept Christine off her feet, and carried her out. Very melodramatic. As the room filled with applause, police chief Tigisi "Tig" Anderson broke away from the crowd and followed the pair. Since fang serum delivered a powerful aphrodisiac, Tig was charged with making sure nothing non-consensual occurred.

The day after the ritual, Christine confided in Cerissa that she found the cowboy quite attractive. Cerissa filled her in on Zeke's past then—his wet work for the government assassinating drug lords, as well as his inability to take no for an answer. Forewarned is forearmed.

Despite her opinion of him, Cerissa understood why Christine might be affected. Bites were powerful things. Just watching the bite had ignited desire in Cerissa—she had wanted to take Henry right home and to bed, and still couldn't entirely shake the image of Zeke sinking his fangs into Christine's neck, along with the sparks deep in her belly the scene excited.

Her own reaction slightly mortified her. Karen was right: the whole tableau had been over-the-top.

"It felt a bit voyeuristic," Cerissa said to her bestie.

"I bet every vamp in the room had a hard-on." Karen laughed. "Come on, let's go back to the waiting room."

Before Cerissa could get up from the table, a buzzing noise caught her attention, and she wrinkled her brow at the sound.

"Is that your phone?" Karen asked.

"You're right. I put the ringer on vibrate."

Cerissa rummaged through her purse and couldn't imagine who would be calling her. It was too soon for Christine to be out of recovery, and this early in the afternoon, Henry would be fast asleep. Perhaps Ari needed something.

When she found the phone, she recognized the area code as local. Probably spam, someone wanting her to renew her car warranty or claiming to be the IRS.

"Hello," she said briskly, ready to punch the disconnect button.

"Ms. Patel?" the voice asked.

"Yes, this is Dr. Patel. Who is calling, please?"

"This is the surgical room coordinator. Are you in the hospital?"

"Yes, is Christine out of recovery already?"

Karen leaned over, alert, trying to listen in on the call. Cerissa tipped the phone to the side to let her.

"We need you to return to the surgical center waiting area. How soon can you be here?"

"A few minutes. I'm in the cafeteria."

"Please wait for me by the door marked surgical center."

"Will do."

The caller hung up.

"Do you think something happened?" Karen asked.

"I hope not." Cerissa nervously fingered the amethyst and moonstone bracelet she wore—the one Henry gave her when they first became mates. "I knew I should have scrubbed in. But they wouldn't hear of it. I don't have surgical privileges here."

She quickly bussed the table with Karen's help and rushed down the hallway to the elevator, repeatedly punching the button. When they arrived at the marked door, an official-looking woman emerged. "Dr. Patel?" the woman said.

"Yes. And this is Karen Turner. What's wrong?"

"I'm Beatrice Rivers. Let's go into one of the family rooms, where we can talk in private."

Cerissa's stomach sank. Talking in private never meant good news. Something must have happened to Christine.

Beatrice led them to a small room and closed the door behind her. After they sat down on the couch, Beatrice pulled a chair over to face them and asked, "Are you Christine's family?"

"We're friends." Cerissa glanced at Karen, who chewed on a cuticle. "And Christine gave me her power of attorney. She doesn't have any family. Her husband died, and she never had children. We're all she has."

"I—I'm sorry." Beatrice's voice caught.

Cerissa touched the woman's arm to let a light flow of aura calm her. "Is Christine alive?"

Beatrice cleared her throat. "She's on life support right now."

"Oh my God," Karen murmured.

Cerissa took a deep breath. This was going to devastate Henry. "What happened?"

"Surgery finished, but we encountered a problem in the recovery room. Are you familiar with electromechanical dissociation?"

"Yes, I am."

Karen furrowed her brow. "Well, I'm not."

"It's rare," Beatrice replied. "But the condition sometimes occurs during or after surgery. The heart can stop contracting, yet the muscle still conducts electrical impulses. To the nurses in recovery, electromechanical dissociation can appear to be an equipment malfunction. They see the heart's electrical readings on the monitors, but blood pressure and pulse stats drop."

Cerissa twisted the beads on her bracelet. "Were you able to restart her heart?"

"Yes. Staff initiated CPR right away and called the anesthesiologist back. Ms. Dunne had been taken off the ventilator before going into recovery, but the doctor encountered trouble intubating her again due to edema. They finally inserted the tube. She's on a ventilator now, and her heart is beating on its own."

"If her heart started again, why is she on a ventilator?" Karen asked.

"Because Christine isn't okay," Cerissa replied. "Brain death?"

"We don't know yet." Beatrice gave a hesitant shake of her head. "You're a medical doctor?"

"Yes, but most of my work is research, not clinical. How long was she down?"

"According to the monitoring equipment, almost ten minutes. The next six hours will be critical."

Cerissa's throat tightened. "So she may never wake up?"

"Usually, we don't phrase it that bluntly to family members."

Stress lines appeared around Karen's eyes, and she twirled a strand of her auburn hair. "How soon can we see her?"

"You won't have to wait long. She's being transferred to intensive care right now."

An inkling of a plan began forming in Cerissa's mind. "We want her to have a private room."

"I'll make sure she has one. But don't give up hope yet." Beatrice stood. "I'll come back for you when she's in the ICU."

"Thank you."

Karen looked lost. "What can we do?"

Once the door shut behind Beatrice, Cerissa turned to her bestie. "I can't use Lux medical technology. The Protectors will get pissed if I save another life and risk our exposure so blatantly."

"Can any of your, you know, natural Lux skills help? Your aura or something?"

"Not really." Cerissa ran her fingers over the amethysts and moonstones in her bracelet, worrying the beads as she tried to figure a way around the problem. "A small dose of vampire blood would heal a circulatory blockage. But her whole brain suffered a terrible trauma when it was deprived of oxygen and might be too damaged. The amount of blood she'd need would turn her."

Thirty minutes later, Beatrice returned. "We have her in a room now. Would you follow me?"

They went up four floors and down a long white hallway. Beatrice paused outside a door. "Just remember the surgery was finished, so she's, well—"

"We understand. There will be swelling and bruising on her face."

Beatrice nodded and opened the door. They walked into a room crammed with hospital gear, monitors, tubes, wires...and a bed. Karen let out a gasp.

Even with Beatrice's warning, the sight was shocking. Christine looked like she'd been in a car accident.

Cerissa rushed to the bed and took Christine's cold, lifeless hand, letting her own aura flow into her friend, searching for signs of consciousness. She sensed a distant presence, very far away, and checked Christine's eyes, then tried a few stimulus tests. The results weren't encouraging.

A woman came in wearing a traditional white coat. "I'm Dr. Williams," she said crisply, the same way Cerissa had heard other doctors speak when they created an official persona to keep the pain of endless death from reaching them. "I'm the ICU doctor on duty. We've done everything we can for Ms. Dunne. We'll keep her comfortable. But for now, all we can do is wait."

"Thank you, doctor," Cerissa said. "Ms. Rivers explained what happened. It's tragic, that's all."

"If you need anything, push the red button." The doctor pointed to the call button.

Once the doctor left, Karen asked, "Now what? We just wait?"

"Yes and no." Cerissa glanced at her watch. It was almost four o'clock—an early moonrise would wake her mate soon. "I have an idea, but I need to talk with Henry. I'm going to flash home. Call me if anything happens."

"Okay. I'll tell them you went to the bathroom if they ask for you."

"Thanks." Cerissa hugged her bestie and then slipped into the room's private bathroom to flash back to the Hill.

They couldn't let Christine die. As a community, they'd committed to making her one of them. As a couple, she and Henry had committed to his role in the process, to turning and guiding the new vampire.

Could she convince Henry to act now and not wait? He'd told her how he felt whipsawed by the speed with which everything happened, and she understood, but she also knew her mate—his own nature had him constantly questioning whether turning someone he barely knew was the right thing to do. That would be the true hurdle to clear now.

And using an untested experimental method to do so? He wasn't going to like that part either.

Cerissa took in a deep breath, trying to calm her jangled nerves. Even if she could persuade Henry, the big question remained: would her idea work, or would the process go terribly, terribly wrong?

Chapter 3

FOREVER

Rancho Bautista del Murciélago—Moments later

The moon rose at four-thirty in the afternoon, waking Henry earlier than the predicted six-twenty-three sunset. The first thing he noticed was Cerissa's anxiety channeling through the Lux crystal embedded in his wrist. He grabbed his phone from the charging station next to his crypt's cot, but no messages waited for him.

After shaving and getting dressed, he climbed the basement stairs to find her pacing in the kitchen. "Is everything all right? I sensed your distress as soon as I rose."

"There's been a complication," she said, and explained what happened and how Christine might not survive.

Perhaps it would be for the best.

He frowned at the unbidden thought even though its logic made sense.

He'd agreed too fast to turn Christine. At his age, fang fever—like baby fever—could make a vampire feel physically prepared even if they weren't emotionally ready for the role. And he felt far from ready.

"Are you having second thoughts?" Cerissa asked, breaking the silence.

He looked at her, startled. If anyone else asked, he would dismiss the question. He'd made the commitment, and his sense of duty to the community demanded he live up to his word.

But he owed Cerissa a complete answer. "Yes and no. The desire to procreate is strong, but I've heard others speak of fang fever—the urge will pass. The real issue is this: I'm not sure I want to be tied to Christine for the rest of my life. I only know her professionally, in a business setting. I'd hoped to have time to get acquainted with her on a personal level."

"You've expressed those concerns before." Cerissa took a seat on one of the stools at the kitchen island. "What's the 'no' part? The reason you want to go ahead?"

"I may not have this opportunity again." He eased himself onto the other stool. "The council has cleared the way for Christine. While I'm concerned about our short acquaintance, I keep telling myself most vampires don't truly know their offspring well before turning them. In the past, the urge struck, and the vampire acted. With the treaty's prohibition on creating new vampires, this is a rare chance. It may not come my way again."

Cerissa looked at him intently. "The decision remains yours."

"Perhaps nature made the decision for me."

"About that—I have an idea."

His brilliant mate. Their knees touched as he faced her, sitting on the kitchen stools, and he stroked her cheek, his thumb caressing her jaw line. "Cerissa, you can't do for her what you did for Nicholas. From what you described, she is too far gone for a small dose of vampire blood to revive her."

"Agreed."

"And even if I drove out there tonight, if she cannot feed, I cannot turn her."

"That's why I want to do a five-pint transfusion."

Henry's eyes widened. It took a moment before he choked out his response. "You—you want to transfuse *my* blood into Christine?"

"Absolutely."

Holding very still, he let her proposal sink into his gut. He knew her deep-seated need to prevent death grew from the loss of her father in her early life. He'd accepted that aspect of her—a wound that sometimes drove her to do risky things. So he wasn't surprised. She wanted to do what she always did: use her medical skills to save the patient.

But Henry had lived a different life. In his two hundred years, he'd learned the opposite lesson: some patients couldn't be saved.

He met Cerissa's eyes.

"Have you decided?" she asked, her voice steady.

Despite her efforts to mask her emotions, he could sense the underlying anxiety in her question. She desperately wanted to save Christine. The crystal conveyed the war inside her as she struggled to let him decide the best course. Like the angel she resembled in her Lux form, she selflessly put his needs before her own.

How could he refuse her anything?

Suddenly, he sprang to life, strode from the kitchen island to the stove, began heating water, and took three pouches of blood from the cupboard. "If I am going to give five pints, I need to overfeed. And you will need to drain her before transfusing my blood. But I will have to be there to bite her—we need fang serum to complete the turn."

Cerissa hopped off the stool. "I'll get my gear for the donation."

"We can use my room. Set up by the couch."

"Will do."

Cerissa ran downstairs to the lab and grabbed tubing, empty collection bags, and a sterile donation needle, throwing them into her medical bag. Did she need anything else? What wasn't she considering?

Then it hit her—Marcus Collings, the town attorney, might know if anyone had tried this before. Phoning Dr. Clarke was out of the question. She didn't trust his opinion.

When Marcus answered her call, she explained what happened and what she planned on doing.

"You're out of your mind," Marcus said. "I'm sorry about Christine's condition, but you can't turn her if she's unconscious. A transfusion won't work. The blood must go through the stomach."

Damn. She hadn't realized the digestive system played a role in the turn.

Then she flipped his statement over in her mind. How would the stomach make a difference? Intravenous delivery healed people—she'd used the technique to save two mortal lives. So on what basis did he make his assertion? Hearsay? Direct experience? She couldn't give up without scientifically exploring the question.

"Has anyone attempted it, Marcus?"

"I—well—well, no, but—"

"Look, do me a favor. I'm short on time. Search the database, the one compiled by *Living from Dusk to Dawn*. I need to know if anyone has made a vampire via blood transfusion. I understand your doubt, but I want to check."

Living from Dusk to Dawn, an online magazine created by the treaty communities, maintained a repository of medical research on the vampire condition. The database wasn't large, but she'd learned a thing or two from reading the articles related to her current research.

She kept gathering equipment as the phone transmitted the clicking sounds of Marcus typing on a computer keyboard.

Moments later, Marcus said, "Nothing. I've run four different searches. No one has tried to turn an unconscious person and written up the results."

"Then we don't have any evidence proving a transfusion won't work."

"Cerissa, I'm sorry to say this, but as town attorney, I'm telling you not to attempt this. If the hospital catches you—"

"What's that, Marcus?" She tapped a button on her phone for an app created by Ari. The sound of static dropout invaded the call. "I can't hear you."

She punched the disconnect button. Hopefully, the subterfuge would keep her and Henry out of trouble with the council. Because one way or another, they were doing this.

Minutes later, she ran upstairs to Henry's office, rushed through it to the small, windowless room he used to relax and read, commandeered a shoe rack from his walk-in clothes closet—dumping the shoes on the hardwood floor—and carried the rack into his room to use as a means of support.

Her mate could reorganize the shoes in his closet later. She suspected he'd give her an earful about the mess once he saw the pile, but she didn't have time to tidy up.

She strung the collection tubing through the shoe rack's wire frame, placed the empty bag on the donor scale, and then fastened a collection needle to the tubing. The whole jury-rigged contraption sat next to his black leather chaise lounge. It would have to do.

A short while later, Henry arrived with extra pouches of self-warming blood in his hands, but before he could recline on the chaise lounge, his phone rang.

"Don't answer that!"

"Why not?" He placed the pouches down and took his phone off his belt. "It is Marcus."

She couldn't let Marcus coerce Henry into stopping. "He's going to forbid you from going through with this. But if you aren't aware of the prohibition..."

Henry frowned. "Cerissa, there is one thing you may not have considered, and perhaps Marcus has. Because of the brain trauma Christine has gone through, she may never rise, or alternately, rise deranged."

The idea had occurred to her, but they had to try anyway, right? "We'll deal with the outcome when we get there."

"Just so you are prepared." Henry relaxed back on the sleek lounger. "The council will not tolerate a mentally unstable vampire. Unenlightened of them, but they will order her destroyed."

Cerissa didn't like the council's stance, but at the moment, she couldn't do anything about their backward thinking. "Would you phone Rolf and ask him to drive to Los Angeles? We're going to need help getting her out of the hospital, and we can use the back of his SUV to transport her to the Hill."

"Of course. I will make the call as I feed."

She wrapped the tourniquet around Henry's arm, and he sipped at another pouch of blood. He didn't even flinch when the silver-coated needle went in. She sometimes wondered if the pain reflex was lessened in a vampire his age.

After she started the process and red liquid flowed through the tubing to the collection bag, Henry tapped his phone and brought it to his ear. "Rolf? Cancel the poker game. We need to leave for Los Angeles in fifty minutes."

"What happened?" she could hear Rolf ask Henry.

Henry explained what occurred at the hospital, then said, "Will you swing by my house and pick me up once the sun sets?"

Cerissa waved at him, trying to get his attention. She would flash him back to the hospital with her.

He held up a finger and shook his head. "Good. See you shortly."

As soon as Henry hung up, she said, "Call Rolf back. I'll flash you—"

"No. If we are going to fool the council, I will need to leave with Rolf, so the guards have a record of my departure. Meet me at the gas station at the last southbound freeway off-ramp for Mordida. We can flash from there to the hospital without anyone being the wiser."

Henry was right. Why hadn't she thought of that? "Great idea. I'll see you there once we finish."

She glanced down at the readout on the donor scale. A pint of vampire blood weighed five hundred grams. The bag had reached its target weight, which meant she had a full pint.

After she finished collecting all five, she took his blood pressure to make sure he was all right.

He gave her a sideways smile. "I'm fine. Let us leave."

She huffed. Big, bad vampires didn't worry about their health. Well, she'd do her job even if he disagreed.

Once she'd assured herself his vitals met the baseline requirements for a healthy vampire, she unwrapped the blood pressure cuff, loaded the bags into a canvas tote, grabbed her med kit, and, after collecting a quick kiss from Henry, flashed to the hospital bathroom without him, dropped the bags there, then flashed back to the gas station he'd specified. It was her usual spot to fill her car's tank, so the location was familiar.

She hid behind the white-painted mini-market where the landscaping became denser and watched the colors of early sunset—yellow swirled with coral—fade to a deeper hot pink, then magenta. She phoned Henry.

"We just turned onto the off-ramp," he said.

"Super. You'll find me behind the building."

She disconnected the call and swatted at some buzzing night insect that'd tried to land on her nose, then tugged at the beads on her bracelet. Time was of the essence. If they were going to return home to bury the body, they had three hours to finish the transfusion and sneak Christine out of the hospital without getting caught.

Peering around the building, she saw Rolf's Escalade pull up. Rolf parked at the pumps and started filling his tank. Henry got out and strolled to the side of the mini-market where Cerissa had told him she waited. After a quick hug, she double-checked the security camera locations and grabbed his hand to move them out of range, then transported him into the hospital bathroom and peeked out the door.

Karen sat in the bedside chair, fiddling with her phone, alone with Christine.

"Hey—"

"Eek!" Karen jumped. "Don't do that."

"I didn't mean to sneak up on you." Cerissa held out the canvas tote bag. "We're green to go."

Chapter 4

Death's Door

Los Angeles General Hospital—Moments later

Henry leaned over Christine. Her face appeared bruised and swollen, pale and flaccid, and the pallor of her skin drew his thoughts to the night his favorite aunt died.

Tía Isabel had been around the same age as Christine. She made the best *Alfajores de Veracruz*, a cookie sandwich with a sweet filling, and she always snuck him a treat even when his mother scolded that it would ruin his appetite. To a little boy, it meant the world. Standing by his aunt's bedside, he'd held her large hand with both of his small ones and prayed, wishing God would let her stay a little longer with them.

He sent up the same prayer for Christine now and stroked a hand along her arm. No response came, and his heart opened to her in sympathy.

Did he really want to do this? And if so, would Cerissa's procedure even work?

He wasn't certain on either count. He wanted more time, and he wanted better odds.

He looked at Christine again, lying there, needing his help, and knew he didn't have the luxury to wait. And Cerissa—he could feel her desire to save the mortal pushing through the crystal, and in response, he suppressed the connection. The choice had to remain his.

Clearing his mind, he couldn't deny one truth: he might never have another chance to make a child. And that wasn't just the fang fever talking—he really wanted a child, someone to mentor and guide in a way his own maker never had with him.

Anne-Louise had been inclined to "throw him in the deep end" and let him flounder. He'd do better by Christine.

He wanted that opportunity. He wanted family, like the aunt he'd loved. He wanted a child.

Straightening his spine, he took another breath and faced his mate. "You must drain her until she is close to death."

Cerissa bit her lip. "She's almost there already. This is going to be tricky."

He stepped aside to allow Cerissa to connect a drain line from a large vein in Christine's arm. After covering that arm with a blanket, Cerissa snaked the tube along the edge of the mattress to mask its presence, and then fed the blunt opening into the fluid collection bag hanging from the hospital bed.

Cerissa hooked one of the donor bags behind a tall monitor out of sight and connected the clear tubing into the IV line. Blood—his blood—flowed through from the hanging bag.

Anxiety flitted in his chest. There was no turning back. "Should I bite her?"

"Not yet. I want to give the healing properties of your blood a chance to work on her brain."

"But I thought she was too far gone."

"She is—for full recovery. The oxygen deprivation injured her brain too much. But if we can heal some of the trauma, it might make the turn easier."

His chest filled with sadness. "Whatever you believe is best."

Cerissa would do what she could now, and he'd do what was necessary if his child woke *non compos mentis*. As much as it would rip his heart out, he'd destroy his own child if he had to.

He stepped aside so Cerissa could apply some blood directly to Christine's face, too. She peeled back the bandages and, using a syringe filled with his life's essence, treated the incision areas, as well as those on her stomach. Twenty minutes later, the swelling and bluish-red color began to fade.

She put the bandages back in place. "In case the doctor or nurse returns."

Once half of the first bag was in, Cerissa performed a series of tests. When she finished, she shook her head. "No improvement." Henry felt her gaze land on him. "It's up to you."

He gently turned Christine's head. His instinct told him a neck bite would be best, and, given her condition, he'd take all the advantages he could get.

Leaning over, he sank his fangs into her. A momentary weight of guilt wormed through him, like he was betraying Cerissa by biting someone else to turn them vampire, but he pushed the guilt away—this was Cerissa's idea as much as it was his.

He left his fangs in long enough to unload a full dose of serum into Christine's bloodstream, and then he pulled back, wrinkling his nose and puckering his mouth at the bitterness. The small taste reminded him of feeding on a fresh corpse—something he'd done regularly before banked blood became available. "She is close to death."

Cerissa nodded, concern in her eyes. "Her blood volume is already low. In a normal turn, how much would you drink?"

"It is not an exact science." Henry removed a vial of Rolf's blood from his pocket and spread a small amount over the bite marks, healing them—a precaution against any hospital personnel noticing the unusual wounds. "The same amount you took from me, more or less. About five pints."

He moved to the door to stand watch.

"This is going to be tricky," Cerissa said from behind him. "I don't want her to die prematurely from heart failure. We need her heart working to circulate your blood."

Cerissa kept the stethoscope on Christine's chest and signaled Karen to open the drain line on the other side of the bed.

A few minutes later, Karen bent to examine the fluid collection container. "Looks like we're at five hundred milliliters."

"And I'm detecting an arrhythmia—her heart is struggling. I'm going to restart the transfusion."

Despite the unknowns, they had to risk sending the blood directly into Christine's circulatory system. Using a nasal tube to deliver it into her stomach wasn't an option. There'd be no way to hide the tube. The ICU nurse occasionally came in to take readings and would notice red liquid being fed through Christine's nose.

For appearance's sake, Cerissa re-established the saline line into the IV, but spun the roller clamp to stop the flow. Too much fluid in Christine's system would dilute Henry's blood.

"Should I keep the drain line open?" Karen asked.

"For the moment, yes. In theory, we need to drain another fifteen hundred milliliters."

Henry jumped away from the door. "Someone is coming."

Cerissa quickly covered the red-filled tube with the edge of the bedsheet.

The doctor strode in and conducted some additional tests. Dr. Williams demonstrated the lack of reaction when she ran a swab across Christine's eye. And Christine didn't respond to pain stimuli. The device monitoring her brain function showed no activity.

"I'm sorry," the doctor said.

Cerissa stood between the IV line and the doctor, hoping to block the view. "We'll stay here with her to the end."

"Of course. Buzz the nurse if you need anything," the doctor said, and left.

Cerissa pursed her lips and checked her watch. Normally, a one-pint transfusion took around ninety minutes because of the risks attendant to transfusing a patient too quickly. But she was fighting the clock now—they needed enough time to get Christine back to Sierra Escondida before sunrise.

Would vampire blood prevent hypothermia and the other side effects of a massive transfusion? She had no way of knowing, but she had no choice.

She listened to Christine's heart again. The arrhythmia was worse. "Stop the drain line."

Karen peeled back the blanket and rotated the lever to block the line.

After opening the transfusion to the maximum rate, it still took them two hours to empty all five bags. Toward the end, Cerissa took Christine's hand, letting a little aura into her, and the response seemed different, as if her presence had returned, but at the same time, something about her life force had changed.

Is the vampire DNA already transforming her?

Karen ran a hand through her hair, fatigue etching lines around her eyes. "How are we going to get her out of here?"

"We need the doctor to declare her dead. They'll take her to the morgue downstairs, and we can retrieve the body there."

Cerissa disconnected all the transfusion tubing, coiled it inside an opaque plastic sack along with the empty blood bags, took her hypo from her purse and dialed in a number.

"What are you doing?"

"I'm giving her a drug to stop her heart. Henry?"

"That should be fine," he said. "The transfused blood should have circulated thoroughly by now. But give me a moment first."

He slid past Cerissa to Christine's side and bit her again. He made a nasty face when he straightened. "I cannot tell if she will rise; she still tastes of death. The additional fang serum may help."

After Henry healed the bite marks, Cerissa waited a few minutes to allow the fang serum to circulate. When she finally pressed the hypo against Christine's arm, the device made a light *hiss*, and, seconds later, the heart monitor alarm sounded. The doctor hurried in to begin heart compressions.

Cerissa laid a hand on the doctor's arm. "I hold her power of attorney. Christine has a 'do not resuscitate' order under these circumstances. You can stop trying."

"Do you want me to call the hospital chaplain?" Dr. Williams asked.

"No, Christine wasn't religious. There is no other family to notify. We're all she had." Cerissa paused, then preempted what she knew would be the doctor's next question. "And I'm sorry, despite the 'donor' release form she signed, she isn't eligible as an organ donor."

Cerissa wove a tale for the doctor—Christine had a pre-existing blood-based illness that ruled her out.

The story was almost true.

The doctor scrolled through the electronic tablet she carried. "Her condition isn't in the chart."

"I'm surprised, as Christine mentioned it before the surgery." Cerissa touched the doctor's arm, letting a little aura push her to believe the lie. "Perhaps the notation is buried in the paperwork somewhere."

The doctor nodded, then called time of death as nine-thirty-six at night. A nurse arrived, and together, they began to disconnect the ventilator.

Cerissa stroked Christine's arm, waiting until she stopped breathing. Her heart would remain motionless, and the vampire blood would marinate into her organs and tissues, giving the powerful DNA time to transform every fiber of her body. With the next sunset, her heartbeat should resume and start pumping vampire blood throughout her body—if they were lucky.

"You can stay here with her as long as you want," Dr. Williams added when her work was done.

"Thank you. We won't be long. But I want to walk with her when you take her to the morgue."

"Are you sure?" the doctor asked gently.

"Yes. I want to make sure she's treated with dignity."

The doctor squeezed her shoulder. "I understand."

Once the medical staff left, Cerissa looked over at Henry and Karen. "Rolf should be here any moment. I'll go with the body, then wait by the front entrance for him. You two go to the waiting room in case he heads that way first. Hopefully, we'll sneak her out with no one the wiser."

Chapter 5

THE HEIST

LOS ANGELES GENERAL HOSPITAL—THIRTY MINUTES LATER

Where was Rolf? Cerissa paced by the hospital entrance, trying to avoid the electric eye that automatically opened the sliding doors, and failed miserably at it. The doors *swooshed* open for the umpteenth time as she again stepped up to look out the tall plate-glass panels, searching for a familiar blonde head.

"Cerissa."

She jumped and spun around to face Rolf. Damn vampires and their sneaking about.

Rolf gripped his own arms tightly and glanced around nervously. "I came in the back entrance."

She couldn't help noticing his body language. "What's wrong?"

"Ach, it's torture being in a hospital. The aroma of fresh blood is everywhere."

A wave of sympathy washed through her. The place must smell like a candy factory mixing vats of molten chocolate to him. The enticing scent would be bad for any vampire, but especially for someone who craved adrenaline-enhanced blood like Rolf did.

"Christine is in the morgue." Cerissa guided him to the room where her partners in crime waited, and they all huddled together. "One of us needs to steal the file with the death certificate. The orderly dropped off the documents with a record keeper on the same floor."

Rolf straightened his back, his face brightening. "Leave that job to me."

Henry gave a quick nod. "I will go with the ladies and carry the body back to the SUV."

Cerissa looked around. "Do you have Christine's overnight bag?"

"Right over here." Karen walked to where the suitcase lay on one of the waiting room couches.

"Good. We'll need to dress her or put her in a bathrobe or something. Please bring it along."

"Allow me." Henry picked up the bag, and Cerissa led them to the morgue. When they went past the records clerk, she pointed him out to Rolf.

A smile ruffled Rolf's lips, and he hung back.

No one was in the morgue when they arrived—at least, no one alive. Cerissa snagged an empty wheelchair from the hall. "You'll find her in number five-twenty-three."

Whoever set the room's thermostat had erred on the freezing side. Cerissa shivered as she rolled the wheelchair over to a table, signaling Karen to join her, while Henry opened the compartment and pulled out the slab.

Christine lay on a cold metallic tray, her bandaged face already looking younger and at peace. "Please bring her over to this table."

Cerissa rummaged through the overnight bag to find the clothes Christine had planned to wear on the drive home. Having never dressed a corpse before, Cerissa found the task harder than she expected. It took her and Karen working together to peel off the hospital gown and pull the knee-length shift over Christine's head, bending her still-flexible elbows to thread her hands through the armholes.

Fortunately, when a mortal went through the turn, rigor mortis never set in, but it was too early to count Christine's loose muscles as a good sign. Even under normal circumstances, rigor took two to six hours after death to manifest. Cerissa decided to hang the sweater over Christine's shoulders once she was in the wheelchair rather than try to work her limp arms through the sleeves.

"What are you doing?" an orderly demanded as he wheeled in another bagged body.

She jumped, a startled "Oh!" escaping her lips. The hospital was having a bad night.

Henry leapt into action, cornered the orderly, and bit him.

Cerissa gulped. At an intellectual level, she knew biting gave a better chance of mesmerizing the orderly and making him forget.

Still, shock jolted through her at the sight of Henry's fangs sinking into someone else's skin, his Adam's apple bobbing as he swallowed, and she was surprised by the light tingle in her core. She tried to shake off the feeling, but Henry pivoted enough to lock eyes with her as he continued to swallow.

Heat rose to her cheeks. He must have sensed her reaction through the crystal. She hated admitting the truth, but she loved the predator in him.

Karen nudged Cerissa, snapping her out of her fascination with the scene.

"Ah, yeah, what?"

Karen motioned at Christine. "We'd better hurry."

"Oh, right. Of course." Cerissa's eyes cut back to Henry before she finished speaking.

He released the orderly's neck, easing the man onto a nearby chair with a breathless "Forget," then shot her a knowing smile as he anointed the bite with vampire blood from the vial he carried.

She ignored her own deepening flush and adjusted the blue-flowered shift to cover Christine's knees, feeling Henry approach behind her.

He lifted the limp body, settled Christine on the wheelchair, and tentatively released her. He caught her before she slid to the floor.

"Do you have anything to hold her in place?"

Cerissa rifled through the bag and pulled out a bathrobe belt. "Will this work?"

With Karen's help, Cerissa wrapped the belt under Christine's arms and tied a knot behind the wheelchair while Henry held Christine in place. When released, she slouched forward, but stayed somewhat upright. Cerissa arranged the sweater to cover the belt from the front.

Henry then took his place behind the handles, his body masking the knot at the back, and rolled the chair to the hallway.

"Where's Rolf?" Cerissa asked, stopping Henry. "He should be back by now."

"I'm here." Rolf appeared at the door with the file in hand.

She snatched the documents from him and skimmed through to confirm the folder contained the right paperwork.

"And I convinced him to delete the electronic records too," Rolf added.

Satisfied with the file's contents, she cocked her head at him and raised an eyebrow. "I thought you couldn't mesmerize someone to do your bidding."

"Not always." Rolf grinned smugly. "But when in the daze, they can sometimes be confused into doing what I ask. In this case, the clerk believed one of the doctors ordered him to delete the record."

From Rolf's rosy color, she suspected he'd made a meal of the records clerk, but she didn't say anything. If Karen didn't object, far be it from Cerissa to stir the pot.

After all, they'd both witnessed Henry feed on the orderly. She couldn't exactly throw stones at Rolf.

"Let's go." Rolf led them down the corridor. "There's an exit this way."

Moments later, they were outside on the sidewalk.

Cerissa looked up and down the street, trying to get her bearings. "We need to roll her to the parking lot."

"Perhaps it would be better if we brought the SUV to her," Henry said. "Stay here."

He and Rolf *whooshed* out of sight.

The street wasn't a busy one, especially this late at night, and by the time the guys parked the Escalade SUV at the curb, Cerissa had untied the bathrobe belt to release Christine.

Henry exited the passenger seat, and Cerissa glanced around, nervous someone would catch them. "Hurry."

"*Ja, ja*." Rolf opened the rear hatch, and Henry lifted Christine into the utility storage area and laid her out, bending her knees so she'd fit.

Rolf pressed the button to close her in. "We'll make it back to the Hill with time to spare."

"Then what?" Cerissa asked. "We wait?"

Henry put an arm around her. "We must bury Christine. She should be able to climb out of the dirt by herself. That is, she will either learn, or die trying."

Cerissa cringed at the horrible process. "Why not lay her out in one of your crypts?"

"She needs to learn how to free herself from the ground."

Karen gestured impatiently at the white SUV. "Time is ticking. The longer we stand here, the greater the chance someone will remember seeing us."

Rolf gave a sharp nod. "Karen will ride back with me."

She swung up into the passenger seat. "Let's get going."

Their friends drove off, and Cerissa parked the wheelchair by the doorway, not concerned over what an orderly might think when the errant chair was found. She then walked briskly with Henry to her car.

When they arrived, he stopped at the car's fender. "Would you like me to drive? You've been through a lot today."

"As have you. How are you feeling after donating so much?" She touched his chest, wanting the connection for a moment.

His hand covered hers, and he lightly squeezed her fingers. "I'm fine. The orderly's contribution helped."

She looked at him a moment longer, and then patted his chest and strode to the driver's side. "Thank you, but I'll drive. You can keep me entertained on the way."

Once they were both inside, she pressed the start button. "But first"—she hit the phone icon on the steering wheel—"I need to call Ari."

On the sixth ring, Ari answered. "Hey, Ciss, what's happening?"

"I just stole a corpse."

The snort that came over the car's speakers sounded, well, liquid. "Fuck, my nose hurts."

"Spraying vodka through your nose will do that," she said with absolutely no sympathy.

"Twenty-five-year-old scotch, not vodka. What a waste."

"Right. Well, I need you to locate the surveillance footage of the morgue at Los Angeles General Hospital and delete the video. Think you can do that?"

"Sure, I can cover your ass. But who's the corpse?"

"The Hill's water attorney."

"Ciss, you're not supposed to take Shakespeare literally—besides, the guy who said 'kill all the lawyers' was the *villain* in the play."

Cerissa rolled her eyes. "Bye, Ari."

Rancho Bautista del Murciélago—Three hours later

Around two-thirty in the morning, they arrived at the Hill's gates. Turning left from Robles Road, Cerissa sped up the paved switchbacks leading to their home.

The SUV blocked the circular driveway by the fountain, so she parked behind it. Rolf stood at the edge of the oak woodlands to the east, apparently looking for a place to bury Christine that wouldn't disturb the cultivated landscaping. Karen sat on the lawn bench looking at something on her phone and yawning.

Henry got out and stretched, then strode over to join Rolf, and they started arguing over the burial location.

Cerissa ran inside to find a sheet to wrap Christine in. The idea of putting her in bare dirt made Cerissa's skin crawl. Without a layer between her body and the ground, Christine would be covered in filth and bugs when she rose. Yuck.

With a midnight-blue sheet in hand, Cerissa returned, went to the back of the SUV, and spread it out. "Henry, please help me."

Together, they rolled Christine onto the sheet and wrapped the fabric loosely around her.

Rolf scowled at Cerissa. "What do you think you're doing?"

"Giving her some dignity."

Henry strode to the garage and came back with two shovels. "Here." He handed one to Rolf. "Make yourself useful."

The two men worked together at supernatural speed to dig a hole about four feet deep.

Cerissa's emotions suddenly caught up with her, sadness and grief tightening her throat. The hospital death had been unexpected and tragic, but at least they now had Christine safely home. As she watched the guys work, a sudden realization sent a surge of fear through her. When Christine woke, her location wasn't where she'd expect to be. Would she rise from her grave disoriented?

Well, they'd be there to calm her. Cerissa would make sure of it.

The guys seemed unconcerned about any of this, instead bickering over the hole's depth. Rolf wanted six feet, and Henry was fine with four. Henry won.

Good. Christine wouldn't have far to claw her way out.

Once they laid Christine in the hole and finished covering her with dirt, Henry dusted off his hands on his jeans and put an arm around Cerissa. She leaned into him, the sadness still weighing on her.

"It is all right, *cariña*. Grief is inevitable. Every attempt to turn a vampire is risky, and this one even more so. The lack of oxygen damaged her brain. I would hate to lose my first child, but we must be prepared for bad news."

Cerissa slumped even more against him. She'd been so focused on getting through the hospital crisis and returning Christine safely to the Hill that she'd pushed from her mind the possibility Christine might never rise. "Is there anything we can do now to help the process?"

He gave a slow shake of his head. "I am sorry."

Karen walked up behind Cerissa and squeezed her shoulder. "You did everything you could. And I'm about to drop dead asleep on my feet." Karen hugged her. "I'll be back here tomorrow at dusk."

Rolf scowled. "No she won't."

Cerissa returned the hug. Her bestie made a great teammate. "Thanks. For everything."

"No worries."

After Rolf and Karen left, Henry scooped Cerissa into his arms, carrying her into the house. Taken by surprise, she wrapped her arms around his neck to hang on. "And just what is this about?"

"You did an incredible thing, *cariña*, regardless of the outcome. But if Christine successfully rises, then tonight is our last night on our own for some time. I want to give you all the attention you deserve." He waggled his eyebrows at her. "What do you desire?"

"You." She winked at him, and suddenly her fatigue vanished. "And maybe some wine."

The corners of his lips twitched. "An excellent choice on both counts."

CHAPTER 6

MANNERS

GAEA'S HOME—AROUND THE SAME TIME

"Oh, Luuu-cy, I'm hoo-me," Ari bellowed as he opened Gaea's front door.

Whatever would she do with him? One would think he learned about relationships from watching television. "Ari, how many times do I have to tell you a gentleman does not yell to make his presence known?"

"You might as well stop now, toots. I yam what I yam." He picked up Gaea and twirled her around. "Besides, I've got news you're gonna wanna hear."

She kissed him. "Well, put me down and come into the parlor."

Fortunately, the contractor had fixed the parlor window, broken by the burglar Seaton killed, and the electricity to the house had also been restored after the fire. The kitchen was still being reconstructed, but the lights were on, which was important so her mortal boy toy didn't hurt himself in the dark.

But instead of putting her down, he carried her into the parlor before letting her feet touch the ground. Even though she was tall and solidly built, he made her feel like a feather pillow in his arms. At six feet, four inches, her lover had broad, muscular shoulders capable of bench-pressing two hundred pounds—he'd demonstrated his skill for her at the Hill's gym.

She glanced at the grandfather clock. "My word, it's after four in the morning."

"This couldn't wait. There was a problem at the hospital—Christine died, and they put her through the turn."

"They *what*?"

"Henry bit her while she was in a coma, and Cerissa drained her and transfused Henry's blood. They returned home and buried her." Ari brushed back the long, mink-colored curl from where it flopped onto his forehead. She loved his curly hair, the way it mirrored his wild personality. "So, tomorrow's the big night. The community may have its first new vampire in, what? Half a century?"

"Indeed." They'd have a new vampire if Christine survived Henry's unconventional approach, but it was too late to raise any doubts about the process.

"Take a load off your feet, toots, while I get a drink." Ari strode over to the sideboard and helped himself to the aged scotch she'd stocked for him. "So Ciss tells me she and Henry are going to be pretty busy for the next few months."

Gaea eased herself onto the plush velvet rocking chair and gave a long-suffering sigh. From her personal experience, "busy" was an understatement. "A new child can take a lot of work to socialize."

"You have, what? Three children?"

"Yes. One is managing my holdings in the U.K. and Europe, the other is goddess knows where, and you've met Winston."

Ari collapsed onto the biggest chair in the room. With his height, he needed it. "Winston was your first?"

"You know he was."

"Yeah, I guess I did, but you've never told me anything about what being a maker was like. You know, the real dirt—deciding to make him your first, and why you two aren't still together."

"Why, Ari, are you jealous?"

He tilted his head back and laughed. "Not at all, sweet cheeks. I'm all the man you need right now. Curious, is all."

She gave a shrug. "Vampires rarely keep their progeny with them for more than twenty years." Gaea crossed her ankles, knowing the move showed off her long legs. "I lived in London at the time I met him—1811. I remember the year because our introduction coincided with the beginning of the English Regency period, and I'd opened the house for the London season."

Ari sipped at his scotch. "London season? What's that? I only know summer, winter, spring, and fall."

"When Parliament commenced their session in the fall, the bon ton would return to town—the women coming with their men. That's when the season began, and the influx made for good feeding."

He gave her a crooked grin. "And it's all about the feeding."

"Not to mention longer nights. We would arrive in November and stay through July at my home on Portland Place. I stole the townhouse from a bankrupt baron at a bargain price."

"Present tense—you still do?"

"I own real estate all over Europe. Lady Ada Fane manages my holdings for me, and we split the income."

"Cool."

Gaea tapped at her chin, considering how much to say. "I threw such outrageous parties for the ton's vampires. My set would converge on London for the season with high expectations, and I presided over all the elegant celebrations." She paused, not willing to share everything with her lover. The London scene was quite different from the humble country origins where she'd grown up. "Greenleaf House sat in the prime district of respectability and was a popular gathering place. Formal dances in the front room, blood thralls in the dining room, and orgies in the back—a little something for everyone."

"I wish I'd known you then."

"I thought the orgies would catch your attention." She smiled sinfully at him. "I met Winston at one of those parties."

"Interesting. He's not exactly a lady-killer."

"Now, don't judge him by today's standards. He's a second son of a duke, and fancied himself quite the peacock, flaunting his lord title even though he'd never sit in Parliament."

"Lord Mason? No wonder he likes being mayor. If he wanted to be in Parliament, being mayor is the closest he can get on the Hill."

"When he strode into my home all swagger to attend one of the dances, his sharp gray eyes were the first thing that drew me to him, but his vulnerability was what held my attention."

"The mayor? Vulnerable? Are we talking about the same guy?"

"It had to do with the way land and titles were passed down. Inheritances were handled different back then—not what you're used to today. The firstborn son received everything. The other sons had to fend for themselves."

"Seriously?"

"Yes, and that's what Winston faced. Being the second son affected his *amour propre*."

"Okay, I see how his self-esteem might be dragged in the mud if his brother got everything and he got zilch."

"At the time I met him, he was over thirty and unmarried. His round face showed the few extra pounds he carried, and his flashy dress hid the hurt of being the second son, although he made a decent living as a barrister. The poor dear even had the potential for a judgeship someday."

"Wait. The mayor's a lawyer?"

"Not like Marcus; he hasn't kept up with American law." She pursed her lips. "Now, what was I saying? Oh yes. I was describing what he looked like when I first met him. He wore the popular Caesar hairstyle of the day to cover his premature baldness and let his bushy eyebrows go wild. Quite dashing in his tailcoat and inexpressibles."

"Ah, his what?"

"Tight pants. He cut quite the picture of manhood."

Ari snickered. "I bet he did, in that outfit. Did you often have mortals attend your parties?"

"By invitation only." Gaea smiled at the memory. "Another vampire, Claire, invited Winston to my party, even though she'd grown tired of him as her blood thrall by then. That's what we called those who were blood-bonded at the time. The bond kept him from speaking of us to the uninitiated. And unlike here, where the mortals pretty much know everything there is to know about vampire life, the thralls were ignorant of the political machinations of our society."

At the time, she had a small fortune in real estate and jewels, but never mixed with mortal society. Her neighbors knew her as the "dowager countess" and gossiped about the exclusive parties she threw, parties to which they were never invited.

And since using human thralls to do daywork was all the rage in her set, adding a barrister to her collection was worth the cost. "Money exchanged hands behind the scenes, and I bought Winston from Claire to add to my stable."

"So why did you turn him? Were you in love with him?"

A good question. She'd turned Winston on a whim once she tasted him. By then, she was going on four hundred years vampire and had never turned anyone. "Something about Lord Mason's blood told me he wouldn't live out the year. At the time, I didn't have a word for it. Now I know the taste: cancer."

"So you brought him over to save his life?"

"Something like that." She tapped her chin dimple. Was it mercy on her part? Or the desire to have a mate, at least for a while? Not that her reasons mattered anymore. "Now, my boy, that is quite enough about my first child. Let us just say I'm experienced enough that if Henry and Cerissa need any help with Christine, please, don't hesitate to send them my way."

"I'll pass along the offer next time I see Ciss." He stood. "Should I wash my glass before leaving, or do you plan on keeping me the rest of the night?"

"Why don't you pour yourself another and bring your drink upstairs with you? I'm going to check on Seaton, make sure he's not up to any mischief, and then I'll meet you in my lounge."

His eyes flashed with desire as he smiled cockily. "You got yourself a deal, sweet stuff. Just leave your hairbrush on the vanity this time. You left me a little bruised after our last round."

"I promise to be gentler with you tonight." As he poured himself another drink, she watched the slope of his shoulders, her eyes following the muscular lines underneath his shirt to the tight, perfectly shaped ass. "Now skedaddle."

When he turned around, he raised the glass and saluted. "Yes, ma'am."

She shook her head, suppressing a grin—it would only encourage him. His flippant attitude was one of the things she liked about him. He didn't intimidate easily, and she enjoyed his confident demeanor.

Not that she was ready to mate him.

No, it would be a long time before she took another mate. Still, they had fun together. She switched off the parlor lights, making sure the rest of the downstairs lights were off, and went upstairs to find Seaton.

He was working at the computer in his study—Ari had given him a series of lessons to practice coding. It pleased her to find him completing them. As it turned out, Seaton had earned a bachelor's degree in computer science before being turned, but didn't tell anyone on the Hill, the lazy sneak.

Before the council laid down the law, insisting Seaton straighten up and become a productive community member, her boarder had played video games all night, but such frivolity wouldn't support a Hill lifestyle.

The poor dear was still uncomfortable around people—especially mortals—and he struggled to fit in on the Hill. But with her guidance and Father Matt's help, he'd find his way. The coding lessons were the latest step in the socialization process.

She moved away from the study and strolled down the hallway to her lounge, stopping outside the door, tapping one finger against the dimple in her chin. How long would she keep Ari? She'd agreed to a non-exclusive arrangement because she knew his reputation.

But all this talk of children had her wondering. Did Ari have something else in mind? Something longer term?

Wait—did he want to be *turned*?

Surely, he didn't want a long-term connection as maker and child. With his short attention span, he'd grow tired of her before the usual twenty years concluded.

Then again, perhaps not. They were having a lot of fun together.

That reminded her a bit of Winston. Her forty years with Lord Mason had been delightful. And it was almost unheard of for a child to settle in the same community as their maker after their time as lovers ended. Still, they'd remained good friends.

Of course, occasionally she had to pull rank and remind Winston that she was his *maker*. He had a few blind spots when it came to his role as mayor, and over the years, she'd had to watch out for them. But most of the time he ran the community well.

She certainly didn't want to be the mayor. Too much work. She much preferred the role of political confidante, whispering in the mayor's ear when an occasional push was needed. In that way, they continued to be a good team together.

She peeked inside her lounge to see Ari naked, reclining on the couch, sipping at his scotch. The smile forming on her face couldn't be fought. Impertinent, yes. But Ari's confidence, his willingness to play as equals, delighted her.

And she would enjoy him while she had him, however short or long their time together might be. Unless he wanted to be turned. She tapped her chin. After all, he *could* fill one of the slots being held open by the Hill. More than a dozen vampires had recently been killed, so the council could authorize the creation of new vampires to replace them, and some of those slots were being held open for mortals who had crucial skills or training. A full-time computer expert was just one of the many essential occupations the town needed to operate efficiently.

Hmm. It was too soon to tell, but what an interesting idea.

Chapter 7

WAITING FOR DUSK

RANCHO BAUTISTA DEL MURCIÉLAGO—THE NEXT EVENING

Henry opened the door at the top of the basement stairs, startled to see Cerissa already standing there waiting for him. He accepted the mug she offered him, wrapping his fingers around the hot ceramic and letting it warm his hands. He sent her a questioning look.

"Shouldn't we go outside?" Her deep emerald eyes pleaded with him as she fluttered her hand, waving toward the side of the house where they'd buried Christine.

Henry checked his watch, and then took a sip of the dark wine. An early moonrise had woken him.

"Dusk has not started yet, *cariña*." Although the sunlight waned, he was still at risk.

"Oops. Sorry. I'm just worried." She bit her lip. "Once the sun goes down, we can wait out there, right? In case she needs help?"

He nodded. Maybe it would be handy after all if Cerissa succeeded in creating a daylight bracelet. "Why don't I make you dinner first?"

An hour later, after they'd both fed, he poured her a glass of Cabernet.

She accepted the wine, then hooked his arm with hers. "It's fully dusk now. Let's go."

Through the crystal, Cerissa's nervousness threaded into him, magnifying his own. Of course, he was just as anxious to find out if Christine successfully rose, but he was realistic that she may not.

Cerissa wasn't. He felt no trepidation from her at that possibility. Her investment in the process, how she'd worked so doggedly to save Christine, gave him cause for concern. It would be terrible for them to have gotten this far only to have his child remain in her grave, but that failure would be particularly hard on Cerissa.

He let out a slow exhale. They'd deal with any tragic outcome together if it came to be. "Christine will not rise until half an hour or so after the sun sets. Twilight must fully end."

"Still, better to be early? We don't want her to wake alone. I placed the patio chairs on the grass by her grave." She tugged on his arm again. "Come."

He chuckled. "Cerissa, staring at her grave won't make her rise any faster."

"Please?"

He gave in, carried a carton of self-heating blood pouches outside, and placed the box on the damp grass next to their chairs. If his child woke, she'd be ravenous—and possibly a bit muddy. It had rained lightly during the day.

He glanced at Cerissa. The way she alternated between sipping her wine and chewing her lower lip, staring at the sodden dirt mound under which Christine lay, was deeply endearing.

At the sound of a car engine, he twisted around to glance over his shoulder.

The Hill's chief of police parked her white van in the driveway by the fountain, accompanied by her second-in-command and mortal mate Captain Jayden Johnson. They had agreed to attend in case Christine became violent and Henry couldn't handle her alone.

This was all new territory for him. Based on his own experience, his child should be hungry enough to drain a mortal, but weaker than him if push came to shove.

Still, better safe than sorry.

Tig and Jayden exited the van and held stun guns at their sides. They were dressed in coveralls, so their uniforms wouldn't get destroyed if they had to subdue Christine.

Unease rustled through Henry. He hoped their precautions proved unnecessary.

When they joined him on the lawn, Henry pointed out the grave—not that Tig would miss the freshly turned dirt.

"Seen any signs yet?" she asked.

"Nothing." Henry rose to his feet, followed by Cerissa, and gestured to the other empty chairs. "Please, sit and relax. I believe we have"—he glanced at his watch—"at least five minutes at the soonest."

They declined the chairs, just as the rumble of Zeke's truck marked his arrival. Henry pivoted toward the sound and hissed in irritation. From behind him, Cerissa pinched his butt. He swung around to glare at her.

Her eyes danced with momentary merriment. "Relax," she whispered. "Zeke is here to help. Let's sit back down."

When she settled into her cushioned chair, Henry did the same, mainly to protect his flank from further attack.

Still scowling in Zeke's direction, he clenched his fists. How could he calm down? Just look at the show-off—decked out in tight jeans with his usual black hat. Shiny diamond shapes encircled the hat's crown on a leather band, and an equally gaudy calico shirt and string tie finished the ensemble. The cowboy was ready for a Saturday night square dance, not the birth of a new vampire.

Besides, Henry hadn't invited Zeke to the party—the cowboy had invited himself by phoning Tig and arguing that he should be included both as a reserve officer and because he'd bitten Christine at the council's request. Tig was swayed by the latter. She thought Zeke's previous bite might give him some influence over the fledgling if Christine became violent.

Solely because he respected the chief, Henry acquiesced to her suggestion that Zeke be included in the welcoming party. Now he wished he hadn't.

Rolf and Karen had stayed home. He agreed with their decision. The fewer mortals present, the better.

When a woman's hand broke through the topsoil, Cerissa gasped, and Henry shot to his feet. His sensitive hearing easily detected the loud, rapid beat of his mate's heart, and beneath the ground, he caught the much softer *ka-thub* of his child's slower heartbeat. Cerissa stood, and he immediately moved in front to protect her. "*Cariña*, please stay behind me."

He had already warned her of the risk. As one of two mortals present, she was in danger. Christine would attack the only food she saw.

Then another hand appeared from the dirt. Christine slowly pushed her head out of the grave, the wet sheet caught on one shoulder, and, gaining leverage, raised herself until she stood, clawing at the fabric edges until she'd ripped the sheet off. Her eyes had yet to focus; her face was slack, her movements stiff—she seemed dazed and disoriented.

Sweeping his fingers behind himself to find Cerissa, he made sure his body blocked the newborn's view of her.

"Christine." Henry stepped forward, and her head swiveled toward him, dirt falling out of her hair. "A problem developed shortly after surgery. We turned you while at the hospital and brought you back to Sierra Escondida."

Christine's dull eyes tracked him as he spoke, but they lacked comprehension. She sniffed at the air. Her head swung in Jayden's direction, and she charged to where he stood.

Tig blocked her. Christine tried to dodge around the chief, but Tig moved too fast for the new vampire. "Henry, call your child back to you. I don't want to stun her."

"Christine, come here." Tearing the corner off one of the self-heating pouches, he waved the opening, letting the scent of dark wine fill the air.

Christine's fangs ran out and she lunged for Henry's hand, clutching the pouch to chug down the blood. She let the wrapper drop to the grass. He opened another for her.

She lunged again, wild-eyed, the intelligence he usually saw in her gaze gone. A moment's grief filled him. Would she come to her senses, or would he be forced to destroy her?

After the fourth pouch, some of the dullness seemed to clear from her eyes, giving him hope. She reached out for a fifth, and he held it back. He must test her now.

"Ask for what you want, Christine."

For a moment, everything within him stilled as he watched her.

"Blood...please."

Relief flooded him. That would do.

It was about all he could expect from a newborn, even in normal circumstances. He handed the fifth pouch to her.

Christine never imagined anything would taste as delicious as a hot fudge sundae, but what the silvery-blue pouches held came close. While she gulped down the next one, she tried to reconcile her memories. A sheet had been wrapped around her, which made sense—after all, she was in the hospital, waking up from surgery...except the sheet was wet and this recovery room smelled like a musty forest.

And why was she demanding blood, guzzling blood, ready to kill for human blood?

She blinked, trying to compel her vision to clear. Cerissa was here, which made sense, but so was Henry. Why did he come to the hospital? And why were these other people here?

She kept trying to force her rational mind to explain what she saw around her. Was she hallucinating from the anesthesia?

Henry held out another pouch like the one in her hand. "Christine, a problem developed with your heart after surgery."

"A problem?"

"You suffered a heart attack in the recovery room."

"Did I die?"

"We turned you before that happened." He waved at her with the pouch. "Take this. You need more."

A compulsion hit her, a compulsion to do what he told her, which sent a momentary rush of fear through her. She was now connected to Henry—and that meant he held power over her.

She wasn't sure she liked the feeling, but she sucked it up for now and accepted the pouch he offered. "Thank you, maker."

Why did I say that?

She downed the contents in three fast swallows. The dark wine was rich, tasty, and filling. When she initially wrapped her head around the idea that she'd drink blood for the rest of her life, she expected the liquid to be something nasty she'd have to tolerate to live.

Boy, was I wrong.

A sense of satiation fell over her, and she swept her gaze across the crowd. Besides Henry and Cerissa, the chief of police and two deputies were standing on the damp grass.

Christine raised an eyebrow, surprised Henry had allowed Cerissa to be present, given the risks. She looked like a tasty, walking hot fudge sundae. So did Jayden.

Restraint.

Henry had lectured her about how a new vampire would feed voraciously. Well, she'd show her control and leave those walking sundaes alone. She dragged her attention away and started brushing the dirt from her clothes and skin. Despite the sheet, filth clung to her, and she wrinkled her nose. "I need a shower."

A faint ripple of laughter ran through those standing around her.

She felt something tugging at her stomach and lifted the collar of her loose dress to look. No bra. A small row of stitches from the liposuction itched where the skin healed around them. She touched her face and found the same.

Cerissa peered around Henry's shoulder. "I'll remove the stitches after you shower."

"Oh, I must look hideous."

"No, ma'am." Zeke took off his hat and nodded to her. "You're a vision of loveliness."

"Ah, thank you?" Christine said, uncertain. Then she zeroed in on Zeke and gave him a head-to-toe once-over, from his honey-blonde hair to his cowboy boots, and back again to the cocky grin on his dimple-cheeked face.

Son of a gun. He was one good-looking man.

Yes, Cerissa had warned her: he wasn't a good person. But Christine had always been attracted to the bad boys.

A shiver went through her when she remembered his bite. Lust filled her, a level she hadn't felt since going through the change—menopause, that was. Now, she'd been through another change.

The memory of Zeke's bite drifted through her thoughts again. Too bad they'd been in council chambers at the time, or she'd have definitely jumped him.

"This is going to be so much fun."

She looked into Zeke's eyes again and smiled a very wicked smile.

Chapter 8

POSSESSIVE, MUCH?

Rancho Bautista del Murciélago—Moments later

Henry snarled in Zeke's direction while holding Cerissa's hands so she couldn't pinch him again. This was Henry's child, his fledgling, and Zeke would keep his hands off her, at least until she found her feet in the world of being vampire.

That, or he'd beat the *cabrón* until he begged for mercy.

"Thank you, everyone, for coming," Henry said, instead of saying what he felt like saying. "Everything is under control. Zeke, you may return home. Tig, I hoped to impose on you a little longer—would you mind standing by while Christine showers? I don't want to leave her alone yet, and for modesty's sake—"

"Fine. I'm happy to babysit."

Christine shook her arms, flinging off the damp earth. "A shower sounds nice. I am a bit dirty."

"I've left clean towels and your luggage in the pool house," Cerissa said, hovering by his shoulder, his body still providing a physical barrier.

Tig took Christine's arm. "Come on. You can ogle Zeke another time."

Jayden fastened his stun gun to his utility belt. "If you don't need me, chief, I'll catch a ride back to the police station with Zeke."

"Go ahead," Tig replied. "I'll meet you there."

Zeke tipped his hat. "Good night, everyone." He strode to his truck along with Jayden.

With them gone, Henry watched as his child walked next to Tig across the grass to the pathway leading under the bright patio lights behind his house.

My child. I have a child.

He opened his arms and hugged Cerissa to him. "Thank you, *cariña*. Without your intervention, she'd be dead."

Cerissa leaned back and looked into his eyes. "How are you feeling?"

"Strange. I'm suddenly responsible for another person's life."

"At least with babies, you have nine months to grow accustomed to the idea."

"Indeed." He cupped her face and reverently kissed her. His beloved had made this miracle happen—a miracle he was only beginning to come to terms with. "I should send out a text, to let Rolf and Karen know all is well."

"You do that. I'm going to refill this." She raised her wineglass. "Should I heat some blood for you?"

"Yes, please. And some for Tig? I'm going to wait in the pool house. Would you mind bringing the dark wine to us?"

Her eyes gleamed in the moonlight. "I'm happy to."

He gave her another squeeze and let go.

Before he could move in the direction of the pool house, anxiety ruffled the hairs on his arms. Did his child need him? He rushed to find out what happened.

When he got there, Christine was in the shower, and Tig stood in the doorway between the bathroom and the living area, keeping an eye on her.

Contrary to what his gut had told him, everything was fine. Henry let out a relieved breath and relaxed back on the couch, resting one arm along the top. "I had planned on giving Christine a detailed explanation of what the transition involved, taking my time to do so while she recovered from her surgery. Now I'm going to provide her with a speed course in being vampire."

Tig shrugged. "She's smart. She'll learn the ropes quickly."

The chief was right. All his worrying was probably for nothing.

He turned at the sound of Cerissa arriving, and his mate offered a mug to Tig. After she took a sip, Tig's eyes filled with surprise. "This is excellent."

"Thank you," Cerissa replied. "It's clone blood."

"You're going to be very popular when you start selling this."

Cerissa's cheeks pinked, and she dipped her head.

His mate still wasn't accustomed to receiving praise, and she sometimes found it hard to stand up for herself. Nonetheless, she'd gotten better at asking for what she wanted in their relationship. "And that other one is for me?" Henry asked.

"Oh, sorry, Henry. Yes." She handed him the mug, then looked around the pool house. "I'll get my medical bag to remove the stitches—"

"No. I don't want her around you. Not yet."

"You'll be there. What could go wrong?"

He ground his teeth. More things than she could imagine. Then he caught sight of Tig's smirk and gave her side-eye. Under the circumstances, he counted on the chief to keep her opinion to herself.

"I'll need to remove the stitches at some point." Cerissa shrugged. "But what if we started slower? When Christine is dressed, bring her to the drawing room. We can all comfortably talk there."

He let out a breath, reconsidering. With him present, Christine would be on a short leash. A conversation at a distance should be acceptable. But for the moment, he refused to allow Cerissa close enough to remove the stitches.

Henry nodded. "Why don't you return to the house and clean the kitchen while she gets dressed?" At Cerissa's urgings, they'd abandoned the dirty dinner dishes in the sink to wait by the grave. "Then I'll determine whether Christine is up for being around mortals."

"Yes, sir," she replied.

He didn't miss the slight bit of sarcasm in her voice, but they had all been on an emotional roller coaster, so he let it slide.

Twenty minutes later, Christine emerged from the bathroom, wearing a long-sleeved shirt with jeans, running her fingers through slightly damp hair. The blonde strands sparkled with silver highlights. "Best shower ever."

Tig cocked her head in Christine's direction. "Do you need me anymore?"

He glanced at Christine, evaluating his child's state of mind from her demeanor.

"We will be fine." Henry stood and shook Tig's hand. "Thank you for staying."

"And thank you for the drink."

"You're welcome." He took the mug from Tig and beckoned to Christine. "Let's go to the main house."

Tig stopped to examine the exterior of the pool house. "By the way, nice job on the windows."

The custom metal work arrived a week ago, and he'd installed the silver security bars across each window to the pool house, along with a folding silver grille. The grille could be extended to close over the French doors from the outside.

"I believe the silver will be enough to keep a young vampire contained," he said.

The whole thing had cost him a pretty penny, but Christine wouldn't be able to escape and hurt anyone. The peace of mind was well worth the cost.

He escorted Tig and Christine past the pool and to the large patio. After they said their goodbyes, Tig veered off to go around the main house to where her van was parked in the driveway. Henry opened the French doors to the drawing room.

Christine stopped behind him on the steps, facing the starry night sky with its wispy scattered clouds and the vineyard trailing over the hills beyond the pool house. She stretched and took a deep breath. "God, everything smells so intense."

"Especially after a rain. Enhanced senses are just one of the many advantages to your new state." He gestured to her and put a little command in his voice. "Come."

Chapter 9

ALIVE OR DEAD?

Rancho Bautista del Murciélago—Moments later

From experience, Henry had no doubt Christine would follow. The compulsion to come when his maker called was all too familiar to him. Over the years, Anne-Louise had compelled him to return to her so she could continue to feed on him, keeping him tied to her, and her reasons for maintaining the bond were so clouded by the lies she told he didn't know the truth of the matter.

Did she really fear becoming revenant, the violent, zombie-like condition that could occur after a millennium of being vampire? Some believed taking the blood of a child granted immunity to the devastating disease. Or was it her joy at having power over him?

The reminder of his own maker's schemes irritated him, and he suppressed the growl welling up in his throat.

Now that he was a maker, there was so much to consider. As time passed, if he continued to feed on his own child, the bond would renew, allowing him to extend the control indefinitely. He had no idea how long he'd want Christine bound to him. In part, the decision depended upon how quickly she controlled her appetite and learned restraint around mortals.

After Christine entered the drawing room, Henry closed the patio doors. "Please, have a seat on the couch."

He didn't want Cerissa sitting next to Christine when she joined them. The heavy, wood-framed armchairs he and his mate usually sat in to read were near the fireplace. By the time Cerissa entered holding a mug of blood, he'd carried over each chair so they could sit across from his child.

Taking the mug from Cerissa, he handed it to Christine, whose eyes lit up as she took big sips. He eased onto his leather-covered chair across from her.

While Christine had lay in a coma, an inkling of fondness, the kind of love that family members shared, began to grow in him. But in all honesty, she was a stranger to him.

His relationship with his own maker began with them as strangers. The difference: he and Anne-Louise had been lovers. Did that change how his maker felt about him? Should he call Anne-Louise and ask her?

Henry shuddered. The thought of seeking help from her repulsed him.

Right now, the primary feeling driving him was obligation—a sense of duty to Christine. Yet he felt something else besides duty, something peculiar. He felt…possessive. Yes, that was the right word. Where did his possessiveness come from?

The possessiveness wasn't that of a lover, even though he'd reacted when Christine made eyes at Zeke.

Was this the sort of possessiveness fathers had for daughters?

When Christine placed the mug on the coffee table, he leaned forward in his chair, putting the palms of his hands together. "There was so much I wanted to teach you before you became one of us, but your medical condition forced our hand. So we might as well get started now. Do you have any questions?"

"Will everything always be this intense?"

Both he and Cerissa chuckled, dispelling some of the tension inside him. "Not always. It will lessen with time, but frankly, all your senses will remain heightened."

"How soon until I can move into a place on my own?"

Prior to surgery, Christine put her furniture in storage and moved her clothes into the pool house. She'd either sell her Los Angeles bungalow or rent the house out later. Under no circumstances could he envision her living on her own, outside the community's walls, in the next five years.

"That will depend on you, but don't count on such a move happening quickly. You have eternity now. We'll take this a step at a time."

"All right. What about my phone? Did anyone bring it home from the hospital? It wasn't in my luggage."

"I have your phone," Cerissa said. "I plugged it in, so it's charged."

Henry held up a hand. "But we don't want you using the device unsupervised. Not until you are past the temptation of phoning a mortal and asking them to come to you."

"Why would I do that?"

"To feed."

Christine glanced at the mug on the coffee table.

He didn't miss the desire in her eyes. "It wouldn't be the first time a new vampire tried to lure a mortal to them. So for at least a few weeks, you'll have no phone privileges."

"But my clients—I need access to my email. I have matters pending I planned on responding to while I recovered from surgery."

"Henry—" Cerissa began, then paused.

Although Christine was his child, Henry valued his mate's advice. He raised one questioning eyebrow in her direction.

Cerissa shrugged. "Perhaps supervised, Christine could access her email."

"Let me consider the matter."

That seemed to mollify Christine for the moment. "What else do I need to know?" she asked.

Henry pursed his lips. He had planned on making a list before events spun out of his control. "First, you are never to be alone with a mortal, including Cerissa. Second, you will be confined to the pool house when you aren't with me or another vampire I trust."

"Wait a minute." Panic filled her voice, and he could hear her rapid heartbeat from where he sat. "I didn't agree to being your captive."

"And you aren't," he said, keeping his voice calm and soothing. "But you are a danger to others."

Christine crossed her arms, giving him the evil eye.

"It is my duty to keep you from hurting any mortal. And these rules are for your own protection too. How would you feel if you attacked and hurt Cerissa or Nicholas?"

"Terrible." Her shoulders drooped and a sigh escaped her lips. "All right, you've made your point."

"Thank you for understanding."

"But how long will all these restrictions last? I'm a fifty-nine-year-old grown woman who is being babysat."

"Precisely. Best to consider yourself a baby. One who needs to crawl before she runs."

Christine didn't look happy at that. "Fine."

"I also want you to stay away from Zeke."

"Now—"

"I saw how you ogled him. Zeke is not an honorable man. I do not want him taking advantage of you in your current fragile state."

"You mean, you don't want me taking advantage of him."

Henry frowned. He wasn't a prude, but he did *not* want her cavorting with Zeke. "You are too new to being vampire to take a lover. Please trust me."

"As you say, I'll think about it."

"Christine."

"Fine." She ground her teeth, her jaw jutting out. "Can I read my email now?"

Cerissa popped to her feet. "I'll get your phone."

Why did she have to volunteer? He would have preferred deferring that a little longer. Now that he was a parent, and she was—what? A stepparent? They needed to work out a strategy together. And besides, he had more experience with vampires than she did. He should be leading them through this.

The doorbell rang. Who could that be? He should have sent out an alert, telling everyone on the Hill about the situation and asking potential callers to refrain from visiting.

Cerissa left the drawing room before he could say anything. Her receding footsteps tapped through the foyer and the front door opened.

"Hey, Ciss, can I meet her?" Ari's unmistakable voice.

¡Dios, dame paciencia! Henry didn't need Cerissa's cousin tempting the fledgling.

"Ari," she said, "now is not the best time."

"Come on, I want to meet the baby vampire." The sound of hurried footsteps on the tile floor of the foyer preceded Ari bursting into the drawing room. "Is this her?"

Cerissa followed, shaking her head. "Christine, this is my cousin, Ari."

Christine stood. "Marcus mentioned you."

Ari gave a big, clown-like grin. "Only good things, I hope."

Christine bit her lip, small fangs showing.

Henry moved fast, *whooshing* between Christine and Ari. "Ari, you would be better off playing with a baby cobra. Christine is too new to be around you."

"Cool, dude. I'll go. I just wanted to see for myself. She's been awake, what, two hours?"

"Something like that. Now please leave."

"This way, Ari," Cerissa said, tugging on her cousin's arm and dragging him back to the foyer.

A few moments later, Henry heard the front door close. Time to nip this in the bud. He'd seen the look on Christine's face when she eyeballed Ari. "I have another rule. Stay away from Ari. You are not ready for any lover, let alone a mortal one."

She cut Henry a look.

"If you need further motivation: Ari is also dating Gaea, and he's not known for his fidelity. I do not want you caught up in his mischief."

"You really are a killjoy."

Cerissa returned with Christine's phone. He stopped her, hooking his arm around her waist and taking the phone away from her. "You will stay six feet away from Christine. Understood?"

Cerissa's irritation rolled through the crystal. "Henry."

"She is hours old. No temptation is better than an accident. Do you agree?"

"Yes," Cerissa and Christine said in unison, both sounding exasperated.

"Now," he said, gesturing with the phone and facing Christine. "You may read your email. If you want to respond, I will read your response before you send your reply."

Christine's eyes grew big. "But what if the communication is privileged?"

"You will hire me as your assistant. I will agree to keep the confidences I learn. And frankly, I'll forget them as soon as I read them. I merely want to make sure you aren't inviting any mortals to meet you."

"You don't have to do that."

"Yes, I do." Henry held the phone next to his chest. "Now, do you agree?"

Christine looked like she wanted to pout. "Yes, fine."

Smart woman. He handed her the phone, and lightning fast, the attorney began skimming through her email.

"What?" she demanded. "Are you going to stand there hovering over me the whole time?"

"I'm going to sit next to you." The rustic couch with its dark brown leather and mahogany frame was big enough that they'd both be comfortable while he monitored her—close without being too close. "I have my own email to go through. But know this—I'll catch everything you do out of the corner of my eye. Do not try anything."

Christine didn't respond, but she wasn't typing—just tapping and reading.

"Cerissa, if you have other things to keep you occupied, you do not need to stay."

His mate raised her eyebrows. "I can take a hint when I hear one. I'm dismissed. I'll be in my lab."

He hadn't meant his comment that way. All the stress of having a newborn child was beginning to show. "Cerissa—"

"It's fine, Henry."

His gaze followed her lovely figure as she left the room, then he settled down and opened the email program on his phone. About twenty minutes later, Christine exclaimed, "Yikes!"

"What is wrong?" he asked.

"The law firm sent out a notice to my clients announcing my death."

"How did they find out?"

"My partner—Patrick Krull—was listed on my hospital forms as a contact. The hospital must have phoned him. He distributed the notice firm-wide, which is why the email landed in my inbox. I need to call him."

"Let me think for a moment. Would it be better if he believed you were dead?"

"And liquidate all my assets? No way in hell. He's the trustee for my estate. I like my nieces, but I'm not ready to give them everything I own. Not when I still need it. We have to call him. Now."

Chapter 10

Visitors

Rancho Bautista del Murciélago—Moments later

Henry checked the time: ten o'clock. Not too late to call. "Put your phone on speaker."

"But—"

"Do you want to call him? I will hear both sides."

"Fine." Christine punched his name from her favorites and hit the phone icon. Moments later, the phone stopped ringing. There was a pause.

"Who is this?" a male voice asked tentatively.

"Patrick, it's Christine."

"Is this a twisted joke? Christine Dunne is dead."

"No, I'm not. I'm very much alive."

"Listen, whoever you are—"

"Patrick! The hospital made a mistake. They got my name mixed up with another patient. It's *me*."

"Okay, then what is your cat's name?"

"Patrick, I don't have a cat. I hate being around cats. Allergic."

"How did we meet?"

"At a conference for city attorneys. You gave a presentation on the regulation of wireless antenna installations."

"Remember the client we expected would end up in bankruptcy court? What did you always say to me?"

"That we were shuffling the deck chairs on the *Titanic*."

The line went quiet for a moment. "Christine, is it really you?"

"Yes, it's me."

"Jesus Christ, Christine, I thought you were dead."

"I know. I can't imagine. I want to murder whoever screwed up at the hospital. But Patrick, you have to send out an email to our clients. Let them know the notice was a mistake."

"Why didn't you contact me before this?"

"Because I've been recovering from surgery. I didn't feel like looking at my phone until this evening. That's when I saw the announcement."

"Where are you? Still in the hospital?"

She looked at Henry, trepidation in her eyes. "No."

Henry nodded at her and said in a low whisper, "Tell him you are here."

"Ah, I'm with friends. Henry Bautista and Cerissa Patel are taking care of me as I recover."

"Wait. The Henry Bautista who is your client in Sierra Escondida? The vampire?"

Henry almost shouted, "The *what?*" but managed to restrain himself.

Christine sucked in a loud breath. "You opened the letter?"

A letter? Henry clenched his fists, ready to thrash her. He could not believe how reckless she'd been to leave a letter explaining to her partner what Sierra Escondida hid.

"Your assistant gave me the envelope. Of course I opened it. I thought you were dead."

Christine eyed Henry's fists and flinched. "Well, I'm very much alive. Please, ignore the letter—"

"I am coming to see you."

"Patrick, really, that's not necessary. You have your work—"

"Christine, I cleared tomorrow on my schedule because I thought you were dead. Surely you wouldn't deny an old friend a visit under the circumstances."

Backed into a corner, Henry checked his phone for sunset and then held up his fingers.

Christine's eyes sharpened. "Fine, Patrick, if you insist. We can meet you at eight o'clock tomorrow night."

"Why so late?"

"You want me to introduce you to Henry and Cerissa, right? Well, they aren't available before eight." She gave him directions and the address. "Please send out the retraction to our clients as soon as possible. I'd planned on replying to emails tonight. I don't want to give them a heart attack."

"Very well. I'll take care of notifying them. Give me thirty minutes."

"Thanks, Patrick. Oh, and bring that stupid letter with you, okay? I'll explain it all when we meet, but I don't want it getting out and embarrassing my Sierra Escondida clients."

"All right, Christine. I will. And I look forward to your explanation."

"Bye for now."

Christine tapped the end button and let out a big breath.

Henry glared at her, barely containing his anger. "What letter?"

"Cerissa didn't tell you?"

He narrowed his eyes at her.

"I guess she didn't." Christine flinched under his glare. "When I first found out you were vampires, I left a detailed letter in my desk drawer for my partner to find in case I was killed."

Henry had to unclench his jaw to speak. "Be that as it may, why didn't you retrieve the letter before this?"

"I intended to—I swear I did. Ask Cerissa. The plan was to leave the hotel and go by my office before we arrived at the hospital. But we got stuck in traffic, so we decided to go after I recovered from surgery."

Rage filled him. The carelessness of their actions. What would the error cost them all?

"I see." He would talk with Cerissa later, both to confirm Christine's story and to ask her how she could neglect this threat. "We will spend the rest of the evening working on a plan for dealing with your partner. Seeing someone who was part of your former life so soon is a bad idea. You have no control over your reactions. Your fangs came out when you caught the scent of Ari's blood. No, this is not good at all."

The doorbell rang. He winced.

Not more visitors.

"Stay here," he said to Christine. He strode to the front door and flipped on the switch for the video monitor.

Ave María Purísima.

The first thing he always noticed about the woman was her short strawberry-blonde hair, which she wore teased into a wild, puffy ball. He opened the door. "Olivia, this is a surprise. I'm a bit busy tonight. How may I help you?"

"Evening, dearie." She held out a large basket. "I brought a welcome hamper for your child."

After spending almost a century in America, Olivia's British idioms and Liverpool accent still betrayed her origins—she had called what she held a hamper rather than a basket. Henry nodded and reached for the gift. "That is most kind."

Olivia snatched back the cellophane-wrapped basket. "I was hoping to give the gift to her in person."

Vendors. As the donor blood franchise operator, Olivia liked to roll out the welcome wagon whenever a new resident arrived. Especially young vampires, who tended to require more blood than older ones, giving Olivia an even larger profit than the average customer.

Henry frowned. "I guess that would be all right, for a short visit. Please come in."

He led the way. As they walked through the foyer and into the drawing room, she said, "I love what you've done with the place. Very old-school Spanish colonial vibe. I feel like I've slipped back in time."

"Thank you." He stopped by the chairs facing the couch. "Christine Dunne, I want to introduce Olivia Paquin. She owns the community dark wine franchise. Her business collects expired blood from the various outlets—blood banks, hospitals—and does blood drives among those who are technically not eligible to donate. There is a lot I haven't had a chance yet to explain, but we cannot catch any diseases, so Olivia can be less picky about donors."

"Welcome to the community, dearie. I brought you a little something for when you're feeling peckish." Olivia handed the basket to Christine. "Here we have blood lollies. Those are quite popular, just a little corn syrup to hold them together, and I stir in the blood as they cool, so the blood doesn't cook. The dried blood jerky is good if you feel like gnawing on something. Satisfies the mouth hunger as you transition to a liquid diet. And here are regular donor bags; I'm sure you've seen these already. And when you're in the mood for a little something special, this one is a donation from a mortal who was drunk. It'll give you a light buzz."

"Thank you." Christine unwrapped one of the lollipops. "I appreciate your thoughtfulness."

"And last but not least, an order form. I'm sure Henry will help you fill one out after he gets a sense of your feeding schedule."

"Yes, I will." He wouldn't, but the woman would never leave if he said that. "Now Christine and I really should get back to her training. You understand, Olivia."

But before he could steer the saleswoman away, Christine spoke.

"Fifty dollars? For a donor bag?" Christine looked in his direction, clearly puzzled. "But I haven't been drinking from donor bags."

"Of course you have, dearie. Henry has probably been serving you blood in a wineglass?"

"A coffee mug."

"Oh, whatever." Olivia wrinkled her button nose, as if a coffee mug were beneath her. "Well, Henry may not have shown you the donor bags yet, but I assure you, you're drinking them."

"Oh. You mean the silvery pouches? Yes, I've seen those."

Olivia's brow furrowed. "Silver—"

Henry cleared his throat. They'd be here all night if he let this continue. "Actually, Olivia, I've been feeding Christine clone blood provided by Cerissa."

"Oh, I heard about your mate's little business. But surely she isn't producing enough blood from clones to feed a hungry new vampire?"

He hadn't spoken with Cerissa about her production capabilities, but she'd expressed no concern about accommodating Christine's needs. Still, he didn't want to put pressure on her.

"So far Cerissa is providing sufficient blood, but perhaps we'll order a little extra from you, just to be on the safe side."

"There you are, dearie. That's right sensible, it is. You don't want to starve a new vampire. And I can easily accommodate her appetite."

"Very well. Please increase my weekly delivery by one bag per day. She should learn to tolerate donor blood in any case. But we'll hold off having Christine place her own order for now."

Olivia's mouth formed a tight grin, her heavy makeup foundation creasing in response. "Only one? Now surely—"

"One will be enough for now."

Olivia opened her mouth, then shut it again. "Ah, well. One extra bag it is, then."

Christine had been watching them intently. "Ah, could we throw in a few more of these suckers? They're divine. And if the rest of the basket is the same, I might need that form after all."

Olivia broke into a relaxed smile. "Chuffed to bits to hear you think so, dearie. Of course, I'll add some blood lollies for you."

"Great."

Henry made a show of checking his watch, hoping Olivia would catch the hint. What part of "short visit" didn't she understand?

Olivia pursed her bright red lips, looking contemplative, before returning her gaze to Henry. "Are you sure only one more bag a day is enough? When I heard about Cerissa's project for Leopold, I'd been led to believe it would be *years* before they were off the ground."

"She is currently producing enough blood for me and Rolf, and now, for my child."

"I see. Well, perhaps collaboration is in my future. Is Leopold's project still looking for investors?"

Henry had to control his smirk. "I'm afraid you should have invested when you had the chance. I believe all the shares have been sold. But if you are interested, I could speak with Cerissa, ask if Leopold is willing to open the offering for additional investors."

"That would be lovely, thank you." Olivia ran her fingers through her fluffy hair, pushing the teased curls out even more, then turned to Christine. "Welcome to the community again, dearie. I'm glad you're joining us. And do let me know what you think of the rest of the goodies."

Christine's gaze flicked between Henry and Olivia. She finally took the blood lollipop out of her mouth and said, "Thank you, I will."

"Now, I'm sure you and Henry have other matters to attend to. I'll just see my way out." Olivia stepped back and turned toward the drawing room door.

"Wait a moment. I'll go with you." Henry wasn't giving her any opportunity to snoop. But first things first. "Christine, can I trust you to take the basket to the pool house and put the contents in your refrigerator?"

She sprang to her feet, holding the basket. "Certainly."

He followed Olivia to the front door. "Thank you for stopping by. Good night."

"You too. Ta-ta."

He'd started to shut the door when he saw Marcus's Mercedes pull up in the driveway and park by the fountain. He groaned. Not another visitor.

"Henry," Marcus said, striding toward the front porch, "I heard what happened. How is she?"

"She is fine. Come in and meet her."

Clapping Henry on the shoulder, Marcus stopped in the foyer. "Congratulations. How do you feel?"

"Strange. Overwhelmed. But happy."

"Well, Cerissa wouldn't listen to me, and I'm glad she didn't."

Henry opted not to acknowledge that they'd failed to obey a direct order from the town attorney. Instead, he glanced out the open door toward Marcus's car. "Where is your fiancé?"

"I left Nicholas at home. Christine is too new to be around mortals."

Excellent. Marcus understood. But it slightly irked Henry that no one seemed to realize she was also too new for all these visitors.

After closing the front door, Henry led the way through the foyer and to the drawing room, pausing just before the doorway. "Go on in. I'll be a moment." When Marcus sent him a questioning look, he held up his phone. "I'm sending out a message. If I don't, the next thing you know, the mayor will be on my doorstep, demanding to meet her. And I don't need Winston's interference right now."

Thumbs flying over his phone's screen, Henry sent a message via the community's listserv, announcing Christine's birth and asking all residents to hold off visiting until she got acclimated to her new status. That should forestall them.

When Henry entered the room, he found Marcus sitting next to Christine on the couch, the two talking excitedly about lawyer stuff.

Henry smiled, but he couldn't allow their chatter to go on for long. He had to return to their main problem: how to keep Christine under control tomorrow night when Patrick visited.

He sighed. Exposing her to mortals this soon was risky, but he didn't have a choice. They had to fix this ridiculous situation.

Hmm. Marcus's advice frequently got them out of trouble. Maybe Marcus might help with the Patrick problem.

Por Dios, he couldn't make the situation worse.

Chapter 11

DEMONS

Rancho Bautista del Murciélago—Around the same time

Cerissa sensed Henry's upset but continued her work in the lab. She didn't want to interfere with his new relationship with Christine. But when his emotions kept hammering at her, she closed the laptop and joined them in the drawing room, only to find Marcus there. Henry then explained the problem they faced.

Crap. She couldn't believe she had forgotten to tell him about the letter. In fact, she couldn't believe she had forgotten about the letter *altogether*.

If only they hadn't hit traffic, this wouldn't have happened. But they had and it had, so it was time to focus on a solution.

Marcus made some great suggestions, and between the four of them, they addressed the crisis with a solid plan. It would entail a few lies—since Christine's face had fully healed, they'd have to tell Patrick the facelift was canceled because the heart arrhythmia started immediately after the liposuction, when in truth both the liposuction and facelift had been finished before the heart attack happened.

After saying goodbye to Marcus at the door, Cerissa returned to the drawing room and asked Christine, "Are you feeling up to going over your memory questionnaire?"

Prior to the surgery, she had given Christine a lengthy list of questions to answer along with a standard personality test so Cerissa could test a theory about the turn—one she'd been arguing with Ari about.

Christine glanced sideways at Henry. "Sure. But then I want to read my client email and respond. I've ignored it too long."

He thinned his lips. "Perhaps. We shall see."

Despite sensing his displeasure through the crystal, Cerissa knew that exact tone of "perhaps" meant he'd begrudgingly agreed. "I'll be right back."

Cerissa dashed downstairs to grab the questionnaire from her lab. She could not *wait* to prove Ari wrong. Two weeks ago, Ari argued that vampires weren't the risen dead, but demons. He didn't expect any true continuity existed between the mortal they were and the vampire they became, instead hypothesizing that a demon took over the body.

"Henry is not a demon," she'd told Ari at the time. "He's Enrique Bautista Vasquez, with the same consciousness and memories he had when he was human."

"Ciss, you say that, but you don't know for sure." Ari looked all smug about it. "Henry may say he remembers being mortal Enrique, but until you can take someone who has been turned and test those assumptions, you have no evidence there is any real continuity of memory or personality."

She scoffed at him. "Whatever a vampire is, it isn't demonic possession. We have the original's DNA."

"Which completely alters the human DNA, leaving room for demonic possession."

"Oh, Ari. You have such a warped imagination."

"Think about it, kiddo. You've morphed into vampire form. What did you have to do to complete the morph?"

"Inhabit a dead life form. Yes, the body of a vampire is not *alive*, not in the sense of any of the life forms I've inhabited before or after. It isn't functioning the way a normal human body does to remain alive. Most of the systems are all shut down. But something does animate them. I can mimic vampirism, even if I don't understand it."

She didn't have to explain any further to Ari—the Lux morphed into what they mapped. No analysis required.

"So whatever keeps a vampire alive," she had continued, "their life force has to have a *rational* explanation. And 'animation by a demon' isn't rational. It isn't based on scientific evidence and doesn't explain anything."

She'd stopped the debate there. Ari was frequently full of shit. But in addition to being her older cousin, he was her Lux supervisor, both of which he lorded over her, and so she cherished any opportunity to prove him wrong.

Christine's turn provided just such an opportunity.

So far, everything she'd observed told her that Christine survived the transition with both her memories and personality intact. All of Henry's concerns over a bad outcome had been unnecessary worrying. But the questionnaire would provide quantifiable evidence that Christine remained herself.

Returning to the drawing room, Cerissa took the chair opposite the couch, where Henry sat next to his child. "How are you feeling, Christine?"

"Not tired at all." Christine shrugged. "It's not like being...mortal. When I woke tonight, I felt rested and energetic—but hungry. Very hungry."

Henry chuckled. "Waking hungry will be true your entire vampire life, but the urgency will lessen with time."

He squeezed Christine's knee in a reassuring gesture, but rather than removing his hand directly after, he allowed it to rest on her thigh. Cerissa noticed the squeeze and was ready to shrug it off, but the lingering presence of his hand resting on the newborn's leg sparked her annoyance.

She eyeballed the offending appendage but bit back the surge of possessiveness rushing through her. Trained by the Lux to put others first, she sometimes struggled with asserting her own needs. And under the circumstances, was this really the time to stand up for herself?

He's probably keeping his hand there in case Christine lunges at me.

It didn't mean she had to like the intimate contact. But they would discuss the matter later, when they were alone. Now wasn't the time.

Henry frowned at her—he must have caught a hint of her resentment through the crystal, yet he didn't move his hand.

Cerissa covered the awkward moment by dropping into her doctor persona. "Well then, Christine, shall we get started?"

Henry squeezed Christine's leg. "Only if you feel strong enough to interact with a mortal. Do you need more dark wine before we start?"

"I'm good." Christine placed her hand over his. "Stop worrying."

Cerissa pressed her lips together to keep from lashing out and focused on her purpose for being there. "I'm going to record our session, so I won't have to take notes."

She set her phone on the coffee table to give the pretense of recording audio. In reality, her contact lenses were already recording both video and audio of their conversation.

"Okay."

Cerissa glanced down at the first question. "What's your last memory before waking tonight?"

"Being in the surgery room and going to sleep under an anesthetic. Counting backward."

"What is the first childhood memory you have?"

Christine's eyes took on a distant look. "A zoo. Seeing sea lions sliding into a pool of water. My mother said I was three at the time."

The simpler questions—like her parents' names and the town where she spent her childhood—were on the questionnaire Christine would fill out shortly. Right now, Cerissa sought the more nuanced memories. "What was your family like?"

Christine glanced at Henry. "Um, I was an only child. My parents were high achievers and expected the same from me."

"Is that why you became an attorney?" Cerissa asked.

"Not entirely. My grades in math and science were fine, but I didn't love those disciplines. English and history were my best subjects, and I excelled on the high school debate team."

"Who was your first love?"

"My husband. We met in high school. On the debate team. We went to the same university for our undergraduate degrees. After graduation, I went to law school, while he got his doctorate in psychology. We were married after we finished our education and stayed together until he died from brain cancer. He was fifty-one at the time."

"I'm sorry, Christine."

"Thank you. It was tough, to keep going afterward, but I managed."

Henry's fingers visibly tightened on Christine's thigh, and hot anger shot through Cerissa. She'd had enough. How could she force them apart without making a scene?

Then an idea struck her. Taking the blank questionnaire and a standard personality test from a folder on the coffee table, she leaned across the table to hand them to Christine. "Here's the—"

Henry's arm shot across Christine's chest and stopped her from standing. His hand then dropped back to her thigh. "I said, no closer than six feet."

"This is ridiculous. I'm supposed to remove her stitches later—I can't take them out from six feet away. And you've been sitting right next to her with your hand on her thigh. She's not going to make it past you."

He snatched back his fingers, like he'd touched a hot stove. Had he not realized what he was doing?

"Newborns are dangerous. I am just being cautious."

She held back the words on the tip of her tongue. She didn't want to accuse Henry of exaggerating the risk because of his possessiveness. "Yes, but we can take precautions while trusting Christine, too, can't we?"

"Thank you, Cerissa." Christine crossed her arms. "That actually brings up something I wanted to circle back on with Henry."

"Oh?" he said, his eyebrows rising.

"Since my husband died, I haven't lived like a nun. You might say I've enjoyed discovering men with the freedom of being a post-menopausal woman. Which is why I can't understand your edict about Zeke." She frowned at Henry, and his face clouded over in response. "I've played the field enough to know what I'm doing. I don't like being told I've lost that freedom."

"It should be enough when I lay down the law. You are my child and should obey me."

Oh boy. That was quite enough.

Cerissa stood. "Henry. The foyer. Now."

She pivoted and strode away. From behind her, he said, "Christine, stay here and work on the questionnaire. I'll be back in a few minutes."

Cerissa stopped under the wrought-iron chandelier, arms crossed, toe tapping, ready to ream him for acting like a jealous lover when it came to Christine.

Henry caught up with her. "Whatever is wrong with you?"

"Me? What's wrong with you? The way you've been ordering me around—"

"Now, *cariña*, I am setting appropriate boundaries for dealing with a newborn."

"And I don't like the way you're sitting so close to her with your hand on her leg."

"Are you jealous?" His notorious eyebrow raised in judgment, his deep brown eyes flashing. "You have no reason to be jealous."

"And you have no business touching her thigh."

He seemed to fight back a smirk. "Cerissa, I love you and only you. You're my mate. She's my child, and no threat to you. I didn't even realize my hand rested on her leg until you pointed it out. Touching her was platonic in nature, paternal."

"Platonic? Paternal? I'm not imagining—"

He moved so fast that she didn't have time to finish. His lips slanted over hers in a soul-scorching kiss. When he pulled back, he stroked her hair. "Truly. I am yours. All yours."

Chapter 12

THE RESULTS

Rancho Bautista del Murciélago—Moments later

When Cerissa broke from the kiss, she read the truth of his words in his intense gaze, in the soft way he caressed her face, in the warmth traveling through the crystal to her heart.

Henry pressed his lips to hers again, gently this time. "I love you. But I have responsibilities now. I thought you understood."

"I do. Just don't touch her so much, okay?"

"I will try. This is new territory for me. I find myself compelled to be near her, not out of love, but from instinct—to prevent her from causing harm and to protect her from harm."

"Okay—" Cerissa's phone rang. "Excuse me."

She slipped the device from her jeans pocket. *Leopold*. Why was her business partner phoning her at this hour? With the time zone difference in New York, he'd be bedding down for the day soon.

She glanced at Henry and said, "I have to take this." She swiped accept. "Good morning, Leopold."

"I'm calling for an update on our project. You're scheduled to go before the town council in six days to obtain approval."

"I know. We've been a little preoccupied here. I mentioned Christine? She almost died, so we had to turn her yesterday. She woke tonight."

"We? You mean Henry turned her."

"I—I had to perform a transfusion. She was in a coma."

"My dear, I'm sure he has his child well in hand. You need to stay focused on the reason I sent you to Sierra Escondida."

"All the building plans are completed. Our architect did a marvelous job on the color renderings for the lab complex. He made all the changes the town requested, including the water conservation plan. The environmental document has been published for the requisite time, with few public comments so far. I'm working on my presentation slides—"

"All very good. But I heard from the mayor. He's been getting some pushback on your project. He implied a small number of objectors are concerned about an influx of unaffiliated vampires into Sierra Escondida." He clicked his tongue. "Some people still carry resentments over the war. He wouldn't tell me who, despite my pressing the matter."

The war? In the 1960s the vampire communities had disagreed over a moratorium on the creation of new vampires, which resulted in a war. The Hill favored the moratorium and fought on the opposite side from Leopold's New York community.

"Influx? I don't understand," she said. "The council is talking about building a short cul-de-sac that would only allow a dozen or so unaffiliated vampires to join our community."

The Hill was just beginning to come to terms with its obligation to open homes for the unaffiliated. When the treaty was signed, those vampires not part of a community were granted a limited time to join a treaty community, and their time to join was running out in a few years.

"I suspect the objections hide something else," Leopold replied. "You're going to need to discover what the issue is and quash it."

"Ah, okay. But even if there are a few naysayers, the councilmembers are quite excited about our project. They like the idea of having a new supply of dark wine. There isn't anything to worry about."

"If they deny the project, it'll be a slap in my face, and I won't give them a second chance. We'll need to try a new location. I've started looking at sites in the Midwest. Lower property values, so we should be able to attract the research professionals you need who don't want to pay California's high prices for a home."

What? No. Her lab had to be in Sierra Escondida. Henry would never move. He'd built this town, he was one of the five founders, and his work—his winery—was here.

"You don't need to shop for a new location," she said, trying to keep the fear from her voice. "I'm sure a few small objections won't be an impediment. I'll make this work."

"See that you do, Cerissa. See that you do."

Henry had remained standing there, listening to her side of the conversation. When the call ended, he said, "I know Leopold can be quick to anger. Is there anything to truly worry about?"

"No." She tamped down her anxiety. Henry had enough on his plate without Leopold's drama making everything worse. "It's just a few objectors. The council is in favor of the lab. I'll figure this out."

"All right. Go work on your project. I have a few things to discuss with Christine." He pulled her tight to his chest and slanted his lips over hers again. "And don't worry. You're the only woman I want."

His love enveloped her through the crystal, warming her to the core. She kissed him deeply, roughly, possessively, and then stepped away. With a glance to the doors leading to the drawing room where Christine sat waiting for him, Cerissa took off for her basement lab.

Time to focus on preparing the slide deck and finishing her speech.

As to Leopold's issue, the solution eluded her. How could she uncover the real reason people opposed the project—if any such opposition in fact existed? The mayor wasn't always forthright, and he'd been known to interfere in Henry's business before. She never understood why Winston resented Henry, only that he did. But so far, none of the mayor's political maneuvering focused on the proposed biotech research facility. Had something changed?

She opened her laptop, stared at the last slide she'd drafted, and drummed her fingers on the lab bench. Should she ignore the complaints, or actively dig to find out who and why?

Both actions had upsides and downsides. Digging might feed the grapevine, but ignoring the objectors might blindside her at the council meeting, leaving her unprepared to defend against their real reasons. Maybe tomorrow, after she wrapped up her slide presentation and the Patrick matter was resolved, she'd reach out to Karen. Karen was the gossip queen, and if anyone knew anything, she would.

Cerissa fell into bed around five in the morning, exhausted. She wished Henry could have spent time cuddling with her, but briefing Christine on her new existence took priority.

Before Cerissa went to sleep, Henry had finally let her get near enough to his child to remove the stitches while he held down Christine's shoulders. Christine smirked at the whole thing as Cerissa clipped the threads and pulled them out with tweezers. The newborn didn't seem tempted to attack.

Cerissa then took a blood sample, part of her plan to monitor Christine's development and track what changes occurred in her body the longer she was vampire.

When Cerissa woke at noon, she reached over to Henry's side of the bed—the side he gravitated to when they cuddled—but he wasn't there.

Why did she expect him be next to her? He'd been clear when he forbade her from sleeping with him. If a vampire sensed danger nearby, they could overcome the power of the sun and rise. He feared he might be startled awake and hurt her, particularly when she woke earlier than him.

But the crystal in his arm wouldn't allow that to happen, wouldn't allow him to cause her harm. She'd told him that a hundred times. Why was he being so resistant?

She picked up her phone from the bedside table and checked the lunar calendar. For at least five days of each month, their sleep patterns overlapped. Sunrise would put him to sleep but the early moonrise would wake him between midmorning and noon—around the same time she tended to wake for the day. Why couldn't they sleep together then?

Her heart ached for him, longing for his presence, his touch, his body nestled against hers. They should share a bed.

The intensity of the feeling gave her pause. Why was she feeling so needy?

Sure, the past forty-eight hours had been taxing. Saving Christine's life, turning her vampire, and dealing with all the details of having a baby vampire in residence, along with Leopold's demands, left her tired and wanting Henry's attention. But the *need* went beyond the norm for her.

Should she mention it to Fidelia? She'd been seeing the Lux psychologist because the earthquake resurrected her PTSD. Was her neediness an additional symptom of her condition?

Perhaps. But she would have to ponder it fully some other time. Her to-do list was way too long to allow for a relaxing day of self-reflection.

A few hours later, she took a break from preparing her presentation for the council meeting, and grabbed Christine's completed questionnaire, placing the answers side by side to compare them.

Not only had Christine retained memories of her human life after being turned, her answers were also sharper and more detailed.

And it was the same with the personality test. While some questions were answered differently, their number was low and within the expected range of deviation. Cerissa could always ask Fidelia for a second opinion, but the results supported a continuity of consciousness.

Cerissa knew better than to make too much out of one research sample—she would need to do this process with a statistically significant group of new vampires before drawing any conclusions.

Still, the results were enough to tell Ari he was dead wrong, something she didn't get to do too often with such clear-cut evidence.

She put in her phone's earpiece and tapped his number. When he answered, his 3-D image hovered over her phone. She didn't give him a chance to say hello. "You were wrong."

Ari sniggered. The video image showed him at a table in an outdoor restaurant with decorative lights illuminating the night. Maybe he'd flashed to his home in Florida, but knowing Ari, he could be anywhere on the globe.

"Okay, I'll bite. What big, bad mistake did I make?"

"Christine completed her questionnaire, and she retained all her memories from before. Looks like your theory of vampires being demons possessing dead bodies was completely wrong."

"So what's your theory?"

She glanced at the completed questions and considered her answer. "Based on what I learned from the original genome, I think the blood exchange does a full DNA edit on the cellular level. So a new vampire is the same entity, the same consciousness, but with the physical advantages and disadvantages of being vampire."

"Yeah, but they're dead, right? No breathing—"

"The way their bodies work is changed, so they appear dead to humans in some respects. Oxygen isn't needed to animate a vampire's body. But maybe 'dead' is the wrong word."

Floating above her phone, the image of Ari wagged a finger at her. "Just remember, when you write up your findings, to include an acknowledgement of my contribution."

Her jaw dropped. "Excuse me?"

"Without my thesis, you would never have been motivated to develop and test your antithesis."

"You know, Ari, your arrogance is sometimes hard to take."

He made kissy lips at his phone's camera. "But you still love me, don't ya, Ciss?"

"Yeah, I guess."

"Oh, and Gaea said to tell you and Henry that if you need help with the baby vampire, she'd happily volunteer."

"I'm not sure Henry would accept help. Right now, he's acting very territorial over his child."

"Well, keep Gaea in mind in case he does. I gotta run."

The line went dead, and his image vanished.

Yeah, she loved her cousin. He was like a big brother to her. But that didn't stop him from being annoying.

Cerissa returned her attention to the presentation slides until she remembered her plan to call Karen. Her bestie picked up on the fourth ring.

"Hi, do you have a moment to talk?"

"Sure." Karen sounded out of breath.

"Are you okay?"

"Just got back from taking Sang and Mort to the vet. Those two are a handful in the car. They love their vet, but there's always a moment when they don't want to get out of the car, and I have to practically drag the duo inside. But once there, they do fine."

"And they're well? No problems with their health?"

"None whatsoever. All routine."

Why did something sound off with the way she answered? Karen usually provided more information rather than less. Cerissa had expected an entire rundown of the visit, moment by moment. She gave it a mental shrug—maybe the vet visit had been too routine even for Karen's storytelling.

"Well, I'm glad to hear the duo are fine. But I called to ask you something specific. Have you heard any rumors about my project? Any Hill vampires who are opposed to the lab?"

"There were the usual assholes who objected to having an unmated mortal on the Hill—meaning you—but once you and Henry mated, they shut up. So no, I haven't heard anything else."

"Leopold got a call from the mayor alluding to some objectors. But the town's only received a few written public comments on the project, which we easily dealt with. I figured we'd sail right through."

"I don't know what to tell you. But I'll keep my ear open to the grapevine for any rumblings."

"Thanks. Okay, I better get back to work. Talk with you later—and give Mort and Sang some kisses from me."

"Don't worry, those two are so spoiled, they don't need extra. Bye!"

Cerissa resumed her work and stopped when the alarm she'd set on her phone buzzed. Now to get ready for Patrick's arrival. She went upstairs to her room, dumped her lab clothes into the hamper, and selected a nice dress to wear after she showered. With any luck, they'd easily convince Christine's partner that everything was well and put him at ease. After all, with the way Henry hovered over Christine, maintaining constant control, what could go wrong?

Chapter 13

SOMETHING FISHY

Rancho Bautista del Murciélago—That night

Patrick parked in the circular driveway, by a fountain of a woman pouring from an urn. Through the windshield, he studied the large, two-story house with its smooth white stucco, arched windows, and terracotta-tiled roof.

Impressive.

Buildings like this were a fixture in California and looked right at home with the vineyards surrounding the structure.

He stepped out of his Volvo sedan, then took his coat off the backseat hanger, slipped into the London Fog, and straightened his tie. The red brick driveway glistened under the outdoor lighting. They'd had a rainstorm during the day, with more rain predicted for tonight—par for the course in unpredictable October. Fortunately, the rain had stopped, so he didn't need an umbrella for the short walk to the porch stairs.

When he first learned Christine died, he'd been devastated. Then he received her surprising late-night phone call. Now, a cross of anxiousness and anticipation churned in him. He rang the bell and waited impatiently.

One of the two paneled doors opened to reveal a lovely woman with dark hair, wearing a long-sleeve plum-colored dress and looking like a business professional.

"Hello, I'm Patrick Krull, Christine's partner."

"Yes, of course. I'm Dr. Cerissa Patel. Call me Cerissa. Please come in."

Patrick entered the elegant foyer, with its black wrought-iron chandelier overhead and a sweeping staircase bordered by a sleek, dark wood railing stopping just short of the middle of the room, and original oil paintings hanging on the walls. The people who lived here certainly had money.

Cerissa closed the door. "May I take your coat?"

"Yes, thank you." He shrugged it off, slipped an envelope from the outer pocket, and handed the London Fog to her. She hung the coat in the foyer's closet.

"Would you like anything to drink? Coffee? Iced tea?"

"I'm fine, thank you. I just want to see Christine."

He glanced at the staircase. Was she upstairs in bed?

"This way, please." Instead of walking to the stairs, Dr. Patel led him though a double-door entry to a large room with a river-stone fireplace. "Here we are."

Relief flooded him when he saw his partner of twenty-five years sitting on the rustic leather couch. "Christine! God, I'm so happy to see you."

He walked briskly over to her, offering his arms for a hug, giving her space to stand, but she remained on the couch and waved him off.

Why did she do that?

He then noticed that sitting next to her was an older man with salt-and-pepper hair who wore his long hair pulled back in a ponytail.

Christine pressed an arm around her stomach. "I'm sorry, Patrick, but my stitches are quite painful. I'll stay here if that's all right."

"Of course, I don't want you to hurt yourself. I'll come to you."

He stepped around the coffee table and began to bend down to embrace her, but the older man shot to his feet and blocked him.

"What the—"

"My apologies." The man lowered his arm and offered his hand to shake. "I'm Henry Bautista. I didn't mean to appear rude; it's only that—"

"Christine should avoid any unnecessary contact," Dr. Patel finished.

As Patrick reflexively shook the man's hand, Dr. Patel gripped his arm, gently tugging him back, breaking the handshake. "It's only that she's still recovering from what happened, and we don't want her immune system under more pressure—common colds, viruses, and the like. Henry is acting on my recommendation, albeit a bit"—she cut the man a look—"forcefully."

"Ah, um, okay," Patrick said, stepping well away from Christine. "I guess that's...understandable."

Except it wasn't. Not really. He'd thought his best friend dead, and now he couldn't even hug her in celebration without a stranger interfering. A stranger who, according to Christine's letter, was no ordinary man—not that he believed the supernatural nonsense in the letter.

"I'm glad you're here," Christine said.

He swallowed, pushing past the memory of his grief. "Even after your call, I've been so worried about you."

"I'm sorry I gave you a scare," Christine said. "Please take a seat. Let's talk."

"All right." He eased onto the large armchair across from Christine, and Cerissa moved away to the leather loveseat on the side of the room. "I must say, once you told me you were alive, I expected to hear you were staying in Los Angeles. What are you doing way out here?"

"Henry and Cerissa are being kind enough to allow me to stay in their guest house while I resettle and recover."

Patrick frowned. That didn't seem right. "Shouldn't you be home, closer to your doctors—in case the problem reoccurs?"

"Please don't worry. It's not a problem being here." She smiled at him, a strained smile. "I'm receiving excellent medical care. Cerissa is a doctor. And this way, I don't have to be on my own."

"Right. Well, I suppose you know what you're doing. You are looking surprisingly healed considering the surgery you described to me, so your recovery must be going quite well."

Christine looked embarrassed. "Well, actually, that's the problem, you see. They stopped the surgery when I developed a heart arrhythmia. They'd completed the liposuction but not the facelift."

"When the hospital phoned me, they said you'd had a fatal heart attack. I don't understand how they made such a terrible mistake."

Christine sighed. "They mixed up my records with another patient in the same recovery room. We both developed problems during our surgeries, and the transcriptionist who took the phone reports typed the death annotation on the wrong file. I had an arrhythmia, but they caught it in time, and I recovered. Honestly, the entire thing is an embarrassing mess—*especially* when I have to explain it to my clients."

She laughed, but the effort was a bit hollow. Maybe her stomach hurt when she laughed? "Well, I'm glad you're fine."

"I'm holding up—but every time I move, the stitches pull," she said, placing a hand over the area again and confirming his guess.

"That doesn't sound pleasant."

"It's not." She pointed at the envelope in his hand. "Is that my letter?"

He'd worked with Christine long enough to recognize the anxiety on her face. Something about the letter upset her. He tapped the white business-sized envelope against his hand. "I opened your letter and was, well, quite flabbergasted that you'd write something like this."

"I can imagine." She gave what looked like a forced smile. Something wasn't right, but he couldn't put his finger on the problem. Christine turned to their hostess. "Cerissa, would you mind getting me some hot tea?"

"Oh, yes, coming right up." Dr. Patel dashed out of the room.

Christine returned her gaze to Patrick. "Anyway, I never meant for you to read the letter. It was just something I played around with. I was supposed to clean out my office before the surgery, but we ran out of time." She held out her hand. "May I have the envelope back?"

"Yes, but you need to tell me what exactly you were 'playing around with' here. You certainly don't look like you're surrounded by *vampires*."

"This is so embarrassing." Christine dropped her hand to her lap when he held onto the envelope a little longer. "The letter is the start of a novel. I had my secretary stash the envelope in my desk to test a theory."

"Theory? Why didn't you email the draft to yourself? I must say, under the circumstances, I was quite disturbed to read that you'd been killed by vampires."

"Yes, the idea struck me as the premise for a novel. A lawyer dies and her partner finds a letter blaming vampires for her death. I wanted to test whether my secretary would keep the secret of a letter marked 'in the event of my death' or feel compelled to tell you about the letter right away."

"But why test that? Why not just leave the letter somewhere the partner would clearly find it—or place the letter in the same envelope as the trust and will. I don't understand why you'd have to test this out."

"Include it with the will! Of course that's a better idea. I'll have to redraft with your suggestion in mind."

Patrick gave her a skeptical look. "I never took you as one who'd write vampire stories. Does the world really need another vampire novel?"

Before Christine could answer, Cerissa returned carrying a tall mug.

"Thank you." Christine accepted the mug and took a big sip. Something about Christine's face looked odd—almost a look of rapture as she drank her tea. "To answer your question, Patrick, vampire romances are quite popular. Writing is one of the things I want to do in retirement."

"Retirement?" he repeated. Was she seriously considering retirement? She'd mentioned nothing about retiring when she scheduled her leave for surgery.

He pursed his lips. It wasn't like her to unilaterally dissolve their partnership and announce retirement out of the blue. She was a planner, through and through. She never made sudden moves.

"Now, I know that look on your face." Christine took another sip from the mug, and her whole face lit up as she did. "I've fallen in love with this hillside valley. I plan on working part time, representing the town, and in my spare time do all those things I've put off doing. Writing fiction is one of them. Even fiction about vampires."

He narrowed his eyes. Her explanation of the letter didn't make sense. Why would she make a convincing and detailed argument to prove vampires ran this town? And the detail—right down to her description of the man sitting beside her, a client, no less. Even if it was for a book, she'd never risk a client's wellbeing or her legal reputation with such a gimmick.

Or was it a gimmick? He had believed the vehemence behind Christine's letter—at least that her clients weren't to be trusted. He hadn't missed the crucifix

Henry wore over his knit crewneck shirt. A storybook vampire would never wear a religious symbol. On the other hand, they'd insisted this meeting be at night.

He kicked himself for even entertaining the idea. Vampires didn't exist. But what if "vampire" was a code word for something else—a call for help based on the shear craziness of the term? Could Henry be involved in a criminal syndicate, and she had to write the message in code to get it sent? He'd known her long enough to know she was neither crazy nor careless.

And the way Henry had stopped him from getting close to her was suspect. Was she now their captive?

"Christine. Are you sure you don't want to come home with me?"

She took another sip from the mug. "Patrick, I'm fine."

"Mr. Krull, I can understand your concern for Christine," Henry said. He took out his phone and looked at something on the screen. "If you'd like to come by tomorrow morning, say around eight, we would happily serve you breakfast before you return to Los Angeles. You can assure yourself of her care, personally."

Patrick could tell Christine was uncomfortable with his doubt. Perhaps this was all in his head? "No, that won't be necessary. If Christine says she's fine, then I believe her. It's just been a few very stressful days."

Christine appeared chagrined. "I'm sorry for worrying you, Patrick, but everything is fine. I want to stay here, even if my move seems rather impetuous. If you'd have someone pack my office and ship everything here in the care of Henry Bautista—"

Henry took a card from his wallet. "Here is my business card. Please have her belongings sent to my winery. There are employees there who can sign for the boxes. That will avoid a problem if neither I nor Christine are home to receive them."

"And you can charge the shipping to my partner account," she added.

Patrick accepted the card. He'd heard of this winery—had tried a few bottles from them and liked their Cabernet. But he didn't understand why this man had opened his home to Christine or had his hand on her shoulder.

Was she involved with Henry? If she was, then why was the doctor staying there too?

"All right," he finally said.

"Thank you. Patrick, please believe me: I wanted to explain my reasons and negotiate an amicable split of our assets in a very different way. I had been thinking of one of our dinners at Musso & Frank's. Unfortunately, the hospital's mistake snarled those plans."

He rose to his feet. "We can go there when you're fully recovered. I'll let you rest now. I'm just glad to see you alive."

Christine laughed. Her nervous laugh. Why was she nervous?

"I'd see you to the door," Christine said, "but..." She waved at her midsection. "I understand."

Dr. Patel stood. "Allow me." She took the letter from him and handed it to Christine. "There. If you'll come with me, I'll retrieve your coat for you, Mr. Krull."

He walked with her to the front door, donned his London Fog, and stepped out into the night.

Something about this whole performance felt wrong, orchestrated. His gut told him that Christine wasn't acting like herself. She laughed at the wrong time and seemed uncomfortably nervous. And the entire "writing a novel" explanation came out of left field. She had *never* mentioned an interest in writing fiction before this.

He got into the car and scratched his chin. Was he overreacting to the situation? He and Christine were close—as friends and business partners. Would she really keep her desire to overhaul her life a secret?

Perhaps he'd conduct his own investigation of Henry Bautista and this community before he returned to Los Angeles. Just to be sure.

Chapter 14

SUCCESS

Rancho Bautista del Murciélago—Moments later

When Henry heard the door close behind Patrick, he let out a deep breath. Christine had passed with flying colors. She'd handled the presence of a mortal without trying to mesmerize or attack him. Impressive, for a newborn.

"I'm proud of you," he said.

She took a sip from her mug. "The blood helps."

"It was good you recognized the hunger and asked for your *tea*. You're doing well."

"Yes, but I'm afraid Patrick is going to be a problem. He wasn't convinced. He suspects something is off about my story."

Henry patted her leg. "I sensed that. But he can suspect all he wants. He has no proof. We have an explanation, however thin, for the letter, which I will destroy." He plucked the envelope from the tight grip she had on it. "And once you're stable enough, you can meet with him—perhaps with Marcus along—to negotiate the split of your partnership. Meeting him out in society will erase his concerns. The restaurant you mentioned could serve for this purpose."

"But I can't eat food."

Henry gave her a reassuring smile. "One of the things we haven't yet discussed. You can dine at a restaurant, but what you consume, you must regurgitate later."

Her eyes got big. "What?"

"It is not hard to learn. With time, you will master the art of blending with mortals."

Cerissa joined them. "Henry, I'm going to make dinner. I'll be in the kitchen."

"Of course, *cariña*. Let me escort my child to the pool house and I'll join you." It still felt strange to name the relationship out loud, although the affection warming his heart told him he was accepting the role. He offered Christine his arm. "Do you think you'll be all right alone for a while?"

Christine walked with him outside. "I'll be fine. I have a few books in my luggage—ones I'd planned to read while I recovered from surgery."

"Good. I hope you can understand why we can't give you unsupervised phone or internet access yet."

"No, it makes sense. I might try to entice a mortal to me if you did."

"Thank you for understanding."

Once inside the pool house, Christine settled on the couch. Henry shut the doors from the outside and slipped on the leather gloves he'd left in the towel cupboard by the pool. With his hands protected, he unfolded the silver grille panels and used a silver chain to fasten them together, wrapping the chain three times through the handholds.

For a fledgling, the silver would work to keep her inside. She had plenty of clone blood available in the small kitchenette, and if she wanted to talk to him, she could go through the underground tunnel connected to the crypts below his house.

Leaving Christine by herself wouldn't be a problem provided she was sufficiently confined. And after the stress of the past few nights, he needed some time alone with Cerissa. Their bickering from last night concerned him. Time alone, time to reconnect, would fix that.

He took a moment to phone Marcus to tell him all went well with Patrick.

By the time he joined Cerissa in the kitchen, she'd changed out of her business attire and into jeans and a casual shirt, and had made a light dinner of yogurt, berries, and nuts. She was already cleaning up.

"Are you sure it's okay to leave Christine unsupervised?" she asked.

"Anne-Louise left me alone frequently after I rose. Something about the relationship creates in our progeny both a fear of and a desire to please one's maker. The two are powerful inducements to good behavior, and the silver barriers on the pool house will keep her inside. Even Tig approved yesterday."

"You're sure?"

"Yes. I can't be with her every minute of every night. Besides, I need to relax. The meeting with Patrick left me much too tense."

She eyed him coyly. "Well, it's my turn to choose. Would you be willing to let me surprise you?"

He cocked his head to the side. They'd decided to trade off leading during lovemaking as a way to explore their mutual desires. She'd thrown herself into their experimentation, and he looked forward to her nights in charge.

Her challenge had him intrigued. "I am willing."

"Then go take a shower and meet me in your room. Ignore the sounds you may hear through the walls."

Sounds? Now, *that* had his curiosity piqued.

He donned a shower cap, not wanting to spend time drying his long hair. From two rooms away, he heard what sounded like an electric drill, followed by the hammering of something—a toggle bolt, possibly—going into the wall.

What was that mate of his up to?

He dried off, spritzed on some cologne, took off the tungsten bracelet he wore to mute their connection, then strode naked from the bathroom, through his large closet, and into the private space he called "his bedroom," only to find she'd done a little redecorating.

The sparsely furnished chamber was smaller than his closet. Intended as a place he could relax when an early moonrise woke him, the windowless room contained a gun safe, a trunk, a chair suitable for reading, a floor-length mirror, and a black leather chaise lounge.

She'd pushed the lounger to the middle of the room, away from the wall where it normally sat, and fastened two padded handcuffs to the wall where an oil painting normally hung. The landscape, which depicted a vineyard and included his home from the late 1800s, had been painted by his vampire sister, and now sat propped against the far wall.

"Let me guess," he said. "You fostered with a family who had a construction business?"

She'd told him about the various human families she'd lived with during her *karabu* stage—an intermediate Lux phase—which spanned almost two centuries. It accounted in part for her vast knowledge and skills, and her ability to blend among mortals.

She returned the electric drill to a tool kit and, using a small hand-broom, swept the shavings into a dustpan, smiling impishly at him. "Why, whatever gave you that idea?"

He waved at the setup. "Professionally done."

"The fasteners release," she said, "so the cuffs can come off, and when you rehang the landscape, the canvas will cover the hardware."

"Indeed. And who is this for? You or me?"

"You."

"But regular handcuffs will not hold me."

"Not any more than a silk scarf would, but it's the idea—or so I'm told. You're bound. You choose whether to break free...or submit."

He raised an eyebrow. She'd become friends with Luis, one of Abigale's mates. Had she learned this from him? Or had she done her own research on the internet, in search of new ideas to try?

Or maybe he should take a closer look at the books she'd downloaded onto her tablet.

He eyed the cuffs again. What *did* she have in mind?

He wasn't sure, but if this was his punishment for neglecting her last night, well, he'd gladly pay the price.

CHAPTER 15

CERISSA'S CHOICE

Henry's bedroom—moments later

Speaking with Henry while he stood there naked sorely tried Cerissa's restraint.

"Come here," she said, and he went into her arms. She inhaled deeply. "Ooh, you smell wonderful."

Woodsy spices and his very masculine scent started a tingle deep in her belly. She ran her hands down his back—his skin was smooth and warm from the shower—stopping at his butt cheeks to squeeze them.

She let out a low moan, then leaned back to look up at him. The intensity in his eyes, those pools of bourbon brown, triggered a flutter in her core. She brought her mouth to his and took full advantage when he parted his lips, probing deeply as she slowly walked him backward until his spine pressed against the wall.

She broke the kiss to look into his eyes. "If I do anything you don't like, say something, okay?"

"I understand." He smirked. "I cannot wait to see what you have in mind."

She smiled as their lips met again.

The leather cuff, lined with sheepskin, had two buckles, with a ring attached to the wall hooks. Without breaking the kiss, she raised his arm and fastened the cuff around his wrist.

Her heart beat fiercely; she was both excited by the images flittering through her mind of what she wanted to do to him, and afraid he might not be pleased.

Capturing his other arm, she fastened the second cuff, sliding the straps through each buckle, then stepped back, admiring what she beheld.

Hot damn.

He was one fine piece of man-candy. Unable to resist the lure, she ran her fingers from his strong collarbone to his firm pecs, circling his taut nipples without touching them, then down to his cut abdomen, massaging each ridge as she went.

Pausing there for the moment, she let her fingers fall lightly over his hips and trail down his thighs, bypassing his erection, which jutted out, begging to be stroked.

When her hands left his skin, he groaned, closing his eyes.

"Look at me," she whispered.

His lids popped open at her command, the pupils already blown out.

Slowly, deliberately, and with a seductive smile, she unbuttoned her blouse, letting it fall onto the couch behind her. The bra was next, and she resisted the desire to play ring toss with his magnificent erection.

Instead, she dropped the scrap of fabric on the floor. After wetting her fingers with her tongue, licking each one individually, slowly, she then cupped her breasts and massaged her own nipples, her gaze never leaving his.

He moaned. "Oh, *cariña*, you are torturing me."

She ran her tongue across her lips. "The torture has only just begun."

The jeans she wore buttoned up. One button at a time, she drew out the process, watching him bite his lower lip, the hunger on his face feeding the flames within her.

Once undone, she pushed the jeans down and kicked them aside, leaving her in a black thong. Playing with her nipples, she eased down onto the couch, lying back and spreading her legs so he had a perfect view of what she had planned next.

Hooking the fabric aside, she ran two fingers around her clit.

He moaned. "All I want to do is break these bonds and replace your fingers with mine."

She locked eyes with him as she continued to finger herself. "But you won't, will you?"

For one long moment, Henry didn't respond.

Then he licked his lips and said, "No, I don't think I will."

Heat rolled over Cerissa in response. She let her fingers slide further down and into her, bringing her slick wetness to where it would do the most good. Rubbing faster and a little firmer, she closed her eyes, feeling his raw desire through the crystal.

When the explosion came, she didn't hold back. She moaned, her hips bucking, her nipples so taut they almost hurt, and she slid her fingers back inside herself to catch the feel of her vagina clenching around them.

"You are so beautiful," he said, sounding breathless. "But even more so when you come."

She rolled off the chaise lounge and sauntered over to him, touching his lips with her drenched fingers, spreading the moisture over them until he opened and took the slick digits into his mouth, sucking hard on them, his erection pressing against her belly, a drop of his moisture smearing across her skin.

"Now," she said, moving away from him to pull the lounger closer. She eased onto the couch's edge, placing her at eye level with his cock. *Perfect.* "Have you ever tried fire and ice?"

She whisked a towel off a tray she'd prepared, revealing a cup of hot tea and a glass of iced tea. She spread the towel on the floor underneath him, raised the glass to her mouth and took an ice cube between her lips, and then rose high enough to run her tongue around his nipple. His skin crinkled hard for her.

"*Madre de Dios,*" he whispered. The look of desire on his face about did her in when she pulled back. "What are you doing to me, *bruja*?"

His imagery set her ablaze. "This witch gets to cast whatever spell she likes."

After sucking on the ice cube again, she tucked it against her cheek and tongued his other nipple, before blowing lightly on his skin.

"Oh, *mi amor*, do not stop."

She chuckled, moving the ice around again to chill her tongue, then licked from his sternum to the most perfectly cut V she'd ever seen, taking her time. His abdomen contracted, and his cock rose with the motion, as if begging for her to touch him.

Soon.

"Spread your legs," she said. After taking a sip of the iced tea—the cube had melted—she knelt between his legs and tongued his balls, feeling them contract from the cold, before once again blowing on them.

He groaned, a deep, manly sound.

Switching off, she took a sip of the warm tea—not too hot—and, after swishing the liquid across her tongue, took first one ball, and then the other, into her mouth, gently sucking on them.

The sounds he made were like applause to her ears.

Had she toyed with him enough? Maybe. She scooted the lounger closer to him, sat down, took another sip of the warm tea, and then ran her heated tongue on the underside of this erection.

He moaned. "Oh, what you do to me."

Next came a sip of the iced tea, and she licked her cold tongue along the same route, then, when she reached his tip, she took him full in her mouth, pushing all the way until he hit the back of her throat.

Slowly she pulled back, sucking on him, rubbing her tongue against the bottom ridge. She paused to take a sip of warm tea then repeated the move, feeling him tremble under her touch.

Now came the cold again, and his cock jumped as her lips touched his head. Her mouth opened wide to take him in.

Henry felt more present in the moment than he ever had. The alternating sensations—heat, then cold—caused his focus to narrow to his *pene*, the desire building to a higher peak without release.

He wanted to rush her, to beg her to finish him. Then again, he didn't want the pleasure to end.

Hanging there, his fangs biting into his lower lip, he resigned himself fully and completely to her control.

Through the crystal, he sensed her excitement at pleasing him, and in return, he sent her all the burning desire he felt.

When her hot lips touched his head again, one warm hand on his *cojones*, the other gripping his shaft, she took him in deeply. Then, instead of releasing him to alternate to cold, she kept going, building speed methodically, until he felt his *cojones* retract and he spilled into her mouth.

Wave after wave of ecstasy convulsed through him as she sucked, taking all he had to give.

"*Mi amor*," he whispered, his mind lost, his heart completely hers.

She released him, placing a kiss on his head when she did, and then took a sip of tea. "Did you like that?"

It took him a moment to recover enough to speak. "You minx. You know I did."

She grinned at him. "But we're not through yet."

What more could she possibly have in mind to top that?

She unhooked each cuff ring from the wall, leaving the cuffs still fastened to his wrists, and went into his arms, her lips open.

Between his fangs, he kissed her deeply, tasting himself and the tea on her tongue.

She gripped his forearm and led him to the chaise lounge. Spreading a soft blanket over the leather, she encouraged him to lie back. "You should rest."

He started to unfasten the cuffs, but she stopped him. "Not yet."

Then he spotted what the blanket had hidden: a board with eyebolts sat on the floor under the chaise lounge, the board's length the width of the cushions. His lounger was a modern open-frame style on four legs, with no armrest, and a cushion at one end in an upright angle to support his back and head, all covered in tufted black leather.

The board with eyebolts wasn't fastened to anything—yet. He had an inkling of what was coming.

Once he lay down on the lounge, she raised the board and, bending his right arm gently, clipped the cuff ring to one eyebolt so his hand rested near his ear, his elbow bent. She stood, still holding the board underneath the lounger's head support, and walked to the other side to fasten the left cuff to the opposite end of the board.

He was again trapped, this time with his hands positioned near his ears. When he tried sitting further forward, the board banged against the cushion's underside. "You call this relaxing?"

She ran a hand down his bare chest, stopping before reaching his *pene*. From a thermos, she poured more tea and warmed her hands on the side of the mug, before returning them to his skin, massaging his pecs, then his glutes, then his abs.

He closed his eyes and gave himself over to her touch until, with one finger, she stroked his *pene*. The bliss brought on by her aura made him instantly hard again.

"Do you need any more time to recover?" she asked.

"No, I think you've taken care of that."

She raised a leg over to straddle him, her knees on either side of his hips, and she held his *pene* poised at her entry.

Dios, she was wet. He wanted to plunge into her, but this was her fantasy.

With her back straight, her hands at her breasts, she played with her own nipples, teasing him. He wanted to suck on those nipples. Would her fantasy welcome a request?

"I'd love to have my lips around those."

She held her breasts, displaying them to him. "You want these?"

"Yes, please."

She bent forward, letting him take a nipple into his mouth. Sucking and flicking the nub with his tongue drew a moan from her.

Yes, that was what he wanted to hear.

She pulled back, and he raised his head, not wanting to let her go, but she shifted to give him the other one. He sucked and nibbled until she seemed on the edge of orgasm.

"Bite me," she whispered. "Bite me right there."

She wanted him to bite the juicy vein on the top mound of her breast? Such a sensitive area. Wouldn't doing so hurt her?

He ran his tongue across the roof of his mouth. The gland, swollen with serum, urged him to bite, and the muscles crisscrossing the engorged sac were so taut that his fangs hurt with the effort to resist. "I don't think—"

She gripped his ponytail and pulled him back. His mouth opened wide with her tug. "When I tell you to bite, you bite. I decide what risks I take with my body."

Why was that so damn sexy? "The lady's wish is my command."

She lowered her breast near his mouth again, letting him choose the precise location. He licked over the tender skin and then slowly, carefully, sank his fangs into the tempting mound.

When his gland contracted and the fang serum shot out, she hissed, then moaned. "Oh my God. I'm on fire."

She tilted her hips forward, pressing down and taking him into her. He rose to move with her—stretched to the limit the cuffs allowed—but he stayed connected, sucking the blood from the bite.

She pumped her hips, and he, helpless beneath her, was unable to get much traction to move with her. Finally, he released her breast and lay back, the fang serum coursing through his bloodstream as well, and he now had enough leverage to meet her motion for motion. With his help, she rode him faster, staring into his eyes until she squeezed her own tightly shut and screamed out her orgasm.

Her scream brought him over the edge, and he joined her with a deep moan, their mutual pulses continuing together.

She collapsed on his chest, her sweat slick against him, and he started to wrap his arms around her when the board clunked against the back of the lounger, startling him.

He was still cuffed.

She stretched to unfasten the cuffs, freeing each hand and letting the board fall to the floor with a *thunk*. He wrapped her in a tight hug. All he wanted to do was hold her all night long.

"I love you, *mi amor*."

"Me too," she said, her breath still coming in pants.

Her head on his chest, she dozed off. He closed his eyes, enjoying the warm feeling, content in his love for her.

Yet as much as he wanted to stay there, something niggled at the back of his mind. He should go check on Christine. He hadn't meant to leave her alone this long.

He began to shift to wake Cerissa when he heard a scream.

Chapter 16

Nightmare

Rancho Bautista del Murciélago—Ten minutes earlier

Christine drank down another pouch and then stretched out on the pool house's comfy couch, a thick book on the history of Lincoln in her lap. If she had to be a prisoner—er, guest—of Henry's, these weren't the worst accommodations.

The pool house was a large room with a king-sized bed against one wall, and a floral-covered couch at its foot to create a sitting area with a large-screen television on a polished wood entertainment center. The breakfast bar separated the kitchenette from the rest of the room—not that she needed to cook anymore. The luxurious bathroom on the other side of the wall included a steam room, a separate shower enclosure with multiple level heads, and a whirlpool spa.

Not bad at all, except for the silver bars on the windows, and the silver grate covering the glass doors. She rolled one of Olivia's lollipops between her lips.

Yeah, being a newbie sucks.

It reminded her of being a first-year associate at a law firm and subject to everyone's whims. But she felt confident time would cure that.

In the meantime, her prison was luxurious at least. And if she wanted anything, she could go through the underground tunnel connected to the crypts, and up the stairs to the kitchen to find Henry.

But she had no need for her maker right now. She closed the book, letting it rest on her stomach, and set the spent sucker stick aside. She didn't feel like reading. She let her eyelids fall, her relaxation deepening, and her thoughts slowly drifted.

In the past, she was always in a hurry, haunted by workaholism and the need to prove herself. She might take up painting, or writing, or both. Maybe photography. Maybe birdwatching.

Now, she had an eternity to do them all. How incredible.

Town Center—Around the Same Time

Patrick whipped the tie from around his neck and undid the top button of his dress shirt as he waited in the town hall parking lot. He wanted a private conversation with Christine before he went out the gates, because if he left, the guard wouldn't allow his return without Henry's permission. Since there were no restaurants or coffee shops in the gated enclave, he waited in the parking lot for her to return his call. He'd tried texting her again, too, but no answer.

Why wasn't she responding to him?

He hadn't liked the way Henry seemed to control her. The man wouldn't even let Patrick hug her, for God's sake.

A recovering surgery patient didn't need to be kept in isolation out of fear of germs.

No, something wasn't right.

After waiting thirty minutes, he started the car and headed back. Would they notice if he parked in the driveway? He'd have to take the chance. Hiking in dress shoes up the rain-slicked driveway, a series of steep switchbacks, wouldn't work.

He parked on the far side away from the front door and walked briskly to the corner of the house. Fortunately, no fence. He snuck around the corner and onto a lush patio surrounding a swimming pool with a diving board. From what he'd learned during their discussion, she was staying in the pool house.

Was it the one with metal bars over the window? He turned around and looked at the main house. No bars on those windows. But why would there be bars on the house Christine stayed in? He rushed to the doors to take a closer look. The grille had chains wrapped around them, holding them shut.

Fortunately, no lock fastened the chain.

He unwrapped the shiny chains and slid back the metal grille. "Christine? Are you in there?"

The curtains parted and her face peeked out from behind the glass. "Patrick?"

Christine looked so pale, much more so than earlier. They couldn't be taking very good care of her if she looked that pasty underneath her makeup. She looked anemic.

He tried the handle and rattled the door. "Christine? Why do they have you locked in there?"

"You shouldn't be here. Please, leave. Now. For your own safety."

"I'm not going without you."

"I–I can't. Please go."

He rattled the door handle again. "Open the God damn door. Now."

She hesitated, her hand hovering over the handle on her side. Something in her eyes told him when she'd made up her mind, and she flipped the lock with a clunking sound.

He opened both doors. "Now let's go."

"Oh my God, you smell so good."

"What?"

"No, no, you have to go." She started to pull the doors shut, and he whipped out his hand, gripping the frame's edge to keep one door open.

"Christine?"

She closed her eyes, a look of fierce concentration on her features. "I can't be around you. You don't understand."

"What have they done to make you so frightened? I swear, if they're holding you prisoner, I'll see them prosecuted *and* I'll sue their asses off."

"It's not what you think. It's..." She took a deep breath and groaned. "Oh...I can't. I can't. Please, Patrick, go. Go now."

He stepped closer, gripping her arms. "I'm not going anywhere, except with you."

She suddenly leaned into him, inhaling deeply through her nose.

Did she just *sniff* him?

Alarmed, he rocked back.

When she straightened, she smiled. What the hell had those sickos done to her teeth? Were those fangs?

He was too shocked to say anything, but she must've seen the look on his face, because she closed her eyes tightly, and her body began visibly shaking, like she was struggling with herself. When she opened her eyes again, he froze. The world seemed to blur, and he lost all control of his body as she opened her mouth, headed for his neck.

The pool house—moments earlier

Christine begged him, but he didn't listen. He had to leave—now. His smell was driving her crazy.

Please, for the love of God, go.

Suddenly he was in her space, speaking to her, but his smell was everywhere.

Her mouth buzzed as her fangs elongated and the first drop of fang serum formed against her tongue, tasting metallic, like medicine, but feeling like velvet, soft and lush as she rolled the small drop around her mouth and swallowed, sending an exciting tingle through her straight to her core. She leaned forward and sniffed his neck, zeroing in on the big, fat vein.

Vein, not artery.

Yes.

A look of shock and disgust crossed the man's face.

She slammed her eyes shut. She had to push him away. Except she couldn't.

When Christine opened her eyes, he was frozen in place.

Did I— Oh my god, I'm so hungry.

Pressing her lips to his neck, she let her fangs sink in. The explosion of flavor across her tongue, at the perfect temperature, dazed her. She sucked and swallowed, over and over and over, until nothing came from the vein.

More.

Pain shot through the ends of her fingers. She caught a glimpse of her own hands.

Claws.

She raised one to his neck and vaguely heard her prey scream at the sight. Ignoring the noise, she sliced into an artery, which pumped a fountain of joy to her mouth. Barely keeping up with the liquid, she swallowed as fast as she could, sealing her lips against the wound so she lost none of the precious liquid.

A light suddenly flashed on, and she flinched at its brightness.

The doors from the drawing room flung open. Her maker stepped onto the pool patio naked and looking disheveled.

"Christine." He *whooshed* to her. "Let go. Now."

"Mine." She carried her quarry inside her room.

"No, Christine, no. Come to me."

The compulsion forced her to obey, and she dragged the body with her.

Henry gripped her arms and unwound them from her prey. Christine whimpered at the loss, watching as her maker lowered the vessel to the ground. But, lightheaded and buzzed, she didn't fight him.

Henry then dragged her backward, just inside the open doors of the pool house.

Only then did she notice a mortal hovering near the drawing room doors with a large black case in hand.

Christine sniffed the air.

"*No*," Henry growled at her, the command heavy in the word. He tightened his grip on her arm. "My mate."

Then he waved the mortal forward.

She knelt by the vessel, touching its neck for a moment. "Patrick's in hypovolemic shock from blood loss—his heart's stopped," she said, her voice rising. "CPR will do nothing—he needs blood first, and I can't transfuse him fast enough to save his life. What do you want me to do?"

The panic in the mortal's voice sent a sharp pang through Christine.

Patrick?

Christine blinked rapidly, feeling like she was coming out of a daze. She saw Henry shake his head at Cerissa. "Nothing can be done now."

The body. It's Patrick?

A horrible feeling descended through her, a feeling she fought against, a feeling that made her want to curl up and die, then and there.

Oh my God, I've killed my best friend.

CHAPTER 17

AWAKENING TO TRAGEDY

POOL HOUSE—MOMENTS LATER

Henry *whooshed* Christine deeper inside the pool house as the blood lust on her face began to clear, fear and grief replacing it. He deposited her on the couch, then, placing the full strength of their bond behind his next command, he said, "Stay here. Do not move. I will be right back."

Returning to Cerissa, who knelt at Patrick's side, he took the pair of pajama bottoms she handed him and stepped into them. She must have snagged the PJs when she grabbed his bathrobe for herself.

"Did you bring a phone? I need to call Tig."

She touched her robe's pocket, but then her lower lip trembled. "Are you sure? Perhaps we just get rid of the body—"

How could his angel suggest that? She always did the right thing.

Then it hit him.

She wants to protect me.

He knelt next to her. "Patrick's car must be somewhere nearby. The guard at the gate would have recorded his entry, but if he remained, as I suspect he did, then there would be no record of exit. There are too many ways this gets traced back to us."

Cerissa nodded. "This is—it's terrible, Henry." She paused. "But the council won't do anything to Christine, will they?"

He could tell Cerissa struggled to reconcile the loss of life, taken by a vampire, against her commitment to saving lives. She was choosing to see the fledging's side of the situation, for him, for Christine. He loved her all the more for it.

"Unlikely," he finally answered. The council wouldn't blame a newborn; they'd blame him. But he didn't want to tell Cerissa that truth yet. "The phone, please?"

She reached into the robe's pocket and handed it to him.

"But Henry? Before you call Tig, I think you should talk to Christine."

She was right. He needed to understand how this happened before calling the chief.

Henry nodded, then strode to the pool house, shutting the French doors behind him.

Christine began speaking the moment he entered. "Henry, I-I told him to leave. I did. I begged him. I tried, but then—" Her eyes squeezed shut. "Please tell me he isn't dead. Please, he can't be dead. Tell me it's not real. It's not true. Please, please, please."

"Christine." Her eyes shot open to look at him. "I'm sorry."

He was. This was his responsibility. He'd promised himself to do better than his maker had for him.

Instead, he'd failed. Failed worse than even Anne-Louise. A dark cloud of guilt rolled through, threatening to overwhelm him, to bring him to his knees. He couldn't let it, and took a deep breath, refocusing on Christine.

She raised her hand to cover her mouth. "Oh my God, I really killed him." Tears began streaking her face. "He's been my best friend for twenty-five years. How—how could I?"

"Newborns have no control. The blood lust—it's too strong." Henry wrapped his arms around her. "What happened is not your fault, Christine."

He didn't understand how he could comfort his child for killing someone, and his sense of moral rightness struggled against doing so. Yet his vampire instincts whispered to provide her with solace, and those instincts won the battle. Christine hadn't meant to kill Patrick. She did what any newborn vampire would do—feed on the first mortal she came across, unable to stop once she started, the blood lust taking over.

"No, no, no. I'm a *monster*."

Swallowing hard, his stomach a mess of knots, Henry compelled a command into his voice to cut through her burgeoning hysteria. "Tell me what happened."

"I was lying there"—she gestured at the couch—"relaxing, and I heard someone removing the chains. I thought it was you. I got up, but when I looked through the curtains, Patrick stood there."

Tears falling down her face, she paused to take a shaky breath. "He called out my name. He said he wanted to get me out of here. He acted like you were holding me prisoner. He demanded I open the door—wouldn't stop until he had it open. I thought if I could show him I wasn't locked in against my will, that he'd leave."

More tears glistened in her eyes. "Only he'd undone his tie, and I could see the vein in his neck pump lightly and the smell of his blood... I pleaded with him to go, but he wouldn't leave, and then there was that *smell*, and the smooth skin, and the blue vein, and then I—I— Oh God, I killed him."

Her body shook with sobs. Henry shivered with the weight of his guilt.

"This is all my fault," she said between anguished cries. "If only I'd never written that damn letter. I wrote it to protect me, and it ended up costing him his life. Oh, Patrick, I'm so sorry."

Henry patted her back, not knowing what else to do, trying to give the same comfort he would have given his long-dead aunt—or any member of his family. After all, she was his daughter now.

His to teach, his to care for, his to...love? And no matter what she'd done, his to protect.

My child.

Those two words had power.

He'd feared the unusual nature of her transition to vampire might leave her impaired, but no, she'd been too coherent and articulate since rising. Mentally, she was fine.

And what newborn could resist the temptation of fresh blood? Her willpower was doomed the minute Patrick came to her door.

"Christine, this wasn't your fault. It is mine. And I promise you I will take care of it."

Henry leaned back, holding her away so he could look into her eyes and gauge her response. "Will you be all right here for a little while?"

She wiped her eyes with the back of her hand. "Yes."

"Read your book." He handed her the large tome from the side table. "Try to distract yourself. I'll return soon."

Henry exited the pool house, pulled out his phone, and hit a number. "Tig? Henry here. We have a problem."

"What happened?"

"Christine killed a mortal."

"How the fuck did you let her get out?"

"The mortal came to her. He was her partner at the law firm. I will explain when you arrive here."

"Is she locked up now? I'm not bringing Jayden if she's not under lock and key."

"I will ensure she is contained."

He ended the call and pocketed the phone, walking back over to where Cerissa still knelt on the ground beside Patrick.

"*Cariña*, you are just as I left you."

"I thought someone should remain by his side." She glanced up at him. "Do you want me to heal the wounds? I have some of your blood encapsulated—it might fix the worst of what she did."

"I don't know what to do right now." He scrubbed a hand across his face. "Tig will know."

"Okay. Why don't you go sit with Christine until Tig arrives? I'll stay here."

"Are you certain?"

"Yes, go."

He nodded, walking into the pool house again. When he closed the doors behind him, he found his child hunched over, crying silent tears on the couch. He gently sat beside her and placed a steady hand between her shoulder blades as they shook.

They sat like that until he heard Tig outside ask, "Where is Henry?"

He straightened his shoulders, knowing where this was likely to lead. He had no choice. Tig would report this to the council, and the council would make him pay the price for Patrick's death.

CHAPTER 18

COYOTES

RANCHO BAUTISTA DEL MURCIÉLAGO—MOMENTS LATER

Tig stopped ten feet away, scanning the crime scene. The pool lights shimmered through the water, the deck expertly furnished with elegant lounge chairs, a gazebo at one end, and the stylish guest house angled at the other side of the pool. So perfect, it'd almost look like a movie set if it weren't for the man's body stretched out on the stone decking near the guest house's glass doors.

"Where is Christine?" Tig asked.

From next to the body, Cerissa replied, "In the pool house. Do you want me to heal the wound? Henry said to wait for you before using his blood."

"How bad is the damage?"

"From what I can see, she bit a vein and clawed open an artery."

Tig scrubbed a hand over her face. "May the ancestors help us. Don't bother doing anything. We'll have to use the coyote plan. We haven't used that ruse in over thirty years, so it should work."

Cerissa's eyes got big. "You're going to blame this on coyotes?"

"Better than that. We're going to take his body and car to the pass and dump them both there. Run out the fuel or fake a mechanical problem and leave him by the side of the road for scavengers to find. In a few days, there won't be much left of his body."

"Then healing his throat doesn't help."

Tig pursed her lips, then bit them together as she parsed the plan. "Actually, it's not a bad idea, just in case the coyotes don't pick the bones clean. Go ahead."

Cerissa took a jar out of her bag and smeared shiny red beads on the open gashes.

"What is that?"

Cerissa rotated the jar to show Tig its label. "Henry's blood, microencapsulated. The process I use doesn't need refrigeration. If you give me a blood donation, I'll make some for you."

Tig considered the offer. If Jayden got hurt, having her blood as a salve would be handy. "Marcus told me about this. How much are you charging?"

"Ah, I haven't been."

"You should. The town has agreed to pay your consulting fee whenever you do DNA analysis for us. You should be paid for encapsulating vampire blood too."

"I'll figure out what to charge later. Right now, I'm too upset."

Tig understood. She took out her phone and called the mayor to explain the situation to him. Technically, the mayor and vice mayor had to approve the coyote ruse before she could implement the plan.

"Go ahead," Winston said. "I'll phone Rolf and clear it with him, but we have no choice."

She ended her call with the mayor, and the door to the pool house opened. Henry stepped out and strode over to her.

"Is your child in there?" Tig asked him.

"Yes. She's quite distraught. The victim, Patrick Krull, was her friend and law partner. He met with us earlier in the evening. After he left, I believe he doubled back and came looking for Christine. I took every precaution to keep her contained inside."

Tig walked over to the pool house. The council would want documentation of the steps Henry took. She'd thought the silver bars and grille were an expensive but adequate solution—but would the council agree?

She took out her phone. Until she was certain that Christine had been properly caged, she'd asked Jayden to remain at the van in the driveway. "It's safe for you to join us," Tig told him. "Would you please bring the camera? We need photos of the barred doors and windows."

"I'll be there shortly."

"Thanks."

Henry joined her by the door. "As you can see, Patrick unwrapped the silver chain that held the folding grille together."

"But no padlock?"

"I had no reason to believe I needed one. Christine would be unable to touch the silver to free herself. And it never occurred to me that the mortal would return and try to take her with him."

Tig *tsked*. Henry should have done more. Even a fledgling like Christine could find something to protect her hands or use a broom handle to unwind the chain, then push apart the folding silver grille without touching the surface. When Tig had first approved of the setup, she never thought for a minute he wouldn't lock the chain shut.

Why hadn't she raised the question then?

Groaning in frustration, she mentally kicked herself. Too few vampires had been created in the past sixty years, and so younger vampires like Henry just didn't have the experience needed when dealing with a new vampire. Like all the founders, he relied too much on the community's gates for protection instead of implementing proper protocol and security measures at the source.

"Do you have any spare padlocks?"

"I should be able to find one."

"Before you leave her alone again, add the padlock."

"Of course, chief."

"I know it's hard to watch a newborn every second. Where were you when the attack happened?"

"I—ah, Cerissa and I were relaxing upstairs."

As much as Tig understood Henry's need to spend private time with his mate, he should have arranged someone else to come stay with Christine for any kind of longer absence. At least until she was a few weeks older and more trustworthy.

Henry folded his hands behind his back. "Christine tried to get the man to leave, but he insisted on rescuing her from us. She didn't attack until he pushed his way in."

As much as Tig sympathized with Henry and his child, her reaction was tempered by the reality lying on the patio: a man had died because of Henry's negligence. He should have stayed focused on supervising and training his fledgling.

"I'll take her statement and include it in my report. But I don't know if her story will make a difference with the council."

Jayden appeared, walking around the corner of the main house. Tig pointed to the pool house, and he acknowledged her with a nod. The flash from his camera soon went off.

"Do you think the council will blame her?" Henry asked.

"Under the circumstances, it's anyone's guess. I've heard most of their stories, and almost to a one they killed upon rising. So they'll understand why she drained him. And I'll recommend no action against her. But with today's sensibilities—"

"They will not understand why I didn't keep her by my side."

"We'll have to see."

Jayden joined them. "I assume you don't want photos of the body."

Tig tapped a fingernail against her lower lip. "No photo. The council will be satisfied with my oral report. I don't want a written or photo record of his death here."

"Got it." Jayden packed the camera and flash away in the kit slung over his shoulder.

"If you'd please get the body bag, we'll put him in the van and take him to the pass." She already wore gloves, so she knelt and carefully searched the dead man's pockets, avoiding contact with the body as much as possible. She pulled out his keys and phone. "I'll drive his car there."

She'd leave the phone in his car—the GPS would track until they got deeper into the pass, where the cell tower signal died off.

But first, she needed a statement. She excused herself from Henry and strode into the pool house.

Christine lay on the couch, tears streaking down her face, but the newborn managed to give a coherent account of what happened, matching Henry's story, and ending, "How am I going to live with this?"

The way she said it about ripped Tig's heart out.

They'd all done things they regretted. Living for many centuries meant more opportunities to screw up. She squeezed Christine's shoulder. "You aren't alone. The community will help, so you'll never go through this again."

When Jayden returned, they placed the body in the bag, and Tig carried the corpse back to the van. Henry and Cerissa followed them. "Henry, you should return to Christine. Jayden and I have this."

"Thank you. Please contact me if there is anything I can do."

"For now, go back and be with your child. She's in a world of hurt."

"I will."

Tig pulled on a clean suit over her clothes, including paper booties for her shoes and an elastic hair cap so she wouldn't leave any trace inside Patrick's car. Jayden followed in the van, and they arrived at the pass twenty minutes later. To make the scene appear more convincing, she pushed the car off the road and into a ditch, giving the tire a nudge against a sharp rock to go flat, and siphoned out the gas, then ran the motor until the engine died.

Patrick's phone showed no bars. She got out of the car and joined Jayden where he'd stopped on the asphalt twenty yards back.

She didn't worry about faking footprints—the rain-washed pavement wouldn't show any. They took the body out of the bag, and she returned the keys and phone to his pocket. Together they left him on his back, one hand over his chest.

With any luck, the tale they'd spin would pass the sniff test. Patrick had gone the wrong way on Robles Road and headed deeper into the community instead of toward the gate. When he realized he was lost, he tried to turn around and ran off into a ditch in the dark. Out of gas, tire flat, he tried to hike back, had a heart attack, and died. His body was eaten by scavengers.

In a few days there would be nothing left but bones, his clothing torn to shreds, the contents of his pockets scattered.

Jayden grumbled something about "disrespectful" and returned to the van.

She glanced after him. The process didn't seem that strange or disrespectful to her. Leaving the corpse to be devoured by animals was how her people, the Maasai, had dealt with death for eons.

She got into the van with Jayden.

"I hate this part of the job," he said, starting the engine.

"I'm sorry. This is our second faked death in a month. It never happens this often. I don't know what's going on."

"Yeah. But these things always come in threes."

"Don't say that. We've had enough turmoil this year alone to fill our quota for a decade. Hell, for a century. The ancestors willing, this will be the last for a long while."

CHAPTER 19

CONSEQUENCES

TOWN COUNCIL CHAMBERS—THE NEXT NIGHT

Cerissa perched on the hard edge of the pew-like bench in the front row of the town council chambers, rotating the beads of her bracelet. A delicate gold chain connected the faceted amethyst gemstones, which alternated with the round moonstone beads, and she played with each type, feeling the different shapes pass under her fingers.

Directly in front of her, Henry and Christine sat together at the defendant's table. The council chambers had no windows, allowing them to start their meetings early or stay later, depending upon what the moon was doing. Expensive maple hardwood lined the room's walls.

The mayor, who ruled from the center of the raised dais, had yet to take his seat behind the polished wood modesty panel, shaped in a sweeping half-circle, which hid the legs of the councilmembers and included a built-in desk for paperwork and microphones.

I hate this room. Almost every time she'd been there, something bad happened.

The notice demanding their attendance at the council meeting arrived shortly before sunrise. When Henry rose at dusk, he excused himself and put Christine in the drawing room, where he could keep an eye on her.

Stress lines crinkled the edges of his eyes and forehead.

Facing him in the foyer, Cerissa had asked, "What's going to happen at tonight's meeting?"

"I do not know yet."

"They won't revoke your parole, will they?" A hundred lashes still hung over his head if he violated the covenant. He hadn't killed Patrick—surely they wouldn't hold him liable.

"I need to speak with Rolf about the council's intent."

"Quique—"

"Please go upstairs or work in your lab, *cariña*. I cannot split my attention any further right now, and I must phone Rolf while I keep an eye on Christine."

Cerissa nodded her acquiescence. She didn't like being cut out of the conversation, but she acceded to Henry's wishes—this time.

Now sitting in the audience, she regretted not knowing what would happen, what deal he had struck. Because when Rolf was involved, there was always a deal.

Why hadn't she stood up for herself? She should have been part of whatever agreement Henry made. Patrick's death was her fault as much as Henry's.

She sighed, worrying the beads of her bracelet between her fingers again.

Gaea and Karen arrived then, settling on either side of her with a few murmured words of encouragement. She barely heard them, she was so focused on watching for the mayor's entrance.

"Excuse me, dearie." A woman hovered over her.

Cerissa rose to her feet to escape feeling trapped by the vampire's presence. "Yes?"

"We haven't been introduced. Cerissa, is it?"

"Yes. But now isn't a good time—"

"This won't take but a minute."

"I'm afraid you'll have to wait until later."

Cerissa moved to sit back down. If she ignored the woman with strawberry-blonde hair teased out like a motorcycle helmet, maybe she'd go away.

Suddenly, the woman gripped Cerissa's wrist. "One minute, love, truly."

"Do not touch me." Cerissa yanked her wrist away and stepped back. She hated it when strangers touched her. "Please."

"Apologies, dearie. I forgot my manners. I'm Olivia. I handle the blood franchise on the Hill."

"Oh, yes." Cerissa frowned. She had too much on her mind to deal with this. "Luis has mentioned you."

"Nothing but wonderful things, I'm sure," Olivia said, fluffing her hair further.

On the contrary. According to the mates on the Hill, Olivia had her nose in the air when it came to mortals. "What do you need? The hearing is about to begin."

"When I spoke with Henry two nights ago, he thought Leopold might be open to new investors. From what I've heard, everyone who's tried your product right loves it. It's going to be quite popular with our residents. Thought I might hedge my bet, so to speak, if additional seats at the table are available?"

This is not what I need right now. Olivia's sense of timing was terrible. "I'll have to consult with Leopold. We sold all the original investment offerings. But we've discussed opening a second tier."

"Wonderful. Please keep me in mind." Olivia squeezed her arm, then backed off like the arm was on fire. "I'm sorry, dearie, force of habit. I'm a toucher."

"Yes, sure," Cerissa replied, returning to her seat on the hard wooden bench, hoping Olivia would take the cue. Her focus drifted to Henry, who'd leaned over to tell Christine something.

"Cheers. And best of luck," Olivia said, and sauntered to a seat in the second row.

Karen leaned over to Cerissa and whispered, "I cannot believe the gall of that woman, talking about investments now. One more second and I was going to shoo her away for you."

Cerissa turned to Karen, a small smile on her face. "Thanks, bestie."

The mayor banged the gavel, and Cerissa jumped.

She wished the hearing was already over so they could go home. Her little family had endured enough disruption over the past seventy-two hours. She couldn't take much more.

Henry glanced at the mayor and then whispered to Christine, "No matter what happens, stay quiet and stay seated."

"But you need legal counsel."

"You're too new to our ways. Stay out of this. I have the situation under control."

The mayor cleared his throat. "I call to order the hearing regarding the death of"—he looked down at the paperwork on the desk in front of him—"Patrick Krull."

Marcus sat at the table reserved for the town attorney, which was situated on the other side of the audience, and began his report. "As you are all aware, Christine Dunne recently joined our community at the request of the council. Mr. Krull learned that his law partner, Ms. Dunne, died after surgery, and insisted on visiting her in person to confirm she still lived. After a successful meeting at Henry Bautista's house, which I approved of in advance, Mr. Krull departed. Later, he returned, snuck onto the property, and freed Ms. Dunne, who attacked and killed him."

The nameplate in front of the mayor lit up. "Let me stop you right there. Am I to understand that Henry abandoned his newly made child, leaving her alone and unattended?"

A stone lodged in Henry's throat. He didn't want to explain what happened.

As agreed in advance, Tig approached the podium and clicked on the microphone. "Mr. Bautista confined Ms. Dunne in a small house behind his. He installed silver bars on the windows, and a silver grille gate blocking the doors."

"Then how did she escape?"

"Mr. Krull removed the silver chain that bound the gate closed."

"You're telling this council there was no padlock on the chain?"

"No. Because we live in a closed community, Mr. Bautista did not anticipate that a mortal would penetrate our community walls and try to free her."

The mayor *harrumphed*. "Not very responsible of him."

Henry agreed. He'd been negligent to leave Christine on her own. Prior to the meeting, he'd spent the time on the phone, talking to Rolf and Marcus, trying to come up with an equitable solution.

There was none. A man died, and his death was Henry's fault.

"Mr. Mayor," Marcus said, "Mr. Bautista is willing to plead guilty to reckless endangerment and pay a fine if his child is not penalized and no mark goes on her record."

There was more to the deal than protecting his child. Henry was willing to pay any amount to save Cerissa from embarrassment. He did not want a full trial, at which the facts might be made public of how he and his mate spent their time while Christine killed Patrick.

"How much is the fine he's agreed to?"

"Fifty thousand dollars."

Almost half of what he received in his settlement from the Mordida Water Company, which had gone to help replenish his dismal reserve fund. But to protect Cerissa—and to take responsibility so his fledgling wasn't punished—he'd gladly sacrifice the money.

"Any discussion from the council?" the mayor asked. "Seeing none, the matter is resolved, and we will accept the fine as stated. Enter your plea."

Henry stood and gestured for Christine to join him. Tig relinquished the center podium, and he took her place. "I plead guilty. Christine pleads not guilty."

Christine looked around wildly. "But what about Patrick's daughter?"

Marcus patted the air, gesturing for calm. "I will be in touch with his law firm as soon as the body is found. He is divorced with one child, an adult daughter who is not involved with the law firm. The town is self-insured and will offer a settlement to his heir for a release of all claims of negligence. The fine Henry pays will go into the insurance pot."

"Oh."

"Christine," Henry said close to her ear, "please, return to the table, sit down, and stay quiet."

She furrowed her brow but didn't move.

"Obey me."

Tig took over, escorting his child by the arm back to the defense table.

"Now, if the matter of guilt is settled..." The mayor turned his gaze to Henry. "Mr. Bautista, you have five days to pay the town clerk. Also, your parole is revoked, thus the previous penalty is automatically reinstated. A hundred lashes. Sentence to be carried out after the hearing closes."

From behind him, Henry heard Cerissa's gasp.

The mayor raised the gavel to adjourn.

"Wait." Rolf's hand flashed out, stopping him. Then his nameplate lit as his microphone came on. "We all know the original sentence was never intended to be carried out. This council voted to conditionally suspend the whipping for two years. If Mr. Bautista didn't violate the Covenant during that time, his parole would end, and the sentence would be nullified. We imposed the sentence to demonstrate that no one is above the law, even a revered founder. But under these circumstances—Henry has repented of his earlier crime and made the woman his mate—carrying out the lashing serves no purpose. I move we commute it entirely."

Henry held his breath. Had Rolf successfully persuaded the mayor? As of their last phone call, he didn't know the answer.

The mayor *harrumphed*. "A unanimous vote is required to change an already imposed penalty. And I will not vote for eliminating the penalty in its entirety. Doing so sends a wrong message to the community. I will, however, support a *reduction*. Fifty lashes. All those in favor."

"No." Rolf shook his head slowly. "Fifteen."

"Thirty-five."

Henry caught Rolf's eye and gave a slight nod. Still horrible, but better than a hundred.

Rolf flicked his fingers, and then cocked his head to look at the mayor. "You can do better than that. Thirty."

The mayor sputtered.

"That's my best and final offer. You do not want to enter the next mayoral race as the man who would impose outrageous penalties—penalties that shock the conscience."

"Fine. Thirty."

Liza leaned forward, eyeballing Winston and Rolf, then flipped the switch lighting her nameplate. "Are you two finished wagging your dicks?" A ripple of laughter ran through the crowd. "If you want my vote, then not more than twenty lashes. And even that is excessive."

"I agree," Rolf said.

Henry appreciated Liza's support. But whether it was twenty or thirty, his back would be shredded by the time whoever served as executioner finished—if they could find someone willing to serve as executioner.

The term applied to the civil servant designated to carry out—execute—physical punishments, which ranged from death to floggings, from brandings to amputations, and the term's broader use dated from before the medieval period. The Hill lacked a standing executioner, and the last time Henry spoke with Rolf, everyone offered it had refused the job.

The mayor glanced to his left. "What about Carolyn? We haven't heard from her."

Carolyn bit into her stick of chewing tobacco. From what she'd told Henry, she'd picked up the habit in her mortal life while harvesting tobacco and continued after becoming vampire—lip and tongue cancer were no longer a concern—and a brass spittoon sat to the side, slightly behind her.

There was also a spittoon in her office where she gave financial advice and managed the wealth of most of the Hill vampires. As a certified public accountant and financial planner, she was a jewel the entire community respected. Her shrewd *independent* analysis had been key in keeping the town financially solvent. Her mate and business partner, Ken Mitchell, handled Henry's accounting.

Henry hadn't phoned Carolyn when they were working out a resolution to Patrick's accidental death. Carolyn had opposed the original punishment, and he couldn't afford to offend her independent streak. So he counted on her intelligence to fight the mayor's unreasonable bias against him.

"Well?" the mayor asked.

Her nameplate lit up. Now all four council microphones were live. "You heard my opinion when all y'all sentenced him the first time. Whipping ain't civilized." Carolyn pointed at the mayor with her stick of tobacco. "Not one of y'all has ever been strung up to the whipping post. I'm the only one among ya who has, havin' been born to slavery and all. Until y'all feel the lash yourself, you have no business metin' it out as punishment. It's barbarism, plain and simple."

"Yes, but unless you vote to modify his sentence, he's facing a hundred lashes."

"Ya think you're gonna twist my arm that way, *Mr. Mayor*? It ain't gonna happen. Read your rule book again. It has to be unanimous of those attendin'. And if I leave, you still got a quorum to do your dirty work."

"Very well. We know where Carolyn stands. In the interest of justice, I'll vote for Liza's proposal if my vote gets this done. Are you two agreed?"

"Yes," Rolf said.

Liza huffed out a breath. "For the record, I agree with Carolyn. Completely. But I'm only voting yes to reduce an already cruel and unfair sentence."

The mayor then turned to Carolyn.

She puckered up and spat a precise wad of tobacco juice in his face. "I'm leaving, like I said I would."

The mayor groped around for something to wipe his face.

Carolyn marched from the dais and down the center aisle—stopping to pat Henry on the arm. "I wish I could do more."

Before he could thank her, she continued her march to the double doors, opened both, and slammed them behind her.

Liza crossed her arms. "In the next election, I'm running for mayor. Winston's been leading our council like we're still in the Dark Ages. No more."

"Well," Rolf said, "with the mayor temporarily unable to speak, I'll note for the record that the vote was unanimous by those councilmembers now attending, and the penalty is reduced to twenty lashes." He banged the gavel. "We are in recess so the mayor may wash his face."

CHAPTER 20

EXECUTIONER

Town council chambers—Moments later

Cerissa stared at the back of Henry's head. He knew. He knew all along. He made the deal and didn't tell her. But how could he agree to this? Only primitive cultures used physical punishment. She'd heard the reason the vampires still did, something about long imprisonments not possible in such a small community.

Guilt crawled up her spine. His long absence from Christine was all her fault. She'd enticed him away from his duty. None of this would have happened if they'd stayed in the drawing room, keeping his child with them.

"Henry," she whispered.

Despite the cacophony of voices surrounding them, he must have heard her, as he left the podium to kneel before her and cup her cheek. "We both understood the threat hung over me. Rolf and Marcus tried to persuade Winston right up to the last moment. Apparently, they failed. The reduced sentence was our fallback position."

She swiped at her eyes, clearing the tears. They needed to talk this out in private. She stood. "Henry. Let's go—"

Christine let out a sudden sob, and Cerissa stopped in her tracks.

"No, the council, bring them back," Christine said, hiccupping. "It should be me. They should punish me. I don't deserve to live."

"Calm down, child." Henry placed a hand on her shoulder. "Come, we will find a room where we may speak in private."

Cerissa caught Gaea's eye. "Please join us. Ari said you offered to help."

"Of course, my dears. Lead the way."

Cerissa dodged past the residents who stared at their small group as they left the council chambers and entered the lobby. "Let's find a conference room. Preferably one with walls that aren't glass."

Christine continued making anguished noises, and Gaea put a soothing arm around her shoulders. "Now, dear, we all understand," Gaea cooed as they walked down the hall. "This has been a terrible experience."

Cerissa opened the door to a small, empty conference room, relieved to be out of the public eye. "In here."

Once they filed inside, Henry took Christine's hands. "Look at me."

Her gaze remained fixed on the ground. "I killed Patrick, not you," she mumbled. "I should be destroyed."

"Look at me." She finally did, and he continued. "All of us, almost every vampire in that room, killed to feed their hunger after being turned. You are not at fault. You should not be punished. I want you to go with Gaea—"

"Why?" Christine asked, her eyes wide with panic.

"The sentence will likely be carried out tonight. You don't need to be here to witness the lashing."

A frisson went through Cerissa. She restrained herself from entering the conversation—she'd have her own talk with Henry after he finished with his child.

"But it should be me." Christine shook her head. "You didn't do anything."

"Do you remember your law school lessons on wild animals in captivity and strict liability?"

Christine rocked on her feet, appearing startled by the question, but it seemed to knock her back into her lawyer persona. "Ah, when someone keeps a wild animal in their backyard, they are strictly liable if it gets out and hurts someone. The person who is hurt doesn't have to prove any negligence on the owner's part. The mere keeping of a dangerous animal is a special risk for which the owner is held liable for all damages."

"Well, in this case, I'm the owner and you're the tiger."

"Oh my God."

"Precisely. Now, as I said, I want you to go with Gaea and sleep the day with her. You'll return to my place tomorrow night, and I'll make arrangements so you're never left alone at any time for the next few weeks."

Christine bit her lip, looking uncertain.

"Come with me, dear," Gaea said. "We'll leave now and go to my place."

"And you have those pouches in your purse if you get hungry," Cerissa said. She'd made sure Christine had enough in case the council meeting dragged on.

"Not to worry," Gaea said. "I have plenty of dark wine in the refrigerator."

Cerissa shrugged. At some point Christine would have to learn to drink donor blood. She hadn't expected the moment to arrive this soon.

After the two of them left, Cerissa hugged Henry tightly. "I can't even comprehend this. Rolf had a sound argument. Why didn't it work?" Tears stung her eyes. "After all you've done for this community, how can they reinstate the whipping?"

Henry sighed. He wanted to get the sentence over with. But Cerissa needed his help to understand.

"Because it was my duty to ensure she did no harm. I took on the responsibility when I turned her. I failed in my duty. Now, I face the consequences, which includes the revocation of my parole." He kissed Cerissa's cheek, which was wet with tears. "Do not cry for me. The punishment will be over quickly."

"There shouldn't be a punishment like this at all."

There was no point in arguing with her. He stroked her hair again. "I want you to go home and use your phone to shut down the crystal. There is no reason for you to experience this."

Her head shook against his shoulder. "No. I won't abandon you. If I've learned anything over the past six months—we're stronger together than apart."

His brave mate. "And nothing I can say would change your mind?"

"I'm staying. And don't block the crystal. If this is to happen, we'll go through it together."

"But you should be spared feeling—"

"No. Don't block the crystal. I'll be there with you. I—I won't abandon you."

He leaned back to look at her, and she swiped at the tears streaking her face. Covering her mouth with his, he kissed her deeply, tasting the salt.

When the kiss ended, he caught a tear with his thumb. "You are braver than I am."

"You are the bravest man I know."

"What you see is yourself reflected in my eyes." He gave a wry grin. "And do not forget, this is not my first time being whipped."

"The first time you chose the punishment as penance. This time, it's being forced upon you."

He cringed at the memory. In the late 1800s, he'd accidentally killed Sarah, his mate, and the guilt over her death compelled him to seek a way to expiate his sin.

"I just don't understand why," she continued. "Why is the mayor so—"

"Intransigent? Winston is hoping I will take the coward's way out and leave the community instead of acquiescing to the council's ruling."

"Why does he hate you so much?"

"He doesn't hate me. He hates that he wasn't one of the founders. He hates being second tier, even though he's now mayor. And nothing will ever change for him unless he can drive us out. He figures if he does this to me, then ultimately my sister and Marcus will leave. Then he only has to deal with Abigale—"

"Doesn't he realize it's a losing game? That everyone, working together, is what makes this community great?"

"No. He—"

A loud banging on the door interrupted his answer.

"Are you in there?" Rolf asked. "The mayor wants to get this over with."

Cerissa took a tissue from her purse and dried her face.

Henry kissed her softly and then opened the door. "Lead the way," he said to Rolf.

When they got back into the council chambers, the mayor glared at Henry. "Nice of you to join us." Winston tapped the gavel to reconvene the session. All four nameplates remained lit, even though Carolyn had left. "The penalty will be carried out in the amphitheater tonight after we adjourn. Chief Anderson—"

From the back of the room, Tig shot to her feet, her fists clenched. "I told you before—I'm in charge of enforcing the laws, but I'm not your executioner, and I refuse the job. Hire someone else."

She strode out, slamming the chamber doors behind her.

"Well, in that case, Zeke Cannon—"

Zeke bounced to his feet from where he sat in the audience. "Can't, mayor. Same reason Tig gave. Plus I'm a-wooing Christine. Call it a conflict of interest—being at the giving end of the lash to her maker would nix the deal before I got started."

He raised his hat, which had been in his lap, and tipped it at the council, before making a quieter exit than Tig had.

"Liza—"

"Don't even ask," Liza said with a sneer.

"Rolf—"

"Mayor, I told you from the start this was a bad idea. I too must decline. Conflict of interest—he's my business partner."

Henry held his breath. If they could find no one to carry out the punishment, then Winston would have no choice but to commute the sentence.

"Well, well. I feared this would be the result." The mayor glared at Henry. "I know how well respected you are in the community, but you aren't above the law. So I made arrangements last night to bring in someone from the outside."

The outside? A frisson of uncertainty ran down Henry's back.

The mayor rose from the dais, strode over to the door leading to the council's private conference room, and opened it. "Please come in. We're ready for you now."

Henry strained to see who appeared, but the dais blocked his view. As the mayor returned to his seat, he said, "Henry's maker, Anne-Louise, will carry out the punishment of twenty lashes."

Heat surged through Henry's body, an anger so intense he clenched his fists to keep from exploding.

How dare he.

Cerissa's anger surged through the crystal as well, matching his.

Anne-Louise appeared from behind the dais. Carved wooden hair combs held back her curly black and gray hair, making it easy for Henry to see the haughty displeasure on her face.

"I traveled all this way for a twenty-lash sentence? Next time, Winston, don't call me if you're going to cave to public pressure."

CHAPTER 21

THE SPECTACLE

TOWN AMPHITHEATER—MINUTES LATER

Henry removed his sports coat, tie, and white dress shirt, leaving them on a bench to the side of the amphitheater's stage. The pants would be ruined by the blood splatter, but at least he could save the rest of his garments from destruction.

Keeping the most stoic look on his face he could muster, he climbed the steps to the stage. Someone had erected a large cross, with cuffs attached.

Probably the mayor.

The *pendejo* had been jealous of Henry's status in the community for *years*.

This is Winston's chance to humiliate me, and he's gone all out for the occasion.

Henry wouldn't give him the pleasure of reacting.

Then he saw Anne-Louise already on stage, wearing black jeans and a long-sleeved black blouse with ruffles flowing from where two strings tied together in a bow at the neck as she practiced with the whip.

Acidic anger shot through his veins. "*Puta*," he whispered at her.

She made a sharp puffing sound at him—her signature chuff. "Truly, Enrique, you are my most ungrateful child. You should be thanking me. You don't want to know who was going to be Winston's next call if I didn't agree."

His anger sizzled out, a cold chill replacing it.

"The Butcher?" Among the treaty communities, the Butcher was a legend, a sociopathic sadist who would leave Henry's back a bloody pulp with just twenty strikes.

"*Oui*. I decided to save you from that. Magnanimous of me, no?"

"Very." He took a deep breath. She'd dropped everything to travel from New York with less than twenty-four hours' notice to spare him that. Perhaps this time, Anne-Louise did have his best interests at heart. "And where did you get the whip?"

She pulled the ancient cat-o'-nine-tails through her fist, dark blood dried on the braided leather, and let the braids fall from her hand.

"I believe Winston bought it at auction on the internet. The cords were a bit rotten. Silly me, I tried to fix them, and the metal tips all fell off."

Old-fashioned whips had metal barbs tied to each tail. The knots in the cords, designed to lacerate the skin, would cause enough damage without the metal barbs slicing him open as well. "Thank you for that."

"See, you can be civilized when you want to be. Now, shall we get this over with?"

The mayor came striding to the side of the stage. "You forgot the bowl."

"*Beurk*," Anne-Louise scoffed at him. "Winston, I told you to forget the garlic. I will not tolerate being hit with the backsplash of that foul rose."

If Henry understood correctly, the mayor proposed dipping the whip in crushed garlic to make the welts more severe.

"But the rules call for—"

"Take the bowl away. Now. Before I pour the contents on your bald head."

The mayor scowled at her, but dumped the liquid in the bushes and, leaving the bowl behind, returned to his seat in the front row.

"Now, my dear boy, you know what to do. Assume the position."

Before he did, Henry pulled out his wallet, handing her the hundred-dollar bill he always kept there. It was considered good luck to tip in advance.

Anne-Louise laughed, a high, tinkling sound he knew too well, and tucked the folded bill into her bra. "Not the first time you've paid me for service," she quipped, then motioned with the whip to the crossbeam.

He gripped the wood. "You do not need the cuffs."

"I didn't think I would." She held out a piece of soft leather. "But you should bite on this. You don't want to crack your teeth. The healing takes forever and is more painful than the whip."

"Thank you," he said, and before his mouth closed, she'd shoved the leather in. He bit down and prepared himself for the first lash.

He didn't have long to wait.

The whip's sound crashed through him. The pain, like fire, spread across his back, and the audience counted in unison.

He tuned them out. He tuned out the sound of the next crack.

He tuned out the pain and the burn and focused his mind entirely on Cerissa's love.

Town amphitheater—A short time earlier

Cerissa left through the council chamber's front door while Henry was escorted out the back. Pushed and jostled by the crowd, she walked past the parking lot and saw Gaea and Christine standing by Gaea's car arguing. Concern flared within her for a moment, but she didn't have the bandwidth to worry about why they hadn't left yet. She had to trust that Gaea had Christine in hand. Focusing on Henry, she kept the crystal's communication open and absorbed his anger, acting like a sponge to give him the freedom to let go.

She made her way down the garden-lined sidewalk and stopped behind the audience on the high, grassy mound, loath to move any closer to the tableau unfolding in front of her. Almost all the Hill vampires attended, sitting in the amphitheater's rising half-circle tiers of seats, with their mortal mates next to them.

The only mortals missing were Karen and Shayna. Rolf had told Karen to go home. Cerissa understood why—Karen had been through enough personal violence, and witnessing this could add to her trauma. And Yacov's widow would have been there, except she had gone to Beverly Hills to meet with the probate attorneys on a matter related to Yacov's estate.

Standing to the side of the crossbeam post, Anne-Louise flicked the whip, practicing how to use the damn thing. Henry's maker may be shorter than him by a few inches, but she was much older, and would be able to put power behind her swing.

Cerissa couldn't stand the thought of him being in pain. But knowing Henry, it wasn't so much the pain he resented. No, he'd hate being humiliated in front of his community.

Anger and helplessness cascaded through Cerissa, binding her in their strands. She wanted to leave the community and never return, and at the same time, she wanted to do something, anything, to stop this travesty of justice.

If she transformed to her Lux form, she could land on the stage and fly him to safety. Except she couldn't. Exposing herself in front of this audience would lead to far greater punishment from the Lux Protectors. And even beyond that, Henry wouldn't want her to. He'd see it as cowardice.

She tugged at her lip with her teeth, still not believing what was about to happen. Then she caught a glimpse of her cousin striding toward her. "Ari, what are you doing here?"

"Gaea phoned me, and I came right over. The mayor wouldn't let me attend the hearing. He was acting pissy about it because I'm not a community *member*."

She squeezed his hands and whispered, "Thank you for being here, but you must be quiet. I need to focus."

"On what?"

"On channeling all the love I can through the crystal."

With any luck, she'd be able to form a cushion between Henry and the pain. Her offering wasn't much, but it was all she could do. When he climbed the short staircase shirtless, her heart ripped open. He looked so proud, so strong and fearless, as he joined Anne-Louise and placed his hands on the crossbeam.

Cerissa held her breath as the whip cracked for the first time, and she sent a burst of love, hoping to reach him before the nine braided tails did.

She let out her breath. "I swear, if I get the chance, I'll kill him."

"Who?"

"You know who. Karen told me this was all the mayor's doing. He's been trying to humiliate Henry for years. He's the one who imposed this ridiculous sentence on Henry for dating me without the council's permission. And now, he's managed to bring it back from suspension—insisted on it, demanded it."

When Anne-Louise snapped the whip back again, Cerissa held her breath, sending more love. Another *crack*. The audience counted two. Anne-Louise was stretching them out.

Red streaks formed on Henry's back. Cerissa turned away. "I can't watch."

But she could still hear the meaty thud of another strike, the roll like an inharmonious musical chord as the whip's tails slapped individually.

Ari wrapped his arms around her while she buried her face in his chest and drew on his aura to boost her power through the crystal.

Even though she'd asked him not to, Henry tried to block her. But between her surging emotions, and the next crack of the whip, he grunted, and his shields dropped. She took advantage of the opening to flood him with her love.

She could feel his gratitude in response.

After the fourth strike, the audience became restless. The mortal mates, in twos and threes, left their seats to stand with her. Some placed soothing hands on her back and arms.

Nicholas Martin, the assistant town attorney, patted her shoulder. "We're here for you, Cerissa."

Haley Spears, the person leading the mates in lobbying for mortal rights, stood behind Ari and cringed when another strike hit. "We have to do something to stop this."

"We will," Luis said, his tone catching her attention. One of Abigale's mates, Luis Garcia was the mortal candidate for the open council seat. His statement sounded like a promise.

But would Tig intervene?

Cerissa looked around and glimpsed Jayden speaking to the chief. Tig nodded and walked off. Jayden approached their group.

"Where's Tig going?" Cerissa asked between strikes five and six.

Jayden squeezed her shoulder. "Home. Zeke's gone too. If we interfere, no one is here to stop us. Liza won't."

By the sixth strike, no mortals remained in the audience. The chant of the strikes had died off, the vampires growing quiet.

A flurry of instructions ran through the group surrounding her. Cerissa couldn't split her attention anymore and listen to them, not while cradling Henry with her love. She had to trust in her friends to act.

Just before the next strike, Ari whispered, "Ciss. Turn around. Look."

Luis rushed to the stage, leading the other mates, who swarmed behind him. When he reached Henry, he stuck his arm out between Henry's back and Anne-Louise's whip. Anne-Louise stopped mid-swing, snapping the cat-o'-nine-tails back so as not to strike the mortal.

"What is the meaning of this?" she demanded.

"You're done. We're not going to stand by and allow this to happen. This isn't justice." He glared at the mayor, who cowered in the front row. "This is some sick, twisted revenge fantasy. And it ends now."

"Well, well, I never—" the mayor stammered.

"We won't leave until you stop this."

The mayor looked around, befuddled. "Where's the chief? Someone, get those mortals off the stage."

The vampires in the audience sat with an eerie stillness—no fidgeting, no whispering, no motion at all. Humans moved constantly. Vampires didn't.

The silence felt like cotton enclosing Cerissa. She held her breath, her vision narrowing as time stretched. If the vamps wanted to, they could rush the stage and clear the mortals away in seconds using their supernatural speed and strength.

Suddenly—movement. Abigale stood and began applauding. Slowly, other vampires joined in, except for a handful. Cerissa made a note of who they were—Henry had a few enemies on the Hill.

Liza bounced to her feet then. "I say the sentence is complete. Who on the council agrees?"

Rolf lazily waved his hand in the air.

"Well, I don't," the mayor said.

"Two against one," Liza snapped. "Majority rule can overturn the chair once the penalty starts. We're done here."

The mortals on the stage joined the clapping. Anne-Louise dropped the whip and said something to Henry that Cerissa couldn't hear.

Standing straight despite the torn muscles in his back, Henry strode across the stage to the stairs, grabbed his clothes, and took the path to the parking lot.

Cerissa started to run to him, but Abigale *whooshed* out of the stands and caught her arm. "Don't. We'll take you home. Give Henry his dignity in this. Driving on his own is showing the mayor what he did had no effect."

Cerissa bit her lower lip. As much as she wanted to rush to his side and do whatever she could to alleviate his pain, Abigale was right. She nodded. "Ari can drive me home."

"Excellent. I'll stay here for Luis." Abigale patted Cerissa's back. "I'm sure Henry is proud of you. You did well."

"As did Luis." Cerissa let out a long breath, the tension leaving her body. "He's a shoo-in for the council seat."

"Indeed." Abigale raised an eyebrow, leering in her mate's direction. "Quite masterful, stopping the proceeding. I do believe he'll teach the mayor a thing or two about leadership. Just give him time."

Chapter 22

WHAT TO DO?

Gaea's house—Fifteen minutes later

Gaea pushed the button to close the garage door and hoisted herself out of her Mazda Miata. Getting out of the sports car always reminded her how low to the ground the chassis sat.

She would check on Christine and Zeke later. They were upstairs in the family room, watching television. Or, at least, they were supposed to be.

She'd had a devil of a time convincing Christine to leave the community center. Once they were finally in the car and on their way home, Henry's child became uncontrollably upset, reacting through the bond to what was happening to her maker at the amphitheater.

Gaea had phoned Zeke to help. The cowboy agreed to babysit and met Gaea on Robles Road, taking over Christine's care, which allowed Gaea to return to the amphitheater, hoping beyond hope that she could prevail on Winston to halt his nonsense. By the time she arrived, the mortals had successfully stopped the terrible spectacle.

My, oh my, oh my. How did all this happen?

Winston had no business taking his frustrations out on Henry.

It won't do. No, it won't do at all.

Gaea thinned her lips and slammed the car door shut, the noise sounding very loud with the garage door closed. Or maybe she'd put more force into the motion than she intended.

What if Cerissa and Henry pull up stakes and leave for New York?

Would Ari leave too?

Not that she was in love with the handsome young man with his wavy hair and charming insolence. Still, he filled certain *needs*.

She stomped over to the corner of the garage they used for a makeshift food prep area. The contractor was still rebuilding her burned-out kitchen—too slowly in her estimation. She stood staring at the garage cabinets next to the refrigerator, tapping a finger on her chin.

Where did I leave that box?

At the end of Cerissa and Henry's engagement party, Ari had grabbed a carton of spiked blood pouches from the serving room. They contained a blood alcohol level of point-one-five.

Gaea opened the cabinets, door after door, fishing around for the box. It had to be here somewhere. She'd hid them well to keep Seaton out of them—so where were they?

The fifth cupboard she opened held emergency food supplies for mortals, but right behind the canned goods, the carton peeked out. Rising on her tiptoes, she pushed the cans aside and brought down the box, popped the seal, and took out a pouch.

She filled a pan with water from the utility sink, placed it on the hotplate, and turned up the heat, tapping her foot. The adage that a watched pot never boils annoyed her. She didn't want the water to boil. She wanted it hot enough to dunk the pouch in to warm the blood.

The shelf over the hotplate counter held the glassware she'd purchased to replace what the fire destroyed. She took down a crystal highball glass and, when the water was finally hot enough, dunked the pouch in for a minute, then dried the outside, tore the serrated corner, and poured the dark wine into her glass. She took a long, satisfying drink.

Marvelous. Simply marvelous.

Cerissa had outdone herself with the clone blood she produced, and this spiked specialty had the perfect amount of alcohol to produce a mellow effect.

Gaea needed something to calm her nerves before she phoned that whelp of hers. Because if she spoke to Winston in her current mood, she'd do more harm than good.

She wandered into the house, touched a match to the kindling under the log in the fireplace of her formal living room, and relaxed in a tall wingback chair covered in beige linen with large turquoise and pink flowers. The warmth from the fire further eased the tension from her bones as she drank, and a sigh escaped between sips.

The story she'd told Ari wasn't the full picture.

Even though Winston's gray eyes and strutting confidence had always intrigued her, she hadn't fallen in love with him, hadn't felt true love for him even in all their years together. No, they'd been more like a long-term friendship with benefits, as the young people would say today.

In some ways, she and Winston were opposites. She was sensuous, and he was cerebral. She was an earth mother, and he, an administrator at heart. But in one way they clicked perfectly—they both loved to garden.

Gardening was how she got her name. The Irish vampire who turned her renamed her after the old earth goddess because of her love of plants. She'd spent much of her mortal life tilling the soil in Ireland. She grew oats, the main crop, but also a veggie garden of cabbages, onions, garlic, and parsnips. And then came the cows. From fresh milk to buttermilk, from sweet curds to sour curds, from onion butter to bog butter—milk products were a big part of her diet back then.

She hadn't seen her maker in decades. But gardening—the love of coaxing the plants to thrive and the act of turning the soil, releasing its rich scent to the air—still defined a core part of her identity long into her immortal life.

She sighed again, thinking of makers and children. She took another sip of her drink, and remembered the taste of Winston after she turned him. An offspring's blood tasted quite mortal for the first twenty or so years. After that, the desire to bite and have carnal knowledge of a mortal became overwhelming. Yet, even so, she and Winston remained a couple for forty years.

Maybe she really did love him. She accepted his foibles until she couldn't tolerate living with him anymore. As he grew into his own as a vampire, his tendency to be bureaucratic and autocratic irritated her to the point that she ended the romantic side of their relationship.

But even though they parted ways romantically, they frequently traveled together, both moving to New York when they became bored with London, and on to Los Angeles in the early 1900s. She appreciated his willingness to take care of the intricate details of globetrotting along with the tedious task of establishing a safe residence—those chores bored her. He even joined her when she decided to buy her spot in Sierra Escondida.

And a good thing they did, too. While Los Angeles was a sparkling, fun place and the early Hollywood crowd an absolute riot, the onset of the Great Depression squeezed the joy out of city living. A return to a simple—though elegant—country life was just the ticket, drawing revenue from her investments and supplementing her income by growing grapes for the Hill's vintners. Thanks to Carolyn Cubbage's financial guidance—the councilwoman was very shrewd—Gaea had more than enough for a comfortable lifestyle.

Winston, on the other hand, eschewed being a common grower. Having long ago abandoned his career as a barrister, he invested in large swaths of land when the owners went broke during the 1930s and made his fortune in mining and forestry.

As time passed, Winston resented not being in a position of authority in the small vampire community. She remained surprised the founders didn't kick the lordling off the Hill early on, what with the way he tried to bully everyone into getting his own way.

When she and Winston first joined the community, Henry held the title of mayor. Although Henry credited the other four founders too, the whole idea of Sierra Escondida was his, and it brought him status—along with Winston's aristocratic resentment of being ruled by a commoner.

After grabbing power when the 1972 vampire treaty forced the founders off the council, Winston replaced Henry as mayor, and that was when Winston's envy emerged for all to see.

In whatever way he could, Winston took potshots at Henry. The founder tended to ignore the new mayor, and when that didn't work, he'd either intimidate or placate Winston, depending upon the situation.

Henry was nothing if not flexible in his approach to solutions.

Over the years, she'd seen Winston's envy create new problems. She'd counseled him in the past to cease his petty, vindictive behavior.

But tonight? Tonight, he'd gone too far.

The front door opened, and Ari appeared in the archway leading into the formal living room. "Hey, sweet cheeks, whatcha doin' in here all by your lonesome?"

"I have a phone call to make to the mayor. What are you doing back so quickly?"

"I dropped Ciss off—she didn't think Henry would want company, so I didn't go inside."

"Then please go upstairs. I'll join you when I'm finished."

"Not without a kiss."

She waved him off. "Later. Now go."

He blew a kiss at her instead.

Gaea *tsked* and leaned back in her chair, staring into the fire. This wasn't going to be a pleasant conversation. Finished with her drink, she checked the time on her diamond-encrusted watch, retrieved her phone from her purse, and tapped her child's number.

When he picked up the call, she didn't give him an opportunity to say hello. "Winston, just what do you think you were doing?"

"Keeping the peace."

"With that spectacle? Not only have you outraged every mortal mate at a point when we we'd finally got them calmed down, but you also managed to infuriate most of the Hill's permanent residents."

"What would you have me do? Give Henry special treatment?" He *harrumphed*. "Do you have any idea how many of our permanent residents would have resented the decision if I had commuted the sentence entirely?"

"But with their mates now upset, those same residents will turn against you." Gaea wasn't even sure why she'd called. The horse had bolted. "Mark my word, Winston. Your actions tonight will be the end of your political career."

"Then it's a good thing I have my gardening to keep me occupied. You needn't worry about me." The doorbell rang in the background. "Speaking of which, that's how I plan on spending the remainder of the night. My Casa Blanca lily bulbs came in today. Good sleep."

The call disconnected, and Gaea *tsked* again. She recognized Winston's bluster for what it was—a man unable to take responsibility for his mistakes. She just hoped the community didn't kick him out. Despite his faults, she preferred having one of her children around. The loneliness that came with immorality weighed a little less heavily on her then.

CHAPTER 23

OUTTA HERE

MARCUS AND NICHOLAS'S HOUSE—AROUND THE SAME TIME

Marcus barreled through the doorway of their temporary home with Nicholas in his wake. "Start packing," he said, consciously lowering his voice, when what he wanted was to yell at the top of his lungs so the entire Hill heard him. "We're leaving."

Nicholas flopped onto the couch. "But I thought we were waiting until Christine—"

"I don't give a flying fig anymore. I've dedicated my life to guiding those pompous idiots on the council—and this time, they have gone too far."

"But the mayor's going to need help." Nicholas kicked off his shoes. "Help writing his resignation letter."

"He can go to blazes for all I care. He'll never resign. He'd rather go down in flames at the next election than give up any power prematurely. And I will not spend another moment toadying to the mayor's resentment of Henry and me and the other founders. This has gone far enough. I won't be roped into Winston's baseless feud any longer. Now get off that tacky couch and start packing."

Marcus sighed as he waited for Nicholas to move. At least they had something to pack. He and his mate managed to retrieve clothes and personal belongings from their earthquake-damaged home, but much to his disappointment, the only temporary place available for them to move into had belonged to Kim Han, one of the Hill residents killed by the VDM. The homey, middle-class décor the house came with, including the furniture, was like a bedbug nipping at his toes.

Nicholas didn't move from the navy velour couch where he lounged, looking right at home. "We should speak with Father Matt before making any serious changes. Why don't you phone him, ask if he has time to talk with us?"

Marcus scowled. He wanted to drop his own resignation letter on the mayor's desk and leave tonight. Let the idiot sail himself out of the political storm heading the council's way. Winston would be lucky if the mob didn't stake him for what happened in the amphitheater.

And Marcus had no intention of standing between the mob and the mayor.

"Please?" Nicholas added.

Marcus let out a huff. "Fine. I'll phone Matt."

Fifteen minutes later, Nicholas sprang to his feet and answered the knock at the door. "Thanks, Matt, for making a house call." He escorted the psychologist to a chair across from the couch. "I was afraid if we got in the car, Marcus would drive us out the gates and not stop until sunrise."

"I'm happy to visit you at home. I really suspected the house call I'd make tonight was to Henry, but he hasn't phoned. If he does, I may need to leave."

"Understandable," Marcus said, offering his hand to shake.

Once Matt was seated in the occasional chair across from them, Marcus eased onto the couch next to Nicholas.

Matt adjusted the traditional Episcopal priest's collar he wore through the neck of his black shirt, which signified his other profession. "So, how may I help?"

Nicholas glanced at Marcus and then looked over at Matt. "I guess I'll explain. Marcus is upset about what happened and wants to move. I'm on the fence. Yes, tonight was terrible. But what the mayor did unified the mortals—even the few who held back their support in the past. This is going be a watershed moment for the community, and I don't want to miss it."

Marcus crossed his arms. "And I refuse to hold the mayor's hand through the turmoil. That jackass got himself into this—he can get himself out."

"Okay, I get the picture," Matt said. "Before we dig into those issues, I first want to say that you both have been making wonderful progress with your trust exercises. And if you ultimately decide to move, I'm happy to continue to work with you via videoconference, or I can refer you to a professional in the community of your choice."

That was excellent news. Marcus let out a breath, tension leaving his body along with the air. They'd have options.

"So let's brainstorm," Matt continued. "What I've heard Marcus say repeatedly is that he needs a break from being town attorney."

Marcus furrowed his brow. "True—"

"And you have a ton of unused vacation time," Matt added.

"You think I should take a vacation, not resign?"

"Now may be a perfect time for a trip. Instead of a letter of resignation, email the mayor that you're taking, what, a two-week vacation?"

Marcus nodded slowly. "In order to give me time to cool down?"

"And to let Winston resolve the situation on his own. He ignored your advice—"

"I didn't say that—I didn't reveal any attorney-client conversation to you—"

"Easy, Marcus." Matt raised his palm. "My guess is you wouldn't be this angry about what happened unless the mayor ignored your advice."

Marcus turned to Nicholas. "What do you say? We could pack our bags and leave tonight." He glanced at his watch. "If we start driving now, we could be in San Francisco and checked into a hotel before dawn. Catch a few shows, enjoy the sights, and then keep driving. Would it feel like a busman's holiday to you if we went to Napa?"

Nicholas squeezed his hand. "I think you have a wonderful idea. But can we leave tomorrow night? I want to visit Cerissa during the day, lend her my support. I can make the reservations for us and then we can take off as soon as it's dark."

Marcus returned the squeeze. "That makes perfect sense. But I'm sending my vacation notice tonight."

"No argument here."

Matt's phone buzzed. "Is there anything else you want to talk about now? I have a feeling once I answer these messages, I'll be headed out to help someone else."

Marcus stood to escort him to the door. "Go ahead and see your other clients. We appreciate the visit on such short notice, but we'll muddle along fine from here."

Indeed, they would. As soon as Matt was out the door, Marcus switched his phone to refuse all calls, and sent an email to the council telling them he and Nicholas were on vacation.

The mayor could go to hell for all he cared.

Chapter 24

PROTECTION

Rancho Bautista del Murciélago—Thirty minutes earlier

The Viper stood in the driveway when Cerissa arrived home, wet blood glistening on the black leather seat under the outdoor lighting, the driver's door open. She slammed the door shut as she passed by. Later, she would wipe down the seats and move the sports car to the garage. Seeing to Henry's wellbeing came first.

She found him lying on her bed, face in the pillow. "How are you feeling?"

"I will heal." The pillow muffled his words.

His back was *shredded*. The whip tore muscle from the bone, leaving large, bloody gashes. She touched the pulse point on his wrist and counted, not surprised to find his heart rate elevated. "Would vampire blood help? I have a donation from Rolf in the lab refrigerator."

"I cannot."

What did he mean, "I cannot"?

She huffed. "Of course you can."

"Someone may check later," he mumbled. "I can't use blood for rapid healing."

His long hair lay plastered in his bloody wounds. As they spoke, she gently loosened the strands, moving them away before his body began healing, and trapped them under the skin.

He lifted his head and took a deep breath. "Is Christine still with Gaea?"

Ari had spoken with Gaea and updated Cerissa when he drove her home. "Ah, Gaea was halfway to her house when your child became hysterical in the car during the...ah, flogging."

He sighed. "I tried to block her, but it was too much for me to handle. What happened?"

"Gaea called Zeke, who took Christine to Gaea's house, and then Gaea returned to the amphitheater, thinking she could stop things. By then, you'd left."

Cerissa found a hair scrunchy in the bedside table and redid Henry's ponytail into a topknot to keep the hair from touching his back. "Zeke will spend the night with her."

"Great. Just great. I do all I can to slow down her infatuation with him, and after I put myself at the whipping post to protect her, she runs to him."

"Not that I'm interested in defending Zeke, but from what Ari told me, Christine lost it over what they were doing to you. Gaea could do nothing to calm her, and when Zeke arrived, he had a foothold—perhaps because of the ritual bite. He was the only one who could stop her hysterics."

"The connection to her maker is strongest when the fledgling is young. She felt my agony. I could do nothing for her."

Cerissa stared at his back. "This is barbaric."

"This is our way. Nothing is served by bemoaning the situation."

The doorbell rang. Cerissa hissed and shot a look in the direction of the foyer. "Who the hell is stupid enough to come here tonight?"

"Would you please go see? I'm in no shape to stand."

She kissed his cheek and went downstairs, pressing the button to turn on the surveillance camera monitor first.

Of all the stupid—

"Let me in." Anne-Louise pounded on the door. "I can smell you there, Cerissa."

"Go away. He doesn't want company."

"He'll want mine. Let me in, or I'll take the door off its hinges."

Vampires! Cerissa unlocked the deadbolt, cracking the door. "What do you want?"

"I have to check on Enrique or Winston will come here himself and do it."

"Fine." Cerissa swung the door opened and stepped aside. "He's upstairs in my bedroom."

Anne-Louise gracefully ascended the stairs in her all-black outfit.

From behind her on the staircase, Cerissa called out, "Henry, fair warning, Anne-Louise is on her way to you."

"*Oui*. Which room?"

"The open door straight ahead of you."

Anne-Louise strode in and stopped by Henry's bedside, examining his back. She took out her phone and snapped a photo.

"What the hell are you doing?" It took all of Cerissa's willpower not to swing her fist at Henry's maker.

"I must—proof for the mayor. He wants evidence Henry is still wounded. Now shut up and let me send this."

Anne-Louise focused on her phone, as if she was having trouble making the technology do what she wanted it to do.

"There." She punched another button and put the phone to her ear. "Winston, you have what you wanted. Now, do not bother us again tonight." She paused, listening. "Listen, you *putain de connard*, if you come to Henry's, I will beat you to a pulp. What I gave Henry will seem like a love tap in comparison. *Comprendre*?"

She stabbed at the phone, ending the call. "There. That is done. Now, be a good girl and find me a towel and a sharp blade."

Cerissa eyed her warily. "Why?"

"I'm going to heal his back. No one will come here, and if they do, they'll have to go through me."

"Henry, do you want me to help her?"

"Please. She seems to have the situation under control."

Cerissa found some dark brown towels in the hall closet—those would hide blood best—and grabbed her medical kit. A scalpel would be the easiest way to open a vein.

Anne-Louise took the towel. "Rise," she said to Henry. "Enough for me to feed the towel under you. Those sheets are too pretty to spill blood on them."

Grunting with pain, he used his forearms and knees to lift himself, and Anne-Louise slid the towel under him.

"Now, dear girl, where is the blade?"

Cerissa narrowed her eyes at Anne-Louise, saying nothing. Even though Henry seemed to trust his maker not to further hurt him, she wasn't so sure.

Into the silence, Anne-Louise chuffed. "Do not anger me, Cerissa. I see the suspicion in your look. I've done everything I can tonight to protect him, and now I will heal him."

"Protect him?" she yelled. "At the council meeting, you sniped at Winston for reducing the sentence."

"I acted the part your mayor expected of me. Is she really this naïve about how the game is played?" Anne-Louise asked Henry.

He growled. "Do not criticize my mate."

"Fine. But this nonsense ends." Anne-Louise held out her palm. "Give me the blade."

Cerissa handed her the scalpel. Anne-Louise sliced her wrist, following a vein, and let the dark, thick blood run onto Henry's back. The first gash began to heal.

Cerissa gasped, feeling Henry's pain as his back arched, and a groan escaped his lips.

"Stop," he ordered Anne-Louise, and blindly reached out his hand to Cerissa. "Give me your phone."

"It's all right—"

"Give me your phone, now. I won't ask again."

"Fine." She took the device from her pocket and handed it to him, and he tapped the application to shut off the crystal's connection.

"*Qu'est-ce que ça a fait*? What did that do?"

"None of your business," Henry said, the pillow again muffling his voice, and tossed the phone onto the nightstand. "Now, please, finish healing my back."

More blood drizzled down Anne-Louise's wrist and onto his open wounds. "Really, Enrique. Winston has had it out for you for years now. When are you going to stop ignoring his pettiness and do something?"

"I am. Rolf is running against him for mayor. I'm backing him."

"That is all? Not enough, *mon bébé*, not enough by…how do you say?"

"A long shot?" Cerissa offered.

"*Oui*. Not enough by a long shot. Perhaps I should eliminate him for you."

"*Cingao puta de madre*," Henry swore. "I don't need you to fight my battles with Winston."

"Then who, since you're clearly unwilling to do what is necessary? Cerissa? I think not," Anne-Louise scoffed. "No. This has been enlightening. You need to do something. Now. Not tomorrow. Not next week. Not the next election. Tonight, you must figure out how to stop him. Because I guarantee he is already planning his next move."

CHAPTER 25

SURPRISE

RANCHO BAUTISTA DEL MURCIÉLAGO—A FEW MINUTES LATER

Cerissa crawled into bed, curling up next to Henry. The large gashes on his back, despite the boost of Anne-Louise's blood, weren't healing fast.

Why was it taking so long? The time he cracked his ribs, drinking vampire blood had healed them quickly.

This time, the damage was to skin and muscle rather than bone. Did that make a difference? Or was it because the blood had been applied topically, rather than swallowed?

She stroked his arm. Now wasn't the time to ask him.

Anne-Louise said good night and went downstairs to guard against further intrusions. At least they'd stopped bickering over the mayor for now. Henry needed to rest.

Once his maker left the room, Henry murmured, "I'm sorry, Cerissa, I will not be much company. I am still fighting the pain."

Her medical kit lay where she'd placed it on the nightstand. Reaching inside, she pulled out a white blood pouch with a red cross label. "Then drink this."

"What is it?"

"A painkiller, processed through my clones. The same one I gave Yacov. The medication may make you drowsy." She rushed into the bathroom to get a glass, poured the blood, and brought the glass to him.

"Thank you." He pushed himself off the pillow and gulped down the liquid. "I'm going to stay here for now. You may sleep next to me, if you so desire, but I do not want to talk. Rising to speak...intensifies the pain."

He let himself return to lying facedown on the pillow.

"Of course, Quique." She wrapped her hand around his, leaned over to gently kiss his fingers, and then dozed off.

At some point in the early morning, half-asleep, she heard the front door close.

"Anne-Louise is returning to the guest house on Rolf's property," Henry murmured. "Until I can afford to build the promised house on our land, she will stay the day at Rolf's."

Cerissa kissed his cheek, and with Anne-Louise gone, she fell into a deeper sleep.

When she woke, the bedside clock displayed the time: after ten-thirty in the morning. Henry still lay next to her on his stomach, his back mostly healed. The corners of her mouth lifted. She was glad he hadn't gone downstairs.

The fact he didn't breathe when asleep momentarily unnerved her. While he had to breathe in air to speak, he didn't need to otherwise. Since he was so good at maintaining the illusion of being mortal when awake, she had to remind herself that his failure to breathe while asleep wasn't a medical crisis.

She moved quietly so as not to disturb him, resisting the urge to lean over and kiss him. She closed the bathroom door, brushed her teeth, and threw on some sweats, one task foremost in her mind: she wanted to clean Henry's car seat of blood and put the Viper into the garage to spare him the blatant reminder when he woke.

Thirty minutes later, she'd finished, then speedily showered and dressed, finally ready for breakfast. She'd sat down to eat at the kitchen table when her phone rang.

Karen.

"Hi, what's up?" Cerissa asked.

"Are you okay? Is Henry?"

"We're both fine. We made it through the ordeal."

"Good. I'm glad to hear." Karen paused. "Can you come to my house?"

"Why?"

"Ah, there's a groundswell happening among the mates. They figured I was the last holdout and landed on my doorstep an hour ago."

"You're not making any sense."

"Get over here as quick as you can, and it will."

"Okay, after I eat. Give me twenty minutes."

"Done deal."

The line went dead. She put her phone aside and chowed down, then brushed her teeth again, grabbed her purse from the foyer table, and arrived at Karen's with seconds to spare.

Karen opened the door while Cerissa parked. Other cars filled the driveway.

"What's going on?" she asked, walking into the entryway. From there, she could peer into the huge formal living room. Members of the mortal rights subcommittee—Nicholas and Haley—waited for her, as well as Luis and Jayden.

Cerissa blinked, the significance of their presence sinking in.

The four mortals who led the march onstage to stop the whipping came over to greet her with a group hug. Karen then excused herself, rushing off to the kitchen to rescue something she was baking before it burned.

"How are you feeling?" Nicholas asked.

"I'm all right, I think. Hard as it was to witness, I couldn't abandon him. Afterward—" She stopped. She couldn't tell them about Anne-Louise's visit. "I stayed with him all night."

"What they did to Henry was brutal," Haley said, the anger lighting her blue eyes.

"I couldn't agree more." Cerissa wrapped her arms around herself, still stressed by the whole thing.

"I'd be absolutely pissed if they did that to Vishon." Haley shook her head vehemently, her long blonde hair swishing over her shoulders. "Vampire or mortal, physical punishment should be abolished."

"I agree with Haley," Jayden said. "Physical punishment should be off the table—full stop. There are other options for dealing with criminal wrongdoing."

Nicholas brushed his hair back. "Hmm. Let's put a pin in what to do about physical punishment. But one thing I think we can concur on—the council has too much discretion over what penalties are imposed."

"Amen to that," Haley said.

Cerissa glanced around the group. "I appreciate the support, but why are we here?"

Nicholas gestured to follow him. They all took seats in the living room. "We'd like to discuss with you what to do next. But we should wait for Karen to begin our discussion."

The heavenly smell of freshly baked cinnamon rolls tickled Cerissa's nose, heralding Karen's return. Cerissa stood to help her bestie with the tray and passing out plates.

"They look wonderful," Cerissa said, taking one. "Did you bake them this morning?"

"The dough was in the fridge when everyone else arrived. I had to do something to kill twenty minutes."

Karen waved in Nicholas's direction. "Can you give me a hand with the iced tea and glasses?"

"Sure."

Cerissa enjoyed her first bite into the roll as she waited for her friends to return. Jayden, Haley, and Luis chatted about what happened at their homes after the flogging was stopped. Tig, Vishon, and Abigale, each in their own way, were royally ticked off at the mayor.

When Karen and Nicholas returned, they placed the tray of glasses on the coffee table and started pouring from the pitcher.

"Now that everyone's here," Nicholas said, taking his seat on one of the white silk couches, "we want to discuss change. Anger over what happened last night has energized our movement. Everyone's upset, and we want to ride this wave and make larger systemic changes happen now—which includes appointing a mortal to the council."

It was about time. Cerissa placed her glass on the coffee table. "Okay. So, what are we discussing first?"

"I think we need to talk about the elephant in the council chambers. The hundred lashes they originally imposed was wrong by any standard of punishment. It wasn't imposed because Christine's law partner was killed. The council imposed the whipping because Henry dated Cerissa within the gates without the council's permission. It was too extreme of a punishment."

"Tell me about it," Cerissa mumbled.

Nicholas leaned toward her, a look of concern in his eyes. "First point—she is a grown woman, who wasn't mated to a vampire, who could make her own choice, and we see how demeaning the council's attitude was to her."

"Thank you."

"Second point—the goal of the rule is to prevent duels between vampires over mates. But Cerissa wasn't mated to another vampire. So Henry broke the letter but not the intent of the law. An extreme punishment—which any physical punishment is—might deter others, but it isn't rehabilitative, and there was no ongoing threat to the community by Henry dating an unmated mortal within the Hill's walls to justify its implementation."

Cerissa held up her hand. "Wait a minute. Are you saying physical punishment should be allowed in some cases?"

"I am, mainly because part of the problem is we don't have a way to incarcerate a vampire for a long term. If you confine them to a coffin, they go crazy after a while with no food. You have to let them out to feed. But only letting then out to feed and locking them in a coffin the remainder of the night also drives them insane. It's worse than solitary confinement. So, it's cruel, but also gives you a mentally unstable immortal as a result."

Nicholas took a deep breath. "All that said, I know several of you disagree with me on that point, and we don't need to resolve those details right now in order to discuss our next actionable steps."

Cerissa opened her mouth to argue, but then decided he was right. They would have time to debate the details. "So what are the next steps?"

She glanced from Nicholas to Haley. While they were both on the mortal rights committee, and she appreciated Nicholas's legal knowledge when it came to vampire law, Haley had been leading things before.

Haley sat forward. "Here's the plan. First, we push the council to fill the fifth seat with Luis." She tapped a manicured nail against her palm. "We need mortal representation with modern-day views. Second, the mortal rights subcommittee is already proposing elimination of the 'no dating' rule. Who you date and where you date them is personal, and shouldn't be decided by the council."

"What about dueling?" Cerissa asked.

Haley gestured to Nicholas, and he jumped in. "Penalize the act, yes."

"Third," Haley said, "we need to curtail the council's power to penalize how they feel in the moment. This can't happen again." She glanced over. "Nicholas can explain his idea."

"The subcommittee will include in its work plan a preliminary list of crimes and the *maximum* penalty the council may impose. The unlimited discretion must end."

"Okay," Cerissa said, reaching for a second cinnamon roll. After all the stress, she deserved another one. "How do we get those three things into motion?"

Haley's eyes sparkled. "We ride the wave of outrage and let it carry Luis into office. Something much more achievable with your help, Cerissa."

"How can I—" Then it hit Cerissa. After what she'd been through, as Henry's mortal mate, if she publicly supported Luis, her experience might persuade the fence-sitters. She took a deep inhale. "Luis already has my support."

Luis smiled at her. "Thank you, Cerissa."

Nicholas motioned to Karen. "What about you?"

"What do you mean, what about me? You want me involved?"

"I think," Cerissa said, "as the vice mayor's mate, your support might sway other vampires—they might read it to mean Rolf supports Luis."

"Oh." Karen hooked an auburn strand behind her ear. "Sure. Why not? Rolf was as much at fault for voting months ago for the penalty, trying to keep you and Henry apart. He'll have to accept a mortal on the council as his punishment."

"Woo hoo!" Ashley shot from her seat to high-five everyone. "How do we get word around?"

"An endorsement letter signed by every mortal mate—with Cerissa's and Karen's signatures at the top—should do the trick," Luis said. "And with Karen's marketing experience, she might have some suggestions for phrasing, ways to sell our plan to the vamps."

"Great idea," Nicholas said. "Let's start drafting. I bet we can have this ready and signed before Marcus and I leave on vacation tonight. If we deliver a *fait accompli,* we'll win because the few vampire holdouts won't have time to fight back."

Cerissa raised her iced tea glass. "To Councilmember Luis," she said, and they all clinked glasses.

She just hoped it went as smoothly as Nicholas thought it would, because she had her doubts. If life had taught her anything, it was that some unexpected event always mucked up her agenda no matter how well she planned things out.

CHAPTER 26

RECOVERY

RANCHO BAUTISTA DEL MURCIÉLAGO—THAT NIGHT

Henry opened his eyes to find his face smooshed in the pillow and his beard regrown, making his skin itch where the whiskers pressed in. He slowly rolled over. His back, although healed on the surface, still ached. The white ceiling surprised him, since he expected to see the unfinished stucco in his crypt. Then he recalled staying in Cerissa's bed at sunrise.

He got out of bed, moving carefully, and worked his way to his room. He couldn't wait to shower and toss the pants he wore into the trash.

He stripped off the pants and held them out. Tan. A bad choice. The light color showed where bits of flesh and blood had splattered his butt with every twist back of Anne-Louise's wrist, creating a gruesome Rorschach. Not that he would have tried to clean and reuse the pants even if they were black.

A good thing he'd had the foresight not to wear a two-piece suit, though, or both the jacket and pants would have gone in the trash, since a suit coat couldn't be worn with other pants—at least not in his fussy estimation. A sports coat was different. He could buy another pair of solid-colored slacks to complement one of the subtle colors in the coat, which was exactly why he'd worn the plaid sports coat in tan and claret in the first place.

He wadded the pants into a ball, shot them into the trash can on the other side of his closet, and picked out a brand-new outfit—slacks and a soft button-up shirt in blue tones. Emphasis on soft to protect his back's delicate skin.

But first, to shave. It took him five minutes to rid himself of the bushy beard, regrown during the day, that was just like the one he'd died with. Now shorn, he readied for his shower, pulling Cerissa's scrunchy from his topknot, a light smile forming when he recalled her tender care.

He opened the glass door and stepped into the shower. The warm water felt like magic. The new skin on his back was sensitive, but he didn't mind the steaming hot water warming him from head to toes.

He stood under the showerhead, letting the spray wash the shaving cream from his face, his eyes closed. Suddenly, the memory surfaced of the whip striking his back, the pain radiating through him. He flinched, gritting his teeth, willing the flashback to fade away and not return.

After drying his hair and tying the long strands back with a leather string, he heard Cerissa arrive home. Dressed in his new clothes, he slipped on a pair of loafers and went downstairs to greet her. His only plans for tonight were to get his child home and maybe check his winery email before it became too late to respond.

His employees were accustomed to his odd hours, but he tried to get business completed by eight as a courtesy to them. He'd tested a scheduling program to send his emails during business hours, but then everyone wondered why he waited until after sunset to respond to their answers.

He found Cerissa in the kitchen. "Good evening, *querida*." He pulled her into his arms, pressing his lips gently to hers. "How was your day?"

She held out a sheet of paper. "The mates are rushing to get Luis appointed to fill the council seat. I just came from Karen's house."

He raised an eyebrow and read the typewritten page. The reasons for making the change were well laid out, and he understood the rush. After the way the mates stormed the stage, they had momentum.

His eyes widened when he read Cerissa's name at the top of the signers list. "I'm proud of you, Cerissa." He hugged her again. "Would you like to join me while I make your dinner? I have a new chicken recipe to try."

"I would love that." She leaned back. "How are you feeling?"

"I am fine. A little sore—the new skin is tender, but otherwise healed."

"Good. Have you heard from Christine? When will she be here?"

"In about an hour. Gaea texted me."

When the doorbell rang, Henry straightened up from loading the dishwasher. Cerissa had finished dinner and stood at the sink, rinsing off the skillet.

He took the skillet from her and placed it on the dish rack to dry, then slid his hand around hers. They answered the door together.

"Hello, dears," Gaea said. "I'm returning Christine, safe and sound."

Henry gave a bow. "Thank you. Christine, why don't you go to the kitchen and warm some blood for yourself?"

His child nodded then strode to the alcove, tight-lipped and miserable-looking as she disappeared into the kitchen.

"How is she doing?" he asked Gaea.

"Not well. The poor thing blames herself for what happened to you last night, and for killing her friend. The guilt she's living with is eating her alive."

"Thank you again for taking care of her. I hope you don't feel it rude of me not to invite you in, but I want to speak with Christine alone."

"Not at all, not at all, dear boy." Gaea patted his shoulder, and he worked hard not to flinch at her touch, more from skin memory than any real pain. "Go and take care of your child. I left Ari at home waiting for me."

When Henry returned to the kitchen with Cerissa at his side, he found Christine at the mahogany table sipping from a tall glass tumbler filled with dark wine. One night away from him, and she was already adopting Gaea's habits.

Henry took the chair opposite Christine. "Cerissa, please sit at the island. I want you to stay, but I also want to be between you and Christine."

Christine looked up at him. "You don't trust me."

"I'll risk no more accidents."

A shadow passed over her face, and she lowered her gaze to the glass. "How are you feeling—after last night?"

"My back is healed already. The advantage of being vampire. But emotional pain doesn't heal as fast. My own will take much longer to resolve." He paused, studying Christine's reaction. "As will yours."

She took another sip and precisely centered the glass on the table in front of her. Staring at her drink, she said, "Henry, I think I made a mistake. Becoming vampire—it's not right for me. I—I want you to help me...end it."

"Absolutely not."

How could she ask that of him? He'd only begun to reconcile his feelings over suddenly having a child—his possessiveness and protectiveness had been growing nightly.

And even beyond his visceral instinct to keep his child alive, this was not the way to react to tragedy. One mistake did not define her long life.

"Please, you must help me," she said. "Every minute I'm awake, I see Patrick's face, the frozen look of horror as I—before I bit him. I'll never forget it." She gripped her stomach. "I can't live with the pain."

Henry understood. *Dios mío*, did he understand. "Some things cannot be fixed, but they can be borne. You will learn this truth for yourself, and we, this entire community, will support you in the effort."

Christine buried her face in her hands. "If you won't help, can Cerissa?"

Henry's brow furrowed. "Cerissa will support you alongside—"

"No, that's not what I mean."

Cerissa's heart wrenched at the pain Christine expressed, but she couldn't begin to imagine what his child had in mind. "Christine, what are you asking?"

"Can't you create one of your magic potions and make me forget?" Christine asked, her eyes plaintive.

Magic potions?

Cerissa wanted to go over to her, to touch and comfort her, but Henry held up a cautioning hand, so she remained seated. "There isn't anything I can make in my lab to fix this for you."

"But you're a witch, right? That's how you woke Henry during the day—and you used some sort of magic to get him past the court's security, didn't you?"

Oh no. Cerissa couldn't explain how she used Lux technology to flash Henry into the courthouse bathroom, thus avoiding security. She made eye contact with him. "No magic was involved. Only science."

"No. It was a trick of some sort." Christine glared at her, gnashing her teeth. "You're a witch. If vampires exist, then witches do. And you have a magical crystal ball."

The touchstone. She believes the memory-reading touchstone is magic.

"The touchstone is technology, not magic. And through experimentation, I learned I could wake Henry during the day if I made him feel like he was in imminent bodily danger." Cerissa paused, looking her in the eye. "You must believe me, I'm a scientist, not a witch."

"But—"

Cerissa clasped her hands together, squeezing them tightly. This was going to be harder than telling her the truth about the Lux.

"Think back to your history lessons. Women accused of witchcraft were the early doctors and scientists of their day, observing nature and testing theories, trying plant-based medicines to heal patients."

Christine had stopped crying, but her face said she wasn't buying it.

"Some of those women were beer makers," Cerissa continued, "with the cauldrons and pointed hats of their trade, adding needed calories to their family's diet, and making a life-saving potion in areas where the local water was unsafe to drink. Boiling the water as part of beer-making sanitized it. But jealous men who wanted the brewer's trade for themselves falsely accused those women of being witches."

"I don't believe you. You are a witch." Christine picked up her glass and chugged down the remainder. "I've been following scientific developments for a long time, and nothing—not a single article I researched—even hinted at what your touchstone can do. It must be magic."

Cerissa let out a long exhale. "We haven't published the science because the process hasn't been patented yet. We don't want others—"

Christine pounded her fist on the table. "Why won't you help me?"

Cerissa bowed her head. All she wanted was to relieve Christine of her pain. But it wasn't within her power. She looked back at the fledgling. "I'm sorry you're going through this, Christine, but I don't have anything to magically take away your pain."

CHAPTER 27

SORROW

RANCHO BAUTISTA DEL MURCIÉLAGO—MOMENTS LATER

"No," Christine said, shaking her head. The memory stabbed through her like a hot knife, over and over, with no end in sight. She needed relief—magical or otherwise.

She'd take *anything*.

Though maybe Cerissa told the truth about the touchstone. In a way, her explanation made sense. Why would the touchstone be written up in scientific journals if they hadn't patented the device yet?

Still, she didn't believe being a research scientist was the whole truth about Cerissa. But as her mind scrabbled to form a coherent thought, she couldn't create a better explanation.

In her frenzy to make sense of her reality, all she could see was Patrick's face frozen as he died. And if Henry's mate couldn't help her, no one could.

Clutching her chest, pressing against the pain festering there, Christine locked eyes with Henry. "You think I can learn to live with this?" she asked, her voice breaking. "No. I won't...I can't."

She was better off destroying herself—permanently.

"Christine, every vampire I have ever met has accidentally killed someone to feed their thirst. When I first rose, I drained dry a priest from a nearby mission who was working late in the fields near the cemetery where Anne-Louise abandoned me for the day. Back then, we didn't have bagged blood. I killed many more mortals before I learned to control my thirst."

Many. He'd killed many. "How do you live with the guilt?"

"I was raised Catholic. Confession helped. Repenting of my sins—sins I could not stop myself from committing—helped. You aren't a religious woman—"

"No, I'm not."

"But some of the principles can apply even outside the faith. I would like to reach out to Father Matt and ask for his help. He's a psychologist as well as a priest. He understands the mind, and how someone in your position may be guided to cope with this difficulty."

Christine locked her fingers, twisting them tighter together, letting the physical pain focus her mind. How could a priest help her, even one trained as a psychologist? She'd never trusted religious leaders or head doctors in the past.

"The pain...the pain is clawing me from the inside, trying to get out, not letting me think of anything else." She gripped her own throat and started hyperventilating. "I can't breathe."

Henry took her hands, untwining her fingers from her neck. "You don't need to breathe. Relax. The panic will pass."

"Don't tell me to relax. You don't know how I feel. You killed strangers." She wiped a hand across her eyes. "I killed my best friend."

Henry squeezed her arm, then glanced in Cerissa's direction where she sat at the kitchen island. She nodded at him.

What was that about? Psychic communication?

Henry gave a little tug on her arm, and Christine returned her eyes to his. "You are right," he said. "I don't know what that feels like exactly. But I do know what it is like to kill someone you love. In 1889, I killed my mate."

Christine's mouth dropped open in shock before she snapped her jaw shut.

"I— It was an accident," he continued. "But the accident wouldn't have happened if I hadn't let jealousy and anger drive me. It took years for me to move beyond her death, to learn to live with the grief, to carry the pain without being overwhelmed by the loss, to feel like I had paid a sufficient penance to experience joy again."

Christine looked away from him. "What I'm feeling—this heartbreak, this misery—feels bottomless."

"I understand. I do. I am sorry you're going through this, but if you come to see what happened clearly, with time, the experience will temper you, like fire tempers metal. You will learn to forgive yourself, and in doing so, learn to forgive others."

"I'm not you, Henry. I don't believe I can forgive myself this."

Henry fell silent a moment. "Let us try. Before you decide that being a vampire is wrong for you, let us try a few other options first."

"I don't see what good it will do."

"Your solution is permanent. We can always return to your plan. Let's attempt something less...final. Agreed?"

Christine's lip trembled. "Turning me wasn't your idea; it was mine and Marcus's. So if you want me to try—"

"I do."

She pulled her hands out of his and sat back. "Then call your shrink."

Henry gave a little bow and took Cerissa with him. Minutes later he returned and stopped by Christine, squeezing her shoulder. "Father Matt is sending over two of our younger vampire residents. They're part of a support group." He stepped over to the stove. "Let me warm some more dark wine for you before they arrive. It will help you feel better."

Fat chance. All the blood in the world wouldn't take away her pain.

Fifteen minutes later, she stared at the half-full glass on the table. Her first time tasting dark wine had produced an explosion of flavors, enchanting her with its richness.

Now, she wanted to throw the glass against the wall.

Henry had finally stopped talking at her, stopped trying to convince her to live. He now stood at the kitchen sink loading the dishwasher, and Cerissa stayed at the kitchen island, the two chattering about something the mortals planned to do.

With no one talking at her, she could finally slow her mind and think.

From what Marcus told her, starving a vampire, or draining all their blood, wouldn't kill them. It took a stake or silver bullet through the heart, beheading, or silver poisoning...or the sun. Can't forget the sun.

Well, beheading was out—she didn't have the means to build a guillotine without being caught, even if she could bring herself to submit to the blade. Same with the sun. Every instinct forced her underground and into a crypt long before sunrise. To overcome her instinct felt impossible.

And they weren't likely to let her obtain aqueous silver, or a gun loaded with the deadly metal. Those things were banned from general possession on the Hill and required a special permit.

Could Cerissa have something in her downstairs lab that would work? Silver nitrate powder, perhaps? Christine would have to wait for Henry to drop his guard—right now, he watched her too closely. But maybe in a few weeks she could sneak away to search the lab for what she wanted.

Something about having a plan to destroy herself calmed her, buying her a moment's peace.

And maybe she had another option. Silver ammunition was strictly regulated, but Henry was a founder, and, from what she heard, a reserve police officer. Did he own a handgun with silver ammo? If so, where would he hide the gun?

Not in the basement crypts. He'd given her a thorough tour of all the sleep rooms, and no gun safe resided in any of the crypts.

But he *did* own guns. Whenever he went off the Hill, he carried a gun in a back harness. They'd discussed his carry license when she prepped his testimony. She'd impressed on him that he couldn't bring a weapon into court, no matter how ingrained the practice.

Hmm, these options are complicated. Is there anything simpler?

Making a stake—that would be easy. The material was irrelevant. Wood, metal, stone—any material strong enough to impale.

Did she have the physical strength to kill herself? She could fall on the stake and maybe gravity would provide enough force. Or would her natural instincts take over and make her miss the target? Maybe a crossbow. She could point the arrow at her chest and find some way to pull the trigger.

She needed an airtight plan—a plan that couldn't fail. One botched attempt, and they'd watch her too closely. She'd lose her chance then.

The doorbell rang, and she vaguely registered the sound.

Of all the options, aqueous silver remained her first choice—even if sneaking around entailed some planning. If she drank a generous amount, no one would be able to save her. One bad night, and her life would be all over. Or drink the solution right before sunrise, and not feel a thing as the silver worked during the day to kill her.

Yes, *that* was the best choice.

A sense of calm enveloped her. She had a plan.

"Christine."

She jerked in her seat, looking up, startled. Henry stood with Cerissa and two other people across the table, staring down at her. She'd been so focused on the glass and her thoughts that she hadn't realized they'd arrived.

"This is Evelina Odegard and Chris Atherton," Henry said. "They are from the support group. But they're also in a band. You'll hear them play at the monthly dances."

Automatically, she said, "Nice to meet you."

"If you'll excuse me"—Cerissa scooted to the basement stairs—"I'll be in my lab."

Christine's eyes tracked her—the smell of mortal blood continued to be a distraction.

Once the basement door closed, Christine focused on the two vampires. They were *young*, in their twenties when turned. God, was she always going to be surrounded by youth here? Being so much older in appearance bothered her more than she'd thought it would, even though the surgery—and turning vampire—successfully removed ten years from her face.

Chris—the man—stood taller than Henry and looked much thinner in tight jeans. He wore his black hair streaked red and shorter than Henry's, but still long, below his pierced earlobes. He must reapply the dye every night. Hair coloring didn't last long on a vampire.

"Call me Wolfie," he said with a gentle grin. "Everyone else does. I'm the lead singer and can really howl."

Christine's eyebrows rose. "Seriously?"

"Doncha know, he wants you to believe he was named for his crooning," Evelina said, slapping his back. "Truth is he got stuck in his wolf form for a week and went around begging for blood."

The woman had a touch of Minnesota in her voice. A little shorter than Wolfie, she was still tall and willowy, with straight flaxen hair and vivid, dark blue eyes. She took the chair across the table. "Anyway, we hear you had an accident."

Of course they'd heard. Marcus reported the whole disaster at the council meeting. Everyone knew what she was—a murderer. "Um, don't take this wrong, but you're too young to understand."

Both Evelina and Wolfie chuckled. "I'm sixty-two—in vampire years," Wolfie said.

Evelina fist-bumped Wolfie's arm. "And I'm his senior. Last week, I reached eighty years from the day I rose from the soil." Evelina lifted an eyebrow. "You're, what, fifty in mortal years?"

"Fifty-nine."

"You look great. I was twenty-six when turned, and he was twenty-two. It's great to have someone in your age group represented. It happened more in the seventeen and eighteen hundreds—you'll see for yourself as you meet more of us. But by the time Wolfie and I were turned, doncha know, the cult of youth had begun."

Christine dropped her gaze to her glass. Why couldn't they shut up and go away, so she could continue planning her own demise?

Evelina dipped her chin, making an exaggerated effort at eye contact. "So, Henry tells us you're having a rough time dealing with the accident."

Christine momentarily met Evelina's gaze, then quickly averted her eyes. She couldn't look at these strangers and say the words out loud. "I killed my best friend."

"How do you feel?"

"Seriously?" Christine lifted her chin. "You're asking that?"

Evelina gave a reassuring smile. "I won't know if I don't ask. Everyone's experience is different."

"I feel terrible. I don't want to go on living, not with this guilt." As soon as the words were out, Christine cringed internally, tightening her grip on the glass. Maybe she shouldn't have said that to these strangers.

"Are you thinking about ending it, then?"

No matter how personal the question, having opened the door, she couldn't lie. "Wouldn't you? I killed someone I cared about—loved like a brother. I don't deserve to live."

Tears started to fill her eyes again. Christine had cried last night on Zeke's shoulder, then again after the sun set tonight.

This can't be happening to me.

The agony pierced straight through her again, reminding her it was real.

"Do you want to hear about the men I killed?" Evelina asked.

Christine froze. Plural. "You're... You killed multiple times?"

"Yup. I was a bit-part actress in the early 1940s. I'd moved from Minnesota to California—I dreamed of being a movie star." She struck a self-mocking pose as she spoke, one hand at her hip, the other with fanned fingers touching her head. "Anyway, I did land some small parts. And I met this guy who said he could help my career. Turned out he lied about everything except one—he told me he had a way I could stay young and beautiful forever. When he turned me, he let me loose in Hollywood and aimed me at his enemies."

"That's horrible."

"Could be worse. I found the strength to stop after the third one died in my arms. The asshole tried to force me to kill again, but I wouldn't. Finally, he gave up and let me go."

"But that's not your fault. You didn't seek out those men—"

"Uff da, of course I sought them out. He gave me the addresses and I went. I hated myself when I couldn't stop feeding on the first one, when I realized I had no control. But that didn't prevent me from going to the next on the list and draining him."

Wolfie cleared his throat. "Evelina's point is that all new vampires are overpowered by blood lust. I killed the drummer in my band. He and I'd gone to high school together. I still think of him."

"Why didn't anyone tell me? Why didn't they warn me?"

Evelina patted her hand. "Gosh darn it, doncha know? They thought they could save you from it—protect you so you were never left alone with a mortal during your first few weeks. If you get past then, you should be home free."

"Why did Patrick have to come back?" Tears clouded Christine's vision. "No—I know why. It's my fault he came looking for me."

"No, Christine," Evelina said with a click of her tongue. "It was old-fashioned bad luck—nothing more."

"That it was," Wolfie said. "If it'd been a week later, you might have been able to resist. But your second day? Come on, no one has that kind of willpower."

Christine brushed aside the tears. "I used to."

"Ya, sure," Evelina said. "I heard you were a high-powered attorney. As a mortal, you probably had willpower comin' out your ears. But as a vamp? You're gonna have to relearn that control. And we'll be here to help you."

"You and Wolfie?"

"Our whole support group. You're the first baby we've had since the treaty moratorium was passed prohibiting the creation of new vamps. So the other eight are looking forward to meeting you."

"But after what I did, how could they want to help me?"

"Oh, fer cryin' out loud, we *all* did what you did. And the one thing I learned from all this is you can't go it alone. If you accidentally kill someone, it's a terrible weight on your shoulders, but together, we can lift each other's burdens."

"I don't see how—"

"That's what our group is there for. You're invited to our once-a-month meetings at the chapel—but right now, I want you to call one of us every night. Don't let yourself slide into the morbs. The hardest thing can be picking up the phone. But you can do it. Good grief, if you can argue a case in court, you're brave enough to phone one of us when you start going down the rabbit hole."

Evelina took a piece of paper out of her purse and unfolded it. "Here's our phone list. You can call any of us, anytime. We'll be there for you."

"I don't know what to say."

"Say, 'Thank you, Evelina. I'll call. I promise.'"

Chapter 28

REACTION

Tig and Jayden's home—Around the same time

Tig glanced over at the squeak of Jayden's trainers. She'd been reading the daily reports on her home computer.

"Looks like we aren't getting a Saturday night off together," Jayden said, leaning against the doorframe of her home office and looking as sexy as hell. He wore tight, straight-leg jeans and a t-shirt that showed off every muscle of his chiseled body.

Tig didn't need to ask the question. She could guess well enough. The mayor had stirred up the hornets' nest—the insects were bound to bite back. "What happened?"

"The mates got together today and signed a letter demanding the council appoint Luis to the open spot vacated by Frédéric Bonhomme's death. It's been three months. The council's had enough time."

"Did you sign?"

"Sure. I have an in with the police chief." He grinned confidently as he strode across the room to kiss her. "Figured my job was safe."

"Yeah." She kissed him back. "I'm glad you signed it. So what's the problem?"

"We've started to get domestic disturbance calls."

"Oh shit." Tig ran her fingernails through her short afro. "Who?"

"The usual suspects. They aren't happy about their mates being involved. Hell, I'm surprised we didn't get a call about Rolf."

Rolf had his problems, but domestic violence wasn't one of them.

Wait, that means...

Tig's eyes went wide. "Did Karen sign?"

"Yup."

"Praise the ancestors. Glad to see that gal showed some backbone."

"Me too. Cerissa signed first, with Karen's signature next."

"I'm not surprised Cerissa signed." Tig's heart went out to both the mortal scientist and her mate. "Did you talk to her? How is she doing?"

"I saw her at Karen's house. She's doing okay under the circumstances. She's not happy with what the council did."

"That sounds like an understatement. She's justified in being furious with them." After pretending to leave during the whipping, Tig had stayed at the rear of the amphitheater near Cerissa, ready to keep the peace if it became necessary. She'd felt it best to look the other way at their intervention but wasn't willing to risk anyone getting hurt. "I'm glad you and Luis and the other mates stepped up and stopped the flogging. The mayor's an idiot sometimes."

"Anyway, I sent Zeke out on the first domestic response. Liza agreed to go on the second call. So far, no physical violence, just loud arguments."

"Good." Because a vampire who hit their mate—non-consensually, that was—would be facing the whipping post, and they'd had enough of that nonsense for now.

"If we get a third call," Jayden continued, "that leaves you and me."

"I'd put Rolf in the rotation, but he and the mayor have a meeting scheduled for tonight."

"We could press Henry into service. He's still a reserve officer."

"And who would watch Christine? No, after all he's been through, we leave him alone. We take the call."

"Yes, ma'am." He gave a salute. "But I'm staying in civvies. No reason to throw on a uniform."

"I think we can bend protocol on your day off."

Tig's phone rang, so she picked up the device. Rolf's name appeared on the screen, and she swiped the answer button. "Yes?"

"The mayor didn't show for our seven o'clock meeting."

"So why are you telling me?" She glanced at the time. The mayor was twenty minutes late.

"I've phoned him repeatedly, and he doesn't answer."

"Maybe he forgot and went into town. It is a Saturday night, after all."

"Bah, I know very well what tonight is. Karen is pissed I'm at town hall, and I promised to return home in thirty minutes. The mayor is going to make me break my promise."

Tig rolled her eyes and spotted a spider crawling along the ceiling. She let the arachnid be. In the cow-dung-and-mud hut she'd been raised in, she became used to sharing space with insects. Her attitude toward them hadn't changed in four hundred years, even though she now lived in a dwelling that would seem like a palace to her childhood self.

"And again, why are you calling me about this?" she asked. "Do I look like Winston's babysitter?"

"Because I want you to go by his house for a welfare check."

She clenched her jaw and counted to ten.

"Are you still there?" Rolf asked.

"If you honestly believe twenty minutes of tardiness demands a welfare check, then why don't you go look for him?"

"Because if I leave town hall, I might miss him, and then we'd be going in circles."

Grr. She couldn't ignore a request for a welfare check. "Fine. I'll go. But then I'm off the clock. If he's not there, someone else can go track him down. And if we get any more domestic calls, you'll have to respond."

She disconnected the call and eyed Jayden. "What say we check on Winston, and then go catch a movie?"

"Great suggestion. There's another Avengers movie out."

Jayden loved his superheroes. The pricy comic books he collected were framed and hung on their family room walls.

Tig pushed back from her desk. "Grab your jacket. We'll take my car. Once we track down the mayor, we'll head into Mordida. Let's go."

CHAPTER 29

KNOCK, KNOCK

WINSTON'S HOUSE—TEN MINUTES LATER

Tig parked in front of the mayor's house. The lights were off. Her first guess had probably been the right one—Winston went into Mordida.

He liked opera. She should have checked what was playing at the local opera theater to save her the trip. But since they were there, it was faster to see if he was at home.

"Let's go," she said to Jayden.

No answer when she knocked or rang the doorbell. She tried the door handle. Locked. "Should we check the back door or leave a note?"

He glanced at his watch. "We have plenty of time. Let's check."

She appreciated his thoroughness. No protocol required them to go any further with a welfare check, but it wasn't a big sacrifice, either. While she drove them to the mayor's, Jayden had used his phone to find the movie start times. They had at least thirty minutes, so he could afford to be relaxed about their detour.

The side gate was unlocked, so she went in, Jayden trailing her. It'd been a long time since she'd been at the mayor's house. His backyard was a beautifully manicured English garden, with roses, hedges, and night-blooming flowers. He'd done a marvelous design job, creating inviting spaces, with benches and arbors for intimate conversations.

She waited while Jayden tried the sliding glass door. "Hey, Tig, it's open."

"Not everyone locks every door all the time."

"Mayor? Are you home?" Jayden called out as he walked in and turned on a light. He looked over his shoulder at her. "I've got a bad feeling about this."

Just as Tig opened her mouth to tell him not to tempt fate, an odd scent hit her nose, the dry, not-quite-rotten smell of mummified remains, but with a sweet, perfume-like overlay coming from the garden.

She rushed up the patio steps, but instead of following Jayden inside, she swung around, using the added height to scan the garden. Locking her gaze on a break in one hedge, she followed the direction of the bent twigs until she saw the brown mass in the shadow of a huge night-blooming jasmine bush.

The flowers' sweet scent had entwined with the sickly odor of death.

"Jayden," she called. "Over here."

Avoiding the damaged hedge, she crept along a parallel path, approaching from the other side, her gun in hand, and on alert for any danger.

He joined her in a snap, his own weapon drawn. "Do you think that's the mayor?"

"Presumably." The face was withered, the skin a mottled gray and black, ashes blowing off him in the evening breeze, making an immediate identification difficult. She glanced around—could the killer still be here? "Cover me."

She made a circuit of the yard perimeter. No sign of the perp except for the broken branches of the hedge.

Then they made a quick search of the house in case the perp was hiding inside. Nothing.

Returning to the body, Tig bent her knees to rest back on her heels to get a closer look.

Lying on its back, the mummified body outlined the mayor's shape—short legs, thick, round hips, a hefty paunch, and a wide chest. Reaching across the body, she used a writing pen to move the left sleeve.

"The wristwatch looks like his. It's the one he uses when he doesn't want to date himself by pulling out a pocket watch. And the sweep hand is still running, so the timepiece doesn't help to fix the time of death." She used the same pen to point at the metal tip sticking out of his chest. "Looks like some kind of rod was used to stake him."

"How do you want to approach this?"

"Crap. This is so not good. Henry's got motive. As does Cerissa. Even Liza. Or Carolyn. The two councilwomen were pretty angry about the way he put them in a corner last night." Tig scrubbed a hand over her face. "Then again, those are only the recent community members he's pissed off. Dammit, every member of the Hill could be a suspect."

Jayden held up his hands. "Before we begin making a list, maybe we should get the police van and start processing the site."

He was right. Tig sighed, releasing the mixture of sadness and anxiety invading her chest. "Normally, I'd ask you to take my car and come back with the van, but I don't want to be left alone with the body. Not under these circumstances. Everyone at the meeting heard me tell him off. So we do this by the book. I'll call in Zeke. As far as I know, he has no reason for wanting the mayor dead."

"Sounds like a plan." Jayden ran a hand over his shaved head. "We have gloves in the car and a camera in the trunk. I'm going to document the scene while we wait for Zeke and a search warrant."

Tig frowned. "We don't need a warrant to search his house—it's the scene of the crime."

"This is the crime scene." He waved his hands around. "Not in there." He pointed at the house. "It's one thing to clear the house. Exigent circumstances allow us to enter to make sure a perp isn't hiding on the premises. But a search for evidence? There is no crime scene exception. What if the mayor has a girlfriend on the Hill, one we don't know about? What if she resided with him, even part-time? Then she has a privacy interest in the house, and the warrantless search might get thrown out and the whole thing become one big, effed-up mess."

She rose to her feet. "Fine, fine."

Why am I fighting him on this? I'm the one who said "by the book."

"Go ahead. Text Marcus." Then she recalled seeing the email from Marcus and Nicholas. "Shit. They left on vacation. Let me call him instead."

After Marcus said, "Hello, Tig," she put the phone on speaker so Jayden could hear and asked, "Where are you?"

"On vacation. We've got the car packed and are about to leave—"

"There's been a development."

"No, I don't care what screw-up happened now. I'm getting in the car, and going to San Francisco, so—"

"Marcus, it's serious."

"Tig—"

"You're going to want to hear this."

There was a frustrated sound, and then Marcus said, "Tell me."

"This may come as a shock—"

"Tig, I don't have time for any dancing around. What happened?"

No way to sugarcoat it, really.

"We believe the mayor is dead. Murdered."

The silence on the other end was unusual. The town attorney never needed time to think. "You're sure?" he finally asked.

"I'm standing by his withered body in the garden behind his house. He's wearing a Tissot sports watch. Seventy-five percent sure it's him. We need a Mincey warrant."

Marcus let out a long exhale. "I'll write the warrant. Send me the details. But I need to speak with Nicholas before I cancel my vacation."

"Understood. Goodbye."

"Let's get the kit." Jayden took two steps in the direction of the police car and looked over his shoulder. "Are you coming?"

"Yeah—" A shiny object lay among the purple blooms of the creeping thyme next to the body. "Wait. What's that?"

He returned. She squatted on her heels again and used her pen to lift the shiny object.

"Don't do that," he said, gripping her arm. "Let me photograph the scene first. Come with me."

Together they went to the car to retrieve the gear they had with them. Tig surveyed the area. The mayor had the only home on the street. No visible cameras on his property. The Hill originally planned to open new homesteads to fill out Winston's cul-de-sac, but when the North American treaty was signed, *no expansion* became the council's new watchword.

City utilities plus the isolation of country living—the mayor had the best of both worlds. Unfortunately, it also meant no witnesses nearby who might have seen the murder, and the tall cypress trees separating the mayor's property from the wild fields beyond gave the perp plenty of places from which to enter the backyard and hide.

They hurried back to the crime scene as she phoned Zeke and instructed him to bring the police van. About ten minutes later, the cowboy arrived, and Jayden finished with the photos. "Okay, you can use your pen to lift the bracelet."

"Bracelet?" she repeated.

Tig sank to her knees in the dirt, crushing some tiny flowers she didn't recognize, hooked the jeweled chain with her pen, and raised it to eye level. An amethyst and moonstone bracelet with the chain broken where it attached to the latch, the amethyst beads faceted, the moonstone beads round and smoothly polished. It most likely belonged to one of the Hill's mortals, as the moonstone would mark a mortal as being mated to a vampire.

"Shit, shit, shit," Jayden said.

"Do you recognize the bracelet?"

"Yeah. It looks like the one Henry gave Cerissa when he mated her. I've never seen her without it."

"Jayden's right, chief." Zeke stood to the side, his eyes sad. "That sure does look like Cerissa's bracelet."

Jayden held out a clear evidence bag, and Tig let the bracelet slide off her pen with a light rattle of the chain. He then sealed and signed the bag.

Tig gave Jayden a hard look. "Was she wearing it today when you saw her?"

He scrubbed a gloved hand over his face. "I don't remember. She had on a long-sleeve shirt."

Tig locked eyes with Zeke. "You can't tell her. You can't tell anyone. As of right now, everything you've seen is confidential."

"I know my duty, ma'am."

"Good." Her phone rang. *Rolf.* After swiping to accept the call, she said, "The mayor won't be meeting with you tonight."

"Why?"

"You'll have to take my word for it. I'll phone you later. Go home, Rolf."

The night had begun as a normal Saturday. In under an hour, it'd spun upside down.

Cerissa worked for Leopold, the New York community's CEO. If Cerissa killed the mayor, the political ramifications were going to be horrific. Wars had been started over less. And Tig couldn't turn to the vice mayor for counsel. Or even Marcus. They were both too close to Henry.

What in the name of the ancestors am I going to do?

CHAPTER 30

POSTPONED

MARCUS AND NICHOLAS'S TEMPORARY HOME—TWENTY MINUTES EARLIER

As soon as the phone call with Tig ended, Marcus sank onto the tacky couch. No matter how many times he'd sat on it since moving in, the navy velour always felt foreign under his fingers. Now, the polyester's velvety texture would forever be associated with the mayor's death.

Nicholas bounded into the room, in slacks and a polo shirt, looking youthful and happy over the trip. Marcus hated to burst that joy.

"Okay." Nicholas came to a stop in front of him. "All my bags are in the car. I want to grab my pillow and we can leave. I might catch some sleep while you drive. Are you ready?"

"Sit down." Marcus tapped the cushion next to him.

"What's wrong?"

He closed his eyes and summoned the will to say the words. "The mayor's dead."

"Wait, what?"

"Tig found a body at Winston's house." Marcus opened his eyes and, taking his mate's hand, stared into his beautifully dark irises. "She needs a Mincey warrant."

The warrant was named after the defendant in the first Supreme Court case to determine that an accused murderer could assert a privacy interest in a crime scene location. Marcus paused, slowing his thoughts. His mind tended to rattle off legal facts whenever he was in a crisis. The law was calming when reality was harsh.

But the Mincey warrant was a good idea on Tig's part. They'd have to be very formal in this investigation.

"She may need other search warrants," Marcus continued. "Do you mind if we delay our vacation by one night?"

Shock played out on Nicholas's face. "Ah, no, I mean, we have to stay now. You work on the warrant, and I'll call the hotel and rearrange things."

Marcus slowly rose from the couch. He'd known Winston for close to a century. While not a founder, Winston had guided the community for fifty years, and despite the mayor's recent bad and infuriating decision-making, his influence over the town council had kept them prosperous and stable since 1973.

Marcus's home computer was in one of the back bedrooms, and he plodded down the long hallway to reach the den. He clicked the mouse, the screen saver disappeared, and he opened a form warrant. He filled in the probable cause information Tig provided and wrote a comprehensive search area—the garden and any buildings on the property. Marcus couldn't recall if the mayor had a gardening shed separate from the house, so he erred on the side of expansiveness.

He then checked his contacts. He couldn't use the local judge in Mordida. Not with a dead vampire as the corpse. Too touchy for the mortal courts, this matter required an insider's assistance.

One thing the North American treaty established was a system for approving search warrants. Marcus had fought to have someone in each community designated as a judge to review and authorize warrants, hopefully someone with legal training. He himself served that role for other communities on occasion.

He hit the number for his contact in the San Francisco Lodge.

"Good evening, Marcus," Diana Lindel said. "How may I help you?"

"Do you have time to review a warrant?"

"Certainly. But I must say, your little community has been having a lot of turmoil lately."

"Unfortunately, true. And this situation is bad, very bad. Our mayor was murdered. For the moment, Tig is embargoing the news until we get a handle on who killed him."

"I'll keep my review confidential. Email me the details."

"It's a simple Mincey warrant. Shouldn't take you too much time. But I suspect we will need other warrants. Are you available tonight?"

"I am. Send them as needed."

Marcus said goodbye and then wrote the email. Tig should have her answer soon. Diana was fair and reliable.

Finished, he went looking for Nicholas. For some reason, Marcus needed a hug. Badly. Did the mayor's death remind him how close he came to losing his mate in the earthquake?

He found Nicholas where he'd left him: sitting on the couch in the living room and talking on his phone to the hotel. When he hung up, Marcus pulled him to his feet and wrapped him in a bear hug.

"Are you okay?"

"I don't know." Marcus took in a long breath. "It feels like the Hill is crumbling. All I want to do is get in the car and drive. I can't deal with the insanity."

"Who do you think killed him?" Nicholas stepped back, looking stunned. "And is it personal to the mayor, or is this another attack, like with Oscar's group?"

Marcus tugged at his mustache. "I hadn't considered the VDM. They've been killed, jailed, or otherwise dispersed. My mind immediately went to Henry. He has motive."

"Don't say that."

"I dislike suggesting his guilt even to you, but everyone else, well, their minds are going to go there."

Nicholas flopped onto the couch, slouching, and buried his face in his hands. "So what do we do now?"

Marcus sat down next to him and stroked his back. "All we can do is wait for the warrant and pray to God Henry is innocent."

CHAPTER 31

INTERROGATION

RANCHO BAUTISTA DEL MURCIÉLAGO—LATER THAT NIGHT

Henry resented the ringing phone but answered anyway. Evelina and Wolfie had gone, and he'd been sitting with Christine at the kitchen table, supervising while she read her email. "What do you want, Tig?"

"I need Cerissa to come to the police station."

Anger crawled up his throat. "And my family needs to be left alone."

"I understand. But I must insist—"

"No. I have paid my debt to the community, and we will not be at the town's beck and call—"

Tig's loud huff cut him off. "Someone killed the mayor."

He made eye contact with Christine, to make sure she was listening. "You want Cerissa to run a DNA test? Tonight?"

"No." Silence. "I need to interview her."

His brow slowly furrowed. "I do not understand."

"She may have information about the murder."

"Wait." His stomach sank, but his voice rose. "You're calling me because she's my mate and you expect me to deliver her to you?"

"As required by the Covenant, I had to inform you first. My next call will be to her."

"No." He scrubbed a hand over his face. How could things go from bad to worse? "I will tell her. We should be there in thirty minutes."

Henry tapped the "end call" button. He took a step, but suddenly staggered, grabbing the kitchen counter. For a moment, blind fear overwhelmed him.

Tig had left him with no choice. The Covenant was clear—he had to bring Cerissa to the police station for questioning. The implications churned his gut.

Madre de Dios. Why did Tig suspect Cerissa?

He forced his mind to focus. Christine would have to come with them. He couldn't leave her alone at home. Besides, there was a reason they needed another attorney on the Hill, one who could act as defense council. He never would have guessed the need would arise this soon or strike this close to home.

"Stay there," Henry said to Christine. "I'm going to trust you with your phone. Don't send any emails while I'm gone."

Her eyes looked so sad. "I won't."

Henry ran down the basement stairs and found Cerissa in her lab. He knocked—he'd learned the hard way not to barge in. When she opened the door, he said, "I have bad news. The mayor has been killed."

Cerissa crossed her arms. "That's good news, not bad."

"I understand why you are angry, but never say anything like that. Because he *is* dead."

Her eyes got big. "Are you serious?"

"Very."

"How?"

"I do not know."

"Why would anyone kill—"

"There's more. Tig wants to interview you."

Her jaw dropped open, and she paled. "Me? Why?"

"Tig wouldn't say. But she must have something, some evidence to tie you to the crime."

"That's ridiculous. She's grasping at straws. When does she want to interview me?"

He took a breath, relieved she wasn't overreacting to Tig's summons. Blind fear had engulfed him a moment ago, but they both needed to remain sharp.

"Tig wants you at the police station now."

"Idiots! I have more important work to do." She shrugged off her lab coat and tossed it on a hanger. "Wait. What about you? Do you believe I suddenly became an avenging angel?"

"Of course not, but what I believe doesn't matter. Tig may suspect you committed the crime. We should leave, so you can answer her questions and she can move on to find the true culprit."

"Fine. Let me go change into something more comfortable for a police interview."

On the drive over, they speculated what this might be about, yet nothing made sense. He parked outside the police station and, staying between Cerissa and Christine, let his mate lead the way in. The door buzzed when she opened it, announcing their entry.

Tig appeared from the hallway leading to the offices. "Henry, you and Christine can wait out here in the lobby. Cerissa will come with me." Tig grabbed her arm.

"Hey, what are you doing?" Cerissa exclaimed. "Tig?"

"This way," Tig replied, and began walking Cerissa away from them.

Henry held up his hand. "Wait. Christine and I will come with you."

"I can't allow that, Founder."

Jesucristo. Tig's use of his formal title signaled something was terribly wrong, like a mother using a child's middle name.

"Why not?"

"Because you may be a witness. I'll interview you separately."

"Then Christine will represent Cerissa."

Tig looked like she was about to boil over. "I don't think—"

"Christine stayed at Gaea's all last night and during the day. Zeke accompanied her and spent the night there too. So it is impossible for her and me to be witnesses to something that happened last night."

"Why do you think the mayor was murdered last night?"

"The mayor was alive when he left the amphitheater, at which point Christine was in Zeke's or Gaea's custody, where she remained until eight this evening."

"Fine. She can come." Tig tugged on Cerissa's arm. "Please come with me."

Christine turned to face Henry. "I can't."

"Christine, you can." He placed both hands on her shoulders. "I understand you are grieving, that this is a difficult time for you, but we need you right now. Cerissa needs you. There is no one else we can seek help from."

Fear filled the attorney's eyes. "As legal counsel, I'll have to sit next to Cerissa. After what I did to Patrick, how can you trust me to be near her?"

A dilemma he had no easy answer for, except, at some point, he'd have to trust her. Four days old was a little early, but the death of her friend had left an imprint to bolster her self-restraint.

"Tig will keep Cerissa safe from you, and you will keep Cerissa safe from Tig."

Christine took the seat next to Cerissa in the interview room and removed three blood pouches from her purse, placing them on the table in case she needed them. How in the hell was she supposed to represent Henry's mate in a *criminal* matter? She had only practiced civil law and never served as either a criminal prosecutor or a defense attorney.

Everything she knew about criminal law she'd learned over thirty years ago in the classroom.

Tig placed an audio recorder on the table. "I'm going to record our conversation, do you agree?"

Cerissa looked to her right. "That's up to my attorney."

The answer evaded Christine. She met Cerissa's gaze wide-eyed, the stress too much. Fangs lowered in her mouth, while adrenaline charged her body, shutting down her mind.

Cerissa smiled reassuringly. "You've got this."

Did she? Christine forced her fangs to retract and took a couple of deep breaths. Could she reason her way through this? A recording worked for them as much as against them. At least this way, no one could lie about what Cerissa said.

"We'll allow it," Christine finally replied. "But we want a copy."

"Agreed." For the recording, Tig stated the date, time and who was present. "After the council hearing, did you remain at the amphitheater to the end?"

"I—"

Christine held up her hand. "Wait. Before we answer any questions, you need to tell us why Cerissa is being interviewed."

"No, I don't."

"Then we'll leave. When you're willing to be open with us, we'll return."

Tig glared at Christine.

"Cerissa is free to leave, isn't she?"

"As I told Henry, someone killed the mayor."

"When?" Christine asked.

"We are still investigating time of death."

Cerissa touched Christine's arm. "It had to be after the whipping—"

"Please don't say anything. We'll break to talk in a moment." Christine looked at Tig again, feeling her confidence creeping back. "How was he killed?"

"I've told you all you need to know to continue questioning."

"Not by a long shot. Do you believe Cerissa witnessed the crime?"

"If I could ask my questions, that should become obvious."

"Cerissa is being interviewed as a witness?"

"Again, you have all you need—"

"Is she free to leave?"

Tig tapped her fingers on the table. "No."

Christine eyeballed the recorder. "I see. Is there a place I can talk with my client without being overheard?"

"I can't leave you alone with a mortal."

"My client has a right to consult with her lawyer prior to questioning."

Tig scowled. "That's not happening."

Cerissa laid a hand on Christine's arm. "I trust Christine. And she has those"—Cerissa pointed at the pile of blood pouches, the kind with straws attached—"if she's hungry. The attack on Patrick was a regrettable accident and won't occur again."

Something in Cerissa's touch warmed Christine in the way a shot of tequila used to, her tense muscles relaxing. The sudden calm lowered the barrier she'd erected between her mind and her emotions, and tears pricked her eyes. Cerissa's blind faith somehow made what happened to Patrick feel even more tragic.

Then she straightened in her seat and brushed away the tears. If Cerissa believed in her, she could do this.

Tig slapped the table. "I'm not willing to take the risk."

"Is there a panic button in here?" Cerissa asked.

"She could rip your throat out before you pressed it."

"But she won't. And you won't get your questions answered until you leave us alone."

"Naïve mortals," Tig muttered, then slid the desktop phone over, a large model with lots of options. "It's your funeral. Press the red button here if you get in trouble."

"Thank you."

Tig glared at them, then swept the recorder off the table. As soon as the door closed behind the chief, Cerissa said, "I didn't kill him."

Clients! Christine held up her hand. "Stop. I need you to listen to me. Innocent people go to prison all the time, especially those who don't listen to their lawyer. The interrogation is a game—they have something that makes them believe you or Henry were involved. We need to flush out their evidence while giving them as little as possible, understand? The police are notorious for twisting a suspect's words."

"You think I'm a *suspect*?"

"Yes. Tig tipped her hand when she said you couldn't leave. They have something tying you to the crime."

Christine spent another ten minutes going over possible questions with Cerissa. Once she felt securely in control of her client, she pressed the red button. "Chief Anderson, you may come back in."

Chapter 32

WHO DID IT?

Sierra Escondida Police Station—Ten minutes earlier

Tig used the break time to phone Marcus, asking the town attorney to write a search warrant for Henry's place, including the pool house.

"What should I put as the basis?" Marcus asked.

"Cerissa's bracelet was found broken at the scene, near the body."

"Seriously?"

"Yes."

"What are you looking for?"

"Crossbow, other bolts, silver-melting equipment, silver ingots, communications threatening the mayor or conspiring to murder him. Include the house, all outbuildings, and their vehicles."

What none of the suspects knew—unless they were the murderer—was that Winston's corpse wore his gardening clothes and had been staked from the back. It would take a pretty strong vampire to stab through the ribcage or spine and reach the heart. The metal stake looked like a crossbow bolt, so she and Jayden suspected someone shot the bolt using a powerful crossbow rather than stabbing with it by hand.

"I'll send Nicholas over with the warrant as soon as I have approval," Marcus said.

"Thanks."

With a house the size of Henry's, hiding a crossbow would be easy. The bolt Dr. Clarke removed from the corpse was silver-tipped. From the appearance of the uneven silver coating, an amateur had hand-dipped the bolt, someone not accustomed to working with precious metals. It took a very hot fire to melt silver. A basement lab like Cerissa's might be the perfect place to hide a melting furnace amongst the other equipment—the machine would look innocuous, hiding in plain sight.

And stores rarely sold bolts singly. If the search party found more bolts from the same manufacturer—even if they weren't silver-coated—those bolts would be circumstantial evidence pointing to a suspect.

Additionally, something had left behind scratch marks in the silver on the bolt that pierced the mayor. If they located a crossbow, the weapon might have silver particles in its track if the perp hadn't cleaned the weapon. When a bolt was propelled through the track by the taut bowstring, friction resulted, accounting for the scrapes, leaving silver residue behind and providing more circumstantial evidence confirming they had the perp's crossbow.

When Christine called over the intercom, Tig returned and placed the recorder back on the table, a yellow pad in front of her, a pen in her hand, and a paper bag near her elbow.

Both Cerissa and Christine were smart women. To get at the bottom of this, the police textbooks said to start with broad questions and narrow them down from there. "Please account for your time from when you left the amphitheater last night until you arrived here at the police station."

"After Henry was released, my cousin gave me a ride home."

"Did Ari come into the house with you?"

"No, I went in alone. Henry was already upstairs in bed"—she cringed—"lying facedown, his back shredded."

"How did you feel, seeing his condition close up?"

"About the same way you would if it had been Jayden."

Christine laid a hand on Cerissa's arm. "We are not here to explore how she felt about the events last night. Do you have any other questions related to the alleged murder? Or are we free to leave?"

Tig gave an angry *ha*. No way in hell were they leaving now. She had too many unanswered questions. "So you arrived home and found Henry in bed?"

"Yes."

"What did you do?"

"I stayed at his side. Around a quarter to eleven, Anne-Louise arrived. I let her in and returned to Henry. She took a photo of his back, sent the image to the mayor, and spoke with him by phone."

Tig made a note of the time and then hit an intercom button. She had another witness to secure. "Jayden, would you please contact Anne-Louise, ask her to come to the police station, and bring her phone? If she refuses, send Zeke to retrieve her."

"Will do."

Tig released the button. "How long did Anne-Louise remain with you?"

"Ah—"

"If you remember," Christine said.

With a grimace, Cerissa looked away. "It wasn't long. She left the room and went downstairs, to fend off anyone who tried to disturb Henry."

Tig furrowed her brow. "Why would Anne-Louise do that?"

"In case the mayor showed up."

Something about the answer didn't make sense to her. Tig made a note to circle back later. "And what did you do?"

"I stayed in my bedroom with Henry. I fell asleep next to him. I heard the front door close when Anne-Louise left."

"What time was that?" Seeing Christine's hand land on Cerissa's arm again, Tig added, "If you know."

"I don't. We have blackout curtains in my room, so I can't even estimate. I went back to sleep."

"What time did you wake?"

"Around ten-thirty in the morning. Henry was still next to me."

Tig noted the time. "Is that unusual?"

"Yes, he usually sleeps in one of the basement crypts."

"Did he ever leave the bed before sunrise?"

"No."

On prior occasions, Cerissa had mentioned her envoy training included resistance to being mesmerized. But did her ability to resist extend to her mate? "How can you be sure if you were asleep?"

"He was in a lot of pain—moving made it worse for him. And if he had gotten up, the mattress would have dipped and wakened me."

"Could he have mesmerized you, forced you into a deep sleep?"

Cerissa wrinkled her nose, as if the question were distasteful. "He can't. Impossible."

Tig let that one go. Yes, some mortals were resistant, and with training, could become even more so. But no one was resistant all the time, particularly when stressed out, and their own mate did the mesmerizing. She'd follow up on the question later, probably with Henry.

"What did you do after you woke up?"

"I changed into sweats—I'd fallen asleep in what I wore to the council hearing—and cleaned Henry's car, moved the Viper into the garage, and then I showered and changed clothes."

"You cleaned his car first thing on waking?"

"Yes. His seat, ah, it was covered in blood and flesh from his back. I didn't want him to have to see it."

Tig suppressed the cringe she felt. Was Cerissa's graphic description meant to garner sympathy?

It didn't matter. If Cerissa killed the mayor, she'd get what she deserved.

"And afterward?"

"I made breakfast and received a phone call from Karen as I ate. She invited me over for the meeting with Nicholas, Haley, Luis, and Jayden."

"What time did you meet at?"

"I arrived a little before noon."

"And when you left, what time was it?"

"I don't know, precisely."

"Did others leave when you did?"

"Yes." Cerissa's face brightened. "You're right. Nicholas did."

Tig made another note, this one to ask the assistant town attorney to confirm the time. Jayden had told her he left before the others because he had to return to work. "Continue, please."

Cerissa shrugged. "I returned home, and Henry had just finished getting dressed."

"How do you know he'd just finished?"

Cerissa took out her phone and tapped in a search. "Sunset was at six-eighteen, and the moonrise was later, at seven-forty-two, so he woke when the sun set and couldn't have been awake more than thirty minutes. When I saw him in the kitchen, he was shaved, smelled showered, and in fresh clothes. He made dinner for me, and then Christine returned home."

"What time did Christine arrive?"

"Around eight, maybe a shade earlier. She was pretty upset, and Henry phoned Father Matt, who sent over Evelina and Chris—I mean, Wolfie. They arrived about twenty minutes later. I went back to the basement to keep working, to give them privacy. Later, Henry came down to the lab and relayed your request to come here."

"So you were alone between eight-thirty and nine-thirty?"

Not that it mattered. By then, Tig had found the body.

"More or less," Cerissa replied.

"Did you leave your home anytime between seven and seven-thirty this evening?

"No."

"And in the early morning, prior to sunrise, you and Henry were alone in the house?"

"At some point. I don't know precisely when Anne-Louise left."

"And did you leave the house at any time between when you returned from the amphitheater and the next morning when you went to Karen's house?"

"Only to clean Henry's car. When I finished, I immediately returned."

Tig sat back. Were there any other questions she should ask before digging into the specifics and nailing down Cerissa's statement so she couldn't wiggle out later?

She tapped her pen as she scanned her interview notes. Nope. They'd covered the entire time period in question. Now to narrow the focus. "Do you own a moonstone and amethyst bracelet?"

Cerissa glanced at her right wrist, covering the bare wrist with her other hand. "Yes, Henry gave the bracelet to me."

Christine held up a hand, signaling her to stop. "Why are you interested in Cerissa's bracelet?"

"Where is your bracelet?"

Christine slapped the table. The paper bag at Tig's elbow rattled. "Don't answer that." Christine glared at Tig. "Why do you want to know about her bracelet?"

Tig frowned. "Why won't you let her answer the question?"

"Tell us why it's relevant, and she will."

Tig lifted the paper bag. Christine wasn't going to let her nail down the facts first. Fine. It didn't matter. She opened the bag and took out a glass evidence container with the moonstone and amethyst bracelet visible inside it. "We found this next to the mayor's body."

Cerissa let out a gasp, which told Tig everything she needed to know.

Christine again touched Cerissa's arm. "Don't say a word. We're going to confer first. Please give us a fifteen-minute break alone. I need to feed."

Cerissa coughed. "And I could use a glass of water, please."

Tig felt like breaking the table in two. She'd almost gotten Cerissa to claim ownership of the bracelet before Christine brought things to a halt. Usually, they didn't have an attorney representing the suspect. No other attorneys lived on the Hill except Marcus and Nicholas, who worked for the town. Now, she doubted the council's wisdom in adding another one.

Tig grabbed the recorder and stormed out. This wasn't over. Not by a long shot.

CHAPTER 33

MURKY ANSWERS

SIERRA ESCONDIDA POLICE STATION—MOMENTS LATER

Christine moved to the other side of the table, grabbed a pouch from the pile, and squeezed it to start the heating process. The smell of Cerissa's warm mortal blood was beginning to distract her.

A knock on the door, and Tig popped in to drop off a bottle of water for Cerissa. After eyeing where Christine sat, the chief closed the door again.

Cerissa twisted off the cap and took a healthy drink. "I don't know how my bracelet wound up at a murder scene."

"When was the last time you remember wearing it?"

"I always wear my bracelet. I wore it to the hearing."

Christine poked the straw in the little silver circle designed to be punctured and took a long sip while she listened to her client, grateful for the fortification and strength the dark wine gave her.

"The clasp has been a little flaky recently." Cerissa's gaze dropped, and she rubbed her hand over her wrist where the missing bracelet would have rested. "I've gotten into a bad habit of twisting the beads when nervous. I meant to take it to a jeweler, but with everything happening I didn't find the time—"

"When did you first notice it was missing?"

"When I woke. I don't sleep with jewelry on and thought I might have unfastened the clasp in my sleep and lost the chain somewhere in the sheets. I didn't want to disturb Henry by searching for it. He's impressed upon me that it's dangerous to disturb him while sleeping—not that I agree with him. But after everything he's been through, I didn't want to accidentally wake him."

Christine gestured for Cerissa to stop. There might be a way to explain away the evidence. "Could you have lost your bracelet at the hearing or outdoors at the amphitheater?"

"Anything's possible. I was so upset, I wasn't thinking clearly, and people kept touching me. Unless I'm close friends with someone, I don't like being touched. At the amphitheater, well, I couldn't keep watching Anne-Louise—ah, what she did to Henry—so I buried my face in Ari's shoulder."

Boy, did Christine understand. Through the blood they shared, Henry's torment had almost wrecked her. If she'd had to witness it, she wouldn't have been able to control her rage.

"Go on."

"When I turned my back, the other mortal mates surrounded us, touching me, trying to comfort me before they swarmed onto the stage and stopped the flogging."

"Okay, here's what we're going to do." Christine finished the pouch and tossed it in the corner trash can. "When Tig comes back in, I want you to look at the bracelet. If you can't positively say it's yours, then don't claim it as yours. The bracelet could be a fake to frame you."

"Woah, really?"

"Anything's possible. It's also possible someone found your bracelet, or stole it, last night. We don't know enough. The main point is, don't volunteer to fill the gap. You don't have to explain why the bracelet lay by the mayor's body. Tig has to prove how you lost it at the scene—she has to connect the dots—right now, it's just circumstantial."

"I understand."

Christine started to stand up, and Cerissa said, "Wait. I remembered something."

"What?"

"After Anne-Louise took the photo of Henry's back, she berated him for letting the mayor bully him, and offered to 'take care of Winston' for him, but Henry declined. Should I tell Tig?"

Oh shit. Yes, there was definitely a reason suspects needed an attorney in the room. "I'm glad you didn't tell Tig about the conversation, and we don't want to volunteer anything, either. It goes to your *mens rea*—your state of mind. Anne-Louise may have offered, but the chief could spin it into something else."

"How?"

"Tig could claim that Anne-Louise's comment put the idea in *your* mind, and you ran with it."

Fear and fatigue showed in Cerissa's eyes. "What do we do?"

"If the chief specifically asks about Anne-Louise's offer, then confirm what Anne-Louise said—the only way Tig would know is if Henry or his maker tells her. But don't volunteer the information."

"Okay. I can do that."

Christine grabbed another blood pouch and moved to the chair next to Cerissa, then hit the intercom. "We're ready."

Tig had barely sat down when Cerissa asked, "May I see the bracelet you found at the scene?"

Tig frowned but handed over the container. There was no reason to say no. "Is it yours?"

Cerissa studied the bracelet from all sides. "It looks like mine, but I can't be sure." She furrowed her brow, deep lines forming, continuing her examination. "And the chain is broken from the clasp. See? The two large rings forming the clasp are still hooked together."

"Was your bracelet broken?"

"No. The clasp was flaky—I had to make sure the latch seated—but not like this. This one..." She shook the container. "See how the tiny chain loop has been pulled from the solid gold loop welded to the clasp?"

Tig took the evidence container back. "But your bracelet *is* missing."

"I wore it last night to the council meeting. I normally take the bracelet off at night, but I was so focused on Henry, I didn't leave his side to get ready for bed and fell asleep. In the morning, I realized my bracelet was gone. I thought I'd lost it in the blankets, and I didn't want to disturb Henry."

"Anything else?"

"Ah, a lot of people touched me last night."

Tig could guess where this was going. Cerissa was trying to establish doubt as to when she lost the bracelet. All Tig could do was nail down her story to undermine any attempt to make later revisions. "Did you notice your bracelet missing after they touched you?"

"I don't remember right now—I was pretty stressed out at the time, and I'm very tired right now."

Tig put the bracelet container back in the bag. "I overheard you telling your cousin how you wanted to kill the mayor."

Christine jumped in. "If she said anything like that, the comment was in the heat of the moment—"

"While the mayor was having my mate flogged," Cerissa finished, and side-eyed her attorney. "I didn't kill the mayor. And there's a reason they say revenge is a dish best served cold. Because if you serve it hot, you're suspect number one. Do I look that stupid to you?"

Cerissa had a point. Tig had known the mortal for six months now and had yet to see her lose her cool. Still, the bracelet was pretty damning circumstantial evidence.

"And I don't remember when I lost the bracelet, but I do remember a lot of people touching me last night. I—I couldn't keep watching, and Ari hugged me, my face smooshed against his shoulder, and all the mortals surrounding me touched my back and arms. One of them could have pulled on it without me noticing, or someone snagged the chain, breaking the loop connected to the latch. Then the bracelet fell off, and someone else picked it up. Did you fingerprint it?"

"Not yet. We're going to do that after I finish the interviews. Is there anything else you want to add?"

"Not that I can think of now."

Tig tapped the table, considering her next move. She really had no choice. "Cerissa Patel, I'm placing you under arrest for the murder of Winston Mason."

Christine shot to her feet. "Now, Tig, you have no evidence she did anything. The real murderer is out there and you're jumping to hasty—and erroneous—conclusions."

"She's my main suspect. I'm going to interview Henry, and then Anne-Louise. Until I have a better suspect, she's staying in jail. I have forty-eight-hours to charge her."

Christine stared down at Tig. "When will Cerissa receive a bail hearing?"

"Bail?" Tig said with a scoff. "We don't do bail here. If I charge her, she'll stay there until the trial."

"That's not fair!" Cerissa said.

Tig stood. Confining Cerissa was for her own protection, too. If someone was trying to frame her, they may decide to kill her to close the case.

Christine touched Cerissa's arm. "Be patient. I'll speak to Marcus. There must be some solution we can arrive at."

"In the meantime, Jayden will process you." Tig motioned for Cerissa to join her. "Please bring your purse. He'll inventory the contents and give you a receipt."

"Ah, I can't keep it with me?"

"No."

Fear appeared in Cerissa's eyes. "Then I need to talk with Christine."

"After you're processed, and in your cell, we can make that happen." Tig pursed her lips. Was there something in Cerissa's purse to incriminate her? She looked more frightened now than she had since the interview started. "For now, come with me."

CHAPTER 34

DAZED AND DEPRESSED

SIERRA ESCONDIDA POLICE STATION—MOMENTS LATER

Cerissa held her hands behind her back as Tig fastened the handcuffs. While the cold metal wasn't heavy, the weight tugged at her already drooping shoulders. She walked down the hall, Tig's hand on her arm guiding her, and they went into a large room filled with file cabinets, a couple of desks, a big table, and a whiteboard where Jayden worked.

"Sit there," Tig said, pulling an office chair from a desk and placing it far enough away from the table covered with notes and evidence that a mortal wouldn't be able to read the paperwork.

When Tig took Jayden out to the hall, probably to speak confidentially, Cerissa scanned the table without reading any of the materials, knowing her contact lenses would record everything, and she could read them at her leisure—of which she'd soon have plenty. Without any effort, she listened in to the conversation.

"When you go through her purse," Tig said, "watch for any evidence to link her to the murder. She seemed frightened when I mentioned you'd inventory her purse."

"Got it, chief." Jayden didn't sound happy. He returned alone to where Cerissa waited.

She wanted to scream. Her reaction wasn't because she carried something tying her to the crime. No, her reaction was because she had Lux technology in her purse, including the hypo and her phone. If they scrutinized those too closely, it wouldn't be good.

She watched Jayden dump her purse contents into a plastic tray and make a list of everything there. He held out the hypo. "What is this? How should I log it?"

"Ah, it's an advanced air-pressure hypodermic, also called a jet injector, and is used to deliver medicine subcutaneously or intramuscularly. Be careful handling the device—I don't want you to accidentally inject yourself."

He quickly dropped the hypo onto the tray and made a notation on his list. When he finished with her purse, he uncuffed her. "I need your ring and watch too."

For the first time since she'd arrived at the police station, she started to tear up. She didn't want to be separated from her engagement ring. The three diamonds in Henry's gift symbolized her and the two children she'd have someday—and how he would love all three of them without reservation.

"Look, I'm sorry, but we have to do this."

Her hand trembled as she twisted the ring, working the band off. "I hope the town has good insurance. If anything happens to those diamonds, well, they're valued at close to a million dollars."

Jayden's eyes got big. "I'll note the amount here, and we'll lock the ring in the police safe. Anything else of value?"

"My watch." The watch contained the flash disk. As she unstrapped the wristband, she covertly swiped at the crystal face to deactivate the instantaneous travel mechanism so Jayden wouldn't accidentally send himself to the Lux Enclave.

He put the ring and watch into a smaller plastic box and took them to a large safe in the corner. Moments later, he closed the door and spun the dial.

Her heart ached to be separated from the ring, and by extension, from Henry.

"Okay," Jayden said. "Here's what's going to happen. I'm going to take your fingerprints and your booking photograph, then you'll change into a jumpsuit. What size? My guess is you're a small."

"Probably. Sometimes a medium because of my hips."

"I'll bring both." He took out two folded garments from a closet near the safe, both striped red and white.

"Isn't orange the standard color?"

"It was, until that TV show. We switched because too many people wore orange jumpsuits as a costume. Plus, the red and white colors make hiding in the vineyards hard." He placed the jail clothes on the table. "And your shoe size?"

"Seven."

He pulled a pair of plastic clogs from the same closet.

She stared at the horrible jumpsuit. In that outfit, she'd look like a circus clown.

"Come on," he said. "Let's get you changed."

He didn't handcuff her again, but he did take her arm, controlling where she went. After finishing the fingerprints and mug shot, he took her to a single-occupancy restroom. "This isn't protocol, but I'm going to let you change in here. You have two minutes to use the toilet and change clothes, and then I open the door. Put your street clothes and shoes in this bag."

She took the clear sack, went into the small restroom, and managed to be done and dressed by the time the door handle turned.

He took the clothes bag from her and guided her to another door, which led to the jail cells. She'd been there as a visitor when Marcus was incarcerated, but never expected to be inside one herself.

"Take your pick," Jayden said.

The three cells looked identical. A cot and bathroom facilities—a toilet, sink, and shower in the corner. Unlike most jails, there was a shower curtain she could pull around the bathroom area.

Steel bars covered in silver grille created the enclosures, with the back wall consisting of concrete blocks covered in the same silver grille. No windows.

To one side sat a coffin on a short riser. Yes, she knew "sleep pod" was the more modern term, but she'd be sharing a cell with what was clearly an old-fashioned coffin made from walnut wood with a high-gloss sheen.

How depressing.

When she didn't move, Jayden said, "Some people don't want to be near the door—less disturbance when other prisoners are brought in and out."

She stepped into the first cell. It didn't matter. No one else was in jail—only her.

He shut the door with a clank. "You'll always be monitored via video and audio." He pointed at the cameras. "If something goes wrong, if you need anything, call out and the person on duty will check on you. You can pull the shower curtain closed to shower and use the bathroom, but if it's closed for too long, the guard will check on you. Any attempt to commit self-harm, and you'll lose the right to the shower curtain and bedding, understand?"

She nodded. The hits just kept on coming.

"Would you like something to read? We have a mini-library."

"Sure, thanks."

He brought her a stack to choose from, and she grabbed a romance. Under the circumstances, she had no interest in reading courtroom thrillers or murder mysteries.

"Can I see Henry soon?"

"I don't know. I'll get back to you."

Jayden closed the cell door and left.

She looked around. How did she end up here? In jail. Trapped. Alone.

She'd done nothing wrong.

Looking around at the small, crowded room, the limited furniture taking up most of the space, she touched the coffin's hard, shiny surface.

Will my life on the Hill be buried in this jail cell?

The impulse to *say* the mayor deserved to die after what he did to Henry had been only that—an impulse. It warred against the more ethical part of her conscience, which didn't abide revenge.

With a sigh, she sank down on the cot, leaning against the cold block wall behind her.

Yes, she'd avenged Yacov when she killed Dalbert, but his death had also been in self-defense and defense of others—if she'd let him live, he might have warned Oscar, who would have killed Rolf. So while staking Dalbert was ethically ambiguous, she'd made the decision in the heat of the moment. It wasn't premeditated murder.

And Tig knew nothing about how Cerissa killed Dalbert—Rolf had taken credit.

No, the reason she remained trapped here was because of the amethyst and moonstone bracelet Henry gifted her when they first became mates.

How did my bracelet end up by the mayor's body?

The hallway door opened with a creak, and she perked up, hope growing in her heart.

Are they bringing Henry to see me?

CHAPTER 35

MORE QUESTIONS

SIERRA ESCONDIDA POLICE STATION—TEN MINUTES EARLIER

Henry let himself be directed from the lobby to the interview room, only to find the chairs empty. He pivoted to make eye contact with Tig. "Where is Cerissa?"

Tig pointed to one of the four chairs at the utilitarian table. "Please sit."

"Go ahead, Henry," Christine said, following him into the small room and taking a seat.

He strode to the place Tig indicated. Still standing, he said, "I will only ask this once more. Where is Cerissa?"

Tig let out a noisy breath. "Jayden is processing her."

"Processing?" His eyebrows rose. "That had better not mean what I think it means."

"She's under arrest," Tig said.

He fisted his hands. That was beyond unacceptable. He couldn't allow his mate to be caged. "I want to see her. Now."

"You can't stop this. I have probable cause to hold her." Tig pointed at the chair again. "The best way you can help her is to sit down and answer my questions."

Christine squeezed his arm. "I think you should at least listen to Tig's questions."

He took a deep breath. Getting violent would aid no one, and he lowered himself onto the straight-backed chair. "Ask your questions."

Tig took the seat across from him and set a small paper bag and a recorder on the table. "After you left the amphitheater, where did you go?"

"Home. I was in no shape to go anywhere else."

"When did Cerissa arrive home?"

"Not long after I did, a few minutes, perhaps. And about ten minutes before Anne-Louise arrived."

Tig didn't seem surprised. Cerissa must have answered the same question already.

"Once Cerissa got home, what happened?"

"She joined me in bed and did not leave, except to open the door for Anne-Louise. She fell asleep in her street clothes."

"So you're saying she stayed with you until dawn?"

"Yes."

"And you know it's a crime to lie during a police investigation? If you're covering for her—"

"There is nothing to cover for. Ask your questions or let me take her home."

"Fine. Was she wearing her bracelet when she got home?"

Henry furrowed his brow. Tig had to mean the amethyst and moonstone bracelet he'd given Cerissa when they became mates. It was the only bracelet she wore. "Why?"

"Just answer the question, please."

Christine *tsked*. "They found an amethyst and moonstone bracelet at the crime scene and Cerissa is missing hers."

"Again, was she wearing the bracelet when she arrived home?"

How could he avoid answering? The path Tig led him down would end in disaster. And lying wasn't an option, even if he knew which lie would save his mate.

"Henry?"

He resigned himself to the inevitable. "I did not notice, one way or the other. For the most part, I was facedown on a pillow. The searing pain in my back distracted me."

"When you woke tonight, was Cerissa wearing the bracelet?"

"She had on a long-sleeve shirt, so I couldn't tell one way or another."

"Are you able to mesmerize Cerissa?"

What a rude question. But then, the whole situation was intolerable. "I've never tried. She tells me it isn't possible, but in any case, I respect her too much to force her to do something against her will."

"When you woke tonight, was Cerissa home?"

"No. She came home about twenty minutes afterward."

"Tell me what happened once she was home."

"I made her dinner and she ate it. Then Gaea brought Christine home, and Cerissa and I met her at the door." He explained as tactfully as he could Christine's state of mind, and how they spoke with her together. "After Evelina and Wolfie arrived, I believe Cerissa went downstairs to her lab. I found her there after you phoned me."

"Was Cerissa present when they arrived—if I asked them, would they be able to confirm Cerissa's presence?"

He thought for a moment. So much had happened in such a short time. This was important, and he didn't want to botch the answer. "I believe so. But you should ask them."

"What time did she go to her lab?"

"I'm not sure. Wait. She was in the kitchen when Evelina and Wolfie arrived because she excused herself shortly afterward. They may be able to confirm the time. But she answered the door with me. I wouldn't leave her alone in the kitchen with Christine."

Tig made a note on the pad in front of her. "Do you own a crossbow?"

Henry raised an eyebrow. A crossbow killed the mayor? "No."

"Does that mean if we find a crossbow at your house, the weapon belongs to Cerissa?"

Henry glowered at her. "You will not find a crossbow at my house unless you planted one."

"So you know for a fact that Cerissa does not own a crossbow?"

"There is no crossbow at my house."

"Henry—"

"I *said*—"

Christine touched Henry's arm, and he stopped speaking. "Tig, he's answered the question. Is there anything else you want to ask?"

"Could Cerissa leave her basement lab without you knowing she did?"

How to answer? Cerissa's technology complicated the issue—technology he couldn't explain to Tig. His mate could flash to a different location, but he'd know because of the crystal. That left the tunnels. "She could go to the pool house by way of the basement tunnels, and I wouldn't know unless I checked the alarm system log. The program should log the alert if an exterior door was opened."

"I may need access to the alarm system log." Tig made another note on the yellow pad in front of her. "How difficult is the log to obtain?"

"Not very. I sign in over the internet."

"All right. I want access to the log before the night's over. Please make arrangements—"

"Fine. But what about Cerissa? When will I see her?"

Tig stood and moved to the door, taking the yellow pad and phone with her. "Not any time soon."

His hands fisted, and he shot out of his seat. "Tig—"

Christine's hand landed on his forearm again, and she shook her head. He took a deep breath. She was right. He had to remain calm.

Tig looked at him over her shoulder. "Wait in the lobby, and I'll get back to you."

Sierra Escondida Jail—Around the Same Time

Cerissa's chest deflated when she saw Nicholas enter the jail's hallway alone, until a hopeful idea struck her. "Are you here to release me?"

"I wish. How are you doing?"

She sighed. "About as well as can be expected."

"We can't talk about the case without your attorney being here." He leaned against the cell bars. "I wanted to check on you, make sure you're okay."

"Oh." Her stomach knotted. "Thanks."

"Look, if you killed him, I understand why. If you didn't, then we'll get this cleared up soon. Be patient."

Cerissa crossed her arms. "Why do you think I'm capable of killing in cold blood?"

"If I imagine myself in your shoes—after what the mayor did—I'd want vengeance."

"Well, for the record, I didn't kill him."

"Noted. Look, I'm here to deliver the signed search warrant to Tig. We aren't using a judge in Mordida. One of the treaty community judges reviewed and authorized the search."

"What?" They were going to rummage through her lab. When would this nightmare be over? "I'm not a vampire. How can—"

Nicholas held up his hands, patting the air the way Marcus did. "Your rights are still being protected, but we don't have to dance around the cause of death."

"I guess that makes sense."

"Anyway, Tig wants me to go with Zeke and Bailey to search your house. I know Zeke gave you problems in the past. Is there anywhere you'd prefer I search and keep him out?"

"Yes. Our bedrooms and Henry's office. I, ah, I don't want him rifling through my underwear drawer, and I suspect Henry wouldn't want Zeke looking through his finances and personal records."

Nicholas gave her a sympathetic look. "Got it. Anyplace else?"

"You might take Luis along to help search my basement lab. He'd recognize the equipment easier than the rest of you. And I don't mind if he helps search the bedrooms."

"We'll do our best to be respectful. And if you feel like you aren't being treated fairly, ask Christine to contact me."

"Thanks, Nicholas." She glanced to the side. Maybe he could convince Tig to let her have visitors. "Ah, when can I see Henry?"

"The way Tig was talking, not until tomorrow night." He gave a shrug. "Hang in there."

She grimaced. *Yeah, right.*

He waved goodbye as he left.

She wrapped her arms around herself as sadness inched its way under her skin and burrowed into her gut. The institutional beige hallway, the gray bars, the fluorescent yellow light—all the tedious colors depressed her even more. She couldn't accept any of her captivity.

And then it hit her. The council meeting to approve the lab project was scheduled in three nights. What the hell was she going to do? If she stayed in jail, they'd deny the project, and then what? Leopold would cancel the Sierra Escondida location.

Forgetting about her eye makeup, she rubbed her eyes with the palms of her hands until the mascara's grit smeared on her skin.

Whatever was she going to do?

And that wasn't even her largest problem. How would she maintain the illusion of being mortal if they kept her locked in jail? At least once each day she had to morph to another life form—that, or inject the morphing stabilizer, but using the drug over a long period would make her ill.

And at some point, they might discover she wasn't mortal.

She bit her lip. The Lux would never let that happen. They'd extract her to prevent the vampires from finding out her true nature. But if the Lux arranged her jail break, she'd never be able to return—she'd have to leave the treaty communities forever.

She'd have to leave Henry.

A broken sob escaped her lips and tears rolled down her face. With no tissues handy, she used the cot's white cotton sheet to catch her tears. Black smears of her makeup streaked the material.

This can't be happening.

She'd done nothing wrong. She didn't belong in jail. She had to find some way to convince Tig of her innocence.

The bracelet. Tig's suspicions all turned on the bracelet. Someone had to have planted it. But who hated her enough to leave it by the mayor's body? And how was she going to figure that out sitting here?

Chapter 36

It's Not Possible

Sierra Escondida Police Station—Around the same time

Once Tig finished interviewing Henry, she stepped into her office to phone Marcus. She asked him to write another search warrant—one for the guest house where Anne-Louise stayed.

She said goodbye to Marcus, and a text message *dinged* in from Dr. Clarke. The body had been delivered to his morgue, and from his preliminary exam, he believed the mayor was killed in the early evening. The body showed no signs of having been left in the sun all day to cook.

Tig grunted. Henry either didn't know about Cerissa's involvement or was covering for her as a co-conspirator. His mate could have killed Winston before arriving home, or else arrived home later—and he lied for her.

And Cerissa may have lied when she said her bracelet was missing this morning. Tig took the glass jar out of the bag and studied the bracelet for a moment, then placed it on her desk. She needed to return the bracelet to Jayden to fingerprint the beads using the special equipment they had in the squad room.

His initial forensics report on the crime scene sat in the middle of her desk blotter. She scanned the summary—no fingerprints other than the mayor's and Jayden's on the doorknobs, and only Winston's on the gardening implements. If the perp went inside the mayor's house to steal something, they must have used gloves.

Before leaving, Tig had sealed both doors with police tape. A quick search inside had told her nothing looked disturbed, but in a house as cluttered as the mayor's, knowing what, if anything, was stolen would be impossible without the mayor's help.

But Gaea might know—if it became relevant, they could take her through Winston's house and ask her if she recognized anything valuable missing.

A tap at Tig's office door drew her attention, and Nicholas stuck his head inside. "I brought the search warrant for Henry and Cerissa's place. Here's a copy."

"Thanks. Have you served Henry yet?"

"I stopped in the jail wing to tell Cerissa. He was still with you when I arrived."

"He's probably in the lobby by now. Let's go serve him and get this over with." She stood, and then remembered—based on Dr. Clarke's report, Nicholas just became a potential witness. "Wait. Do you know what time you left Karen's this afternoon?"

"Not precisely. I remember thinking I needed to hurry, so I could finish packing for our trip before Marcus woke. The sun had almost set."

"Was Cerissa there when you left?"

"Yes, but she drove off right behind me. Maybe Karen or the others can nail the time for you."

Tig made a note on her pad—she'd have to draft a timeline very soon. There were too many moving parts.

"Oh," Nicholas continued, "I called Luis. He'll help search Cerissa's lab. Is that okay with you?"

"Yeah, we can swear him in as a reserve officer. At the rate we're disqualifying officers, I'll have to swear in the entire Hill." She let out a loud scoff. "Let's go give the warrant to Henry." She gestured to the door. "After you."

In the lobby, she handed Henry and Christine copies of the warrant with Nicholas at her elbow.

Henry scanned the paperwork. "Who will conduct the search?"

"Because of the size of your house, I'm sending four reserve officers—"

"Zeke. Will Zeke be nosing through my home?" Henry stepped within inches of her. "Tig, this is beyond the pale."

Tig uncrossed her arms, ready for action. "Henry, step back."

"After all I've given this community, to be treated like this is unconscionable."

Nicholas laid a hand on Tig's shoulder to stop her from answering, and she almost snarled at him.

"I'm part of the search team," Nicholas said, and, placing the other hand on Henry's arm, wedged himself between the two of them, forcing Henry back a step or two. "I've already spoken to Cerissa. Luis and I will handle the search of your bedrooms, office, and her basement lab."

The scowl on Henry's face softened, and he gave a sharp nod. "Fine."

Tig looked heavenward.

May the ancestors save me from bulls butting heads.

Christine stood and handed Tig a page from a yellow pad with a website, username, and password written out. "You asked for login information to Henry's home alarm dashboard. This temporary access will expire in a few days."

"You won't find anything," Henry said. "There are no alerts for the time periods you are interested in."

"Thank you." Tig studied the page. She'd have to check to make sure the owner couldn't delete anything from the log.

The lobby door buzzed. Tig glanced over to see Anne-Louise arrive, with Zeke following her.

"What is the meaning of this?" Anne-Louise demanded. "First your captain texts me that I must change my flight, that I cannot leave the Hill. Then this oaf shows up at my door demanding I go with him."

"Zeke is a police officer—"

"I don't care if he's a member of the *Légion étrangère*. I belong to the New York Collective, and I'm a guest of your mayor. I'm not subject to your police authority." She pulled her phone from her purse. "I'm calling Winston right now."

"Go ahead. It won't do you any good—"

"Of course it will. I'm here at his request—"

"He's dead."

Anne-Louise's eyes grew round. "*C'est pas possible!*"

"Sorry to say, it's very possible. He was killed sometime after he left the amphitheater. Now, if you'll come with me, I have a few questions for you."

CHAPTER 37

FRENCH RESISTANCE

SIERRA ESCONDIDA POLICE STATION—MOMENTS LATER

Tig motioned for Anne-Louise to walk down the hall ahead of her, her mind on the fact she'd have to soon notify Gaea that her child had been killed.

Although Gaea and Winston were no longer intimately close, the pair had a longstanding friendship. And regardless of their political disagreements, Winston was still Gaea's child, a circumstance Gaea often reminded Winston of when she publicly criticized him. But she could also be territorial, refusing to allow others the same privilege to speak freely about the mayor's faults.

Despite their differences, this would hit her hard. After what happened with Dylan, Gaea's ex-mate who was now serving a life sentence for murdering Yacov, Tig dreaded being in the room when Gaea got the news about the mayor.

Tig took a glance at her watch. The odds were strong Gaea hadn't heard about the mayor's death yet. Everyone involved in the investigation had been ordered to keep it confidential, and Henry knew better than to make that call. So Tig had time to interview Anne-Louise first.

From behind her, she heard Nicholas leave with Zeke and Bailey, the lobby door buzzing as they walked out. They'd pick up Luis on the way, and Nicholas would swear him in as a reserve officer. As assistant town attorney, Nicholas had been delegated the authority to administer oaths.

Tig escorted Anne-Louise to the conference room. After the New York vampire took the hot seat across the table, Tig sat down and said, "I'm recording our conversation. Do you want legal representation?"

"*Beurk*," Anne-Louise scoffed. "I didn't do anything to need a lawyer. Ask your questions so I may leave this hellhole."

"When you finished at the amphitheater last night, where did you go?"

"To Enrique's. I stayed there until six in the morning. By then, I figured your mayor was unlikely to appear at their door."

"Can you prove the time you arrived?"

"Why should I have to?"

"To make this easier—so we can rule out other possible suspects."

"And just who would those suspects be?"

"Henry, for one." It didn't cost Tig anything to offer his name. After all, his maker couldn't have missed seeing him in the waiting area.

Anne-Louise scrolled through her phone and then plopped the device on the table. "Here. You can see for yourself. I texted Winston a photo at ten fifty-six, and then spoke with him shortly afterward."

Tig opened the photo. *Yuck.* Henry's flayed back. The photo's metadata would establish the time it was taken, and Tig forwarded the image to her phone. She then closed the file and thumbed to the phone call records, which confirmed the connection, and from the length, they must have spoken. So the mayor still lived at eleven. But based on Dr. Clarke's text, Tig already suspected that. Still, it didn't hurt to independently close gaps in the timeline.

Tig handed the phone back to Anne-Louise. "What did you and Winston discuss?"

"I told him to stay away. He was threatening to come over. His presence would have upset Enrique and Cerissa. They'd been through enough."

Tig raised an eyebrow. Why was Anne-Louise protecting them after serving as the executioner? Her behavior didn't make sense. "Did you have any other disagreements with the mayor?"

Anne-Louise's eyes went solid black. "I survived the political intrigue of the Sun King's court. Do you think me stupid enough to admit to having a disagreement with your deceased mayor?"

"Why did you come to Sierra Escondida—"

"Why, why, why! Why is everyone asking *why*? Enrique is my child. I came here to protect him."

"Serving as executioner is a very strange way to protect him."

"No, it isn't. I spared him from the Butcher."

Aha.

Even after two centuries, Anne-Louise's instinct as a maker was to protect her child. Although childless, Tig had known enough makers to understand the impulse. And what the mayor planned to do to Henry if Anne-Louise hadn't appeared was even more barbaric than what Anne-Louise herself served up.

"After you spoke with the mayor, did you feel Henry needed any further protection?"

"I stayed in his drawing room until almost dawn. I wanted to make sure no one else disturbed them. Then I returned to Rolf's guest house."

Tig pressed her pen to her lips. She could check with Rolf to confirm the time. "Let me see your phone again."

She'd learned a thing or two about technology. She checked the device's GPS history, and it confirmed Anne-Louise's story—she left Henry's at six-oh-two in the morning and arrived at Rolf's five minutes later. Sunrise occurred at seven-fifteen. The phone remained at Rolf's until Zeke picked her up.

Of course, as Anne-Louise pointed out, she wasn't stupid. She may have abandoned the phone at Rolf's when she went to kill the mayor.

"Do you carry any weapons with you when you travel?"

"I sleep with a silver knife. It is back at Rolf's."

"Did you bring any other weapons with you from New York?"

"No."

"Did Rolf provide you with any weapons?"

Anne-Louise laughed. "Why would he?"

"Answer the question, please."

"No, he did not provide me with weapons. And I didn't buy any here."

Tig tapped the table. She didn't want to have the murder weapon leaked to the community, so she stopped there. "One of the things we found at the crime scene was the mayor's phone. According to his calendar, you were to meet with him at seven this evening."

He didn't have his phone password protected, so they had access to everything on the device.

Anne-Louise let out a puff of air, much like a tiger's chuff. "As I said before, I spoke with him while I was at Enrique's house. During that conversation, I asked to reschedule."

"What were you meeting him about?"

"He failed to pay me at the amphitheater, claimed his secretary had forgotten to write the check, and he promised to provide payment tonight. I decided I'd have the car service swing by his place on my way to the mortuary, so we changed the time to midnight."

The mortuary—owned by vampires and their mates—would load her into a lockable casket to be delivered by plane to New York during the day.

"Why didn't the mayor note the change in his calendar?"

"How am I to know why? He always struck me as a bit of an idiot."

Tig smirked at Anne-Louise's last comment. She couldn't help herself. "That's all the questions I have for now. Is there anything you want to tell me?"

"What could I possibly add? I know nothing about his murder. May I leave for New York now?" Anne-Louise glanced at a gold watch on her wrist. If Tig wore such a delicate watch, it'd get destroyed the first time she had to tackle a perp. "The car service—"

"Cancel your ride. Whether you like it or not, you're a witness to certain pertinent facts. You'll have to stay."

"Surely I am not a suspect."

"I didn't say you were. Under the treaty, I may hold you here as a percipient witness."

"How unreasonable. I witnessed *nothing*. I'm phoning Leopold."

"Go ahead, but wait here." Tig pushed back her chair.

"One minute. With the mayor dead, someone must arrange for my payment. Travel here is not cheap."

Tig rolled her eyes. She had no time to deal with these administrative details. "How much are you owed?"

"Fifteen thousand, inclusive of travel. But now that I must change travel plans, the cost will be higher."

"Then call the mayor's assistant. She can cut the check for what the mayor previously approved. Any additional payments will have to be signed off by Rolf."

"If this town ever wants a service from me again, someone better pay me in full."

Leaving Anne-Louise in the conference room, Tig stormed to her office. She had no choice now. She had to notify Rolf of the mayor's murder. As of this point, no evidence pointed to him as a suspect—aside from his political rivalry with Winston.

When she finished briefing him on what she found at the mayor's house, his response was typical Rolf. "You couldn't tell me this four hours ago?"

"I embargoed the news until I could interview certain suspects."

"You already have a suspect in custody?"

Tig huffed. As much as she'd prefer to keep it quiet for the moment, he'd learn the truth soon enough from Henry. "Cerissa is in our jail."

"*Scheiße*. I never took you for an idiot."

"Rolf," she said with a growl.

"I don't care what you think you know. I can say without doubt she didn't kill Winston."

When Henry first started dating Cerissa, Rolf objected vehemently to their relationship. What had swung him a hundred and eighty degrees around? Cerissa's help with the rescue of Karen from the Carlyle Cutter? Or the special blood she provided him?

The latter question reminded Tig of Rolf's adrenaline-spiked blood problem, and she resisted the strong urge to razz him about it in retaliation for calling her an idiot. But he would serve as the temporary mayor until they held an election. She had to make nice with him.

Damn. Things were happening too fast. "I appreciate your opinion, Rolf. But until we discover a different theory to explain certain evidence found at the scene, Cerissa is at the top of my list. Now, the real reason I called—what time did Anne-Louise arrive at your guest house this morning?"

"Give me a minute."

It was more than a minute, but when he returned to the phone, he confirmed the same time the countess gave. His security cameras recorded her arrival, and the motion detector hadn't caught her leaving until Zeke arrived to bring her to the police station.

With everything happening, Tig had postponed notifying the treaty communities. Based on Anne-Louise's threat to call Leopold, they had to act fast.

"We need a death notice—especially to New York," Tig said. "Give me thirty minutes to make the next-of-kin notification to Gaea before you release the notice."

"Agreed. It will take me that long to write the announcement and obituary."

After they hung up, she logged the information Rolf provided and leaned back in her chair, pondering everything.

Anne-Louise could have stolen the bracelet from Cerissa, left her phone at the guest house, dodged Rolf's cameras by hiking out the back way, killed the mayor, and returned in time for Zeke to be at her door.

A glance at the wall clock told her she didn't have much time; she had to hustle. Tig rushed from her office and found Jayden in the squad room. "I'm going to Gaea's. I need to give the next-of-kin notice before she hears about his death from someone else."

"Do you want me to go with you?"

"While I'd appreciate the company, I want you to stay and keep an eye on Henry and Cerissa."

"Will do, chief." He gestured at the video monitors, which relayed video of the front waiting room, the interrogation rooms, and the jail cells. Cerissa lay on the cot, reading a paperback book. Henry and Christine sat in the waiting area, whispering to each other. Anne-Louise talked on the phone with someone. Probably Leopold.

She let out a long breath. If Cerissa was guilty, this was going to destroy Henry.

The rest of the town would feel the loss too. The blood her clones produced was a major improvement over the stale donor shit they normally drank. And in her short time with them, Cerissa had become an essential part of Tig's team—the scientist's ability to test for vampire DNA had helped in so many ways. Not to mention the friends she'd made—including Jayden.

It'd be a crying shame if she let her rage get the better of her.

"Oh, and before I go"—Tig placed the jar containing the bracelet on the table—"I don't need this for questioning anymore. Would you please fingerprint it?"

Jayden picked up the jar. "I'm not optimistic. It's unlikely we'll get anything useable from beads this small, but I'll try."

Tig grabbed her phone off her belt. She had one more call to make before leaving for Gaea's. When she finished speaking with Father Matt, she snapped the phone into its case and pulled a jacket over her civilian clothes—the one embroidered with "Police Chief" on the back and the town's emblem on the front—and marched to the station's front door.

Henry jumped to his feet when she entered the lobby. "May I see Cerissa now?"

"No. Probably not tonight. I need to continue my investigation. With any luck, you can visit her tomorrow."

"I'm not leaving until I confirm she is all right with my own eyes."

That worked for Tig. She didn't want Henry to leave before they finished searching his house. "I have to go to Gaea's now. She doesn't know yet. I'll be back shortly."

The anger drained from Henry's face. "Please give her my condolences."

"Under the circumstances, I think its best if I don't," Tig said, and strode out the door to her car.

CHAPTER 38

GRIEF

Gaea Greenleaf's house—Fifteen minutes later

Tig parked her Cadillac CTS-V in Gaea's driveway. Father Matt waited for her in the garden, sitting on the white bench. A small, landscaped area, mostly rosebushes heavy with late fall blooms, separated the driveway from the vineyard beyond the house, where the diffuse mounds of dying yellow leaves and dormant grapevines created dark rows as they crept up the mountainside. Matt hastened to meet her at the front porch.

Tig's shoulders sagged. "I hate death notification visits."

"Wait." He held out an arm, stopping her from climbing the steps to the front door. "You worked closely with the mayor for almost sixty years. That's a long working relationship. How are *you* feeling?"

"I've been so busy since we discovered his body earlier this evening"—she let out a noisy, shuddering breath—"I haven't begun to feel anything yet."

"Both because of your age, plus your military and police training, you may avoid seeking help to process your feelings."

"Matt, I don't need therapy. I need five more trained police officers who know what we are and can take some of the workload when a crisis like this hits."

"That rings true," he said with a wan smile. "But at some point it's going to sink in. You're investigating the death of someone you've worked with closely. If you need to talk, I'm here."

She stiffened her back. "Thank you, but I'm fine."

He nodded and then swept his hand toward the door. "Shall we?"

She returned the nod and led the way up the steps before punching the fancy doorbell. Multiple chimes sounded, followed by footsteps rushing to the door.

When Gaea opened the door, her head swiveled like an owl's from Tig to Matt and back to Tig, eyes wide open. "Oh my word, this isn't good."

"I'm sorry, Gaea, but may we come in?" Tig asked.

The Hill's oldest vampire escorted them into a small room off the hallway, a room decorated with a Victorian flair. Tig recognized the style from her time spent in England during the 1800s. She also knew the room because it was the same one—albeit with a new rug—in which Seaton killed a burglar.

After they were seated, Tig asked, "Are you here alone?"

"Both Ari and Seaton are upstairs. Ari's been working with my problem child, helping him with his computer skills." Gaea's eyes got big again. "Oh no, did Seaton do something wrong again?"

"No, this isn't about Seaton. There's no easy way to say this. Earlier tonight, Jayden and I discovered the mayor's body. He had missed an appointment, and Rolf asked us to make a welfare check on him."

"His b-b-body?" Gaea stammered, her hands rising to cup her face.

"I'm afraid he was murdered."

"No, no, there must be some mistake. Why, I spoke to Winston last night. I gave him a piece of my mind over what he did to Henry. No, he can't be dead, not when I spoke to him—"

"Do you know what time you spoke with him?"

The last incoming call on the mayor's phone was marked "private," so Tig wanted to confirm the call was indeed Gaea.

"I don't really—well, it couldn't have been earlier than eleven. I arrived home from that horrible spectacle, got something to drink, and phoned him."

"I was told Ari drove Cerissa home. Did he come back here afterward?"

"Yes, Ari arrived before I spoke with Winston. Oh dear." Gaea cradled her face in both hands. "He's really dead?"

"I'm afraid so. Do you have your phone?"

Gaea pulled the phone out of a dress pocket and handed over the device. Tig checked the timestamp: eleven-thirteen. Yes, Gaea was the last call the mayor received.

Gaea's round eyes looked lost. "When d-did it happen?"

"We're still piecing the timeline together."

"While we were talking, his doorbell rang. He said it was the delivery of his Casa Blanca lily bulbs. Could it have been the killer? Oh no."

Tig made a note. She'd check with the gate guard to find out if anyone came through with a delivery for the mayor. Even though Dr. Clarke believed the death occurred earlier this evening, he wasn't infallible. Was it possible the killer came through in the guise of a delivery person? Then why was Cerissa's bracelet at the scene? Too many variables to juggle. "And Ari spent the night here?"

"Yes. And he went back to his apartment to work during the day but returned before sunset. He's been here ever since, working with Seaton, mostly."

Tig handed back the phone. Some pieces of the puzzle were falling into place. She now had a better idea of who had a decent alibi—and who didn't. "I will try to keep you updated on the case, to the extent I can."

Gaea bowed her head. "Something else happened. Around six-forty this evening, I felt a sharp pain, and then it faded."

Tig noted the time. "I have to ask an indelicate question. Do you still take Winston's blood?"

"Not for almost a hundred years. He's my first child, you know...we were lovers once upon a time."

So the blood bond was long dead. It was surprising she felt any pain at all when he died—if indeed the pain was related to the mayor's death. But the information provided one more data point to help confirm time of death.

Gaea lifted her chin. "Are you sure the body is Winston? There could be a mistake—"

Tig looked over at Matt. She didn't know which she hated more—family members who clung to denial like a lifeline, or those who went into crying hysterics. She was ill-equipped to deal with either.

Matt took Gaea's hand, moving to a chair next to her. "Gaea, I'm going to stay and help, if you'll let me."

"Help with what?"

Matt clasped her hand between his. "Would you please ask Ari to join us? I'm sure his support will be a comfort, once he hears the news—"

Gaea teared up. "There is no news for him to hear."

Tig took out her phone and hit the contact for her computer consultant.

"Hey, my favorite client," he answered. "What can I do for you, chief?"

"Ari, I'm in Gaea's..."

"Parlor," Matt said.

"I'm in Gaea's parlor. Would you please join us?"

The *thump-thump-thump* of Ari running downstairs was distinctive. He swung around the doorway, grabbing the frame to pivot, and stopped. "What's up?"

"Someone murdered the mayor. I need to return to the station and continue the investigation. Matt's going to stay and help—Gaea is refusing to accept—"

"I'm not refusing to accept anything." Gaea shook her head vigorously. "You've made a mistake, and you won't admit it."

Ari sat down on the other side of Gaea, taking her hand. "Hey, sweet stuff, what can I do?"

"You can tell these people they're wrong."

Ari caught Tig's eye. "Do you have a body?"

"At Dr. Clarke's surgery center—in the morgue behind the main building."

"Got it. Let Matt and I handle this. But if you could give Dr. Clarke a heads-up? We'll be coming by."

Tig stood. "Will do." She took a deep breath. "Gaea, you have my deepest condolences."

A single tear overflowed, running down Gaea's ivory cheek.

Tig pivoted toward the door. She couldn't deal with strong emotions in the best of times. Right now, Gaea's grief risked derailing her focus. She couldn't allow that to happen. She had to solve this crime—for all their sakes.

Dr. Clarke's morgue—Fifteen minutes later

Gaea paused, looking at the "Morgue" sign. In all her years on the Hill, she'd never been to this door.

Ari turned the knob, his other hand holding hers. "We don't have to do this if you don't want to."

Gaea threw her shoulders back. "No. I must see him for myself. I must be sure."

Ari had offered to drive, and in her state, she hadn't wanted to be behind the wheel. Something about Ari made her comfortable with his seeing her vulnerable, even though they'd only dated a short time. She just felt, well, more peaceful around him than she had any right to feel under the circumstances.

Father Matt hadn't joined them—she'd thanked him but didn't need a large audience. He'd offered to make himself available later if she needed to talk.

Would she?

Ari pulled the door open, and she stared at the white, sterile hallway ahead of them. Interior doors lined the space.

One opened. "This way." Dr. Clarke gestured to match his words, a clipboard in one hand.

For the first time since she'd met Ari, the young man refrained from his usual flippant remarks. His somber demeanor doubled her growing anxiety, and her throat tightened over what she might find beyond that door.

Dr. Clarke stepped aside, and she led the way in. With a hand resting gently on her back, Ari joined her in the room.

The shiny metal table on which Winston lay looked cold and unforgiving. Despite his withered appearance, she recognized him the instant she saw the body, though she found it hard to articulate why.

Was it the clothes? The body wore Winston's gardening overalls. Although difficult to do in California, where water was precious and not as plentiful as in the English countryside, he'd done his best to landscape his backyard in a traditional way—reminding her of the estate they'd long since abandoned.

Or was it the signet ring? He'd always worn the ring emblazoned with his family's crest, even though he initially changed his name to make hiding from his kin easier. But then, years after they turned to dust, he'd gone back to using Mason.

Lord Mason. Mayor Mason. Always a title to make him feel a little worthier.

Or was it simply the shape of his body? His shape had never changed once she seduced him. And despite the mummification process brought on by death, enough of his face remained. She could see the bones of his cheeks, the set of his lips, the sparse hairline.

Aah, Winston. How could you let anyone do this to you?

"Where is the stake?" she asked.

"The chief has taken the implement and bagged it as evidence," Dr. Clarke replied. "Can you confirm—"

"It's him. It's Winston."

Dr. Clarke noted something on the clipboard. "I'll report your identification to Tig."

Now she understood why all the mortals hated Dr. Clarke. He had the empathy of a tombstone. In that instant, she resolved not to show any emotion in front of him.

I won't cry. I won't cry. I will not cry.

Ari squeezed her shoulder. "You're sure it's him?" he asked in a hushed voice.

"My dear, he was my first child. I know every line, every mark, every contour on his body." Despite her resolve, a tear slid from her eye, landing with a splat on the morgue's stainless-steel table. "You never forget your first."

CHAPTER 39

DISTRACTIONS

SIERRA ESCONDIDA POLICE STATION—FIFTEEN MINUTES EARLIER

After leaving Gaea's house, Tig returned to the detective squad room, relieved to be in a workspace where she felt fully in control—until Jayden gave her the bad news: he had been unable to raise any useable fingerprint fragments from the bracelet during her absence.

"Dammit," she said.

"My thought exactly." Jayden picked up the bracelet jar and walked it to the evidence room. Returning, he asked, "What now?"

"Let's go over the suspects we have so far." She picked up a red electronic pen and listed Cerissa, Henry, and Anne-Louise on the whiteboard, explaining her reasoning to Jayden as she wrote.

When she stopped, he asked, "What about Liza and Carolyn?"

"What about them?"

"Both were pretty angry at the mayor. Carolyn spat in his face, and Liza said she'd run against him in the next election. What if one of them was pissed off enough to do something?"

Tig wrote the names on the board. "But why frame Cerissa? If Cerissa didn't lose the bracelet at the scene, then whoever framed her must have a motive for doing so."

"You know what else doesn't make sense?" Jayden asked.

Tig turned back to him, the red pen still in her hand. "What?"

"If the killer used a crossbow, shooting the mayor in the back, they would have stood a few feet away, at least. Cerissa's bracelet lay right next to the body. There would have been no reason to get so close and no struggle to break the bracelet from its latch. The killer could have watched Winston die from wherever they hid."

"Maybe she wanted a good look at his face to make sure it was him. And the bracelet may have caught on his clothing when she turned him over." Tig shrugged. Nothing was coming into clear focus yet. "Someone turned him onto his back. Most likely the killer."

"Cerissa's a smart cookie. Losing her bracelet at the scene of a crime doesn't fit her profile."

"No matter how smart she is, in the stress of the moment, she may not have noticed the bracelet catch and break."

Tig had seen perps do stupid things before. Even smart perps.

"I still think someone framed her. It might not even be her bracelet."

Tig wasn't satisfied with his deduction. They had no evidence pointing to a frame-up—yet. "Cerissa couldn't remember losing her bracelet, so it's probably hers."

"Yeah, but—"

"Why would the killer leave a duplicate at the crime scene? All Cerissa would have to do is produce the original to clear herself."

"Okay. I still think she's been framed."

"Wait." Tig waved the red pen, a new thought occurring to her. "I'm willing to keep an open mind. But if it is a frame-up, why her? Who on the Hill hates her?"

"Maybe Anne-Louise? Karen said there's tension there. From what she's seen, she suspects Henry is still tied to his maker, and the situation caused some issues between Anne-Louise and Cerissa."

You could have knocked Tig over with a feather. "Seriously? He's over two hundred years vampire, and his maker still feeds on him?"

"Yup, at least, that's the rumor. Why do you think Anne-Louise visits so frequently?"

"Frankly, I never gave any thought to the matter." Tig wrote "Hates C" on the whiteboard, drew a red line under it, and added the countess's name to the new list, even though it remained unsubstantiated speculation.

Jayden made a *hmm* sound deep in his throat. "Despite the tension early on in their relationship, I've heard that Cerissa and Anne-Louise get along well together at times now, and their chumminess annoys Henry to no end."

"Who told you that?"

"Anne-Louise's other child."

Méi would be in a position to know. Tig scrubbed a hand over her face, then she added a question mark after the name. "Could Anne-Louise want him back as a lover? Might she be threatened by his impending marriage? The rumor you heard could be a smoke screen. Anne-Louise strikes me as someone who plays the long game with her political maneuvering."

"She wasn't invited to the engagement party. I guess she could hold a grudge over the snub."

Tig stared wide-eyed at her mate, amazed by how closely he kept his ear to the mortals' rumor mill, even more surprised they felt safe enough to dish the dirt to a police officer. She noted the info by Anne-Louise's name. "So who else hates Cerissa?"

"Rolf did."

"Yeah, but not anymore," Tig said. "You should have heard him defending her on the phone."

"But maybe he defended her because he's the real killer."

Tig laughed. "He wasn't faking. His response was too adamant, too spontaneous. And if he was the real killer, he would have blamed her."

And she couldn't see Rolf risking his comfortable position on the Hill—not when he had a chance to beat Winston in the next election.

"Okay," Jayden said. "I don't know who else might hate her enough to do this. But it's worth asking around."

"In the morning, call Karen and talk with her. She and Cerissa are as thick as thieves. See what she knows. I don't want to start rumors, but we need to nail down any possibilities."

"Will do."

"There's one more thing we should do right now." Tig handed Jayden the page Christine had given her. "Here's the website, username, and temporary password for Henry's alarm system. Based on Dr. Clarke's analysis, time of death occurred after sunset tonight. Gaea had a pang around six-forty p.m., too. But check both windows of time, morning and evening. And make sure the owner can't delete alerts."

"Gotcha." Jayden started typing. Five minutes later, he said, "Okay, we have a log entry for when Anne-Louise left via the front door at six-oh-two in the morning. The front door opened again at ten-forty-six and again at eleven-oh-eight—most likely Cerissa going out to clean Henry's car, and then returning."

"Keep going."

"The door opens at eleven-forty-two. That aligns with Cerissa going to Karen's. Then the front door again at six-fifty in the evening when Cerissa arrives home. Another front-door log entry for seven-fifty-two, which would correspond with when Gaea dropped off Christine. By then, we'd found the mayor's body. No other doors triggered alerts during the time period in question."

"What about deletions?"

"I couldn't find anything in the interface to allow the owner to delete an alert. I'll contact the alarm company and tell you if their answer is different."

"Okay."

"But something you should know—the windows aren't alarmed, and the second-floor balcony doors aren't listed either." Jayden furrowed his brow. "So I guess Cerissa could have used a fire ladder to climb from the balcony to the pool patio."

"It's possible." Tig tapped her lip with her finger. "And while Henry has security cameras, he told me he uses them for live monitoring only. They don't record. He claims to like his privacy too much to record everyone who comes and goes at his house."

"You said Gaea felt something around six-forty?"

"Yeah." Tig nodded. "Could Cerissa have left Karen's after sunset—which started at six-eighteen—driven to the mayor's and killed him, and returned home by six-fifty? Would thirty-two minutes be enough?"

Jayden leaned back in his chair, hands behind his head, looking deep in thought. "If everything went smoothly, the drive time to the mayor's house isn't long, and if she saw him through the bushes, then maybe."

"How did she know he'd be outside gardening?"

"Maybe Gaea told Ari about the bulbs being delivered, and he told Cerissa?"

Tig raised an eyebrow. "Or maybe the plan was to ring the doorbell and catch the mayor off guard, only she got lucky and found him in the backyard."

"Yeah, some luck," Jayden said. "Still, for the timing to work, the sequence of events would have to unfold perfectly. And no plan ever runs perfectly."

Tig snorted. Yeah, most criminals got caught when the fates interfered and screwed up something. "There is another possible explanation. Henry covered for her by opening the front door, thus setting up an alibi, giving her plenty of time to return before Christine got home."

"I'm not buying your theory, not with those two," Jayden said. "Oh, and I heard back from both Evelina and the guard gate. First, Evelina verified she and Wolfie arrived at Henry's house around eight-twenty-five, and Cerissa was there. Not that it matters—we found the body at seven-thirty. The killer would have been long gone by then. Second, the guard gate confirmed the delivery service took a box from Grow Bulbs to the mayor's house around eleven, which is consistent with what Gaea told you."

Tig tapped her fingers on the worktable, hating this case more by the minute. Neither piece of new information pointed to a suspect.

She'd left Anne-Louise in the interrogation room, and Henry sitting in the waiting room with Christine when she returned from Gaea's. "What do we do with those two?" Tig gestured at the surveillance camera screens monitoring them. "I don't want to lock Henry in the cell next to Cerissa; they might try to work on reframing their alibis."

"You don't have probable cause to arrest Henry or Anne-Louise. The only evidence supporting Cerissa's arrest is the bracelet." Jayden rubbed his eyes, looking very tired. "Has the search team finished at Henry's residence yet?"

"I haven't heard back."

Footsteps sounded outside the squad room door, and Tig *whooshed* across the room. Was someone spying on them? She pulled the door open.

A startled Ari stepped back with his fist raised, about to knock.

Tig shoved him into the hallway. "You can't be here."

"Hey, no need to get handsy. Why do you have my cousin locked up?"

She didn't have to ask how he found out. Tig hadn't mentioned it to Gaea, so Henry probably called him. "I can't discuss this case with you, Ari."

"Well, have you heard from Dr. Clarke yet?"

"No. Did Gaea identify the body?"

"Yup. We'd just left the morgue when I got the text about Cerissa. But you can't cut me out of the investigation." He crossed his arms. "If you need computer help, who you gonna ask? Not like you have a lot of choices."

"We're not there yet. When we are, I'll decide what to do."

Ari swiped at the curly hair on his forehead, pushing it back. "Can I see her, at least?"

"We're a bit busy here," she said, with a shake of her head.

"Fine. Just tell me if you let her take her injection kit with her."

"Her what?"

"Ah"—Ari pursed his lips, pausing for a moment—"can I tell you something confidentially?"

"Ari, if what you tell me involves the case, it won't be."

He crossed his arms. "Federal law covers people in custody. HIPAA means you have to treat it confidentially. And you're gonna wanna know this."

Tig scowled at him. "Tell me."

"She has a medical condition. Needs regular injections. She carries the kit in her purse. Do you have her purse?"

If Cerissa wasn't guilty, depriving her of medication she needed wouldn't sit well with the remaining council, who mostly liked the scientist. The bagged contents of Cerissa's purse were on the table in the squad room. Tig cracked the door. "Jayden, please turn off the whiteboard and cover any notes. I'm bringing Ari in."

A moment later, he replied, "All clear."

Tig turned back to face Ari, waving a finger in his face. "No snooping. No trying to find out what we know. No touching anything. You come in, I dump out her purse's contents, you tell me what Cerissa needs. Got it?"

"Whatever." He raised his hands in surrender. "I only want to make sure she has her medication for the night."

Tig opened the door wider, and Ari went in. She dumped out the evidence bag, and he pointed at a silver cylinder. "That's the jet injector—she calls it a hypo. New technology she's been testing. The medicine is in the hypo."

"And what is this medicine?"

"If she wants to tell you, that's up to her. But she and I have the same inherited condition, and we both require the same medication. Marcus already knows that. I didn't tell him the name of the condition, and I'm not telling you, because our medical info is none of his business, and it's none of yours."

Tig picked up the silver cylinder. "Anything else?"

"Her contact care kit—that little zippered case. It has the saline solution she needs."

Tig grabbed the black case as well. "Jayden, please update the inventory and re-bag the contents. Note that I'm bringing these to Cerissa."

"Will do, chief."

"After you." She gestured for Ari to go ahead of her. "You may come *if* you behave."

"When do I ever misbehave?"

Tig shot him a glare, and he only smirked.

When they reached the desk outside the jail wing's door, Florence looked up from her phone. The vampire was married to Lieutenant Bailey and filled in for him because they were short-handed. Florence had received *some* training in handling prisoners, but Tig was really wringing out the blood bag to use her.

Tig glanced at the video monitors on the desk and saw the empty cell. Her heart shot into overdrive. "Where is Cerissa?"

Florence shrugged. "How am I to know? She didn't come out this way."

Tig swung open the heavy metal door leading to the jail hallway and charged in, Ari hot on her heels.

Was she sleeping in the coffin? The big box had been swung around, so the lid opening faced away from the hallway camera. Why? Tig unlocked the empty cell door, walked four steps to the coffin, and opened the lid. "Cerissa, I—"

A cougar sat up and blinked at her, then hissed.

CHAPTER 40

HERE KITTY

SIERRA ESCONDIDA JAIL—MOMENTS LATER

Tig jumped back, letting go of the lid. It banged shut. She swung around to face Ari. "Did you see that?"

He gaped at her. "See what? You dropped the lid before I saw anything."

"There's a cougar in there, and Cerissa is missing."

Ari stared at her like she was crazy. "Are you sure?"

"Of course I'm sure."

"Well, I didn't see a cougar. What color was it?"

"Like one of the mountain lions that roam our foothills. Beige with black ear tips. The cat hissed at me. How could you not hear the hiss?"

The box rattled, and Tig swung back around. The lid opened of its own accord.

"Why did you slam it shut?" Cerissa asked testily, rubbing her forehead. "I was trying to sleep."

Tig stared at her. "Where is the cougar?"

"What cougar?" Cerissa asked, making a face and cocking her head to one side.

"The one that was in this, this"—Tig waved at the coffin, but chose the politically correct term—"sleep pod."

Cerissa scowled. "Are you feeling all right? I'm the only one in here. And I can assure you, there is no cougar in here with me."

"But I opened the lid and saw—"

"Hey, Tig." Ari tapped her shoulder, and a floating peace invaded her, slowing her rapid heartbeat. "You've been under a lot of stress lately. Do vampires hallucinate?"

"Absolutely not."

Cerissa gave a grim chuckle. "Then I don't know what to tell you."

Tig took a step closer and inspected the box. Empty, except for the prisoner. Maybe the stress of everything was playing with her mind. "Why are you in there?"

"I can't sleep well in light, and there's no way for me to turn the lights off. What was I supposed to do? Besides, the mattress in this thing is more comfortable"—Cerissa motioned at the spartan cot—"than that. Why did you wake me?"

Ari pushed past Tig. "Hey, Ciss, are you okay?"

Cerissa threw her legs over the side of the box and stood, reaching out to hug her cousin. "I'm fine. Tired, but fine."

"Tig brought your hypo and your contacts kit."

"Oh, thank the Goddess." Cerissa glanced at the clock on the hallway wall. "I'm kind of overdue."

"I can tell." Ari turned to Tig. "May she keep the hypo with her?"

"No. How frequently does she need the medication?"

"Once a day, usually at night." Cerissa held out her hand. "May I have it?"

Tig passed over the device, and the silver cylinder made a light *hiss* when Cerissa pressed it to her arm.

Finished, she gave it back. "Thanks."

"What about your contact lenses?" Ari asked.

Cerissa waved him off. "I'm fine, Ari."

"Ciss, how long have your contacts been in?"

"I wore them to the…council hearing."

"Did you sleep in them?" Ari glanced at Tig. "She's always doing that."

"Yeah, I guess I did."

"Then it's time for them to come out, don't ya think? Bad for your eyes."

"Oh. Oh, yes." Cerissa nodded vigorously. "I need to take them out."

Tig furrowed her brow. That was the strangest exchange between the two of them she'd ever seen. Why was Ari so familiar with Cerissa's habits?

"I can see the gears in your head spinning," Ari said. "Cerissa and I spent our childhoods together. I've been watching out for her since she was a tiny pup. Honestly, I know her better than Henry does."

Cerissa opened her mouth, then shrugged.

Tig didn't have time to figure out what that was about and huffed a breath as she glanced at her tactical watch. "Are we done here?"

"Ya need to hand her the contact kit so she can take them out."

Tig passed over the black case. Cerissa unzipped it, removed her contacts, added solution to the kit, and squeezed some saline into her eyes. Once the case was closed, she handed it back.

"Tig, can Ari take the case? They need to be cleaned, and I don't have the cleaning solution with me. He can bring them back tomorrow morning."

"Fine." Tig couldn't see any harm in letting Ari have them. "Here," she said, plopping the black kit into Ari's open palm. "Now, are we finished?"

"Can I speak with Cerissa alone?"

"Nuh-uh. No visitors until we wrap our investigation."

"That's not very fair," Ari said, sounding petulant.

"Look, I've bent the rules as much as I can right now. You have to leave." Tig looked at Henry's mate. "Do you need anything before I go?"

"Ah, I generally eat again by now. Can you or Ari bring me food?"

Ari opened his mouth, but Tig cut him off. "We'll take care of feeding her. I'll send Florence in to get your takeout order. That's the best we can do on short notice."

Besides, Jayden might want something to eat too. It looked like an all-nighter for both of them.

"Thank you," Cerissa said.

Tig grabbed Ari's shoulder, spun him to the exit door, and clanged the cell door shut. "Time for you to leave. I have real work to do if I'm going to finish this case tonight."

He stopped in the hallway and turned to her. "I'm taking Gaea back home. She's waiting in the car. If you need to find me—"

Tig pushed him through the doorway, then closed and locked the jail's door. "I won't. Good night."

Sierra Escondida police department—Fifteen minutes earlier

Gaea stayed in the car when Ari stopped by the jail to give Tig confirmation that the body was Winston's. He was hesitant to leave her alone, but for some reason he wouldn't explain, he had to go in person rather than phoning. The chief probably needed computer assistance with her investigation.

Dabbing at her eyes, Gaea didn't want anyone to see her like this. She twisted the handkerchief around her fingers as she waited, unable to rein in her thoughts. Winston had been such a troubled child for so long. As much as he brought order to the Hill, he aggravated those around him with the need to prove himself.

Over and over again, she'd counseled him to be a tad more flexible. His lack of self-esteem only contributed to the problem.

It was probably what got him killed.

Or was that victim blaming? If it was, she couldn't help herself. She needed someone to blame, and the killer was a faceless entity right now. But after Winston's performance at the council meeting last night, including his intransigent refusal to commute Henry's sentence, he'd angered quite a few people.

But enough to–to kill him?

When Ari finally came bounding out of the police station, Gaea had no idea why he took so long. Or had it been long? Time seemed to be moving…strangely.

She stuffed the wrinkled handkerchief into her purse. Once in the car, Ari delivered her back home and took her upstairs to the private lounge, the one with pink roses on the wallpaper and vermillion carpeting.

He helped her lie back on the upholstered divan, the one with matching pink roses, and then he ran back downstairs. Minutes later, he returned with some heated spiked blood in a brandy snifter—which almost got a smile from her—and sat down beside her.

"Do you want to talk?" Ari asked.

She sipped from the glass as the pain tightened inside her, growing worse. "What is there to talk about? He's *dead*." Something in her chest cracked on the word like an ice sheet splitting open over a frozen lake. "Someone—someone did that to him."

"Gaea—"

A simmer of rage rose from the cold that had encased her since she first saw Winston on that slab. "A monster ended the life"—*crack*—"of a good"—*crack*—"decent"—*crack*—"beloved child."

My child.

Sorrow pushed between the cracks in her icy control, making her hands shake. She knew that if she allowed it to come, it would flood her mind, the pain drowning her. And who then would make sure her child was honored as was his due? Who would protect his legacy? She had a memorial service to plan.

No, she'd not crack open now.

"Until Tig knows more, there's nothing else to discuss, my dear."

"You loved him?"

She closed her eyes at the words, burying the answer deep within her. She pressed the grief down by sheer force of will, resealing the ice that encased her heart. The coldness of the feeling carried through in her sharp reply. "I said there's nothing to discuss, Ari."

"Okay..." His green eyes met hers. "I'm not real good at this stuff. Ciss will tell you. I'm not good at guessing what to do. So okay, but if you need something, tell me."

Gaea immediately softened at the warmth in his words. But not enough to bend.

"I never expected to outlive Winston, to outlive my child. And I'm not ready to talk about it, my dear one." She placed a hand on Ari's. "Please don't ask me again."

"That's fair. I'll stay, though, in case there's a way I can help."

Should she ask him to leave? Was it better to be alone or to remain occupied?

"Perhaps I should go to Winston's house and start cleaning out his things. He has no children to inherit his estate, and the Hill will want to make the home available to another vampire. No stranger should throw out his belongings or trample his beloved garden. I can't abide the thought of it."

Tears started to form, and she fought them.

In a flash, Ari grabbed a box of tissues from the nearby bathroom and came back, holding out the box.

She refused to take one. If she did, the tears would begin falling, never to stop. And she had a duty to do.

She gently pushed the box away.

CHAPTER 41

THE MISSIVE

SIERRA ESCONDIDA POLICE STATION—LATER THAT NIGHT

Once the signed search warrant came through, Tig dragged two other part-time officers—both mortals—out of bed to conduct the search of Rolf's guest house, looking for a crossbow or bolts.

Two hours later, the two search parties returned empty-handed from both Henry's and Anne-Louise's, and she sent the part-time officers home. The mortals would split shifts during the day to compensate for lost sleep. Jayden went home as well.

Tig sequestered herself in the squad room, staring at the whiteboard and thinking over the one piece of evidence tying Cerissa to the crime.

A knock at the squad room door alerted her, and Tig *whooshed* over to crack the door open an inch.

Christine.

"May I speak to Cerissa? I want to confer with her before the sun rises. I also need to know when Henry and Anne-Louise can leave. If you aren't detaining them, then Henry will want to escort me back to his place."

Tig checked over her shoulder to make sure no confidential evidence lay on the worktable, and, finding none, opened the door wider. "The mayor's secretary delivered payment for Anne-Louise. I'll give her the check, and she can leave. Henry is free to go after you speak with Cerissa. When did you last feed?"

"A few minutes ago."

"Good. I'll bring Cerissa to the other conference room. You can talk to her there."

Since the jail cells were constantly monitored, the prisoner and her attorney couldn't have a confidential conversation there. Tig showed Christine to the smaller conference room, then paid and dismissed Anne-Louise for the night.

Tig returned to the jail desk.

"She's in the sleep pod," Florence said without looking up from her phone.

Tig acknowledged the statement and pulled back the heavy door to enter the jail hallway. "Cerissa?"

The lid popped open. Cerissa crawled out of the box and ran her hands through her dark hair, brushing back the long waves.

"Christine wants to talk with you before she beds down for the day."

"Okay." Cerissa looked sleepily at her.

Tig unlocked the pass-through and took out a pair of handcuffs. "Hold out your hands."

"Is that really necessary?"

"Do you want to talk to your lawyer?"

"Yes."

"Then the cuffs are necessary."

Cerissa rubbed her eyes before sticking her hands through the slot. Tig cuffed them, opened the cell door, and escorted her to the smaller conference room.

Tig sat the prisoner at the table across from her lawyer.

"I'll need food too. A sandwich would be fine, preferably turkey or chicken."

"How often do you eat?" Tig asked, looking at the mortal incredulously. Cerissa wasn't skinny, but she wasn't overweight, either.

"Four to five times a day."

"All right. I'll see what we can do for you." Tig moved the desk phone closer to Cerissa. "Same protocol. If Christine makes a move for you, hit the red button."

SIERRA ESCONDIDA POLICE STATION—MOMENTS LATER

Bottled water sat on the wood-patterned laminated conference table. Cerissa opened one and took a healthy swig. "Okay, I'm awake, I think."

She yawned, still feeling disoriented from the abrupt morph back to mortal form. Even though she'd taken a dose of the stabilizer earlier, she had been catching more cougar time when Tig woke her.

"What's happening?" she asked Christine.

"They searched your home. Tig won't say if they found anything, but from the body language of the search party, I'd say they discovered bupkis."

"What was listed on the search warrant?"

Christine beamed at her. "Smart girl. Crossbow and bolts, silver, implements for melting silver—evidence, I assume, relating to the murder. And your bracelet. I suspect they are trying to determine if the one at the scene is a duplicate."

"Well, I don't own a crossbow or arrows—"

"Those are called bolts, not arrows."

"I've never seen Henry with them either."

"Excellent. He told me he doesn't own a crossbow."

"And I don't own a duplicate bracelet."

"Hmm. Tig's insisting on keeping you here during the day. Henry and I are returning home. But the real reason I wanted to talk to you is this."

Christine removed an envelope hidden underneath the pages of the writing pad she carried and slid it across the table.

Cerissa opened the envelope and read the enclosed letter. Ari had taken her lenses, downloaded the videos they recorded, and found the answer to who stole her bracelet.

Olivia.

According to Ari, the video showed Cerissa wearing the bracelet on her wrist moments before Olivia accosted her in the council chambers. The video caught a glimpse of Olivia's hand on Cerissa's wrist, and once Olivia left, the next time Cerissa's arm moved back into camera range of her lenses, no bracelet.

A great weight lifted off her chest, and Cerissa kissed the letter.

She didn't understand why Olivia had framed her—Cerissa had met the vampire for the first time right before the hearing—but she would consider the "why" later. Right now, she wanted to get up and dance around in joy. She finally had something to help prove her innocence.

"What's that all about?" Christine asked. "Ari swore me to secrecy."

Cerissa folded the letter and placed it back in the envelope. "I can't tell you how he found out, but Olivia stole my bracelet. The problem is, if I tell Tig now, she'll never believe me."

Christine looked skeptical. "Yet every minute we delay gives Olivia more time to ditch the crossbow and cover up her involvement—or help the killer do so, if she's merely an accomplice."

"Should we call in Tig and tell her?" Cerissa held out the envelope.

"Let's talk this through." Christine slid the envelope back between the pages of her notepad. "You said Olivia accosted you in the council chambers, right?"

"Yes."

"Nicholas made an offhanded comment when he came back from the search, and I didn't realize the connection. Now I do."

"What did he say?"

"The town council meetings are recorded. Video-recorded. There are cameras facing the councilmembers, as well as two pointed at the audience."

"So we tell Tig and ask her to pull the videos?"

Christine's eyes gleamed. "No, I have a better idea. It's so close to sunrise, if you tell her now, she won't have time to do anything. And the way the mates have been protesting unequal treatment, you're better off waiting until morning, so you can bend a more sympathetic ear, one who will be awake during the day to act on your information."

Cerissa wrinkled her brow, not immediately taking the hint.

Then her mind clicked.

Jayden.

He'd help her, wouldn't he?

Cerissa squared her shoulders.

She was innocent. He had to.

CHAPTER 42

DIGGING DEEPER

JAYDEN AND TIG'S HOUSE—THE NEXT DAY

After way too little sleep, Jayden rushed to get ready and then made breakfast for Cerissa and himself. If she remained confined in jail beyond today, he'd arrange to have food delivered on a time schedule that made sense. For now, he hoped she liked scrambled eggs, toast, and coffee.

As he cooked the eggs, he phoned Karen, per Tig's orders.

"Jayden! What's happening? Rolf's asleep—"

"I wanted to speak with you. I hope it's not too early."

"Nah, this is fine. What's up?"

"You listen to the gossip mill. Have you heard of anyone talking trash about Cerissa? Anyone who hates or resents her?"

"Why do people assume I'm a gossip?"

He scrubbed his hand over his shaved scalp. In his fatigue, he'd been too blunt. "Uh, I'm sorry, I didn't mean to offend. Tig guessed, being Cerissa's friend and all, you might have heard something and not shared it with Cerissa, not wanting to hurt her feelings."

"And why are you asking?"

The toaster's timer *dinged*. He took the toast and started buttering it. "Rolf didn't tell you?"

"Didn't tell me what?"

"Cerissa is in jail."

"What? Why?"

"She may have killed the mayor."

"*What?*" she screeched in his ear.

He moved the phone away. "Tig told Rolf last night, a little after midnight."

"That explains it. I went to sleep early, around midnight. I was exhausted after our meeting to draft the support statement." Karen *tsked*. "And Tig seriously thinks Cerissa killed the mayor?"

"The evidence points to her involvement."

"There's no way she did it, evidence or not. She just wouldn't."

"Which is why I'm asking whether anyone hates her enough to frame her."

Karen fell silent for a moment. "Jeez, Jayden. I desperately want to help, but I can't think of anything I've heard to suggest that."

"I mean, anyone—say like Anne-Louise? I know the history."

"Then you know they've patched things up. But if anything occurs to me, I'll call you back. Count on it."

Sierra Escondida Jail—Ten minutes later

Inside her cell, Cerissa bounced to her feet and gripped the bars as soon as she saw him. By the clock on the wall, it was almost eleven in the morning. "Jayden, oh thank the Goddess, it's you."

He carried a breakfast tray for her in one hand, and keys in the other. "I didn't know you would be this hungry, or I would have been here sooner."

"It's not the food. I remembered something. Something important."

"Can you wait until your attorney wakes up tonight?"

"No, I'll waive Miranda rights, whatever you need, but I have to tell you, now."

He paused, as if considering the matter. "Okay, let me take you to a conference room where it's easier to record the conversation—for both our protection. Do you want to eat first?"

"I can eat while we talk."

Jayden clipped his keys back on his belt, juggling the tray. "I'll be right back."

When he returned, he handcuffed her, and they moved into the conference room. Jayden started the recorder and confirmed Cerissa's limited Miranda waiver.

She uncovered the tray and scarfed down a triangle of toast. As much as she urgently wanted to tell Jayden her news, her growling stomach took precedence.

"Okay, what did you remember?" he asked.

She awkwardly shoveled in a bite of eggs, trying to feed herself despite the handcuffs, then took a sip of her coffee to wash down the eggs and began. "Something odd happened at the hearing. Olivia came up to me."

"Why is that odd?"

"I'd never met her before, and under the circumstances—I mean, Henry and Christine were on trial, and here she approaches me to invest in the clone blood venture."

"Olivia isn't known for her sensitivity toward mortals."

"No kidding. I tried to get rid of her quickly. Instead of leaving, she grabbed my wrist—it struck me as odd at the time. I don't like to be touched by strangers, and this was our first time meeting socially, so I yanked my arm out of her hand."

Cerissa stopped to take another bite of her breakfast. "I know I wore the bracelet to the hearing, because I'd been playing with the beads and twisting the bracelet around my wrist. And this morning, when I woke up, the memory hit me: the memory of glancing down at my bare wrist, my eyes blurred with tears, after Henry's sentence was reinstated. The bracelet was gone. I only vaguely noticed. I didn't have time to do anything about it or even think about it again because we had to rush to a conference room—Christine became hysterical and we had to make plans for her—and then I forgot about it altogether because of the flogging and everything that came after. But I know I lost the bracelet in the council chambers, and she was the only one who touched my wrist while I was there."

"Hmm." Jayden leaned back in his chair, and she took the opportunity to scarf down her eggs. When he sat forward, he pursed his lips, like he'd made up his mind. "The council meetings are recorded. There are two cameras facing the audience, to video whoever is at the audience microphone. If this happened before the hearing started, the odds of catching the interaction on video with Olivia aren't high."

"But you could check?"

"Yeah, don't worry. It's easy enough for me to do. I'll contact the town clerk's assistant to have him send over the recordings."

"Thank you. Thank you so much."

He stood. "Hey, they might show nothing."

"I understand, but it's worth trying."

Sierra Escondida Police Station—Shortly after sunset

Jayden had the video cued and waiting when Tig arrived at the police station for the night. He met her in the hallway leading to her office. "I have something to show you."

"Did you get a break in the case?"

"Yes and no. We need to bring in Olivia for questioning."

"Why Olivia?"

He led the way to the squad room and had her sit at the computer monitor. "Watch this."

The video quality wasn't great. He had to zoom in a lot, and the graininess made the details blur. After Tig finished viewing it, he moved the cursor back to the starting point and ran the video again.

"To me," he said, "it looks like Cerissa is wearing her bracelet, Olivia grips Cerissa's arm, and when she takes her hand away, the bracelet is gone. What I can't tell is whether she palmed the bracelet, or if it fell into Cerissa's purse. This flash here"—he paused the video—"that could be the bracelet falling. But without Ari to help with enhancement—"

"If we need to, we'll send the video to Mordida's crime lab." Tig leaned back in the chair. "You're right. The priority now is to bring Olivia in for questioning."

"I've called Zeke already—he's on standby to hear from you."

"Good. Ask him to cruise by Olivia's place and pick her up. I'll call Nicholas for a search warrant. We'll then send Zeke back with Nicholas to search her house while she's here with me."

Jayden already had the group text composed and hit the send arrow. "Done." Taking Tig in his arms, he gave her a deep welcome kiss. "I'll be glad when this is over."

"It can't happen too soon."

He checked his phone. "I'm going to drive to the gate. Dinner for me and Cerissa should be there waiting." His phone buzzed. A text, and he laughed when he read it. "Ah, if you think Anne-Louise was testy last night, wait until Zeke gets here with Olivia."

"Why?"

"According to Zeke, Olivia is 'as mad as a rattler and twice as ornery.'"

Tig smiled smugly. "Well, we'll see how long she stays that way after I finish with her."

CHAPTER 43

A NEW SUSPECT

MARCUS AND NICHOLAS'S HOME—AROUND THE SAME TIME

Marcus had been awake for forty minutes, and repeatedly phoned both Nicholas's cell and his town hall office with no answer. Worried, he paced in the living room. His next call would be to Tig.

Then it occurred to him to check Nicholas's bedroom.

He *whooshed* to the door and knocked, despite the desire to burst in.

"Come in," a sleepy voice said, immediately making him feel like an idiot. How could he not think to check this before?

His mate never napped at this hour. That was why. "What are you doing in bed? Are you ill?"

Nicholas rolled over, looking so cute with his messy bed head and bare chest. "Hey, hi there. I'm okay, but it's not like the moon and sun control my sleep." He yawned and sat up. "I didn't return from filling out all the paperwork on the searches until after you were tucked in for the day."

Marcus eased onto the edge of the mattress. "And what did you find?"

Nicholas stretched and grinned like a smug cat. "I don't know if I'm supposed to tell you. Tig swore me in as a reserve officer for the search."

"I'm the town attorney. Of course you can tell me."

Nicholas reached for his phone, which was charging next to his bed, and tapped the button to unmute the ringer. "Maybe I should ask Tig first."

Marcus intercepted the phone, taking the device from him. "There is no need for that. Now tell me."

"All right, all right. The answer is: nothing. We found nothing incriminating." Another big yawn. "No crossbow, no silver ingots, no bolts, no melting furnace, nothing. But we also didn't find Cerissa's bracelet, so the one Tig has is probably hers."

Marcus let out a long breath. That was good news, but not perfect. "Which means Cerissa is still a suspect."

"Yeah. I don't entirely like the results, but it is what it is."

The phone Marcus held began ringing. He looked at the screen. Tig. "Your new boss wants to speak to you."

Nicholas took the phone and tapped the speaker icon. "Hello?"

"I need a new search warrant, and I want you to be part of the search team."

"Okay." Nicholas rubbed at his eyes. "Give me a second." He pantomimed to Marcus to find pen and paper.

Marcus grabbed the items from the small nearby desk and brought them to him.

"Go ahead, Tig. I have Marcus on the call, too."

"Perfect. We need a search warrant for Olivia Paquin's home. Same implements as the other warrants."

"And the basis?" Nicholas asked as he scribbled down the information.

"It appears she took or accidentally acquired Cerissa's bracelet at the council meeting."

Hell's bells. Olivia? Marcus tugged at his mustache, his mind spinning as he parsed all the ramifications. Olivia supplied an essential service to the town. If she killed the mayor and used the bracelet to frame Cerissa, who would take over the expired donor blood deliveries?

Nicholas looked hesitant as he said into the phone, "That's good news, right?"

"It's messy news." Tig paused. "So when can you be at the station?"

"Marcus just woke me. Give me twenty minutes for a shower and coffee. Marcus will draft the warrant while I get ready."

"That works. See you soon." The line went dead.

Nicholas swung his legs over the bed and stood, a bit wobbly. "I haven't felt this beat up since I pulled an all-nighter in law school."

"I'll prepare the warrant, send the paperwork off to the judge, and meet you in the kitchen. Would you like a toast and fried egg sandwich to go with your coffee?"

"Yes, thanks. You're a life saver."

Fifteen minutes later, the judge returned the signed warrant. Marcus had started the coffee and was frying two eggs when Nicholas appeared in the kitchen looking beautiful, dressed in jeans and a long-sleeve t-shirt, his hair partially damp from the shower.

The toast popped up. "Grab that, please."

Nicholas placed the two slices on a plate and smothered them in butter, which always struck Marcus as odd, considering how fit he was and how picky about nutrition he could be. But that was how he liked his toast.

Marcus slid the spatula under the over-easy eggs and delivered them to the waiting toast. "I was thinking."

"Yeah?" Nicholas poured a large travel mug of coffee. "About what?"

"We should delay our vacation until Tig closes the case."

Nicholas's shoulders drooped, and he took a bite of his egg sandwich. "I understand, I do. But then there will be something else—"

"No. I won't let our trip be put off again." Rebuilding their trust and love were too important to Marcus, and keeping his word about their vacation plans was part of that process. "By the time the case is closed, Christine should be ready to take over for me. She can handle whatever arises."

"And if the case is never closed?"

"Then we'll leave in a month. Christine shouldn't need a babysitter by then."

"Okay, you've got yourself a deal."

Nicholas leaned over to him. Marcus opened his lips, inviting a deeper kiss. He wasn't going to seal the deal with anything less and didn't mind the taste of egg.

"I should get going." Nicholas wrapped his sandwich in a paper towel and took an extra to catch crumbs. "Oh, but there is one interesting thing I learned at Henry and Cerissa's."

"What was that?"

"I'm not sure I should tell you," Nicholas said with a teasing flutter of his long eyelashes.

What game was this? "Just tell me."

"Well, if you promise to keep it a secret."

"Nicholas—"

"Let's say, from what I found, Henry and Cerissa are into more than vanilla sex."

Nicholas waggled his eyebrows, offered another quick kiss, and, with coffee and sandwich in hand, rushed to the front door to grab his keys.

Marcus *tsked*. Nicholas shouldn't gossip, even with him. Then an idea occurred to him. Was his mate hinting at something?

Hmm. Maybe they could discuss it on their vacation.

Marcus was happy with their sex life—more than happy now that they were mated—but he was always open to upping his game, within limits.

CHAPTER 44

MURKIER

SIERRA ESCONDIDA POLICE STATION—TEN MINUTES LATER

Tig took the chair across from Olivia in the small conference room and started the recorder. She placed a file folder on the table, the one holding the search warrant Nicholas had dropped off. "Thank you for coming in to talk with us."

Olivia gave her a dirty look. "Bloody hell. It's not like I had any choice, dearie. Zeke insisted."

"We're talking with potential witnesses. Let's begin with when you last saw the mayor."

"At the amphitheater. I stayed for the whole show."

Tig held her tongue for the sake of the investigation, but the way Olivia characterized Henry's flogging as entertainment disgusted her. "Did you leave before the mayor did?"

"I stuck around to the end." Olivia waved her fingers haughtily, the tip of one finger wrapped in white. "Took forever to muddle along through the crowd to my car."

Tig narrowed her eyes at the flash of the white bandage tape. "What did you do to your finger?"

"Oh, this?" Olivia displayed her index finger wrapped in gauze. "I was carving a new bust. The chisel slipped on the marble and took off my fingertip. Hardly ideal, but the tip will grow back."

Olivia was well known for her sculptures. She'd carved the mayor's bust from white marble, which sat in the alcove leading into the council chambers, and she'd sold pieces through the art gallery Henry and his sister, Méi, owned.

Odd, though. For Olivia to slice off her fingertip, to cut though the bone, the chisel's tip would have to be near her finger, a rookie mistake. But mistakes could happen to anyone. "I hope your hand heals quickly."

"In a few days, it'll be as right as rain." Olivia splayed her fingers nonchalantly.

Yeah, regrowing bone took longer than flesh wounds to heal—they were the exception to day sleep returning a vampire to their former appearance. "Now, you said you saw the mayor at the amphitheater. Did you speak to him last night?"

"No chance to, dearie. He was right busy."

"When was the last time you had any private discussions with the mayor?"

Olivia looked thoughtful for a moment. "Why, two nights before. I met him in his office."

If nothing else, the information helped fill in the timeline around the last days of the mayor's life. "What did you discuss?"

"My blood franchise. The ten-year license is up for renewal in fourteen months. Never too early to start discussing the terms."

Tig made a note of the topic. If the mayor opposed the renewal, Olivia would have a ton of motive. "Did he mention anything to lead you to believe someone had it in for him?"

"Now that you ask, he did mention something. He planned on voting against Leopold's project."

"You mean Cerissa's project?"

Olivia flipped her fingers dismissively. "She's just a mortal who works for Leopold. It's Leopold's project."

Olivia's condescending attitude toward mortals was well known. "What did the mayor say?"

"He didn't like the idea of over a hundred mortals working for her lab, even though they'd be outside the walls."

Hmm. Tig had spoken with him about the changes a biotech facility would bring to the community, with the possibility of hiring additional officers for the sub-station to police the business district. Winston never mentioned any opposition to the project.

"How did the topic come up?" Tig asked.

"Well, dearie, I hadn't paid much attention to what Leopold planned on doing. When I stopped by to welcome Christine to our ranks—and I dropped off a lovely gift hamper, too—Henry said his child exclusively drank the blood produced by clones Cerissa created."

Olivia paused with a smirk, as if the conclusion of the story was obvious.

Tig rolled her eyes. "Go on."

"You see, since the mayor opposed more mortals being involved, I suggested we combine distribution under my franchise if Leopold's project was approved—for a percentage of the profit, of course. We don't need extra mortals on the Hill doing deliveries because of *Leopold*."

"And what was the mayor's response to your proposal?"

"Why, he agreed with me. When my franchise comes up for renewal, I plan to sort it nice and tidy. I'm sure whoever the new mayor is will also agree." Olivia's smirk turned into a big, self-satisfied grin. "With the proposal to bring in a dozen or two unaffiliated vampires, we're going to need more supplies, dearie. I can tell you that. I don't collect enough donor blood to feed those extra mouths."

Was there any way to confirm the mayor's position on Olivia's franchise and Cerissa's project? Tig pursed her lips. They may need a warrant for Winston's office at town hall. She made a note to remind herself. "All right. Think back two nights ago—after you left the amphitheater, where did you go?"

"I drove straight home. Quarterly closing, I had accounting work to do. Was in the thick of it until last night. Never left the house, not until Zeke stopped by tonight."

Tig looked up from her notes. "Do you always do your hair and makeup even if you aren't going out?"

Olivia made a point of fluffing her reddish-blonde hair. "Of course, dearie. A lady always likes to look nice. And besides, I'm going to headquarters later to make sure everything is in tiptop shape for tomorrow's delivery."

Olivia owned a warehouse located outside the gates in the business district. The massive refrigeration units kept the blood cold until delivery. "When was the last time you went to your headquarters?"

"Oh, about four nights ago? Zeke let me take my own car here, so as soon as this business is settled, I'll drive over there."

Which meant the car wouldn't be searched, since it wasn't at her home, and the car wasn't specifically called out on the search warrant. She texted Jayden, asking him to contact Marcus and add Olivia's car and business location to the warrant.

Tig took the bracelet out of the bag, having saved the key evidence for last, because if anything might trigger Olivia to lawyer up, the bracelet would. "Have you ever seen this before?"

"Why yes. At the council hearing, I said hello to Cerissa, and she wore a bracelet very much like the one you're holding. Somehow, the beads or the chain must have caught on my purse strap. I found the bracelet in the side pocket when I went to refresh my lipstick and returned it to her."

Tig fisted her hand around the pen she'd been using to take notes. Olivia had an explanation for everything. "When did you give the bracelet back to Cerissa?"

Olivia stared into space. "Ah, I believe, yes—when everyone left the council chambers to go to the amphitheater. We were outdoors, and she was quite distraught. I handed the bracelet to her as we walked. She didn't even say thank you, the ungrateful minger. She stuffed it in her purse, and that's the last I saw of it."

Dammit. No surveillance cameras were installed outside the council chambers, so she had no way to confirm Olivia's story. "Was anyone else around when you gave the bracelet to Cerissa?"

"I can't say for certain. We were all packed next to each other like sardines." Olivia furrowed her brow, which caused her drawn-on eyebrows to squish together. "Why is the bracelet important? Don't tell me it has something to do with the mayor's murder?"

Tig knew better than to answer Olivia's question. "Thank you for coming in." She removed a copy of the search warrant from the folder she'd carried into the interview room. "This is for you. While we've been talking, my officers have been searching your home."

She blinked. "You're taking the piss."

"No, I'm not joking, Olivia. Read the warrant yourself."

Olivia screeched in pure fury. "This is a shocking cock-up, even for you!"

Ignoring Olivia's outburst, Tig continued, "My officers will also search your business and car. You are not to leave the Hill until they finish. We'll provide a list of what they find. Thank you again for coming in."

CHAPTER 45

CATCH AND RELEASE

SIERRA ESCONDIDA POLICE STATION—A SHORT TIME LATER

After the interview, Tig ushered Olivia out to the lobby, where she rendezvoused with Jayden. "Did the new warrant arrive?"

He held out a folded document to Olivia. "Here's your copy of the revised warrant. If you'll come with me, I need you to open the door to your car."

Olivia ripped it out of his hand and flapped the paper in the air. "I'm calling the vice mayor. This is an absolute invasion of my privacy."

"Be my guest," Tig replied. "In the meantime, assist Jayden, or we'll be forced to break into your car."

"Bloody wankers," Olivia spat, and stormed out the door.

Tig motioned to Christine, who sat in the lobby with Henry. "Please come with me. Henry, wait here."

The founder started to stand. "But—"

"Nope. Not happening yet. Please be patient."

Tig placed Christine in the conference room, then took Cerissa from the jail cell—handcuffing her first. Once everyone was seated, Tig drummed her fingers on the table, staring at Cerissa and frowning. She had to ask the question, even though she suspected what the answer would be. "Did Olivia return the bracelet to you?"

Cerissa looked offended. "Absolutely not. But that means you found the video of her stealing the bracelet."

Damn. Tig ground her teeth. Having a scientist for a suspect meant tiptoeing on eggshells so as not to reveal too much. "That's an exaggeration. What we found was video of the bracelet missing from your arm after Olivia spoke to you."

"Same thing."

"Why would Olivia try to frame you?"

"She has the donor blood franchise. Maybe she sees clone blood as a threat."

"That doesn't make sense." Tig shook her head. "With the proposal to expand the community, to create more vampires *and* open up homes for the unaffiliated, we're going to need both the donor blood she provides and the clone blood your business will offer."

"Stop," Christine said, holding up her hand. "It's not Cerissa's responsibility to figure out Olivia's motivation. That's your job."

Why was Christine blocking this line of inquiry? Cerissa might have an idea why Olivia framed her, and so far, the lack of motive made Olivia an unlikely suspect.

Tig looked at her notes. "You had your purse with you when the mortals surrounded you?"

"Yes."

If Olivia told the truth—if she did return the bracelet—any one of those mortals could have lifted the bracelet from Cerissa's purse. But why would one of the mortals want to frame her? Then something struck Tig. "When you arrived home afterward, did you carry your purse inside with you?"

"Yes, of course."

"Where did you put your purse?"

Cerissa furrowed her brow and cocked her head to the side. "On the foyer table, where I always do."

"The table near the front door?"

"Yes. But why—" Cerissa's frown deepened. "I told you, Henry remained in bed next to me the entire time."

"But Anne-Louise didn't. You said she went downstairs, all alone for hours."

"Oh. Oh!" Her eyes grew big. "When can I go home?"

Tig drummed her fingers again, thinking about Cerissa's question as she watched Christine suck blood through a mini-straw. It struck Tig as the weirdest thing she'd ever seen—using a child's generic juice pouch to package dark wine—but on the other hand, the arrangement looked handy when a vampire had to travel.

Crap. With all the stress, her mind had gone off on a tangent instead of focusing on the question she wasn't ready to answer.

Maybe imagining the cougar last night had been her mind telling her she needed a break. Except she had no time to take one.

Christine stopped sipping and cleared her throat. "You have no evidence tying my client to the murder. The only evidence you have is the bracelet Olivia stole from her and planted at the scene."

"And her stated wish to kill the mayor."

"Heat of the moment." Christine waved the pouch, dismissing the idea. "Besides, you have no proof she acted on those words. You don't have probable cause to formally charge her. If you try, we'll challenge it and insist on a bail hearing."

"I already explained we don't do bail hearings here."

"But Marcus did tell me about another option you use: home detention. We live in a gated community. There are guards who would stop her if she tried to leave. There is no reason or basis to keep her locked in jail."

The attorney was right on all counts.

"Fine. With an ankle monitor, I'll let her return home. She can go anywhere inside the Hill, but she doesn't leave the community. If she needs to go outside the gates, she has to clear it with us first."

Cerissa glanced at Christine. "I can live with that."

Squad room—Ten minutes later

Cerissa gratefully collected her purse and clothes from Jayden, who whispered, "Good luck," as he strapped on the ankle monitor.

"Can this thing get wet? Because the first thing I'm going do is take a long, hot shower."

"No problem. It's waterproof to a hundred and thirty feet."

She gave an unladylike snort. "Jayden, there's nowhere on the Hill I can dive that deep underwater. Our pool is twelve feet, maximum."

He finished crimping the flap in place. "Will you be at the council meeting tomorrow night?"

She frowned. They were scheduled to discuss appointments for the open seats.

"After all this, I wasn't sure the other mates would want me to attend." She accepted the small plastic box Jayden handed her. After slipping on her engagement ring, she kissed the stone, and then fastened her watch strap.

"I want you there," he said, escorting her to the restroom. "But maybe talk with Luis or Haley first."

"Thanks, Jayden, I will."

She ducked into the restroom, stripped off the jail's horrible striped jumpsuit, and quickly donned her street clothes. Never had she been so happy to leave a place, almost running down the hallway to where Henry waited. Her smile grew bigger when she spotted him, standing by the door wearing a suit and tie, looking dashing, his deep brown eyes flashing with happiness when he saw her.

She ran right into his arms. "I've missed you so much."

"Come, *cariña*. Let's go home."

Christine came charging along the same hall. "Don't forget me."

"We would never do that, Christine." Cerissa reached out a hand and pulled her into a group hug. "Thank you for all your help."

Henry *harrumphed* and pushed Christine back. Cerissa got the message and stepped to the other side, putting more distance between her and the baby vampire.

All she wanted was to take her small family home and forget about the last twenty-four hours.

Tig appeared in the lobby. "Off the record?"

Christine crossed her arms. "Go ahead."

"Guard her carefully," Tig said, inclining her head in Cerissa's direction.

Henry's face clouded over. "I will not let Christine—"

"Not Christine. If—off the record—someone tried to frame her, they may try something else."

"I see. Thank you." Henry squeezed Cerissa's waist. "She will be protected. You may count on it."

Tig started to leave, and then swung back around. "One other thing. I don't want you talking with other residents about the case, particularly Olivia's potential involvement. We need time to run down all leads."

"All right," Cerissa said reluctantly. Finding the real killer took priority over her feelings. Although Olivia stole her bracelet, she couldn't prove who killed Winston. So, as much as she wanted to shout "Olivia's the killer" from the rooftops, she'd put the community's needs first.

During the drive, Cerissa's phone rang. *Leopold*. When she answered, his first words were "Did you do it?"

"Leopold!"

"I wouldn't blame you if you did. I'd only fault you for getting caught."

Cerissa stared at the screen, not sure how to reply. She had met Leopold over two hundred years ago. He had been enmeshed in European politics, advising mortals, and almost got himself staked for his troubles. She'd saved his life, and he never questioned how she could live such a long life and look so young. A bit of her aura had helped to ease his mind and bring him to accept the situation.

But murder? How could Leopold make such a suggestion?

"I didn't kill the mayor. I don't know who did. I've been released with an ankle monitor and orders not to leave the Hill."

"Do you need me to send anyone to assist? I have attorneys on retainer—"

"Christine Dunne is representing me."

"The new vampire? Let me send someone else to help you. Someone with more experience."

"Christine has been an attorney for over thirty years. She's doing fine. I'm out of jail, aren't I?"

"Yes, yes—but you should never have been arrested in the first place. You're my envoy. That blasted police chief should have accorded you greater respect than to lock you in a cell."

"Leopold, I'm more concerned with the fact that someone is trying to frame me and almost succeeded. When the mayor spoke to you, did he give you *any* clue as to who resented our project? Was it Olivia Paquin?"

"If I had known who made the complaint, I would have dealt with the matter myself. But Winston would not name names, the bastard. Do you want me to send an assassin to kill Olivia?"

"Leopold, no!" The last thing she wanted was Olivia dead. Everyone would suspect her. "Are you trying to get me convicted?"

"No, I—"

"Don't do anything. Just be patient," she said, hoping her racing heart would soon calm down. "I'm sure Tig will get to the truth."

Chapter 46

Hot Water

Rancho Bautista del Murciélago—Fifteen minutes later

When they arrived home, Henry escorted the ladies to the kitchen straight away and warmed blood for Christine. The tightness in his chest relaxed as he worked. All he wanted to do was hold Cerissa, but he had to attend to his child first. It was his obligation.

"How does your back feel?" Cerissa asked, perching on one of the stools at the kitchen island.

"All is well. I'm fully healed, and no longer sore."

"I'm glad."

Henry glanced over as Christine sat down at the table, pleased to see her keeping her distance from Cerissa. His child started scrolling through something on her phone. He no longer felt the need to supervise her phone use. Having a task—in this case, representing Cerissa—had given her both a distraction and focus, but the accident had also changed her level of caution with mortals. He felt confident she wouldn't contact anyone, wouldn't entice someone to her so she could feed.

Besides, she needed to be able to talk with her support group, and with Marcus or Tig about Cerissa's case.

"Evelina and Wolfie are coming by shortly to take me to their group's meeting." Christine looked up at him from the phone. "They scheduled the gathering so the members could meet me. They'll deliver me there, and Zeke will bring me home."

Henry nodded. He would voice his objections over Zeke shortly. Right now, he needed to establish a sense of peace and check in with his child.

"How are you feeling?" Henry placed the mug on the table in front of Christine and leaned against the table, watching her.

"I—I," she began, then looked down at the dark wine. "Defending Cerissa, defending you—my work distracted me from thinking about Patrick."

"Perhaps it is more than a distraction. Your work gives you purpose. You bring value to the community, an asset we couldn't easily replace if you left us."

Christine kept her eyes lowered. "When I'm busy, I don't obsess about what I did. But when I stop, when I'm by myself, the grief and guilt returns." She let out a big breath. "The loss feels like a gaping hole in my chest, as if someone reached in and yanked out my heart."

"That is understandable." Henry squeezed Christine's shoulder, hoping it would offer some comfort. "You are not alone in your experience."

The doorbell rang.

"That's for me." Christine scooted her chair back quickly, grabbing a go-cup to transfer her dark wine into.

"I am glad you are going to their support group"—Henry stepped away to allow Christine to go past him—"but I'm not pleased you are seeing more of Zeke."

Cerissa sighed. He shot her a look not to disagree with him.

Christine screwed on the lid to the go-cup. "I'll have my phone if you need me."

As soon as Christine cleared the doorway, Cerissa laughed. "She skillfully sidestepped your comment. I still can't figure out if a new vampire is like having a toddler or a teenager."

"Maybe both," he replied, stepping over to wrap his arms around his mate. "I am glad to see you in good spirits, *cariña*."

She stayed seated on the kitchen stool but melted against him. "Actually, I'm feeling lightheaded, like I've been trapped in a whirlwind and spun around."

"Being arrested for murder will do that to you."

"Yeah, but it's more than spending the night in jail. It's the fear that whoever tried to frame me will succeed. Or that the killer will never be caught, and I'll always be under suspicion."

Henry's stomach tightened. The same fear had spiked his own anxiety. "Ari told me what your lens video showed when he returned your lenses to me—the case is on your bedstand." He stroked her hair down her back. "Didn't Tig believe you? That Olivia stole your bracelet and planted it by the mayor's body?"

"Olivia said she returned the bracelet to me. I don't remember that at all. But I also didn't remember losing the bracelet in the first place. The whole evening was traumatic—"

"Ask Ari to check the video from your lenses for the time period after the council meeting adjourned and find out if Olivia did indeed return the bracelet."

"That's my point—I should have asked Ari already. But I'm numb and my brain is only working at half speed."

He squeezed her tightly. "You are having a normal reaction to trauma."

"And I feel guilty—both for Patrick's death and for what happened to you. If I hadn't seduced you—"

"No. Stop." He stepped back, making eye contact with her, holding her at arm's length. "Don't ever say that. If anyone is to blame, it's me. I should have called Gaea or Marcus or someone else to come watch Christine so you and I could take a longer break. But I underestimated the risk."

"It still feels like my fault." She turned away on the stool to lean against the kitchen island, guilt in the set of her shoulders, and rested her face in her hands. "Why didn't I fight harder to get a babysitter for Christine? If I hadn't been feeling neglected, with a touch of jealousy thrown in the mix, I wouldn't have agreed so quickly."

"Now you are overreacting—" He stopped, rethinking his choice of words. "You aren't overreacting, but you are taking on blame for events outside your control."

"How can you be so calm?"

"Part of it is my old-world view of sin. Like I told Christine, the process of my faith soothes me: I confessed and accepted my guilt and punishment. I start over, anew."

"Maybe I should try your approach."

"I'll say the same again: it may not work the same for you. Or it may. Everyone is different." He gently pivoted her until she faced him again and brushed the loose, dark brown strands from her eyes. "However, in this case, it is my humble opinion that you have nothing to be guilty about. You raised the question of whether it was safe to leave Christine alone, and I said yes. Christine is my child. The decision was mine, not yours, to make. Weeks ago, when you said we'd be parents, I failed to disagree. But I was wrong not to speak up."

"I participated in the process. We gave birth to her—"

"I am sorry, Cerissa, but if I agree with you, I would be doing you a disservice. It would be like saying the obstetrician was responsible for the actions of all the children they delivered."

"It's not the same thing. I'm kind of like her adopted mother."

"Not quite. Vampires only have one parent."

Cerissa exhaled a loud breath and crossed her arms. "You're not going to let me win this one."

He cupped her cheek. "Are you mad at me?"

"No, not really. You're probably right."

"I'm always right. I just don't always express myself diplomatically. I am trying harder."

She chuckled. "You are trying harder. I'll give you that." The tall stool she sat on put her at hip height to him. He stepped between her legs, which she wrapped around him and tightened, pulling him into a sexy embrace, touching her lips to his. "Thank you, Quique."

"You know," he began, and nuzzled her, pushing her hair back with his nose and whispering into her ear. "I've been fantasizing doing to you what you did to me."

He could picture her helpless, at his mercy, as he licked every inch of her.

Near his lips, the pulse in her neck quickened, but with the crystal still off, he wasn't entirely certain why. After the flogging, they'd used her phone to stop the crystal's transmissions so she wouldn't feel his pain. Now, he missed the connection.

"You made me tingle all over just saying it." She gave a little shiver. "But I feel weird doing anything with handcuffs so soon after being in police ones. All I want is a hot shower."

"And you've had dinner already?"

"At the jail—Jayden got takeout while Tig interviewed Olivia."

"Then perhaps a shower together? I found time to install the grab bars last week."

Her beautiful emerald eyes brightened. "Ooh, that sounds perfect."

Chapter 47

HEALING

Rancho Bautista del Murciélago—Minutes later

Cerissa stepped under the hot spray face first, her hands braced against the smooth stone tiles lining the shower walls. On the other side of the clear glass door, Henry took his time removing his shirt.

She tilted back her head and, closing her eyes, let the water wash over her.

With her eyes shut, the sight of Henry being flayed alive by the whip crawled across her inner eyelids. Other scenes rapidly followed: Christine in the ICU, Patrick lying dead on the patio tiles, the jail cell door closing, locking her in.

As the warm water melted the tension in her muscles, the feelings she'd caged inside rose in her throat, and she let go with a sob.

Henry opened the door and took her into his arms. "Cerissa, what is wrong?"

She leaned into him, the terrible guilt finally escaping. No matter how logical his earlier argument, the feeling of being responsible engulfed her.

She'd failed both Henry and Christine. She'd failed to protect them from the beginning.

She should have insisted on scrubbing in at the hospital for Christine's surgery. She should have insisted Christine not be left alone in the pool house. She should have—

I should have stopped the flogging.

Tears streamed down her face, her wet hair clinging to her back as she cried on his shoulder. Gently, he helped lower her to the shower bench. Kneeling in front of her, he brushed her hair aside and palmed her cheek.

She couldn't stop the sobs as they became hiccups. She hated when that happened, and swiped at her eyes. "I'm sorry. I'm so sorry."

"You have nothing to apologize for."

She wrapped her arms around his neck and pulled him tight to her. "I was such a coward. I couldn't watch. I turned away."

"*Cariña*, you *were* there for me. You never left my mind. Your love sheltered me, gave me strength to endure."

The tightness in her chest choked the air from her lungs. "I—I didn't, I couldn't"—she hiccupped again—"do anything to stop them."

"I'm glad you didn't try. It had to happen. If you'd taken us to the Enclave, flashed us out of there, we would never have been able to return."

She nodded against his neck. She recognized this. She recognized the logic of his argument. She had thought the same at the amphitheater.

After taking in a deep, shuddering breath, she said, "You're right."

She remained pressed tightly against him until her sobs quieted.

"I have an idea," Henry eventually said. "Let's finish showering and go downstairs and light a fire in the fireplace. We have the house to ourselves until midnight. We can wrap up in blankets and cuddle. How does that sound?"

"You're not disappointed?"

"Of course not. We can play in the shower another time. Come. I'll help you wash your hair." He moved the showerhead to the side and squeezed a liberal amount of shampoo into his palm, then worked his fingers through her hair.

She relaxed as he massaged her scalp. The jail's institutional smell permeated everything. The shampoo's herbal scent—argan oil and rosemary—lifted her spirits.

"Lean forward." He took the hand sprayer, flipped the directional switch, and rinsed the shampoo from her hair. After repeating the process, and then using conditioner, he helped her to stand.

She pressed the lever sending the water back to the showerhead, and let the spray take the conditioner away.

"Soap?" he asked, holding out a squeeze bottle of a gentle body wash, similar to baby shampoo.

"Thanks."

But the moment the soap hit her hand, something inside her shifted. Between her tears and the warm water, the tightness in her lungs released, and pressing close to Henry's naked body awakened a different feeling.

Instead of smoothing the soap over her skin, she lathered his chest. As she did, his cock responded.

"Ignore him."

She chuckled, giving him a coy smile. "Hard to do."

She slid her hand down his abs, drawing a fingernail through the sexy trail of black hair leading south, to wrap her slick hand around him. Gently squeezing, she ran her hand back and forth along his length.

"Cerissa, are you sure you—"

"Shut up and kiss me."

His lips slanted over hers. "If you're sure—"

He always had to get in the last word.

She opened to him, letting his tongue caress hers, the taste of him familiar and welcome. She loved the way he grasped her hair, pulling her tighter to him, as his other hand fingered her nipple until the peak firmed so tight that she thought she'd come from his touch alone. The hefty feel of his erection in her hand only ignited her further.

She gripped his wrist, taking his hand away from her breast and pushing his fingers between her legs. The water sluicing over them hadn't washed away the slick wetness, and he slid his index and middle fingers into her.

She moaned against his throat when his thumb found her sensitive bud, and after refreshing the gentle soap on her hand, she gripped his erection again, speeding up the slick back-and-forth. He groaned, his knees softening their support for a moment as he rocked, pulling in and out of her hand.

Clutching the grab bar with her other hand for leverage, she pressed into what his fingers did, deepening the reach of the ones inside her as his thumb drew circles on her swollen clit. The tension built as she let go of everything she'd carried into the shower—all the guilt, all the fear, all the sorrow. She loved him so much, loved how he made her feel, loved what they had together. It was their love that filled her now.

She raised her head, offering her lips, letting him capture the moan that escaped her. He shuddered against her, his breaths coming rapidly as he pumped into her hand vigorously. He thrust one more time with a big shudder, and his hard length pulsed against her hand as he shot his spend against the shower wall.

He sped up his thumb's circles, and she held her breath, feeling the cliff approach, and with one more circle, she fell—fell into his arms, fell into his heart, fell into her own moment of perfect bliss.

He caught her, wrapping his arm around her. "I love you, *cariña*. I love you so much." When she opened her eyes, he smoothed back her hair. "Please keep sharing your heart with me. Don't ever be afraid to open up about what you're feeling. I'll always be here for you."

His love lifted her. "And I'll always be here for you."

Chapter 48

WARMTH

Rancho Bautista del Murciélago—Fifteen minutes later

After drying off and throwing on a pair of black boxer shorts, Henry lit a fire in the drawing room fireplace, using his least favorite sections of the *Wall Street Journal* wadded under the kindling. He didn't subscribe to the WSJ for their sports coverage or the opinions of their pundits. He subscribed for the latest financial news and to keep an eye on his investments.

The paper caught fire quickly, flames licking the kindling, and soon the large log was alight, the scent of burning pine filling the air. The comfy smell threw him back in time. He didn't burn pine too often because it risked creosote build-up in the chimney, but when he did, something about the scent said "home" to him.

After gathering blankets and a sheepskin throw rug, he made a nest for them in front of the blaze, then poured her a scotch. She was still upstairs drying her hair and had looked like she could use something stronger than wine. He made a quick dash to the kitchen to prepare a fruit and cheese plate in case she was hungry, and returned, everything ready for her on the raised fireplace hearth.

When he heard the floor creak, he glanced over at the open drawing room doors to see her standing there, wearing a long cotton nightshirt.

Perfect.

He wore only a pair of black microfiber boxer briefs—the kind that hugged his butt tightly. As much as he liked silk boxers, she'd complimented him heavily when he wore the formfitting ones, and he took the hint.

The only thing puzzling him was the phone she carried. Why bring it downstairs now?

"That looks so romantic," she whispered, her voice airy, like a spring breeze gently swaying the branches.

"Come. Join me."

His heartbeat sped up as he watched her. She'd left her beautiful hair loose, slightly glistening with oil, and wore no makeup, making her look ten years younger than the thirty-two years she pretended to be. She eased onto the fur rug and bent her knees, staring into the fire and laying the phone aside. He took the space behind her, spreading his legs to let her lean against his chest.

"Comfortable?" he asked.

She lifted the glass of scotch, took a sip, and snuggled against him. "Very."

"I'm sorry you had to spend last night in the town's jail. Did Tig treat you well?"

"I have no complaints about how they treated me." She took another sip and placed the glass back on the raised river-stone hearth. "I just wish I wasn't still under suspicion."

Despite the anxiety rumbling in the back of his own mind, he had every confidence in Tig. Given enough time, the chief would find the real killer. So he forced himself to calmly say his next words. "This too will pass."

The firelight on her face made her glow. "There was one funny moment, though," she said, with a soft giggle. "If Tig says anything to you, I want you prepared."

"What happened?"

She leaned her head back, looking up at him. "The sleep pod provided privacy, so I figured I'd catch some cougar time. I was afraid to ask for my stabilizer—I didn't want to answer any questions about the hypo or the drug."

He clenched his jaw. She should never have been made to suffer for want of medication she needed. "I'm sorry."

"Well, Tig came in to ask me something and lifted the lid without warning me. I didn't have time to change back."

Fear ruffled the hairs on his arms. "How did you explain it?"

"I hissed at her, and she dropped the lid. I morphed back, shimmied into the striped jail clothes, climbed out, and acted completely shocked by her comment about the mountain lion. Ari backed my play. All you need to do is act mystified if she asks."

The fear dissipated. Cerissa had handled the situation well, as she did most things, and he could almost picture the look of shock on Tig's face. In all likelihood, Tig would dismiss the event from her mind as too bizarre to be real. "Thank you for telling me."

Cerissa curled her legs under her and snuggled her face against his chest. "What was it like?"

"What, *mi amor*?"

"Ah, the amphitheater, the..."

"You have a difficult time using the word, don't you?"

She nodded against his chest. Clearly, she needed help processing what happened, and he wouldn't deny her, much as he hated reliving the experience.

"Standing up there wasn't as hard as I thought it would be. You would not have been able to hear, but Anne-Louise told me she'd modified the whip by removing the metal tips—so the lashing wasn't as vicious as it could have been."

Cerissa sat up, her emerald eyes growing big. "Metal tips?"

"Yes, historically, a cat-o'-nine-tails included metal tips. More damage would have been inflicted if she'd left those on." He kissed the top of her head, stroking her arm where he held her. "The pain was actually worse afterward. At the time—"

"The adrenaline—"

"And your help through the crystal. Both, probably, kept the pain muted during the actual whipping. Afterward, walking away and getting in the car, well, I wasn't sure if I'd be able to drive, particularly reaching for the stick shift, which pulled at the torn muscle. But I managed. Then climbing the stairs to your room was...challenging. I barely had enough energy to fall face first onto your bed."

"I'm sorry," she said, snuggling in tight against him.

"Don't be." He stroked her hair. "It was my own fault, as I've said before. But now, the sentence is done with, and the threat will no longer hang over my head. With the mayor dead, I doubt any future councils will be imposing such a penalty for a long time."

"Nicholas wants to draft maximum penalties based on the transgression, so the council has less discretion to do whatever they want. The councilmembers' personal opinions about the transgressor shouldn't factor into the decision-making."

"Perhaps such a system would be fairer." He shrugged. "But sometimes the current way has been to my benefit."

He felt her head move against his chest. "Not this time."

"Point taken."

"Are you having flashbacks at all? I, ah, can't tell if you're holding the pain in. The crystal's been silent because you had me cut the app two nights ago."

So that was why she'd brought her phone. "Would you like to turn it on?"

"Yes, very much so."

"Go ahead."

She held out the phone to allow the camera to recognize her face, and then tapped the app to reconnect the crystal. She fell silent, and he took the opportunity to relax and let her emotions mingle with his. Hard as it was to drop his shields, she deserved to know what he felt.

And right now, he felt peaceful, more peaceful than he had since the whipping. Being close to her went a long way toward healing him.

"Have they found Patrick's body yet?" she asked. "What's left of it? Tig wouldn't tell me."

"The coyotes and other scavengers did their work. There wasn't much left but bones, and some of those had been dragged off and found yards away."

"So his family will never know how he really died."

"With Dr. Clarke's report as coroner and 'heart failure' listed as the cause, Tig notified Patrick's next of kin, his daughter. We planted the idea that he had a stroke or heart attack, got confused, drove the wrong direction, and when he tried to turn around, he ran off into a ditch, flattening a tire. Tig siphoned off his gas and let the engine run until the motor died, then left the body a hundred feet away to sell the story. Again, we told his daughter he had started walking back before passing out. Marcus will try to negotiate a settlement agreement and pay the daughter an equitable amount to compensate for her loss."

"On what basis? What did the town do wrong?"

"An accidental death like this, caused by a vampire, is handled by the town. It's part of what we pay taxes, fees, and fines to cover."

"No, that's not what I meant. In the eyes of the outside world, the town didn't do anything wrong. How does Marcus justify the settlement to Patrick's daughter?"

"Marcus will tell the mortal there was a problem with directional signs. But most people will not argue or even ask. Not expecting any payment for the tragic accident, they will accept the money. And if necessary, one of the community's members will be dispatched to *persuade* the mortal to sign the settlement agreement."

"You mean mesmerize."

"Yes." Remembering the orderly at the morgue, he chuckled. She hated his mesmerizing skills until she needed to use them. "Sometimes, when you try to do the right thing, it backfires. That doesn't mean we shouldn't do it."

"I understand, I do. But what about Christine—won't the law firm and Patrick's daughter expect to see her at the memorial service?"

"Christine will send flowers and make a donation in his name. But she will also send her regrets. Her recent surgery will have to be the excuse, even if the mortals involved don't entirely believe her. She is too young to be surrounded by so many of them for so long in such a crowded space."

"That will be hard on her, having the disapproval of her friends and colleagues, not to mention missing the opportunity to further grieve Patrick."

"I know." He ran his hands down Cerissa's back. She had a great capacity for empathy. "But the disapproval will work in Christine's favor. Although painful for her, it will mean a cleaner break from her previous life."

"Yes, there is that." Cerissa brought her knees up, pivoted to face the fire, and reached for her drink again.

He snugged his arms tighter around her, enjoying both the warmth of her body and the warmth from the fireplace as she sipped scotch.

They sat like that in silence for a long while, each in their own thoughts. Then she bent forward to set her empty glass on the fireplace hearth and took a bit of apple from the plate, chewing and swallowing it with a murmured hum.

Suddenly, she turned to him, raising her legs over his and wrapping them around his back, her naked sex pressed against his, separated only by his underwear. Apparently, she'd decided not to wear panties.

Was she interested in another round? The shower had been satisfying, but he missed being inside her, the way they connected when he buried himself deep.

She closed her eyes and tilted her head, parting her lips.

Afraid of overwhelming her, he held back all the passion surging in his chest and gently met her lips. The kiss was a soft benediction to his love for her, a recognition of all the turmoil they'd been through and come out the other side of by working together.

She leaned back, stroking his face. "I miss the beard."

His eyes widened. It was the last thing he'd expected her to say. "Perhaps tomorrow night."

She wiggled against him. "You feel hard."

"Indeed." He mirrored her hand, stroking her cheek. "When my beautiful mate presses against me, I cannot help my natural response."

"I'm glad. Would you like to do something about it?"

He kissed her, deepening the kiss as he touched between her thighs. She was already wet for him.

When they broke, she unwrapped her legs from around him, giving him the space to remove the stretchy boxers and release his *pene*. He then helped her peel off her cotton nightshirt.

Now naked, she wrapped her legs around him again, and the reddish glow of the fire flared at the edges of her body and outlined her hair like a halo.

Mi Ángel.

With his hands supporting her, he helped her rise to guide his *pene* inside. He grunted as she seated him deep within, her legs tightly holding him. With his hands spanning her sexy ass, he lifted her up and brought her down. The warmth from the fire felt soothing, but the flow of cold air from the room still made her nipples pearl.

Or were the buds taut from scraping against his chest as she moved?

"How is this?" he asked.

"Nice," she whispered, and worked with him to rise again.

He captured her lips, this time flicking them with his tongue, and she opened to him, her mouth warm and welcoming, and he could hold back no longer. He devoured her, losing himself in the play of their tongues, the tightness of her around his erection.

He ignored the ankle monitor scraping against his back. The feel of being inside her was so silky, so tight, so perfect, that nothing else mattered.

And when it came to healing, this was what he needed. Making love to Cerissa, reconnecting physically with her, the pain and humiliation of the whipping post faded to a distant memory.

He reached his hand between them, finding her clit and gently rubbing as she continued to ride him.

The slow rhythm kept him hard, tempting him to stretch out their lovemaking, to stay connected like this all night long. His mate safe in his arms, the glow of desire in her eyes. He'd given his heart to her and never wanted to let her go.

The shuddering tension in her body, her belly tightening, told him she grew close. He kept his thumb drawing small circles on her bud until her pumping hips sped up, her eyelids fluttered, and an explosive "aah" escaped, her face a picture of bliss.

He gave himself over to the silken squeeze of her sheath and the ecstasy flowing from her through the crystal. He pulled her tighter to him and sank his fangs through her soft skin. The flood of her goodness into his mouth made him lose control, and he pumped harder and faster into her, until she exploded again, and he joined her for the ride.

His heart expanded, capturing all the love she sent him and cycling the passion back to her, until he couldn't tell where he stopped, and she began. They were one and would be together forever, no matter what life threw at them.

Finished, he laid her on her back, untangling them and covering her with the blanket, sharing small, light kisses.

"I want to sleep with you," she murmured.

"You already do."

"I mean really sleep. In your crypt. By your side."

"The cots are too small for two people."

"That is easily fixed," she said, sounding sleepy.

Her eyes closed, and he kissed her lids.

When she dozed off, he propped himself on his elbow to watch her as the firelight played across her peaceful face. He savored her beauty, her closeness, her seeming...innocence?

Unbidden, a question rose in his mind. The same question had occurred to him when Tig dragged him in for questioning. Cerissa had killed Dalbert to avenge

Yacov. Had she listened too closely to Anne-Louise's warning—that the mayor would keep coming after Henry if she did nothing to stop him?

She could be vicious when someone she loved was hurt or threatened.

He ran his thumb over her lips, and they parted with a sleepy moan.

If she had wanted to, she could have flashed to the Enclave yesterday evening, obtained a weapon, and returned to the mayor's house, then carried out the deed and flashed back to the extinct volcano that the Lux called home, hiding the crossbow where no one would ever find the weapon, before returning to her basement lab.

Yes, she could have.

But would she?

Even thinking the question felt disloyal.

He stroked her jaw line, trailing his fingers along her throat and past the bite.

No. She'd never kill in cold blood. And looking at the peaceful glow of her angelic face, he wouldn't let himself think anything different.

CHAPTER 49

RECOVERING

Hill Chapel—Around the same time

Christine peeked at her phone, checking the time. The meeting would end soon. So far, the group members were trying their best to make her feel welcome, even after her terrible start as one of them.

Would she ever be able to forgive herself for what she did to Patrick?

According to the stories they told, she wasn't alone. When gripped by blood lust—as most new vampires were—killing a mortal was considered an accident by the group.

A terrible accident, but one all the same.

As an attorney, she'd studied the different levels of criminal manslaughter. Where did Patrick's death fall? Was the feeding frenzy she fell into similar to "heat of passion" murder? Although blood lust sounded like the same thing, it wasn't a likely fit, as she had no intent to kill.

As awful as killing her best friend was, maybe what she did qualified as ordinary civil negligence. Terrible, still carrying with it the guilt of causing a death, but no criminal liability.

Was that why the council let her off the hook?

She kept trying to pigeonhole his death in one of the categories she was familiar with but would circle back to a point made by the group: vampires weren't mortals, and the rules and definitions established for mortals didn't apply anymore.

She needed to quit applying those rules to her behavior now, except mortal law was so familiar to her, so much a part of who she was, that she kept dissecting what happened using their moral standards. She couldn't stop herself. The need to make sense of what happened tore at her.

Evelina laid a hand on her shoulder. "Christine, are you okay?"

Christine looked around, realizing the session had ended and people were starting to leave. Embarrassment flooded her, and she raised a hand to cover her mouth. "Oh, I'm sorry. Just woolgathering."

Evelina hooked her hand through the folding chair next to Christine's, adding the chair to the other four she carried. "It's hard to stop thinking about what happened, isn't it?"

"I was listening to all the stories, trying to stay focused, and then I remembered what I'd done, and started parsing whether it was criminal manslaughter or ordinary negligence and went down the rabbit hole."

"You betcha. It's not easy to stop blaming yourself. But we'll be here for you. You'll get through this. And did you hear what Wolfie said about taming intrusive memories?"

"I don't understand how playing Tetris or a word game on my phone—"

"Now, now, mortal psychologists have studied this. It's a way to break the memory trauma cycle thingy. As soon as you start going down the rabbit hole, stop yourself and focus for ten minutes—only ten minutes—on one of those games, and then move on to something else."

"If you say so."

"It's one of many tools we have. And you have my phone number. Don't stay in your own head for too long."

"Yeah, easier said than done." All the other chairs had been put away, so Christine picked up hers. Evelina led the way and stacked the chairs on a wheeled rack in a closet, then adding the one Christine carried.

"I know it's difficult, but you have to start somewhere. Why don't you call me tomorrow at seven? That should give you time to wake and feed."

"I will. Thank you."

"Are we taking you back to Henry's place?"

"Zeke is supposed to pick me up."

Evelina gave a knowing grin. "Let's check if he's here."

Christine backed out of the closet, and when she turned around, Zeke stood at the door, holding his black cowboy hat in his hand, glancing around—probably wondering where she'd gone—and rolling the brim nervously.

Her breath hitched. She liked what she saw. Despite Henry's misgivings, the cherubic cheeks and sky-blue eyes did her in. A real panty-melter, as her sorority sisters used to say in college. And the innocent way he smiled. Oh boy.

Sure, she'd heard the stories. He was far from innocent.

And after what she'd done, she wasn't sure she deserved happiness, even momentary happiness. Part of her thought she should go to Marcus's office and find some legal work to throw herself into. Something to keep her busy and not obsessing about Patrick's death.

Part of her thought that.

"Howdy, miss," Zeke said. "You comin' with me?"

But the other part couldn't resist the way his smile transformed his entire face when he looked at her. "Sure."

Evelina gave her a pat on the back. "I'll talk to you tomorrow night," she said, as she scooted past Zeke with a wink over her shoulder.

CHAPTER 50

YIN AND YANG

Hill Chapel—Minutes later

Christine strolled to the parking lot alongside Zeke. When they arrived, she glanced around for his truck, and her mind flashed back to the night the council ordered Henry whipped.

She'd grown hysterical as Gaea drove her away from the amphitheater and the flogging started. She could feel Henry's pain, and the desire to return to her maker and protect him almost made her crazy. Zeke had responded to Gaea's frantic phone call and arrived in his truck to take Christine the rest of the way to Gaea's.

Standing by the side of Robles Road, Zeke had put his arms around her to prevent her from running away, while Gaea turned the sports car around to go back to the amphitheater.

Once Gaea rode out of sight, he bit her. No request, no consent. The rush of fang serum shot through her, fading the panic and allowing a sense of sexual bliss to overtake her.

He then helped her into the truck and explained his actions.

"I'm sorry, missy," he'd said. "That's the only thing I knew would help you. Your bond to Henry is mighty strong right now, and another vamp's fangs is a temporary cure. But I won't do nothin' else. You're safe with me."

She remembered those words as he walked her to the end of the church parking lot. She still wasn't sure how she felt about his taking matters into his own hands. Pragmatically, the bite had worked to calm her. On the other hand, he hadn't even *tried* to ask for her permission.

She shook off the memory and stopped walking. "Where's your truck?"

"We're not taking the truck."

Then she saw the two horses waiting for them, and her jaw dropped open.

"I thought we'd go for a ride." He grabbed the reins of an Appaloosa mare, beautifully marked with chestnut spots on her white rear, and untied her from the hitching post. A matching stallion stood next to the mare, his nose blowing bubbles in the water trough. Zeke patted the stallion's dark brown neck. "Knock that off. There's a lady present."

She laughed. It'd been *years* since she last went riding.

Earlier in the evening, Zeke texted asking her to wear jeans and boots. She'd followed his instructions, but she hadn't pictured horses, so she'd worn dress boots with a high heel.

"These two need some exercise," he said when she didn't respond. "What d'ya say?"

Christine walked cautiously to the mare and touched her cheek tentatively. "Will I frighten them?"

"Don't worry none about that, Christine. They're used to our kind."

"What's her name?"

"Yin, and this is Yang."

"You're making fun of me."

"No, ma'am. They're a breeding pair, but two horses couldn't be more opposite than these two. The names fit."

"Hello, Yin," she said, stroking the mare's forehead and getting her shirt slobbered on as her reward. Brushing the slime off, she gave Yin one more pat before joining Zeke by the stirrup.

He offered the reins. "Have you ridden before?"

"A long time ago."

"Western saddle?"

"Both."

"Then you'll have no trouble." He held out his hand. "Come on, hold the horn and put your foot in a stirrup, and I'll make sure you get safely seated."

Why not? She hooked her shoulder bag over her head to hang more securely, then accepted his hand and followed his instructions. Pulling herself up and swinging a leg over was easier than she thought it would be—thanks in part to Zeke's hand on her butt.

"Hey," she said. "I didn't say you could take liberties."

"Pardon me, ma'am." He tilted his hat with a cocky grin. "Didn't want you to fall."

She smirked. They *had* warned her about him.

"Where are we going?"

"My house. I'll drive you home from there." He patted Yin's neck. "Now, in case you need the refresher: don't use the reins to steer. Use your legs. Right leg pressure to turn left."

"Oh no, I'm in trouble there. I'm directionally dyslexic."

He chuckled. "Don't think right or left. You want to go that away"—he pointed toward the driveway—"press your knee gently in that direction. She'll get the idea."

Christine applied light pressure, and Yin started a slow walk along the asphalt leading to Robles Road.

Easy-peasy.

Zeke stepped into the stirrup, kicked his leg over Yang's saddle, and soon caught up with her, riding side by side.

She glanced over at him. "Is it okay to take the horses onto the main road?"

"A trail runs alongside Robles. The town built it, used decomposed granite. And the horses won't get spooked by cars. Don't worry, you're safe with me, ma'am."

"I wish you'd stop calling me that."

"Well, Christine seems even more formal."

"Then call me Chrissy. That's what my family did."

"The name suits you much better, Chrissy."

Despite the dark night, she saw almost as well as she used to during the day. Even the night birds flitting through the vineyards were clear to her.

"Why is everything so visible? I mean, I can see details of that ranch house across the street, but being in a lit room doesn't overpower my vision."

"Just one of the advantages to being vampire. You'll get used to it. Hasn't Henry filled ya in on all the differences?"

"His teaching plan got interrupted when I killed Patrick."

Her gaze fell to Yin's mane, and sadness and guilt washed through her, landing in her gut and tightening into a boulder even Sisyphus couldn't move.

"Now, Chrissy, I understand why you feel bad about what happened, but you shouldn't. The accident weren't your fault. Mortals are our natural prey. When you were mortal, did you feel guilty when you ate a steak?"

Her jaw tightened. "It's not the same."

"Nothin' ever is. But it's close. And we're as near to vegan as a vampire can get. As you grow older, stronger, you'll be able to feed without killing. And until then, there's bagged blood."

She patted the purse she'd slung over her shoulder. "I have three pouches with me, in case I get hungry."

"Now that's a fine idea. And I know those meetings you're goin' to are meant to help you. I hope they do. But I'm kind of an old-fashioned guy. Better to embrace what we are than to feel guilty about what we eat."

"Letting go might be easier if I'd killed a stranger." Her voice trembled, choked up with unshed tears. "I just—I can't live with the guilt of killing my best friend."

"I won't lie to you, Chrissy. Ending your life is the easy thing to do."

Her chin shot up and she glared at Zeke, burning the tears away. "Did Henry tell you I wanted to die?"

"No, he didn't need to. It's written all over your face."

"Oh." She hated being an open book. Starting over, learning to hide her feelings—all of it was more difficult than she'd anticipated. And add in Patrick's death...

"Now, sayin' it's easy to end it, that's not meant to be an insult or to shame you or anything," Zeke continued. When she glanced over at him, the look he gave pierced her soul. "It's just a statement of fact."

She looked away, unable to maintain the intense eye contact with him. "I can't live with this pain."

Zeke reached over and patted her leg. "I know how you feel. I thought of doing myself in after I was turned."

She frowned. Because of the support group, she'd heard a lot of stories about accidents on rising, but not many, if any, of the others had considered ending their life. It seemed like a rare reaction—was he lying to manipulate her?

"My maker wasn't a kind man," Zeke continued. "He used me poorly. I imagined I would've been better off if he'd killed me outright."

"I'm sorry." At least Henry was a moral man. He'd never use his position to abuse her.

"Staying alive and working through the pain, living with it even when you can't let the memory go, that is the harder road. I get that. But for the people around you, well, it's the reverse." Zeke fell silent for a moment. "I know for a fact Henry will blame himself if you end your life. He'll carry the guilt forever, along with the grief of losing a child. Again, that's not to guilt you, it's just a statement of fact. The reality. But only you can make the decision of what's right for you. I hope you like me enough to stick around. I can't take away your pain, but I can help you make some pleasant memories."

Pleasant memories? She didn't deserve any. "Henry would recover, wouldn't he? I mean, I'm a stranger to him."

"I wouldn't say that, Chrissy. That man feels everything deeply. He takes his responsibility for you seriously. If you died prematurely, it'd tear him apart." He tipped his hat. "Anyhow, I wanted to say I'm here for ya, if you need to talk about Patrick. I got a good ear for listenin'."

"Thank you." Should she ask? What Cerissa told her about Zeke—she should verify for herself. "From what I'm told, you still kill mortals."

"Now you're talkin' about my government work, are ya? What you need to know is I kill drug lords. Those guys are meaner than a Mohave green—one of the orneriest rattlesnakes God ever created. They torture and murder for money and territory. Some get too big for their britches, and I'm paid to take them out."

"I'm not sure government sanctions make it right."

"Well, Chrissy, I'm a simple guy, and the drug trade's a complex problem. I lived through prohibition. If people want to drink, they'll find a way. Same with drugs. And the government plays politics in nasty ways. They're racist bastards."

She understood what he meant. Powdered cocaine, a more expensive drug used by affluent Whites, had less severe penalties than crack cocaine. Even though two-thirds of crack users were White or Hispanic, over eighty percent of crack cocaine defendants were Black. It meant that Blacks served longer prison terms for basically the same drug. Congress had finally recognized the problem and adjusted sentencing guidelines, but the disparity still existed.

Zeke shook his head. "I don't know the answer to the bigger problem. But I do know the men I kill are evil. I research them before I take a job. Makes my government contact pissed, I'll tell you that. I've turned down jobs when I found out the target weren't deserving of death."

"I see." Even if he did put some thought into it, vigilante-style justice wasn't right.

"Now, we'll have to stop our talk there. That homestead ahead?" He pointed to a long driveway leading to a house set far back on the flat side of the valley. "That's mine."

When they reached the corral, he dismounted and tied Yang's reins to a hitching post. "Come on down, help me put the horses to bed. Then I'll get you back to Henry's, all safe and sound."

Christine swung her leg back to dismount, heard a *whoosh* behind her, and collided with something soft.

"Ow," Zeke said.

Once her foot was planted on the ground and her other foot out of the stirrup, she turned to Zeke. A bright red gouge ran across his cheek.

"Oh my—I didn't mean to— I'm so sorry."

He touched the raw flesh gingerly. "All my fault, Chrissy. I shouldn't have tried to—"

"Grab my ass again?"

"Something like that."

She scrambled to open her purse and rooted through the contents. "Let me see if I have a tissue."

"Well, your tongue would work a mite better."

She jerked away. "My tongue!"

"That's right." He leaned over—the blood had started to run to his jaw. "I don't want it to stain my shirt, and your tongue will stop the flow."

The night breeze brought the delightful smell to her. But should she really?

Even if blood lust took hold of her, she couldn't do much damage to Zeke. He was older than her and, consequently, stronger too. She leaned in and caught the dribble at his jaw line with the tip of her tongue. "Mmm, that's good. But your blood tastes...richer?"

"That's because vampire blood is richer than mortal. And it won't hurt you none. Go ahead and lick again."

She ran her tongue across the scrape. It tasted heavenly. And made her hungry for more.

She stepped back, watching as the flow stopped.

He touched the raw skin again. "It'll heal before tomorrow night."

"That's amazing." She reached into her purse for a pouch of blood. "If you don't mind. Or would you like one?"

"Go ahead and help yourself. I don't feed again this early."

She felt foolish, having to feed so often, and stabbed the straw into the pouch. She took a few deep pulls, kept drinking until she drained the container, and only then looked up at him.

Most definitely, he is *sexy.*

"Why, Chrissy, you have a little blood on your lips. Let me help you with that." He slanted his mouth over hers, his tongue darting out to lick the dark wine away. "Mmm, that's mighty tasty."

A warm buzz flowed through her, a nice reaction even if his was a chaste, teasing kiss. "But you didn't ask first."

"You're old enough to understand—you wouldn't respect me if I didn't try to steal a kiss."

"Well, why don't you steal another?"

He smiled before closing the gap between their lips and kissing her for real.

She let him in, feeling his tongue slide against hers, until she broke from the kiss breathless.

"And now two is my limit. I promised Gaea I'd go slowly." He touched the gouge on his cheek. "But I could show you something else about vampires."

Her eyebrows shot up when he opened his pocketknife.

"Has Henry explained the healing power of our blood?"

"Someone did."

"Would you like to see the healin' work?"

She eyeballed the knife, guessing at what he alluded to. "Okay."

"I promise to be quick." He took her finger in his hand, poked the tip with the knife, and squeezed. The puncture stung. When a bubble of blood formed on her fingertip, he released her and pointed at his cheek. "Smear it on the scrape."

She did. The skin began to crust over, and the gash now looked a day old.

"Wow."

"Give it another half-hour, and it'll disappear." He lifted her finger and wrapped his lips around the tip, sucking, and then moaned. "Oh, that's just as powerfully good as I supposed it would be. But I better stop there before I get carried away and break my promise."

"Your promise to Gaea?"

"And to myself. I promised myself I wouldn't seduce you tonight. Now head for the truck, before I change my mind. It's almost midnight and I should get you home."

"But what about the horses?"

Zeke glanced from the horses to her. "I'm not sure." He shook a finger at her. "Now, you wouldn't be tempting me here, would you?"

She chuckled, and turned it into a *tsk*, like the noise Gaea made. The horses really should be brushed down and their gear removed. "I'll trust you if you'll trust me."

"Well, Chrissy, ya got yourself a deal. Take Yin's reins and follow me."

Chapter 51

TREACHERY

Rancho Bautista del Murciélago—The next night

Cerissa spent the day working in the basement lab, nervous about the upcoming council meeting. The group texts had been flying. The mates were ready to converge in support of Luis, and even had a second candidate in mind. So far, the texts contained no hint the larger group was aware she'd spent the night in jail.

Luis knew. Nicholas knew. Jayden knew. Should she email Haley and tell her?

The way gossip traveled in this town, someone had probably told her already. Probably.

It was three in the afternoon before Cerissa remembered to call Ari. "When you checked my lens videos and discovered Olivia stole my bracelet, how far beyond her thievery did you view?"

"I stopped when you left the amphitheater. Why?"

"Olivia claims she returned the bracelet to me when we were outdoors, walking to the amphitheater from council chambers."

"Hmm. There was a point when she bumped into you—the shoulder slam appeared intentional."

"Is there any possibility she slipped the bracelet back into my purse?"

"I don't have an answer for you. You didn't look down when she pushed by, so I can't tell for sure."

"Thanks, Ari. Will you be at the council meeting tonight?"

"I'm working on getting cleared to attend. Gaea wants me to go instead of her—she'll be too busy getting things ready for the memorial service—so I've got extra leverage this time."

"Please give her my condolences."

"You got it, kiddo. But you're coming tonight to the service, right?"

"That's the plan."

Once Henry and Christine woke for the night, and fed, Cerissa drove them in her car to the town center. The council meeting was scheduled for eight o'clock—an hour earlier than usual—to accommodate the ten o'clock memorial service for the mayor. They arrived like a family, walking through the double-door entrance together.

Cerissa's throat tightened and her stomach roiled as soon as she set foot inside. She'd already hated the council chambers, but now she associated the room with the brutal way Henry had been flogged.

Was this what PTSD felt like?

The intensity of the feeling was worse than the anxiety she'd experienced after the earthquake. Maybe she was overdue for a talk with Fidelia, the Lux psychologist.

Her reaction must have reached Henry through the crystal. He slipped his arm around her waist and, with a squeeze, pulled her closer to him.

Ari came bounding up to them. "I got Rolf to approve my attendance."

They all moved to find an open row with only a few people already in it. When Henry stopped and stepped back, Cerissa took the cue and entered ahead of him. Christine would take the seat on the center aisle, so she could step out if she needed to feed. Her purse held three blood pouches.

The man sitting at the far end—one of the community residents Cerissa hadn't been introduced to yet—glared at her. "Vampire slayer," he spat out under his breath.

Cerissa froze, not knowing how to respond.

"We don't need your kind here."

Haley, who sat on his other side, pulled on his sleeve. "Hush."

The nasty vampire must be Haley's mate, Vishon, and a moment later, Cerissa's contact lenses confirmed the identification.

Another community member approached Henry in the aisle and loudly said, "She killed the mayor. How come she isn't in jail?"

Cerissa had met Mitchell before, in one of Father Matt's groups, and his attitude toward women could win the Neanderthal award. His mortal mate, Aeesha, turned in her seat, her mouth gaping open at her mate's display, her long purple fingernails gripping the pew-like bench.

Reaching around Ari, Mitchell poked a finger at Henry's back. "Take your mate outta here, or we'll stake her. See how she likes it."

Cerissa swallowed hard. What could she do to stop this? She'd promised Tig to stay quiet about Olivia. Now wasn't the time to take a stand.

Or was it?

CHAPTER 52

MEMORIAL PREPARATIONS

The Hill Chapel—A short time earlier

Sitting in the chapel's front pew, looking at the haphazard mess, Gaea sighed. The florist had delivered the flowers during the day, placing them in the chancel, but hadn't put any artistry into arranging the various displays.

Two nights ago, after visiting the morgue and finally having a good cry, she'd moved into action and called Lady Fane. Her child was shocked, of course, but her children were never close, and Ada decided not to fly out for the memorial service, which meant they didn't have to delay the service to give her time to arrive.

Ari helped Gaea pick out two photos of Winston, photos showing different aspects of his personality. The print shop was closed on Sunday, but the young man promised to get the photos blown up and mounted on foam-core board as soon as the shop commenced business on Monday morning.

The chapel doors swung open, and she turned at the sound. Her devilish lover came striding in.

He held up the two poster-sized photos. "Success."

Tears flooded her eyes. The photos were magnificent. She wiped the tears away, then took the photos from Ari, walked briskly to the altar rail, and, juggling the two oversized foam boards, opened the gate where it was hinged. She walked up the steps into the chancel and placed the photos on the two easels Father Matt had provided earlier.

"Thank you," she said as she moved the easels apart, creating more space for the standing flower sprays.

"What else can I do?" Ari followed her into the chancel. "I left the programs on the little table by the doors. I had no problem getting them printed."

He'd helped her to design the remembrance pamphlets last night; they featured more photos of Winston on the front and back, and the simple information about his birth, death, and next of kin inside the folded page.

"Go to the council meeting. I'll be fine here." She bent over to pick up a pot of mums. "I just need to arrange the flowers. The delivery person wasn't very artistic—"

When she straightened, Ari wrapped his arms around her waist and kissed the back of her neck. "Are you sure?"

"I'll be fine, truly I will." She moved away to set the pot on the floor in front of an easel. "Now go."

"Will do, sweet cheeks. Text me if you need something."

She turned around and shooed him away. One of them needed to be at the meeting to see what the council did.

Ari had barely left the chapel when Olivia stuck her head in. "Oh, dearie, there you are. You weren't at home when I stopped by."

"I'm a bit busy." Gaea wasn't close friends with Olivia. Why was the woman looking for her? With the service tonight, a condolence visit could have waited. Or maybe Olivia had something else in mind. "If you need to talk with me, we can do so at the reception after the memorial service—"

"Then you aren't coming to the council meeting?"

Gaea waved her hand at the flowers. "I really have too much to do to be ready for tonight's service."

"Of course. Well, I wanted to tell you I'm throwing my hat into the ring." Olivia took a few more steps closer. "I don't believe we should have two mortals on the council, so I'm making the sacrifice to offer myself for Winston's seat."

"Oh." Gaea swallowed. "Isn't it too soon to replace him?"

"The council posted the agenda—both seats will be appointed tonight."

Gaea shook her head slowly, both at the council's haste and at Olivia's announcement. She didn't think Olivia was a good choice, not with her great and well-known distaste for mortals, but then, someone else would likely run as well, so she politely said, "Good luck."

"Well, dearie, there is something else you should know."

Olivia had the sensitivity of a toad. Couldn't she see Gaea was busy? Why couldn't Olivia go away and leave her in peace?

Gaea huffed. "Yes, what is it?"

"I don't mean to be indelicate, but did you hear who Tig arrested?"

"Someone's been arrested already?"

"Yes. Cerissa Patel."

Gaea grabbed the chancel rail, her head light as dizziness overtook her. "What?"

"I suspect Cerissa's bracelet was found by his body. Tig had the beaded chain in a bag, asked if I'd seen it before. So I'm putting two and two together." Olivia tutted. "Looks like she's the killer. But Tig let her out last night with an ankle monitor. Can you imagine that? I don't bloody understand why."

Gaea grew more lightheaded, and her knees started to give out.

Olivia *whooshed* over to her. "Are you all right, dearie?"

"I need to sit."

Olivia guided her down the two steps from the chancel and over to the front pew.

Collapsing onto the hard wooden seat, Gaea murmured, "It can't be true."

"True as can be. Call Tig. She'll tell you."

"No, impossible. Not Cerissa."

"Well, dearie, I heard the mayor was going to vote against her project. And after what happened with her mate, well, it just makes sense."

"No—"

"Anyway, I thought someone should have the decency to tell you. Why don't you call Tig? I have to leave for the council meeting. I'm sorry you won't be there. I was hoping for your support. Are you sure you don't want to come with me?"

Gaea glared at Olivia.

"That was crass of me, I'm sorry, dearie. You take care of yourself."

Olivia turned and strode out of the chapel.

Gaea found her phone next to her purse and, hands shaking, managed to place the call, even though it took her three attempts to tap in the code to unlock it.

"How may I help you?" Tig answered. "The council meeting is about to start."

"Is it true?"

"Is what true?"

"Did Cerissa kill Winston?"

Gaea could hear the big breath Tig exhaled. "I can't discuss my investigation at this point."

"She did, didn't she? You'd deny it if she wasn't a suspect."

"Gaea, please. You know me better than that. Don't jump to any conclusions. I have a lot more evidence to look at before we bring homicide charges against anyone. Please be patient. Once we are certain, I'll be in touch." Tig paused. "I promise."

Gaea stabbed the "call end" button. If the scientist was innocent, Tig would have said *something*, at least hinted at it.

Rage shook her hands. How could Cerissa? After everything Gaea had done for her, how could she murder Winston?

CHAPTER 53

DOWNHILL

SIERRA ESCONDIDA COUNCIL CHAMBERS—MOMENTS BEFORE

Henry growled. The hostility and disrespect aimed at Cerissa sent rage flowing like lava through his veins. He spun around to face Mitchell. He wouldn't let these troublemakers drive his mate from the council chambers.

"Shut up, Mitchell. You have no idea what you're talking about." He scanned the entire room. "Cerissa is innocent. She was with me when the mayor was murdered."

"Of course you'd lie for her." Mitchell fisted his hands. "Everyone knows she killed Winston as payback for flogging your ass. Couldn't do it yourself? Had to have your harpy fight your battles for you?"

Leaning past Ari, Henry stopped inches from Mitchell's nose. "Take that back, or the next thing I do is to remove your head from your shoulders."

Sitting at the center seat on the dais, Rolf gave three rapid taps of the gavel, and over the PA system said, "Chief Anderson, the first resident to take a swing goes to jail, as does the resident he swings on."

"Yes, mayor."

"That's entirely unfair." Mitchell turned to look in Rolf's direction. "Henry's the one who brought a vampire slayer into council chambers."

"Close your mouth, and there will be no reason for Henry to strike you." Rolf brushed his long bangs out of his face.

"Like hell I will. Someone has to say it."

Rolf tapped the gavel. "Mitchell, sit down. Now."

Mitchell huffed and stood his ground, pointing at Cerissa. "I will when that—that *murderer* leaves." He turned to Henry. "I'll say it again: take your stinking harpy outta here."

That was enough. No matter the penalty, Henry couldn't allow Mitchell to insult Cerissa any further. Fists clenched, jaw set, eyes stinging from turning fully black, he lunged to charge around Ari.

Ari sidestepped—cutting Henry off—and splayed his hands on Henry's chest. "Dude, it's not worth it."

A twinkle in Ari's eye should have warned him. Ari pushed hard—harder than a mortal could—forcing Henry to step back to catch his balance. Then Ari spun around, bringing a right hook under Mitchell's chin and sending him sprawling. Very calmly, he leaned over the dazed vampire. "Don't speak to my cousin that way."

Before Mitchell could *whoosh* to his feet, Tig grabbed him with one hand and reached with the other for Ari.

"Hey, Tig," Ari said, pulling out of her hand before she could tighten her grip. "I'm not a resident. Winston made that clear when he wouldn't let me attend the last meeting. And this mayor said the first *resident* to swing goes to jail."

"Ari," Tig said, her voice low and growly, "quit being a jailhouse lawyer."

Rolf pounded the gavel. "I did say resident. Chief, please take Mitchell outside, and when he can control his mouth and show the decorum this council demands, he may return. Now, everyone else, take your seats. The meeting is called to order. Any disruptions will be fined—heavily."

Henry slid past Cerissa to sit next to Vishon, just in case the *pendejo* decided to take another verbal jab at her. Ari eased onto the bench on her other side, followed by Zeke and then Christine.

After the usual rituals—pledge of allegiance, approval of the minutes from the last meeting—Rolf opened for discussion the only order of business on the agenda: appointing temporary replacements for Winston Mason and Frédéric Bonhomme.

Whoever they selected would have to run again in next year's election, but the appointees would gain the incumbent advantage.

Henry had almost thrown his name in the hat. Almost. But between the flogging and Cerissa's arrest, they were too much in the spotlight already, and not in a good way.

Haley slid out of the row, walked to the audience podium, and, not being very tall, adjusted the microphone, which squeaked with the movement. Her black pantsuit and white blouse lent a professional air. "Now that the chest bumping is over—"

A titter ran through the room, and Henry raised an eyebrow. Really? How dare Haley be dismissive of his defending Cerissa? Then he reconsidered. Was the dig at her own mate? The mortal hadn't sounded happy when Vishon sniped at Cerissa.

Rolf didn't even bother to bang the gavel. Instead, he waved his hand in a "hurry up" circle.

"First, on behalf of our coalition, I want to offer our condolences to Gaea Greenleaf and the council."

"Thank you," Rolf said.

"I can say with assuredness that no mortal meant the mayor any harm."

Grumbling among the vampires filled the room.

"However," Haley continued, raising her voice to speak over the noise, "the council has two seats now open, and we propose they both be given to mortals. Luis already declared his intent to run for a council seat, and we agree he should be appointed to one of the two seats. For the second seat, we nominate Maggie Leigh."

Henry frowned. The chief's clerk? Why would Tig's clerk be interested in serving on the council?

Then it occurred to him. Both Rolf and Liza had worked closely with the mortal. They always spoke highly of her, which made her a smart nominee, politically speaking.

"Two excellent recommendations," Rolf said, his voice warm and encouraging. "Anything else?"

"We hope you will consider both our candidates. Our nominations are supported by the entire contingent of mortal, er, guest residents. To save time, we decided to present the proposal as a package and not have everyone take a turn at the podium, although Luis and Maggie are here if you have any questions for them."

Haley turned off the microphone with a *click* and returned to her seat.

"Thank you. The council appreciates your suggestions, and your respect for our time."

Henry raised an eyebrow at the change in his business partner's demeanor. Had Rolf become a new person upon taking over the mayor's role, suddenly polite and politic? Why hadn't Rolf been this diplomatic all along?

"Is there anyone else who wants to speak?" Rolf continued.

Olivia rose, and her high heels tapped on the tile floor as she raced to be next at the podium. "Mr. Mayor, honorable members of the council, as you all are aware, I have the franchise for the most important service provided to our community."

A light *harrumph* escaped Henry's lips. While delivering blood was an important service, it wasn't the only important one the town provided.

Not to mention she had probably killed the mayor and was attempting to frame Cerissa.

Henry made eye contact with Marcus and inclined his head in Olivia's direction. Marcus nodded briskly, confirming what Henry had already surmised:

the town attorney knew Olivia was a suspect even if the rest of the Hill wasn't aware. Marcus's job involved obtaining the search warrants, after all.

"And given my community service," Olivia continued, "I'm nominating myself to the council."

That brought a smattering of applause from the audience. Henry gritted his teeth and started to rise to object, but Cerissa stopped him.

"We can't prove Olivia killed the mayor, not yet," Cerissa whispered. "From what Jayden told me, the council wasn't briefed. They don't know Olivia is a potential suspect. Liza and Carolyn were kept out of the loop because they challenged the mayor at the last meeting, and Rolf wasn't told either, because of his connection to you. If you say something now, it'll look like you're defending me again."

He fisted his hands, fighting his desire to act. Olivia was the most likely suspect—if they could only prove her guilt. "Fine."

Perhaps Marcus would find a way to stop this travesty.

Rolf raised an eyebrow at their whispering. "Thank you, Olivia. Anything else?"

"No, dearie."

"Are there any additional nominees from the floor?"

While a murmur rose through the audience, no one stood. Had everything happened too fast for the various factions on the Hill to coalesce behind a fourth candidate?

Rolf tapped the gavel. "Very well. I'll close the nominations and open discussion."

Carolyn reached over and clicked on the microphone in front of her. "Olivia's always done a mighty fine job of delivering what we all need. I have no problem with her joinin' our council."

Liza rolled her eyes, and her nameplate lit. "I'm not sure we are ready for *two* mortals on the council. And Maggie is essential to the police department. We've never had a better assistant and can't afford to lose her."

Henry crossed his arms. Yes, everyone on the dais was being diplomatic tonight.

"For those reasons," Liza continued, "I would support Luis and Olivia's nominations."

Rolf steepled his fingers together and looked at them thoughtfully.

Madre de Dios, was he mimicking Winston?

"I concur with Liza and Carolyn," Rolf said, "with one concern. Every ten years, this council decides who will receive the blood franchise. Mr. Town Attorney, would you please explain the problem?"

Marcus stood. "Until now, Olivia's bid has always been accepted. If Olivia wins re-election in a year, her franchise will come up for renewal during her term. Under state law, this is a major conflict of interest."

Henry let out a relieved breath. Marcus was on top of the problem.

"Thank you." Rolf looked over at Olivia. "Are you willing to surrender your franchise when it expires?"

Olivia popped up in the audience, not bothering to go to the microphone. "Yes, dearie, I am. But I've also been told by another lawyer that there are ways, legal ways, around those laws. I figure we'll cross that bridge when we come to it."

"Does the council have any further questions or discussion?" Rolf paused, waiting. "Hearing none, is there a motion?"

"I move we appoint Luis and Olivia," Liza said.

"Is there a second?"

Carolyn seconded the motion.

"Hearing no objections, the motion is passed unanimously. Luis and Olivia, welcome to the town council. You'll be seated at our next meeting."

Henry nearly groaned. Why hadn't Marcus done more? With Olivia on the council, Tig would have a harder time proving the blood franchise holder killed the mayor. Everyone would view the investigation as a political attack. He shifted to look at Cerissa.

"Not here," Cerissa whispered, squeezing his hand. "We'll talk later."

He trusted Cerissa's instincts. She was right. This wasn't the time or place.

But he vowed then and there that he'd do whatever was necessary to protect his mate. If Tig didn't clear her name, he would.

Chapter 54

Uncertainty

Outside council chambers—After the council meeting

Cerissa fumed over the outcome as they joined the crowd headed to the parking lot. How could Tig stay silent while Olivia, suspect number one, was elevated to a position of power? Yes, she understood Tig didn't want to tip her hand if an accomplice helped kill the mayor or until she had more solid evidence.

But couldn't Tig have said something? Anything?

At least Luis got the appointment. But why had Rolf given in so easily and allowed a mortal on the town council? In the past, he hadn't been too keen on the idea.

Then the truth smacked Cerissa in the face, and she growled to herself. Luis would be serving on the council next to his employer. From Rolf's point of view, the mortal would be intimidated, afraid to buck his boss. And Olivia was well known for her distain toward mortals. So her appointment would appease the vampires who didn't want a mortal on the council.

Politics.

This was the very reason she hated them. Everyone constantly maneuvering to satisfy their base, to keep their voter support, never putting the group as a whole first. And when Rolf officially ran for mayor, he could play the story both ways—one of the first to welcome a mortal on the council, and at the same time pleasing the vampire supremacists on the Hill with Olivia's appointment.

Grr.

Once they were outside in the parking lot, Ari gave Cerissa a hug. "Hey, kiddo, don't let it get you down. These things have a way of working themselves out."

"Yeah, right."

"Look, I have to skedaddle. Gaea texted me. A late delivery of flowers arrived at the guard gate, and the guards wouldn't let them through. I have to pick them up for her."

She waved him off. "Go on. We'll see you at the service."

During her goodbye with Ari, Henry took the front passenger seat, appearing to trust Christine to behave herself in the back seat.

Cerissa got behind the wheel and closed the door. "We need to find out who spread the rumor about me. Too many people knew I'd been questioned. Jayden told me there was no announcement to the community about my detention—Tig doesn't do press releases. Given the subject of tonight's meeting, I doubt my mortal friends spread the rumor to their mates either."

And now everyone had heard it at a public meeting. Being accused was almost as bad as being convicted. The suspicion would worm its way into everyone's hearts until she had no friends left and her life in Sierra Escondida would be over.

"Why don't we leave the car at the chapel and go for a stroll?" Henry suggested. "The loop through the park shouldn't take more than twenty minutes. We can discuss ideas for proving your innocence as we walk."

"I'd like that."

"Are you okay with taking a walk, Christine?"

"Of course. Do you think Zeke will be at the memorial service?"

Henry rolled his eyes. "Probably."

"May I sit next to him?"

Cerissa reached out a hand to touch Henry's leg. "Yes. If you like, he can drive you home."

Henry growled.

"She's a grown woman. If she wants to be with Zeke, you have no business stopping her. Maker or not."

"Cerissa—"

"Henry."

"Fine." He puffed out a deep, put-upon sigh. "Christine may sit with Zeke."

Council chambers—Around the same time

Once the public meeting adjourned and everyone cleared out except for Marcus and the council, Tig joined them for a closed session. She stood at the audience podium to make her report.

"I have nothing new for you on the mayor's death. We're looking at certain persons of interest. We believe we know what murder weapon was used, but we haven't found the weapon yet, and I've assigned detectives from the sub-station to contact the places these weapons are sold to check if they had recent sales."

"And what weapon was used?" Liza asked.

"For now, that's all—"

Rolf gave a sharp scoff. "It's not a secret, chief. Olivia told me you searched her place for a crossbow. The search warrant for her properties and my guest house listed the same thing."

"And Olivia told me y'all found Cerissa's bracelet by the mayor's body," Carolyn said.

Great. Just great.

Liza clicked on her microphone. "You should know, chief, Olivia is the reason everyone reacted to Cerissa's presence. Olivia made house calls to obtain support for her appointment to the council seat and used the opportunity to spread the rumor about Cerissa and all the details about the weapon. She strongly questioned why you released Cerissa when, in Olivia's words, 'she was clearly the killer.'"

Tig rubbed her eyelids with one hand. The weight of the investigation made her want to crawl in a sleep pod and stay there until spring. Was Olivia trying to deflect suspicion from herself, or being true to character, spreading hateful gossip about a mortal? Either was possible.

"I appreciate the information, Liza. I'm not happy because I wanted those details kept confidential, as this is an ongoing investigation."

"Hard to do when Olivia's involved," Liza added.

"Well, I hope I can count on the council to show some discretion. Do not confirm or deny Olivia's rumors. As I said, we have multiple persons of interest—"

"Not suspects?" Rolf asked. "I thought you made an arrest."

"Early in the process, we took a suspect into custody. However, as more evidence surfaced, reasonable doubt was raised, and we released that suspect without charging them. When we are ready to charge a suspect, I'll notify the council."

"But I heard Cerissa was under house arrest," Carolyn said.

Tig scrubbed her face. "That's an overstatement. Given the circumstantial evidence, she's a person of interest. We've asked her to wear an ankle monitor and not leave the Hill without permission. As her lawyer pointed out, we don't have enough evidence to bring charges before the council yet."

Tig excused herself and left the closed session meeting, her frustration mounting. She took a deep breath of the night air to clear her head. The short walk to the police station would give her time to think.

Right now, the investigation boiled down to a battle of credibility—Cerissa versus Olivia versus Anne-Louise. Cerissa said the bracelet wasn't returned. Olivia said it was. Tig had phoned Anne-Louise after learning Anne-Louise had the opportunity to access Cerissa's purse, and Anne-Louise denied knowing anything about the bracelet.

When it came to motive, Cerissa had plenty. Olivia didn't—at least, so far, Tig hadn't discovered any clear motive, but they still had to follow up on Olivia's meeting with Winston. And Anne-Louise's so-called desire to protect her child seemed inconsistent at best. After all, she'd shredded Henry's back, even if she claimed it was to spare him worse.

At the police station, Tig collected Jayden, and, wearing their dress uniforms, they drove the short distance to the chapel. She circled the parking lot, trying to find an empty space. Everyone on the Hill must be attending.

Then Tig noticed Cerissa's Malibu.

Not good.

As much as they may want to pay their respects, after what happened at the council meeting, Henry and Cerissa should have stayed home. When Tig finally found an open space, she parked and sent a group text to Liza, Rolf, and Zeke, asking them to be on the alert. If things went sideways at the service, they'd be ready.

CHAPTER 55

REQUIEM FOR THE DEAD

Hill Chapel—Moments Later

Cerissa entered the vine-covered walkway leading to the historic chapel's entrance. The gray river-stone building, weathered by time, had been the site of too many funerals lately. She walked somberly with her arm hooked through Henry's, Christine following them.

Anxiety thrummed through her. Despite the clear night sky, the fresh scent of old oak trees, and the pleasant sound of night insects, their stroll in the park hadn't done much to calm her. No new ideas to clear her name had occurred to them, and a text from Rolf to Henry confirmed Olivia was responsible for the rumors.

Now the whole town knew Cerissa was under suspicion for the mayor's death.

All thanks to Olivia. If Cerissa had doubts before, those were gone. Olivia *never* returned the bracelet. No matter what Tig suspected, Anne-Louise would not have rifled through Cerissa's purse to find something to leave at a crime scene. It just wasn't her style.

Cerissa sighed. If only she hadn't agreed to stay silent. She should have shouted the truth from the rooftops the moment she was released from jail: Olivia stole her bracelet and planted it at the crime scene. Rather than accede to Tig's demand, why hadn't she put herself first for a change? Why had she placed the community's wellbeing above her own?

Now, it was too late.

As they approached the chapel, a couple of vampires who passed by glared at them angrily. When the vine-covered walkway ended, Cerissa pulled Henry aside. "Maybe we should go home."

"And what would Gaea think?" Henry brushed a hand over her hair, smoothing the strands caught in the evening breeze. "That we do not care?"

"With all the rumors, I'd rather have her misunderstand than to attend and upset her."

"*Cariña*, your concern is valid, but we should not let those rumors drive us away. I've known Gaea and Winston too long to abandon her at this time. And I can't imagine Gaea would believe such evil gossip about you. She'd seek an explanation."

Cerissa glanced up into his confident eyes. "Only Gaea matters right now."

"Exactly. And she needs our support in her time of grief."

Still holding his arm, she climbed the stone steps to the open double doors. Haley passed out remembrance programs and wouldn't make eye contact when Cerissa accepted one.

Once they'd stepped through the narthex, Henry whispered, "Everything will be all right. Tig will solve the case and clear your name."

"But what happens until then?"

"We hold our heads high and carry on."

Then why did her churning stomach urge her to leave? They slowly walked down the center aisle, following others who turned aside to take their seats in the pews, and Christine peeled off to sit next to Zeke. Cerissa felt the stares drill into her back like heat lasers.

Flowers filled the raised area beyond the rail, ranging from tall displays of cut carnations to live potted lilies and mums in colorful bloom, a lavish display of grief.

Henry had sent a large floor-stand spray of gladiolas and white roses on their behalf, and two oversized photos of Winston stood on easels among the flower arrangements. One showed him in the typical suit he wore to town council meetings, and the second was of him gardening.

The mayor had gardened? That was news to her. Come to think of it, Cerissa knew very little about him as a person. She'd first met Winston when she arrived on the Hill—and that initial introduction had left her with a less-than-stellar impression of him. She never tried to learn more.

When they reached the row reserved for Hill founders, she took the seat one in from the aisle. Marcus, Méi, and Abigale, along with their mates, were already there and had saved the two end seats for Henry and Cerissa.

The arrangement placed her in the row behind Gaea. Ari sat next to the bereaved, an arm around her shoulders.

Cerissa gripped Henry's hand tightly. Something about funerals brought tears to her eyes even when she wasn't close to the deceased. But she didn't want to cry, afraid the tears would be misunderstood, and struggled to swallow her feelings.

Olivia marched down the center aisle to the front pew where Gaea sat. She wasn't going to horn in to take a seat near Gaea, was she?

Instead, Olivia knelt next to Gaea and leaned in very close, whispering something to her. Gaea spun around to glare at Cerissa, then patted Olivia's hand.

Olivia rose and went to another pew. With a squeeze to Ari's shoulder, Gaea whispered something to him.

He shook his head. "Gaea, don't."

She pointed at him, as if to say, "Stay there," and strode to the end of the aisle where the founders and their mates sat.

When her gaze landed on Cerissa, Gaea's eyes narrowed. "It's not enough that you murdered him? You also have to show yourself here tonight?"

A sharp pain gripped Cerissa. How could Gaea believe her capable of murder? If only Gaea had more faith in her, the way Henry thought she would.

Cerissa swallowed her feelings and responded in a clear and sure voice. "I didn't kill him, Gaea."

Gaea snorted and pointed at the ankle monitor. "That says otherwise."

"Please believe me. No matter what you've been told by some people, it's not true."

"And after everything I did to help you when you first arrived here. I argued on your behalf, urging Winston to let you stay. I should have told him to kick you out. If I had, he'd be alive today."

Henry stood, putting himself between them and gripping Gaea's shoulders. "We are here to pay our respects to the mayor and to offer you support in your grief. Cerissa is innocent of these accusations."

Gaea narrowed her eyes at him. "For all I know, the two of you conspired together."

"I understand you are upset." Henry continued to face Gaea, his hands on her shoulders. "But you have known me for far too long to believe such nonsense. Neither of us had anything to do with his death."

Gaea knocked his hands off her, took a step back, and pointed at the exit doors. "Leave, now."

Henry gave a short bow. "We will do so, but only because we respect your feelings in this moment. In your heart, you know we had nothing to do with Winston's death."

Henry stepped to the aisle and turned around. "*Mi amor*," he said, and offered Cerissa his hand.

Remembering Henry's words, she kept her head held high and walked out on his arm. It wasn't until she reached the car that she let the first tear fall, her heart breaking, and they continued to stream down her face the entire way home.

Chapter 56

GRAND-MÈRE

THE HILL CHAPEL—AFTER THE MEMORIAL SERVICE

A sense of relief ran through Christine when the memorial service finished. The conflict between Gaea and Henry initially had her hyperventilating. But when Gaea returned to her seat—instead of marching over to Christine and kicking her out too—her pulse had slowed to normal.

Zeke, clearly attuned to her turmoil, had patted her hand at the time and said, "Don't worry, Chrissy. The drama's done and finished."

Luckily, he was right. Yet the rest of the service gave her the odd feeling of being an interloper. She'd only met the mayor once or twice, and it felt odd to be there, witnessing the deep grief of a relative stranger. So she was glad to leave on Zeke's arm after Father Matt said the closing prayer.

Once she got into his truck, Zeke stepped up on the running board, tipped back his hat, raising the brim high, and kissed her lightly. Then he went around to the driver's side and drove them out of the parking lot and onto Robles Road.

"I hope you don't mind, Chrissy, but I got to take you straight back to Henry's. I don't have time to take you to the funeral reception. Tig asked me to come by the station to help out."

"Maybe we could get together later when you finish?"

He smiled at her. "If I'm lucky, we might be done by two or three."

She chuckled. "I'm still not accustomed to thinking of three in the morning as a normal time to socialize."

"Tell you what, I'll text you when I'm free. We'll see how you feel then."

"That sounds good to me."

Zeke dropped her off. Moments after she waved goodbye—and barely before Henry opened the front door for her—Anne-Louise arrived in a rental car.

The older vampire parked and joined them on the porch, taking Christine's hand. "My dear, I'd like to invite you back to my temporary abode for conversation and companionship."

Christine glanced at Henry, letting her eyes ask the question. She hated needing a babysitter. But everyone on the Hill seemed to be reaching out, offering help, in one way or another.

"It's all right." Henry gripped her shoulder while glaring at his maker. "Just be cautious what you say to her."

The countess chuffed at him, but Christine thought it good advice under any circumstances. After all, Anne-Louise was still a potential suspect. This might be a good opportunity to listen for any clue to help Cerissa.

She turned to face Anne-Louise, more than a smidge nervous. "Um, okay then."

Anne-Louise led her by the hand to the car. The countess's attire seemed out of place for the Hill—an empire-waist full-length dress in a bold royal blue—and she'd worn the dress to the memorial service. Perhaps the formal was the nicest dress Anne-Louise packed for her trip.

Christine got in on the passenger side and continued to study her grandmaker. Anne-Louise's salt-and-pepper hair with big, soft curls was held off her face by wooden clips, and her hazel eyes shone with a certain sparkle. Pale white skin bore the same agelessness as most vampires, so Anne-Louise didn't look old, but she did look more mature than Henry.

When they arrived at Rolf's guest house, Christine entered ahead of Anne-Louise into a sitting room. Her eyes widened, the room reminding her of a French chateau she'd stayed in some fifteen years ago while her husband was still alive. Her chest tightened at the memory. The trip to France had been their last together.

A blue velvet settee, framed in carved wood, stood opposite two chairs, with an oval coffee table between them, periwinkle flowers hand-painted on its surface and coated in a shiny varnish. From Christine's experience working with Rolf, the décor seemed an odd choice for him. Perhaps Karen picked out the furniture.

She went over to stand by the white limestone fireplace—a fire was already sparking on the grate—and she rubbed her arms. The power her grandmaker emitted made her skin crawl.

"Are you cold, *chère*?"

She dropped her hands to her sides. "Ah, no. I'm adjusting to being—"

"You'll grow accustomed to the chill of death." Anne-Louise patted the cushion of the settee. "Come, child, sit. You are safe here."

Yeah, right. Despite the elegant décor, Christine felt like she stood before a judge in chambers for the first time.

"You look so stiff, *chère*. Relax. I want to get to know you. You're part of the family now. We've never had a lawyer in my line. Your skills may come in handy. Tell me about yourself."

Christine took a seat on the far end of the settee, the velvet soft under her fingertips. "Well, I graduated from Stanford in 1984. I spent a few years at a big firm, and then opened my own. I specialized in water law and public law, which is why I represented Sierra Escondida Water Company at the trial."

"I see. So you're very analytical. Henry must like that. He likes smart women."

"We aren't lovers," she blurted out. Marcus had briefed her. Most makers and their children began as lovers, and she didn't want rumors about her and Henry floating around.

Anne-Louise laughed. "Of course not. Rolf told me the deal. But still, even when you are not lovers with your maker, it is important to like each other. The relationship of maker to child lasts a lifetime."

Christine had only viewed Henry's guardianship as a temporary thing. She really didn't want a permanent parental relationship out of the deal. She had one set of parents who'd already passed away—that was enough for a lifetime—and she had expected her connection with Henry would end when she got her hunger under control.

Her stomach rumbled. Even thinking about hunger made her hungry. "Anne-Louise, do you mind if I feed? I brought my own."

"Go ahead, *chère*. And call me *grand-mère*. It is our way."

Grandmaker seemed weird enough. To call this stranger grandmother when she looked to be in her early forties was just bizarre. Christine opened her purse, pulled out a pouch, and tore the wrapper off the straw.

"I am glad Cerissa is providing you with clone blood. Much superior to the *merde* Olivia delivers."

"Agreed." Christine had tried bagged blood at Gaea's. She far preferred Cerissa's clones. After taking a deep sip, she released the straw. "But the suckers Olivia makes aren't bad."

Anne-Louise laughed again, the high-pitched sound making Christine uneasy. "We were speaking of lovers. I hear you are seeing Zeke, yes? A beautiful man."

Christine took another sip of blood to delay her response, not sure she wanted to talk about Zeke with Anne-Louise.

"Of course, I prefer mortals, myself," Anne-Louise continued, wrinkling her nose as if the thought of bedding Zeke was disgusting. "Though even if I were to consider a vampire lover, he would not be on the list."

That piqued Christine's curiosity. "Why?"

"I prefer penthouses, and he prefers barns."

"Perhaps I could look for a mortal boyfriend—"

"No. You, *chère*, are too young to date mortals. Taking a vampire lover first would be a good experience for you. Learn what it means to be vampire from an experienced man."

At her age, Christine never thought she'd hear anyone say she was too young to do anything. "I already drink this." Christine held up the pouch. "How much more is there to learn?"

"To begin with, you do not instantly become vampire. Think of a young woman—she takes ten years for her body to fully mature, to start her cycles and fill out." Anne-Louise gestured to her own breasts. "For the hormones to reshape her."

"Ah, do vampires have cycles?"

"Not of the type you're speaking of. We cannot become pregnant, and we do not carry disease. Both excellent reasons to explore sex with a vampire lover."

Christine exhaled a long breath. "I'm not sure Zeke is the one to explore with. Henry doesn't approve."

"*Beruk*." Anne-Louise wrinkled her nose as if smelling something disgusting. "Ignore Henry. His standards are too strict. Besides, you are not looking for a mate—you are too young for the bond. But regular sex? *Oui*. And Zeke is quite charming, with his wavy blonde hair and eyes a color that would make a bluebird jealous. Not to mention the muscles. And I have seen him with horses. He has a way with animals."

"But what about his wet work for the government?"

"Aha, *chère*, I heard that about you—that you are a very ethical attorney."

"What did Henry tell you?" He tended to be tight-lipped. Would he really tell his maker about the deal they made, which was protected by attorney-client confidentiality?

"Enrique? He tells me nothing. No, my daughter, Chen Méi, keeps me up to date on all the gossip involving this little, dreary place. And she tells me Zeke has been looking for a reason to stop his wet work. It is getting harder for him to hide his identity, with all the electronic gadgets the government has now. He hasn't been gone from the Hill for months."

That was interesting news. "Why are you pushing me toward Zeke?"

"Because I like Cerissa. I wouldn't want Henry to be tempted by you."

Christine let out a laugh. She'd seen the way Henry looked at his mate. The idea was ridiculous. Henry would never be tempted by her—by anyone other than Cerissa.

"Believe me, there is no temptation there."

"But with Zeke as your lover, well, it would shut the door tighter."

Was this really a concern? Or was this whole conversation an attempt to deflect, to get the suspicion for Winston's murder away from Anne-Louise by her pretending to care about Cerissa?

Henry had warned Christine not to trust what his maker said. To verify everything.

"So, what would you like to do?" Anne-Louise asked, interrupting her thoughts. "Do you play Faro?"

"I've never heard of the game. I do play bridge."

"We'd need another two players at least. And Rolf is a terrible bridge player—don't tell him I said that—so perhaps something else? Chess?"

"I'm a bit rusty, but sure."

Anne-Louise gracefully rose from the couch, all smooth muscle and elegance, and returned with a chessboard, which she placed on the oval coffee table.

She arranged the pieces, moving the white king and queen into place. "Now, you must not let Henry boss you around too much. You're a strong woman. Don't let him take that away from you."

"He isn't the problem." Christine sighed. She'd forget for a little bit, and then the memory would come flooding back. "The problem is what I did to my friend."

"Yes, most unfortunate. But his death was Henry's fault, for not watching you closely enough. But we must not cry over spilt milk. You cannot bring your friend back by focusing on his death. You must look forward, not backward."

Easier said than done. "Some of the younger, ah—"

"It is all right to say the word, *chère*."

"Some of the younger vampires have invited me to their group—we talk about our...accidents. Talking helps. To know I'm not alone in killing a friend."

"They understand what you've been through, and at such a young age. I am glad you have ones around you who understand."

"So am I."

"And if you ever need anything, reach out to me, even though I'll be in New York." Anne-Louise used both hands to brush back her curls and reset her combs. "If you get tired of Henry's bullying, you can come stay with me for a while."

"I'm not sure Henry would agree. And I'm supposed to join Marcus's law practice. It would be hard to do so from New York."

"Still," Anne-Louise replied with a coy smirk. "If you ever need a break, know that I'm just a phone call away."

Chapter 57

Circling Back

The Hill Chapel—An hour earlier

Tig watched Henry and Cerissa leave the memorial service together. Thank the ancestors she didn't have to intervene. But if Cerissa wasn't guilty—and it was starting to look like she wasn't—Gaea was going to regret publicly shaming her.

Once they settled down and the mayor's service started, Matt gave an excellent sermon, and various community members spoke for a few minutes each on what they cherished most about Winston. Listening to them, Tig battled to hold back her own grief. Sadness tightened her throat and tears pushed to emerge, but she didn't have time for these feelings—not with a killer or killers still out there. She had a community to keep safe and a culprit to hold responsible.

After the memorial service ended, Tig drove the short distance from the Hill Chapel to the police station, Jayden in the passenger seat next to her. Staying for the after-service reception wasn't in the cards.

When they arrived, she grabbed the reports from her assistant's desk and headed to the squad room, where they took seats at the worktable.

Watching Gaea grieve over Winston had been hard. And despite how much work Tig had to do, it wasn't easy to switch gears, so she started with a softball question. "Anything new?"

"I already scanned through those"—Jayden gestured to the reports she held—"and the local sporting goods stores weren't much help. They've sold crossbows within the past few months, but some were paid for in cash, and the ones paid for by credit card didn't ping a Sierra Escondida address."

"Were any purchased in the last week?"

"A few. I already obtained a warrant for security camera video for those stores. But it's a long shot. You can also buy a crossbow over the internet. Complicating things, the brand of bolt the killer used is a popular one."

So that didn't narrow down anything. Tig frowned. "What do you suggest?"

"Approach the research from the other side. Get a warrant for our suspects' credit cards. Start with four people: Olivia, Anne-Louise, Cerissa, and Henry. That's a lot of paper to go through, but Marcus and Nicholas could help with the review."

"Shouldn't we include Liza and Carolyn?"

"Sure, but I'd prioritize the first four."

"Perfect. Call Marcus and ask him to draft the search warrants. Anything else?"

Jayden leaned back in his office chair and ran a hand over his shaved head. "Maybe we're going about this wrong."

She pinched the bridge of her nose, fighting the tension headache forming behind her eyes. She didn't feel like she had the energy to think any harder about all this, let alone switch directions. But Jayden's insights frequently hit pay dirt. "What do you mean?"

"Instead of looking for the weapon, we should be looking for the motive."

"Well, Cerissa has a motive."

Jayden puffed out a long exhale. "You're never going to convince me. You get a sense of people, and Cerissa didn't strike me as the type to kill in cold blood for revenge. And what purpose would it serve? She or Henry would be suspect number one. No, she's too smart. I don't buy it. Add in the fact she lost her bracelet at the council meeting—"

"Then you think Olivia or Anne-Louise killed the mayor?"

"Possibly," Jayden said. "Olivia has a thing against mortals, so leaving Cerissa's bracelet, trying to pin the crime on her, would be consistent with Olivia's attitude. And Cerissa's lab is going to produce blood, which may cut into the donor blood revenue."

"Not if we expand our numbers."

"I know, but Olivia's so-called agreement with the mayor doesn't ring true. Luis told me Olivia doesn't want us to expand our numbers—so why would she agree to deliver clone blood for the biotech lab if the increased quantity enables the unaffiliated to move in? And the bunk she fed you about putting delivery of Cerissa's product under her franchise? The mayor can't make a commitment without getting the council's vote—I checked with Nicholas. But with Winston gone, all we have is Olivia's word on their discussion."

Now Tig understood the avenue Jayden wanted to pursue. "You think the mayor didn't agree with her and she's lying about their conversation?"

"That would be par for the course with Olivia."

"Then we need to search both his town hall office and his home for anything we can use to contradict Olivia—a notebook, a diary, anything. I'd already made a note to do that, but I gave first priority to the search for the weapon used."

"The night we found the body, I locked the mayor's office and put police tape over the door. The mayor's secretary agreed to contact me if they needed anything out of the room. From what I gather, Rolf is continuing to use his vice mayor office."

She lifted an eyebrow. Rolf wasn't in a hurry to claim the mayor's office? Now she'd heard everything. "Well, we can't ask Liza to help with the search. She's on our list as having motive."

Jayden frowned. "But there's no connection between her and Cerissa's bracelet."

"I know. And I like Liza, but I can't chance it. What if Cerissa dropped the bracelet, and Liza found the damn thing after everyone else left the council chambers? Or Carolyn?"

"That leaves Zeke and Nicholas."

"Precisely." She glanced at her watch. "Zeke should be here any minute. I asked him to come by after paying his respects to Gaea."

"What about using Rolf?"

"Because of his relationship with Henry, I don't like the optics. If we find something implicating Olivia, people will say Rolf planted the evidence."

"Being a small town makes this difficult."

Tig snorted. "No kidding."

"Maybe we should ask for outside help."

Leave it to Jayden to nail the problem on the head. If things continued this way, she would have no choice. She'd have to reach out to San Francisco with a request to send some of their security officers to assist—for an outrageous fee.

Tig tapped on the table. "Before we blow the budget bringing in outsiders, we could use Bailey again. He did okay on the first search—and he's detail-oriented when it comes to paperwork. And like you said, Nicholas, of course."

"All right. I can get behind that." Jayden stretched. "And Anne-Louise wants to leave for New York. She keeps texting me."

Tig chuckled. "I love how she bugs you rather than me. Like she thinks she can bully you. Fat chance."

Jayden's tired eyes looked merry for a moment, then turned serious again. "We haven't cleared her, and if Olivia really returned the bracelet, then Anne-Louise could have stolen it at Henry's."

"But why? What's her motive?"

"What if she wanted Henry back?"

Tig shot him a skeptical look. "Seriously?"

"Well, Anne-Louise still takes his blood. Jealousy is not out of the realm of possibility in that scenario. Add that to her feeling slighted about her omission from Henry and Cerissa's engagement party…"

"Okay, okay. Next time I have the opportunity, I'll ask Henry why Anne-Louise wasn't at the party. But where would she have gotten a crossbow from?"

"I don't know. Maybe she carries one in her luggage?"

"If she did, she dumped the weapon somewhere afterward." Tig added the question to the whiteboard and stared at the list.

In any case, she was beginning to come over to Jayden's side. The bracelet had been too easy. She'd had the same feeling Jayden voiced: Cerissa wouldn't kill the mayor this close to the flogging—she'd wait. And Olivia looked like a serious suspect—if they could only find the evidence they needed to prove it.

"Let's draft a warrant request for the mayor's office at town hall." Tig shuffled through the file of warrants and found what she wanted. "Marcus wrote the Mincey warrant broad enough to include the office inside of Winston's home. So we're good there."

The night they found the body, her team conducted a thorough search of the backyard, but only a spot search of the residence, and found no obvious clues inside, so they left the home sealed with police tape. The way she figured it, after they had a handle on what they were looking for, they could make a second run through the house.

Tig slipped her phone off her belt and called Marcus to explain what she needed, including the warrant for credit card information on all six suspects, and how she wanted Nicholas and him to review the paperwork.

Marcus groaned. "Look, Tig, I agreed to cancel my vacation and handle the warrants you need. But I'm not doing your grunt work."

"Someone has to," she said. "And I'm running out of police officers."

"I can contact the law firm in Mordida we use, and have their junior associates conduct the document review."

She considered his suggestion for a moment. The credit card records were unlikely to reveal what the Hill hid. So using uninitiated mortals wasn't a problem. "Time is the key. I need this done now. How quickly could they start?"

"Well, I, um, I imagine it may take a day or two for the outside attorneys to commence their work."

"No, this is too important. We need to begin the review as soon as we get the records tomorrow. And I need someone I trust doing the review, not a bunch of junior attorneys just out of law school."

"Tig—"

"You don't want anyone else to die because we delayed."

"Fine," Marcus said. "Nicholas and I will do it."

Once the call ended, she sent a text to Zeke asking him to pick up Lieutenant Bailey and Nicholas along the way and report to the mayor's house to start the search. Then the phone buzzed. She expected Zeke's response, but instead, a new message popped up.

A text from a number she didn't recognize: *What you seek is in Patel's car.*

What the fuck?

Tig showed Jayden.

"Another attempt to frame Cerissa?" he asked.

"Or an attempt to get us to spin our wheels so we're looking in the wrong direction while the real perp gets away with something else."

Jayden jumped to his feet. "Let me check the number."

He dashed to the computer and searched the reverse directory. Results for a burner phone appeared, one not associated with a username yet.

Tig sat there thinking and tapping her fingers. They had searched Cerissa's car when she was in custody and found nothing. Only Zeke, Bailey, Nicholas, and Jayden knew that. So if this was a frame-up, whoever concocted the bogus lead wouldn't be aware the results for the car came back clean—no weapon, no blood, no mud from the garden.

Still, she couldn't ignore the message. She had no choice but to follow up on the tip.

She shot to her feet. "We need to update the original warrant for Cerissa's car. Damn. I'll have to call Marcus again and try for a verbal okay based on the text."

"He's going to get tired of hearing from us."

"Too bad. We need to move on this, fast, before whoever sent the message does something while our backs are turned."

Chapter 58

UNWELCOMED VISITOR

Rancho Bautista del Murciélago—A short time later

Cerissa pushed the switch on the security monitor to check who'd rang the doorbell. She wasn't expecting company.

What are they doing here?

Tig and Jayden stood on the porch, wearing their dress uniforms. They must have gone straight to work after the service.

Henry's footsteps on the stairs told her he'd heard the doorbell too. "Who is it?"

She waved at the video monitor, feeling like she wanted to find a large shipping box, curl up inside as a cougar, and ignore them.

Henry opened the door. "Chief, captain," he said with a nod. "How may we help you?"

Tig held out a page entitled "search warrant."

"We're here to search Cerissa's car."

"Didn't you already do so?"

"We received a tip and need to check for additional evidence."

A tip? Cerissa felt a mixture of anger and disbelief flash through her.

"Do you have the keys?" Tig asked when Cerissa continued to stare at her.

Cerissa retrieved her purse from the foyer table, took out the keys, and handed them over. "Here." She couldn't imagine what they thought they'd find. "But you don't need the key. I don't lock the car when it's in the garage."

"Cerissa, what have I told you—"

"Not now, Henry. Besides, you have an alarm system."

"Still, leaving the Malibu unlocked is a bad practice."

"Henry—"

A sharp laugh shot from Tig, and she shook her head. "Which garage is the car in?"

"The second from the right stall."

Cerissa led the way. The garages didn't connect to the house. Henry had told her the story months ago. When his house had first been built, horses—not cars—used the garage area. No one wanted the smell of a barn against their home. When he rebuilt the barn into a five-stall garage, he gave each stall its own door, and the horses were relocated to Rolf's property.

Housing the animals at one location turned out more cost-effective for the partners, as the horse manager could care for all of them at once. Besides, Rolf had more room, more flat land than Henry did, though Henry retained a better view of the valley, which was exactly why he chose the current parcel.

A keypad was mounted on the side frame of each stall. Cerissa reached out to enter the code for hers.

"Wait," Tig said, *whooshing* over to block Cerissa's hand. "When did you last touch the numbers?"

"This evening."

"Let's confirm you were the last one in here—Jayden, please print the keypads for all five doors."

They stood there silently watching as Jayden worked, and Cerissa read the new warrant, which listed the same items as the first one. She wanted to ask Tig why they were looking in her car, but with a quick finger-swipe at his throat, Henry motioned for her to be quiet.

When Jayden finished, he said, "Only Henry and Cerissa's fingerprints are on the pads."

Tig turned to them. "Does anyone else know the combination to the doors?"

"A few," Henry replied. "Rolf does. My mechanic does. I haven't given the code to Christine yet."

"What about Anne-Louise? Does she have the code?"

He looked thoughtful for a moment. "I don't recall. I gave her the garage code at one point, but I can't recall if I reset the code afterward."

"Great, just great," Tig muttered. "I want a complete list of who has access to your garage."

"I will phone you if I recall any others."

"All right—open the door."

Cerissa punched in the code on the pad for her garage door. The door raised normally.

Tig *tsked*. "Damn it, Henry, of all people, I thought you'd know better."

"Pardon?"

Cerissa bit her lip. She thought he'd be pissed off by the reprimand. But he looked more startled than offended.

Tig strode into the garage and, taking a pen from her pocket, flicked the white woven string hanging from the track the opener rode to lift the garage door. "This cord is attached to the quick-release mechanism."

"So?" Henry cocked his head to one side and furrowed his brow. "I don't understand."

"Search 'garage door break-in.' You'll understand in about six seconds."

An angry scowl fell over Henry's face. "Tell me now."

"Fine. When the garage door closes, the release mechanism rides the track"—Tig flicked the attached string with her pen again—"and this cord arrives next to the closed door. A thief can wedge a coat hanger through the seam at the top of the door, hook the cord from the outside, and pull it through. A sharp tug, and the lock is released, and the door can be raised manually."

"Thank you for the education." The amount of pink on Henry's cheeks surprised Cerissa. "I will correct the error."

Tig narrowed her eyes at them. "So anyone could have gotten in here."

"Not precisely. If both Cerissa and I are asleep—as sometimes happens—I arm the alarm."

"But the rest of the time, the door is not armed?"

"True, but if someone raised the door, it would register on the alarm company portal as having been opened."

"This is the same portal you already gave me access to?"

Henry pressed his lips together and nodded.

Cerissa crossed her arms. She hadn't realized how all the security precautions Henry took created an electronic trail of their comings and goings, tagging them as well as any potential burglars. Not that she planned on any wrongdoing, but she disliked the idea of being surveilled by Henry's devices. She had lost enough privacy with the contact lenses the Protectors required her to wear, recording everything she saw, everywhere she went—except in bed.

"I'll need to check the portal again," Tig said. "Don't change the password you gave me."

"I set your original password to expire in five days. Contact me if you need it longer."

Tig turned to Jayden. "Would you please try opening the car's doors? Are they unlocked?"

Wearing purple nitrile gloves, he used one finger in an uncommon spot to pull the door's handle. It opened with a low *click*. "I'm in. If we find anything, then I'll dust for prints."

"Start your search."

Cerissa stood there, watching, gnawing on her lower lip as Jayden worked. Why had they returned? What happened to trigger another search?

Tig had said "a tip" led them back here.

Had Olivia managed to do something else to frame Cerissa? She couldn't say anything to Tig right now—it'd look too defensive.

"Nothing in here," Jayden said.

"Pop the trunk, then we'll check the undercarriage."

As soon as the trunk lid popped open, Cerissa gasped. A long, black zippered bag filled the width of the trunk. Based on its size, the bag could hold multiple rifles or golf clubs, with shoulder straps designed for easy carrying.

I always thought all those precautions Henry harped about were to keep thieves out—not to prevent killers from framing me.

Since thieves rarely got past the Hill's wall, she'd gotten lax in her precautions. But clearly, the biggest threat came from those inside the walls. The whole situation had opened her eyes to the true meaning of "nasty neighbors."

"What's in there?" Tig asked.

Cerissa shrugged. "I have no idea. I've never seen it before, and I don't know how it got in my trunk."

Tig said nothing, maintaining her standard working glare that Cerissa had seen too many times in the past few days.

Jayden dusted the zipper flange and the bag's exterior. "No fingerprints."

"Go ahead," Tig said.

He pulled open the zipper. Inside lay a folded crossbow and nine silver-tipped bolts. "The case smells of cleaner—like someone wiped it down."

Tig swung her gaze to Henry. "You said Rolf has the code."

"You don't think—"

"He benefits by becoming mayor."

"Rolf would not kill for power, and he wouldn't do this to Cerissa, either. His opinion about her has changed. She is helping him with his…problem. If she is gone, no one would be able to help him control his need."

Cerissa rested her hand on Henry's arm. Sure, Christine said not to volunteer information. But this was important. "Don't forget we took my car to the council meeting, and then to the memorial service afterward. My car was parked in the town parking lot during the meeting, and in the chapel parking lot for about thirty minutes while we took a walk."

"Are you suggesting someone planted the weapon while your car was in the public parking lots?" Tig huffed her annoyance. "Jayden, please secure the crossbow as evidence."

"Wait," Cerissa said, pointing at the open bag. The rust-colored substance on the bow's string had jumped out at her. Why hadn't they seen it? "Take a closer look. The string is darker in color there."

Tig leaned over the string and sniffed. "Blood. Dried blood. Let me see your hands."

Cerissa held out her hands, relieved. Tig wouldn't find any cut or wound on her to account for the blood.

The chief took out her phone. "I need photos of your hands, front and backs. Both of you."

Cerissa cooperated, holding out her hands. "Jayden took photos when I was jailed. You won't find any wounds on my hands in those either."

"We'll check," Tig said, snapping the shots. "But Henry's blood could have healed an injury before he brought you to the station—so the lack of visible wounds doesn't let you off the hook."

Cerissa didn't bother arguing the point. She was allergic to vampire blood in mortal form, but mentioning her allergy would raise a whole nest of vipers she'd rather leave alone.

When Tig finished, Cerissa dropped her hands to her sides. "Do you want me to analyze the DNA on the crossbow?"

"You're not going anywhere near that weapon," Tig said sternly.

"But I'm the only one who can test for vampire DNA."

"No. Absolutely not. We'll test the evidence using Mordida's lab. And I will need a sample of your DNA for comparison."

Cerissa ground her teeth together. She couldn't give a DNA sample. "Why do you need my DNA? I'm the one who pointed out the blood. Would I do that if it was mine? Not to mention the lack of cuts on my hands, arms, neck, or face. I'm betting it's vampire blood."

"We'll save time if we start with your DNA when the lab runs the test. Besides, I'm not giving you a choice."

She had to stall. "Do you have a warrant?"

Tig crossed her arms and growled. "We can get one."

"Come back when you do." Cerissa hurried across the driveway toward the house.

"Please close the garage door when you are finished fingerprinting the car," Henry said.

Once the front door closed behind them, he asked, "Why did you run off?"

Cerissa strode to the kitchen. "I need to figure out how I'm going to give Tig a DNA sample."

"I don't understand. Can you not morph your DNA to resemble human?"

They stopped at the basement door. "Henry, vampires have a third strand of DNA, the strand that screws up forensic tests, so the machines report their DNA as a corrupted non-human sample. Do you recall where vampire DNA came from?"

His eyes lit up. "The Lux."

"Precisely. My DNA will create the same error as vampire DNA, and when that happens, Tig will start digging into what I really am."

"Can you create fake cheek cells?"

"Huh?"

"The DNA tests the police use take a cheek swab."

"Do you know what the kit looks like? Or the manufacturer? If I had that information, I could order the kit, doctor a swab, and swap it out for the one they use. Maybe."

"And whatever DNA you create, you would have to be able to produce it over and over again."

"Right. Wow. I've never thought this through before." Cerissa ran down the basement stairs. "How long will Tig take to obtain a warrant?"

"Fifteen minutes? Or an hour or two? It depends upon the judge."

"Fifteen minutes?" she shrieked, and rushed into her lab, scanning the room and then throwing her hands in the air. "I can't solve the problem here. I don't have the right tools."

"Then call Ari. Or another Lux. Or reach out to Agathe. You cannot be the first of your people to face this issue."

"I might be—few of us get as embedded in a small community as I have, and police departments only started using DNA machines during the last thirty-five years, which isn't a long time to the Lux. With my luck, I'm the first to be suspected of a crime."

"Speaking of which, you cannot flash there with your ankle monitor."

She glanced down at her leg and scrubbed a hand over her face. "You're right—but at least I know who to call to fix *that* problem."

Chapter 59

TICKING CLOCK

Rancho Bautista del Murciélago—A few moments later

Cerissa sank onto a stool at the lab bench and tapped the contact button on her phone for Ari. Henry left to go check the alarm company portal, to find out when the garage door was last raised.

"Hey, Ciss, what's up?" For some reason, he had the video on his phone turned off, and she couldn't see him. "You're not back in jail, are you?"

"Not at the moment."

"That sounds ominous."

"Tig wants me to give a DNA sample."

The laughter on the other end of the line went on for at least a minute.

"And what did you find so funny about that?" she asked.

"You helped the community by decoding their DNA. Now you're about to be hoisted on your own petard—you know, blown up by your own fart."

She groaned. Yeah, she could always count on Ari's twisted sense of humor. "Thank you for that image."

"You're welcome."

"So you've had your fun at my expense, but what the hell am I going to do?"

"First, you'll develop a DNA you can use. That's the easy part. You know that already, you're just upset."

And she had every reason to be upset. "I need to go to the Enclave lab, but this ankle monitor—"

"Aha. You've come to the right place. I'll use the back door into Tig's computer system and figure out what you need to do."

"My main question is: will I trigger an alarm if I morph and slip off the monitor?"

"Shouldn't if you don't cut the strap, but let me check. Hang on."

She glanced at the time. If Tig took an hour to get the warrant, fifty-five minutes were left. If Tig took fifteen minutes, Cerissa was doomed.

"Okay, I'm back," Ari said. "Morphing to slip off the monitor won't trigger anything, but I've put myself between the monitor and the alert—I'll know if something happens and override, so Tig will never see it."

"Perfect." She morphed her leg into a thin tentacle and slid the ankle monitor off. "Okay, it's off. I'm free. See anything?"

"Not a peep."

"Super. Now, what's the second thing?"

"How much do you know about magic?"

She rolled her eyes. "Magic isn't real."

"No, not *that* kind of magic. I mean illusions, tricks, sleight of hand—the kind of magic mortals use."

"A little."

More than a little. She'd spent some time with a family of magicians in the early 1900s.

"Misdirection and belief," Ari said. "Write the misdirection script in your head and believe it. Trust me. That's how you'll fool Tig."

Yeah, right. "Goodbye, Ari."

After disconnecting the call, she tapped the flash disk in her watch and arrived at her bedroom in the ancient, and mostly dead, volcano housing the Lux Enclave. A selection of lab sarongs hung in her closet. She grabbed one, not thinking about the color, and tied the sash around her neck before morphing into her true form. She rushed down the corridors and with long, slow flaps of her wings, flew up the narrow flight shaft five floors to her high-tech bio lab.

Twenty minutes later, she'd completed gene surgery on a sample of her own DNA to remove the strand donated by her human father, duplicated it, and then done the nanosurgery necessary to entwine the two strands. The resulting DNA would still read as female because she duplicated the X chromosome, but a human grown from the DNA would resemble her father's mother.

Not that anyone living today would know what her human grandmother looked like—she died over two hundred years ago.

The next and more time-consuming step—coax the DNA to grow buccal epithelial cells, the cells lining her mouth.

That process took another thirty minutes, and she counted every second, not knowing when Tig would return.

Finally, she slid the petri dish into the replicator to speed cell reproduction. Forty minutes later, the amount grown was the size of an eyelash. She needed more than that to fool a DNA test. But at this point, the reproduction would grow logarithmically, multiplying faster with each passing minute.

Another twenty minutes and the replicator buzzed. She took out the petri dish. The contents filled the dish, about a half-inch high, and looked like jelled goop. Now to test, to determine whether she'd been successful.

Her phone rang. "Hello," she sang, and paused as the app translated her Lux speech to English.

"Tig is at the front door," Henry said.

"Damn." Her heart went into double time. What to do? "I'm not ready yet. Stall her."

Chapter 60

No Cooperation

Rancho Bautista del Murciélago—Moments before

Tig rang the doorbell, still grinding her teeth over Cerissa's insistence on a warrant. Marcus wrote the request quickly, but because they would use the Mordida police lab to process the samples, a Mordida judge had to sign the warrant, and the judge took his bloody sweet time. The mortal judge didn't understand the time pressures imposed by the impending sunrise, which was only six hours away, and he gave Jayden a hard time over being awakened after midnight. All told, it took nearly two hours to get the warrant approved.

"Why would Cerissa make us go through all this procedural foolishness?" Tig grumbled. "I start to believe she's innocent, that she's been set up, and then she does something like this."

Jayden gave her a tired smile, holding the testing kit at his side. "I'm sure she has her reasons. Maybe Christine instructed her to."

Tig shrugged. "Could be." The door opened, Henry standing there. She held out the warrant. "We're here for Cerissa."

"She is downstairs in her lab."

"Well then, let's go."

Except Henry didn't move. Instead, he held out both arms, gripping the doorframes and blocking the door. "That isn't necessary. I'll get her for you."

Tig pushed past him and marched into the foyer. "Take us to her now, or we'll go there ourselves. Jayden knows where Cerissa's lab is."

Henry held up his hands. "Now, Tig, there is no reason to be unfriendly about this."

Tig scowled. Yeah, gesturing for her to be calm wouldn't get him very far.

"If you'll wait in the drawing room"—he started to lead the way—"I'll go downstairs and bring her to you."

"You're not understanding me." Tig stopped in the foyer. "I am this close"—she held her index finger and thumb an inch apart—"to revoking her parole and locking her up so I don't have to go through this run-around again."

Henry made a disgruntled sound. "Very well. Follow me."

He took them through the drawing room and down a hallway that seemed like a long way around to reach the kitchen, finally arriving at a door, where he stood, blocking the way.

"At least allow me to go first and warn her," he said. "She's very touchy about people bursting into the lab when she's working."

Tig was ready to put them both in jail for obstruction of justice. "I don't care if she's about to have a scientific breakthrough. We're going down there."

He didn't move. "Tig—"

"Out of our way, now."

He opened the stairway door. "Cerissa," he called out. "Tig and Jayden are on their way to you."

"She *is* in the lab, right, Henry?"

"Of course."

Tig pushed past him, racing down the stairs, Jayden behind her. Something about this raised her hackles of suspicion. If Cerissa had decided to bolt, she had a two-hour head start on them. And with all the nonsense over the warrant, neither Tig nor Jayden had checked the ankle monitor's tracking program.

The door to the lab was closed. Tig didn't knock. When she swung open the door, Cerissa stood on the other side of a lab bench and looked up at them, eyes wide, her mouth in an O. She wore a sarong-like dress. The outfit struck Tig as odd. She'd only seen Cerissa wear a lab coat over street clothes when working. But then again, Tig had never barged in on her at home before.

"Here's the warrant for the DNA test." Tig slid the paper across the center island lab bench.

Cerissa skimmed the order. "I guess it's okay. Christine isn't back—"

Jayden was right. This is the lawyer's fault.

Tig rapped her knuckles against the tabletop. "We're taking the sample now. Come here."

"Fine. But I have a sensitive test running." Cerissa hooked her thumb in the direction of the lab bench against the wall behind her. "I'm going to stay right here, where I can continue to observe it."

Tig motioned for Jayden to go around the island to where Cerissa stood.

Before he could reach her, Cerissa let out a big *achoo*, raising her arm to cover her face. "Excuse me." Three more rapid sneezes followed. "Jayden, would you please hand me a tissue from the box behind you?" She pointed to a side counter and sneezed into the crook of her elbow.

Jayden grabbed the box off the counter and brought it to her.

"I'm sorry." She took a tissue and blew her nose. "Fall allergies."

Jayden pulled on nitrile gloves and unpeeled the wrapper from the test kit, exposing a large white swab. "When you can, open your mouth and I'll take the sample. Won't be but a second."

"Okay, I think it's safe." She wiped her nose one last time, then held her mouth open.

He swiped her inner cheek on one side and then the other. "That's all."

He inserted the swab into the plastic tube and snapped the two parts together, then took a moment to write on the label.

While waiting for him to finish, Tig looked at Henry, who'd hung back by the door. She'd checked the alarm log when Jayden went to get the judge's signature, and something she'd read didn't make sense.

The garage door to Cerissa's stall had been opened and closed twice tonight, and three times last night. For every car trip, there would normally be an even number—open and close to leave, and open and close upon returning.

The one thing everyone knew about Henry: he was a stickler for taking care of his cars. He'd never leave one out all night and day unless he had a very good reason. Nor would he leave his garage door open unattended.

"Last night, how many times did you open and close the garage door to Cerissa's stall?"

"Last night?" Henry furrowed his brow. "When I went to the police station to check on Cerissa, and then a second time to return home with her."

The printout had them arriving home at eight-fifty. "Did you go out again around nine-eighteen?"

"No. Evelina and Wolfie picked up Christine about fifteen minutes after we arrived home. Cerissa and I stayed in. She showered, and then we relaxed in the drawing room. Christine came home a bit after midnight, brought by Zeke."

So someone else may have opened the garage door and planted the crossbow in Cerissa's trunk. Tig unfolded a page from her pocket and showed it to Henry, pointing at a time in the alarm system report. "What does this error code mean?"

"Someone opened the garage door without using the keypad or a remote opener. The alarm system uses that code to report the occurrence as faulty or suspicious."

It made sense—if Henry was telling the truth. She would have believed him instantly had it not been for Cerissa's insistence on a warrant, but she couldn't think of a better explanation for the error code. Still, she'd have Jayden confirm with the alarm company when they opened for business hours.

Bolstering his story was other information she'd gleaned from the alarm report. Once Henry and Cerissa returned from the jail, their home doors stayed closed until Christine left, but no doors opened around the time the garage door reported an error code. The simplest explanation: someone broke into their garage and hid the crossbow in Cerissa's unlocked car while Cerissa showered.

Henry gestured toward the door. "Do not take this the wrong way, but if you have no further questions, please leave. We have been harassed enough for one night."

Tig scoffed. Lucky for him she wasn't the sensitive type, though she grudgingly understood Henry's need to protect his mate. She hoped Cerissa's DNA didn't match the blood on the crossbow. She signaled to Jayden to join her, and they left.

As soon as she heard Tig and Jayden begin to climb the stairs, Cerissa hobbled to the sink, spitting into it. "That tastes vile."

She took a healthy swig of water from a cup, swished, and spat into the sink again.

"I'll be back in a moment," Henry said. "I want to make sure they leave."

She waved at him. "Go."

Looking through the cupboards, she found some tongue depressors and, using the edge of one, scraped the slimy coating off her inner cheeks.

When Henry returned, he joined her by the sink, a comforting hand on her back as she rinsed her mouth a third time. "They are gone from the house," he said. "Now tell me—"

She gargled and spat. "I hope the stuff works. I had no time to test it."

"You were able to grow cheek cells?"

"I hope I did."

"But how did you—"

She gestured to the petri dish. "Do you see that goo? Buccal epithelial cells. But they won't stay in place for long—saliva washes them away in a couple swallows."

"The sneeze."

"Yup. An old magician's trick—misdirection. It was Ari's idea. I'd trained with a magician a hundred years ago. When he reminded me, I thought it was useless advice, but once I produced the cheek cells, it made sense. I stuck my finger in the goo, then used the tissue as cover when I spread the vile stuff along my inner cheeks, and no one was the wiser."

"From where I stood, I didn't notice anything at all."

"Neither did Tig or Jayden—they naturally focused on the tissue box when I scooped up the cells. And if the test comes back as corrupted DNA, we can always blame the results on sex."

He rose an eyebrow at her.

"Your blood or semen residue in my mouth could explain an abnormal test."

"Good thinking."

"Once I calmed down, I realized we had a decent way to explain away any abnormal test results."

"I hope we won't have to," he said, hugging her.

She squeezed him back. "Me too."

When they released each other, she hobbled back over to the table.

"Are you injured?" he asked.

She raised the long white skirt of her Lux lab sarong, revealing a purplish tentacle—like an octopus's arm—where her foot should be. "I arrived back here seconds before you called out, warning me they were on their way. I'd already morphed my foot to slip on the ankle monitor when they came through the door, and I couldn't slide the strap on in time, so I dropped the monitor and grabbed it with this."

She curled the tentacle's tip through the strap and used her hands to pull the monitor higher up, then morphed back to a human foot. "There." She wiggled the strap along her ankle, so the plastic sat more comfortably. "I was afraid to move. I didn't want to drop it."

"I'm glad the subterfuge worked."

"Now all we have to do is wait until the test clears me."

Henry's worry snaked through the crystal. "But whoever left the crossbow in your trunk, well, the blood may be intentional. It could be my blood. All they'd need is the whip Anne-Louise used to do a contact transfer."

"Oh damn." She would have uttered a stronger word, but Henry hated hearing certain swears. "I hadn't considered the possibility. They framed me already. Now they might come for you. Who took the whip?"

"I believe Anne-Louise returned it to the mayor."

Her heart sped up, panic surging through her chest. "Then you need to stop Tig, now. She has to find and secure the whip."

"If I run after her, Tig is not going to be happy with me since I kicked her out."

"So apologize—but you have to raise the issue before the DNA test of the blood comes back abnormal." She pushed at his back, directing him upstairs. "Go!"

Chapter 61

Another Twist

Rancho Bautista del Murciélago—Moments later

Tig accompanied Jayden to his car. They'd taken separate vehicles so he could drive the sample to the Mordida crime lab. The forensics technician promised to expedite the results, since the investigation involved a murder.

Jayden placed the sample in the passenger seat, shut the door, and leaned against the car, arms crossed.

"What's next?" he asked.

"I'm joining the search team at the mayor's house. It'll take all of us to complete a rapid search."

"All right." He kissed her. "I'll drop this off at the lab and meet you at the mayor's, then?"

"Perfect." The front door opened, and Tig pivoted at the sound.

Henry came racing down the porch stairs. "I'm glad you haven't left yet."

She raised an eyebrow. Minutes ago, he'd told her in no uncertain terms to leave. "What do you want?"

"We know the residue is not Cerissa's blood. And I know I did not kill the mayor."

"So—"

"I am concerned with being framed. Did you find the whip?"

Tig immediately understood where his mind was headed. "You're concerned blood from the whip was wiped onto the bowstring."

"Precisely."

Ancestors be damned. Just when she'd finally discovered some incontrovertible evidence, her hope went up in smoke. "We haven't found the whip yet. Did Anne-Louise keep it?"

"I believe she returned it to the mayor," he said. "I have not had the opportunity to talk with her—"

"Don't. I'm on my way to the mayor's house. If I don't find the whip at his home or in his office, I'll expand my search. But I want to be the one to speak to Anne-Louise."

He bowed. "I will defer to your judgment."

"Oh, one other thing I meant to ask earlier." Mention of Anne-Louise had reminded her. Keeping track of all the bits and pieces wasn't easy. "Why wasn't Anne-Louise at your engagement party?"

"She had a scheduling conflict. In all bluntness, I didn't want her there, but Cerissa thought we should extend the invitation. Cerissa phoned her, and it worked out well when Anne-Louise declined. We didn't bother mailing a formal invitation."

His answer aligned with Jayden's view of the situation. "I see."

"I can't speak for Anne-Louise, but knowing how she feels about Cerissa, she wouldn't frame my mate. Just believe me when I say neither Cerissa nor I had anything to do with the mayor's murder."

Tig felt like screaming at him. Yes, someone might be framing Cerissa, but it was ridiculous for Henry to think she'd take his word as evidence of their innocence.

Civilians.

No one was above suspicion. Nothing but hard evidence could rule them out.

The minute Henry ran to catch Tig and Jayden, Cerissa gathered the materials she needed for her presentation. Tomorrow night, the town council would either thumbs-up or thumbs-down her land use project to build the lab.

She'd worked so hard to put everything in place. The hearing had been scheduled weeks ago and the requisite notices posted. She'd had plenty of time to prepare. But between Henry's flogging and the mayor's murder, her plan to be prepared had been sidetracked like a freight train switched to the wrong rails, and the lack of preparation barreled down on her.

She wrapped her arms around the rolled oversized development plans and pinched the printout of the presentation slide deck between two fingers, managing to carry everything as she walked upstairs, through the kitchen and foyer, and into the dining room. She would spread out everything on the dining room table.

Henry returned inside, closed the front door, and followed her. "Cerissa, let me help you with those."

"I've got them." She scurried to the dining table, dropped the pile, and sorted things out. "Did you tell Tig?"

"Yes. She will search for the whip." He walked behind her and squeezed her shoulders. "Under the circumstances, why don't you postpone your presentation? We could phone Marcus and ask if there is some way to delay the land use hearing."

"I've already spoken with Nicholas. We can't postpone without incurring another thirty-day delay. And in any case, the council must open the hearing in person to approve the postponement. I can't waste the time. Leopold is getting antsy and won't tolerate any delay."

"I understand. But the hearing may be tense, given the rumors—"

"I thought of that. By tomorrow, Tig will have the DNA comparison run and be able to confirm my blood isn't on the crossbow. She can tell the council." Cerissa unrolled an oversized tract map showing the project location and used heavy drinking glasses from the china cabinet to hold down the four corners. "The suspicion around me will then be lifted and we'll be good to go."

"Are you sure?"

His fretting only increased the anxiety pumping through her. "Yes, I'm sure."

"You don't have to work on your presentation now." Stepping beside her, he leaned in close and brushed her hair aside, his breath tickling her skin. The soft press of his lips sent a distracting tingle through her. "Rest. Sleep. You have all day tomorrow to work on what you'll say at the council hearing."

She pushed the pleasant feeling away. "You don't understand. I have too much to do."

"I've looked through your presentation. You're ready. You may not feel prepared, but you are. Your architect did a fantastic job designing the project." He gave her shoulders another squeeze from behind. "Get some sleep now and begin fresh in the morning."

He had more confidence than she did. "Give me an hour now. I'll sleep better if I get a head start on the work. The prep tomorrow will feel more doable then."

"All right. But come kiss me good night before you go to bed."

She turned around and pressed her lips to his cheek. "Guaranteed."

The Mayor's House—That Night

Three hours into searching the mayor's house, Tig located Winston's handwritten appointment calendar in his home office—a tooled leather book with thick linen paper—noting a terse record of whom he met with and the subject.

Zeke found the whip in the kitchen sink. Why in the name of the ancestors would Winston take the damn thing home with him?

The calendar entry confirmed what Tig already knew, but it also built on Jayden's hunch. The mayor met with Olivia on the same night Christine rose. They discussed the blood franchise, but next to the entry, "Denied" was penned.

What precisely did he deny? Olivia's request? Cerissa's project?

The mayor had also noted Olivia's opposition to expanding housing for low-income unaffiliated vampires.

Hmm. Olivia never mentioned the subject when she recounted her meeting with Winston.

If the mayor had denied Olivia's appeal to place the delivery of Cerissa's product under Olivia's franchise agreement, and if the mayor was going to vote to approve the biotech facility—providing extra blood for unaffiliated vampires, allowing them to join the community—and if the entry noting Olivia's opposition to the unaffiliated was accurate, then Olivia had motive to not only kill the mayor, but to frame Cerissa.

Combined, by killing the mayor and framing Cerissa, Olivia would guarantee destruction of her competitor's project and eliminate any possibility of the unaffiliated joining the community. No on one the council would ever vote to approve the biotech facility, even with a replacement mortal running it. The project would be tainted beyond repair.

Two powerful motives in total.

It was Jayden's theory come to life. But the calendar entry was too ambiguous to build a case against Olivia. They needed something more concrete.

Wearing disposable gloves, Tig flipped through the leatherbound book, checking later dates, which were blank. The rescheduled midnight meeting with Anne-Louise wasn't noted either.

The last entry from the night he died summarized his plan to plant fall bulbs. Strange, because Gaea said he was going to plant the blubs before sunrise. Instead, the early-morning hours were blocked off for a review of the agenda packet for the next council meeting. Did that mean he made entries after the task was completed, or about to be done?

So rather than an appointment calendar, perhaps this was an old-fashioned diary, a record of what he did, rather than what he was scheduled to do.

She closed the leather-bound cover and slipped the diary into an evidence bag. They were using so many bags that she'd sent Bailey to the sub-station to restock.

It had taken her and Jayden quite some time to completely search the mayor's neatly cluttered study. She'd been through the entire desk—including a look for any hidden compartments—and so far, nothing, not even his missing laptop computer.

Didn't everyone have a home computer?

She sent Jayden to help search the bedroom as she wrapped up the office.

Finished with the desk, she glanced around. Built-in bookshelves filled all four walls, from top to bottom, with a wooden ladder on wheels allowing access to the top shelves. The large, walnut-stained desk stood in the middle of the room with two guest chairs in front. They'd been through all the books, looking for hidden valuables, hidden notes, hidden anything. Not a single fake hollow book in the lot. What should she do next?

"Over here." Jayden entered the office carrying a familiar leather bag. "Finally found his briefcase in the bedroom, in a closet. It contains his laptop."

"Excellent. A review of his email might prove useful."

Jayden set the computer on the desktop and hit the power switch. "I wish we could use Ari to conduct the electronic search."

So did she. "Not a good idea."

The *brr-ring* of her phone interrupted the conversation. *Mordida lab* flashed on the screen. "This is Tig."

"Hi, this is Ynez at the lab. I have bad news for you."

"The DNA didn't match?"

"Ah, no. I never got to the comparison, because the blood from the crossbow string keeps coming back as contaminated. I tried three times, and each time—"

"Don't feel bad; we weren't expecting much. Thanks for trying. I'm going to swing by and collect the evidence. Please don't throw anything out."

"No worries. I'll have everything bagged and the evidence card filled out by the time you arrive."

Tig swiped off the call and looked over at Jayden. "It's not mortal blood."

"I heard."

A surprising wave of relief swept through Tig. And not just for Henry's sake. She genuinely liked the mortal. Something that was easier to admit when she wasn't questioning whether Cerissa was a murderer. "That means Cerissa isn't a serious suspect."

"Do you want me to mention the elephant in the room? It could be Henry's blood—and he'd have the opportunity to put the crossbow in her trunk."

"You know how strongly you felt it couldn't be Cerissa in the first place?"

"Yeah."

"Well, trust me on this: Henry would never do anything to implicate Cerissa in a crime. That man loves her too much."

Jayden chuckled. "In that case, are you going to have Cerissa run a comparison of the blood on the bowstring to our suspects' DNA?"

"I'll think about it." Tig adjusted the elasticized blue paper cap she wore over her short afro. "We'd need a way to make sure no one can accuse us of evidence planting or corruption if we use her."

"You know what's been bothering me?" Jayden asked. "Even if the red stain was Olivia's blood, how did her blood get on the bowstring? Olivia's finger was bandaged after the sculpting accident—a vampire's wound wouldn't reopen and bleed. Right?"

"Correct," she replied with a frustrated huff. Jayden had nailed a key point. "Why don't you take your team, go to the mayor's office, and start searching there next?"

"Hey, chief," Zeke said, poking his head into the mayor's study. "Do you need me for anything else? Looks like we're wrapped here, and I have a late-night date."

Tig felt like snarling at him. Since discovering the mayor's body, she and Jayden hadn't had any alone time.

"Come on, chief. Anne-Louise is expecting me to pick up Christine, to keep her safe. All in the line of duty, ma'am."

"Yeah, right."

Jayden shrugged. "We don't need him. The mayor's office is small. Bailey can go home too. Three people would be too many; we'd be bumping into each other. Nicholas and I have this."

"Fine. Zeke, take off for your *date*. I'm headed to Mordida to pick up evidence from their lab."

She just had to figure out how to get it tested without Olivia crying foul. Then an idea struck her. She'd call Marcus as she drove and put the plan in motion.

Chapter 62

DEATH WARRANT

Rolf and Karen's driveway—A short while later

Christine hesitated, unsure whether to climb into the passenger side of Zeke's F-150. Anne-Louise stood near Rolf's rose garden, waving her hands, shooing Christine to go.

Was this a smart idea? Sure, her *grand-mère* encouraged her to seduce Zeke. But Henry opposed any involvement with the cowboy, and she trusted Henry.

On the other hand, Anne-Louise could be right. If Christine took a lover like Zeke, a blood exchange repeated over time might weaken the bond between her and her maker and take some pressure off Henry.

She took a deep inhale and let the air slowly out, watching the cold night frost her breath. All this vampire stuff was so confusing. Although she'd absorbed a lot of information about the community and how vampires lived, she didn't know it at a gut level, which made her decision harder.

Christine glanced over at Zeke, who'd gotten behind the steering wheel. Being close to him, seeing his come-hither smile, stirred desire in her.

After what she did to Patrick, did she deserve any pleasure? Anne-Louise suggested she did. As did Eveline and Wolfie.

"You comin'?" he asked.

She let out a big exhale again and stepped on the running board, hoisted herself inside the cab, and closed the door behind her. She sneaked glimpses at Zeke as he drove them down Rolf's driveway.

He sent a glance her way. "What's you lookin' at, Chrissy?"

Warmth rose to her cheeks. "You."

"I was gonna say you look hungry." He returned his eyes to the road as he pulled the truck out onto Robles. "Did you bring any dark wine with you?"

"I have some left in my purse. But I'm really hungry for something else."

Zeke's face brightened. "I like the sound of that."

So did she. But was she ready? "Where are you taking us?"

"Well, before you confessed your hunger, I was gonna suggest we hang at my house."

"I thought you said you weren't going to seduce me."

"That was last night. This is today. But I won't do nothin' until I hear yes from your lips."

"I'm not saying no, but I'm not sure I'm ready to go back to your place, notwithstanding my hunger."

"Well, it's a mite too late for any social events."

She glanced down at her phone. Three-thirty in the morning. "I have to be back to Henry's at least a half-hour before sunrise."

"Hmm."

"Is there any place people park and make out?"

He laughed, a deep, masculine sound. "Happy Gap."

"Pardon?"

"From my childhood. Where I grew up, at the road's pass, there was a rock pile made of large boulders. We did our off-the-books courtin' there. We called the pass Happy Gap."

"You're making fun of me." She lightly punched his arm, like she did to her best friend when he used to tease her. The memory momentarily saddened her.

"I'd never make fun of you."

She sucked back the emotion and tried to center herself. "When were you born?"

"I was thirty-one when my maker turned me...in 1887."

"Wait." She did the math quickly. "You were a child during the Civil War?"

"Yes, ma'am."

Wow. This was the strangest part of joining the Hill—meeting people who'd lived during historical events she'd only read about. "What was that like, to be alive during the Civil War?"

"I don't have nothin' to compare the experience to. My mama and pappy owned a cattle ranch in California. We didn't feel much impact of the war here. But the smallpox plague of 1862 took my pappy and younger sister, and the drought the following year killed our ranch. Three hundred head of cattle died over the summer after my pappy passed away. My older brother Joshua couldn't keep the ranch going. We tried switching to sheep—they don't eat as much—but we couldn't do the change fast enough, and we owed the bank greatly. Around the time of my eighteenth birthday, we lost the ranch."

"I'm sorry."

"Not your fault, Chrissy. We tried moving into town, to scrape through, but there was no work. Joshua moved up north with Mama, and I started hanging with a bad crowd. I was no good at book learning, but I'm good with my hands, and I applied for an apprenticeship, but neither the cabinetmaker nor the blacksmith could take me on—everyone was a-hurtin'."

When they reached his house, he kept driving. Did he have a local Happy Gap in mind as their destination?

"So what happened?"

"I became an outlaw." Zeke shrugged, his gaze still on the road. "That's how I met Nathaniel, my maker. I tried to rob him and got bit for my trouble. Spent two years as nothing better than a slave. At least he turned me rather than killing me."

"Did he finally let you go?"

"Nope, Henry killed him in a duel over a woman."

"What? He never mentioned—"

"He doesn't like having his dirty laundry aired. Could be why he doesn't want you around me. I've learned over the years to keep my mouth shut about it, but I thought you should know the truth."

Christine eyed him. There was more to the story than either Henry or Zeke had told her separately. Henry had revealed how he accidentally killed his mate, so he didn't bury all his past mistakes like Zeke suggested.

Then again, intentionally killing and accidentally were quite different, too.

Should she believe Zeke? Well, there was one way to find out. "Does Cerissa know?"

"I suspect she does. They had a rough spell around the time she saved my life."

"She *what*?"

He made a left turn onto a dirt road. Soon the truck hugged the side of a mountain, going about fifteen miles per hour on the narrow switchbacks.

"Well, the story goes like this. I jumped in front of a bullet to protect her, and the ammo turned out to be silver. She cut me open, took the bullet out—and a good thing, too. The metal had wedged up against my heart. A wrong move and I'd have been a goner."

Wow. Zeke had almost sacrificed himself to save Cerissa. Christine would confirm the story with her, but there was more to Zeke—and his reputation—than she'd heard from Henry.

As a lawyer, she'd learned how people were rarely all good or all evil. In court, the lawyer who could tell the best tale, the more sympathetic story, would win. While she respected Henry, he wasn't perfect. And while Zeke's flaws raised questions in her mind, he wasn't all bad.

"Are you going to continue your wet work for the government?"

"Now, you raise a good question. If it's a deal killer, I could stop anytime. I've been giving a lot of consideration to my future, and I do believe those days are over for me."

Zeke pulled the truck into a turnout where the dirt road widened, just big enough to turn around. He parked with the back of the truck facing the valley, grabbed a blanket from the back seat, and, cocking his head, invited her to join him in the truck's bed.

A beautiful view. Fields of fall-colored vines, a clear night sky littered with twinkling stars, and a valley of brightly lit houses increased her sense of wellbeing, the place beginning to feel like home. They snuggled together, leaning against the cab's back, the blanket wrapped close around them.

Then an idea hit her. If she could accept the good—as well as the bad—in Zeke and Henry, why couldn't she accept the same in herself? What happened with Patrick was certainly horrific—it was the worst moment of her life. She still had a lot of grieving and work to do, but she was also determined to never kill again.

The universe willing, she'd make good on that vow.

"What's ya thinkin', Chrissy?"

"About my future."

"What's you decide?"

"I like it here. I was also wondering something."

"What's that?"

"I was wondering when you were going to kiss me again."

He pivoted on his butt cheeks, turning to face her. "Well, pretty lady, wait no longer."

Sierra Escondida Police Department—Around
the same time

When Tig returned from the Mordida police lab, she locked up the evidence and waited for Jayden in the squad room. He didn't need her looking over his shoulder as he searched the mayor's office. An hour later, he appeared carrying the mayor's desktop computer, looking perplexed.

He carefully set the machine on the worktable. "Were you aware the mayor had two microphones connected to his computer?"

"So?" She twirled the pen she held. "With videoconferencing, lots of people have microphones."

"Yeah, but hidden in a way to catch the voice of whoever is sitting in the guest chair and software for recording audio only?"

"Maybe he dictated his reports."

"Not according to his secretary. She doesn't do any transcription work for him." Jayden plugged cables from a monitor and keyboard into the computer and then flipped the power switch. "If he used them for dictation, then there should be audio files, right? I haven't found a single one. The mayor had two programs for recording audio, but when I conducted a global search for the file extensions, no files were listed in the results."

She didn't like where this was leading. "Maybe someone erased them?"

"That's possible." Jayden rubbed at his bloodshot eyes. His fatigue really showed. "But my guess is the mayor recorded meetings he held in his office and hid them someplace."

"Are you saying..." If that idiot recorded the confidential conversations she'd had with him over the years, she'd dig up his corpse and pound him into dust.

"See that history?" Jayden pointed at the screen to a list of programs last opened. "Right before the council hearing on Henry, the audio program was active for fifteen minutes. But no file. Same over the past week. Twenty minutes here, ten minutes there. I bet he saved them to an external hard drive."

Tig threw down her pen. "How do we prove any of this?"

"We've exceeded my computer forensics knowledge. We really need Ari."

She so hated this case. The convoluted nature of the evidence had her ready to throw her hands in the air and join Marcus on vacation. "You're right. But how would the community view it? After all, I put Cerissa under arrest initially."

"But you never charged her." Jayden leaned back in the chair and locked eyes with her. "We can't give the computer to Mordida's crime unit—we have no idea what's on here." He tapped his fingers against the case. "Someone could have bluntly discussed *sensitive* topics."

Tig scrubbed her forehead. Yeah, like the blood franchise, for one. Or clone blood. Or how they conspired to cover up Patrick's death.

Dammit. A nest of crocodiles she didn't want to disturb.

"Okay, then what do you suggest?"

"To be extra cautious, we bring in Ari and Seaton together," Jayden replied. "Have Seaton do the button pushing, but let Ari help him. Working together, they might figure out where the audio files went. They can watch each other, and we can watch them to make sure there's no funny business."

"And you want the audio files—if they exist—because those files might tell us whether Olivia had a motive to kill him."

"Bingo," Jayden said, giving her an off-kilter smile. "There's a big discrepancy between Olivia's statement and the mayor's diary. I think the recordings—if they exist—will give us proof that whatever the mayor said to her, he signed his own death warrant."

Tig couldn't be prouder. She loved Jayden. Sure, he was buff. But when he showed off his shining intellect, he really made her hot.

"And, if I'm wrong," Jayden continued, "I imagine the mayor had at least one conversation with Anne-Louise in his office, too. Of course, we won't know whether it incriminates her until we find it."

Tig checked the time. Too close to sunrise to start now. "Captain, please phone Ari and Seaton. Tell them we want their help and ask them to be on standby tomorrow night after the council meeting ends. You're right. This may be the break we need."

Chapter 63

READY OR NOT

Rancho Bautista del Murciélago—Around the same time

After working for an hour on her presentation, Cerissa went to bed and spent a few restless hours trying to sleep. When she woke at ten in the morning, her stomach churned.

Some days it didn't pay to get out of bed. Today felt like one of those days.

She texted Jayden to ask about the DNA test, but he didn't answer. She knew the blood wasn't hers and had confirmed the cheek cells tested human, but maybe Tig was holding off the announcement until tonight's meeting. She just prayed to the Goddess that the DNA wasn't Henry's—that Olivia hadn't gotten hold of the whip and smeared his blood on the bowstring.

During the day, Cerissa practiced her presentation five times, then ate an early dinner, and decided to wear her black suit rather than the gray one, along with a soft white shirt. She fussed with her makeup and hair, not sure whether to wear the long waves up or down or whether her hairstyle even mattered.

Once she heard Henry and Christine stirring about in the kitchen, she went downstairs and spent an hour asking her attorney how to field certain questions from the council. As long as she kept working, her nerves stayed under control.

But by the time nine o'clock rolled around, she sat in the front row of the audience waiting for Rolf to call the town council meeting to order. It was then that her anxious thoughts claimed her.

What if the council hated the plan? What if they wanted expensive changes?

Her budget was already stretched as far as it could go without snapping. The town planners had demanded expensive land improvements. The architect made all the revisions the planning division staff asked for, and the uninitiated mortals who worked for the town at the satellite office outside the community's walls were satisfied. The project met all requirements of state and local law and would be a fine addition to the business district. But now she had to persuade the council.

Henry sat on one side of her and Christine on the other. Henry had conceded and allowed Christine to be next to her in case she needed some last-minute legal advice. Cerissa kept touching her wrist to play with her bracelet, until she remembered it was in Tig's evidence locker. Instead, she twisted her engagement ring around her finger and waited.

Finally, Rolf called the meeting to order. Marcus swore in the new councilmembers, filling all five seats.

Rolf tapped the gavel once. "This is a hearing on the land use project for Biologics Research Lab."

Cerissa scooted to the edge of her seat, waiting for the invitation to approach the podium microphone.

Marcus clicked on his microphone. "Before we begin the hearing, Mr. Mayor, we need to deal with a conflict-of-interest issue. Olivia has the franchise for a competing business, which may be affected by the proposed project. For that reason, she should recuse herself."

Olivia's nameplate lit. Since her appointment, someone had handwritten her name on a blank plastic rectangle and slid the sign into the light-box slot. "Now dearie, according to Winston, what with the new vampires who'll be moving in, Leopold's project won't have any impact on my business. And if we're goin' that way, then Luis also has a conflict and shouldn't participate. He works for me."

"She has a point," Rolf said. "If she has a conflict, so does Luis."

"I'm not done yet, dearie. *You* also have a conflict. You're business partners with the applicant's mate."

"But Cerissa's project won't affect my business interests."

"No, dearie, but you're predisposed to be biased in favor of your partner. You'd be a fool to piss him off by voting against his mate's lab, even if it's in the best interest of the town to do so."

"Bah. This has come up before because we're a small community. I'm not biased—I can be objective."

Cerissa crossed her fingers. She'd counted on Rolf's support. He knew firsthand how important her product was for the community.

Marcus flicked his microphone back on. "If Rolf, Olivia, and Luis are conflicted off, we don't have a quorum, so you'd draw lots to determine which of you remains for the hearing."

"Bah," Rolf scoffed. "I don't agree. Seniority should control."

"State law calls for the conflicted members to draw lots," Marcus replied, and flipped the switch to turn off his microphone.

"We've not followed state law to the letter." Rolf gave a dismissive wave. "Being what we are, we can't. I'm the most senior, so I'll stay."

Olivia screwed her face in an angry scowl. "Well, if we aren't drawing lots, then I'm not stepping aside either."

Luis leaned into his microphone. "Either we draw lots for the one seat, or everyone stays. And to make this cleaner, I officially resign from my position with Olivia's business."

"What?" Olivia shrieked. "You can't resign. Who will replace you?"

"You should have considered that before raising the issue. As of this moment, I no longer have a conflict."

The *pop* over the sound system meant Marcus had turned his mic back on. "Luis is correct. You no longer need to draw lots. Olivia and Rolf shall leave the dais."

Olivia straightened in her seat. "I refuse."

Rolf gave a dismissive wave of his hand. "If she isn't leaving, then neither am I."

Marcus stood. "Please, I ask you to reconsider. Any decision you make could be subject to challenge—"

"Let's find out if Olivia and I make a difference first." Rolf waved for Marcus to sit down and then looked over at Cerissa. "Dr. Cerissa Patel, please approach the podium and explain your project."

She swallowed hard. The fight over who'd stay on the council had grown a rock the size of a boulder in her throat.

Where is Tig? Why isn't she here to clear my name?

Henry had tried phoning the chief before the meeting started, but no answer. He squeezed Cerissa's hand. "You can do this. Don't worry."

She walked to the podium, Christine at her side in case she needed legal advice. Her presentation slides had been loaded on the town's projection system in advance.

"Mr. Mayor and members of the town council," she said as she clicked to the first slide. An artist's rendering of the six-story building appeared on the screen. "Dark wine is the lifeblood of our community. But the quality of the dark wine currently available is poor, suffused with additives to preserve it and frequently stale. Biologics Research Lab has developed a solution to provide fresh dark wine. The land use project you are considering will involve the construction of facilities to produce the community's preferred beverage, to conduct research to find ways to further expand the supply, as well as providing forensic lab assistance to the Sierra Escondida Police Department and to the treaty communities."

She changed slides to one listing the various approvals needed. "Biologics Research Lab is requesting a zoning change to manufacturing and office use, along with a conditional use permit and environmental review to build the project. Town staff chose a mitigated negative declaration as the form of environmental review, which sets forth the methods the project will use to alleviate the environmental impacts identified by staff and public comment."

The next slide detailed the solar panels on the roof and the automated exterior screens, which would block the sun from heating the building in summer. "As you can see, the building will be state of the art, with a platinum LEED rating for saving energy."

She clicked again. "As shown in this diagram, the parking lot has been designed to capture rainwater runoff and direct it underground, to be used to provide water for on-site landscaping."

Another click, and the slide showed a landscape plan and sidebar key explaining each plant. "Drought-tolerant landscaping will be used. We have met all the standards that staff has set for a project like ours in light of the earthquake and resulting water restrictions. For these reasons, we ask for the council's approval."

With that, she flicked off the microphone switch and mentally crossed her fingers.

"Thank you," Rolf said. "Does anyone have any questions?"

"I do," Luis said. "When will your project start producing dark wine for the community?"

Cerissa turned the microphone back on. "We expect construction will take a year. After that, our plan is to begin producing dark wine for consumption right away."

Luis nodded. "The subcommittee is considering a recommendation to build homes to satisfy the state requirements for low-income housing. Planning staff estimates it will take two years to obtain the permits and build the homes. So by that point, you'd have production started and be able to provide dark wine for the new residents?"

"Yes, your projection sounds about right. And if those new residents are qualified, we could offer night employment. We plan on being a twenty-four-hour business."

"Thank you." Luis sat back from his microphone looking satisfied.

"Any other questions?" Rolf asked.

"I have one," Liza said, sweeping her fingers through her short black hair, her face inscrutable. "Dr. Patel, if you become unavailable, who would replace you?"

"I have no plans to leave."

"But you're mor—er, I mean, you're a temporary resident. If something should take you away—"

Cerissa pursed her lips, trying to anticipate where Liza's question was going. "Like all well-run businesses, we have a contingency plan in place. Another trained envoy would replace me."

Liza's face remained unreadable, but she had no follow-up questions.

"Anyone else?" Rolf asked. "Hearing none, we move to our discussion of the project. Personally, I believe Biologics Research Lab will be a fine addition to the Hill. We've all sampled the dark wine the lab plans on producing, and it's of high quality."

Olivia tapped her mic's windscreen. "Well, dearie, until we see these so-called clones, how do we bloody well know where the dark wine comes from?"

"I could bring one—" Cerissa began.

"Don't interrupt." Olivia narrowed her eyes. "I'm not done. Setting aside the question of whether these clones really exist, we can't rightly approve a project for someone who killed the mayor."

"That's not true," Cerissa said before Christine's hand landed on her shoulder, stopping her from saying anything else.

Olivia gave a disgusted snort. "Winston told *me* he was going to oppose your project because he didn't want to expand our numbers. The unaffiliated who were turned after the war shouldn't get a free ride into our community. They bloody well should be destroyed. We didn't fight a war to prevent a Malthusian catastrophe only to allow low-income gobshite freeloaders to drag down the Hill."

"Now, Olivia," Marcus said. "We—"

"Mr. Town Attorney, don't interrupt me. As I was saying, given the mayor's position, Cerissa is the only one with motive to want him dead, especially after what he did to her mate." Olivia's eyes locked on Cerissa. "What, no comment, dearie? Is that a confession?"

Christine leaned into the microphone. "My client is innocent, and we demand that this slander stop now."

"Cerissa is still wearing an ankle monitor." Olivia gave a condescending sniff. "I mean, why do you think that is?"

Cerissa flinched. Why had she worn a skirt? A pantsuit would have worked to cover the monitor, leaving the matter in doubt—only she didn't own one, having always preferred skirts.

When Jayden had first strapped on the tiny device, the monitor had been a lifesaver, letting her leave jail. Right now, it was about to sink her boat. How could one small device represent such opposite meanings?

Christine glared at the councilwoman. "Tig has been too busy to remove it."

"Then why don't we ask the chief herself?" Olivia pointed to the back of the council chambers. Cerissa spun around to see Tig standing near the doors. "Do you have anything new to report?"

Olivia's condescending smile made Cerissa's stomach turn, and she swallowed against the nausea.

She's fishing to discover whether Tig found the crossbow.

Rolf banged the gavel. "Chief Anderson, can you shed some light on the status of your investigation?"

Tig strode to the podium, and Cerissa stepped aside. "At this time, I don't have a public report to make. I'll meet with the council in closed session after this hearing is over."

Olivia puckered her lips, looking frustrated. "But can you confirm why Cerissa is still wearing an ankle monitor?"

Tig scowled at Olivia. "I will not confirm—"

"But you won't deny it's because she's still suspect number one, will ya, dearie?"

"If you would like to recess this hearing, I would be happy to brief the council privately right now."

Olivia scoffed. "I think we know everything we need to without going into a secret meeting. I'm voting against the project for the same reasons the mayor opposed it."

Liza's eyes looked sympathetic. "I'm sorry, but I agree with Olivia. If Cerissa is a suspect, we shouldn't approve this project."

Cerissa cringed, her stomach twisting into a knot. She'd counted on Liza's support. "Please, Tig," she whispered, "say something. Tell them it's not true."

Tig stood there, remaining silent.

Why? She knew the cheek cells tested human. Why wouldn't Tig speak up?

Liza tapped her microphone. "I'm not ready to have a stranger come in and take over the project before it's even built, which would happen if Cerissa is guilty," Liza continued. "I don't want to approve a project that will be run by a mortal we've never met."

Carolyn pursed her lips, eyes narrowed, pausing for a moment. She then leaned forward. "I'm gonna agree with Liza. Wouldn't be prudent to approve the project if the applicant is a suspected murderer."

"Why don't you take a recess and listen to what Tig has to say first?" Cerissa pleaded.

Olivia snorted. "It won't change anyone's mind, dearie. It's rather clear your time is nearly up. You should sod-off while you still can."

Luis made a motion to recess and reorder the agenda, but it failed to pass. When Rolf officially called for a vote to approve the project, three voted against—Olivia, Carolyn and Liza—and two in favor—Rolf and Luis.

"I'm sorry, Cerissa," Rolf said. "Your request for project approval is denied. You can reapply in six months once your name has been cleared. Meeting adjourned."

Chapter 64

A Deep Cut

Town council—Moments later

Tig hated the vote results, but catching the killer took priority. She'd do damage control when the investigation wrapped. And frankly, despite her gut feeling, she couldn't fully rule out Henry as a suspect—and by extension, his mate as an accomplice—until they completed the blood DNA comparison.

Hard evidence, not instinct, was what the council needed from her.

Tig pulled Cerissa aside before the scientist could leave the building.

"I need to speak with you and Luis."

Tig motioned to Luis, who joined them, and then she found an empty conference room, rushing the two mortals inside.

A closed session of the council would start in fifteen minutes. She didn't have much time.

"Wait." Henry stood with a hand blocking the door as Tig tried to close it. "You're shutting us out? You shouldn't speak to Cerissa without her attorney."

Tig pushed his hand off the door. "This isn't about her guilt or innocence."

Christine wormed her way past Henry. "If you're going to question Cerissa about the murder, I should be present."

"I don't need you in order to speak to one of the town's paid consultants in the course and scope of her job," Tig said with a growl. "Step back. Now."

Christine moved back. "This is most irregular."

"Everything about our community is irregular." Tig shut the door and turned to the scientist. "I'm sorry, Cerissa. I couldn't reveal how I knew your guilt is in doubt."

"I—I can't believe you said nothing when Olivia began spewing her hate. Why won't you take off the ankle monitor? By now, you must know my blood wasn't on the bowstring."

"Be patient. We'll get there."

"Patient?" The anger in Cerissa's eyes gave way to desperation. "You don't understand. Leopold will pull the project from the Hill and insist we locate elsewhere. You'll all lose out. We have to go back in there, ask the council to reconsider. There must be something you can say."

Tig shook her head. She felt awful about refusing to remove the ankle monitor and motioned for the two mortals to sit. "I can't say anything yet, not in open session. If we're wrong about our possible suspects, I don't want to tip off the real killer or their accomplice. The less the community knows about the evidence, the better chance we have of trapping the real culprits."

Plus, no matter how much Tig suspected Olivia, she needed to keep the council in the dark until she sprang her plan on them in closed session, especially if it was one of them.

"Do you have any idea what a six-month delay is going to do to us?" The distress in Cerissa's voice was heartrending. "And Henry—"

"I understand. I'll do whatever I can once we prove who killed the mayor."

Luis patted Cerissa's shoulder. "Let's hear why Tig wanted to speak to us."

Cerissa let out a noisy breath. "Fine. Why are we here?"

Tig took a seat across from them, folding her hands on the table. "Right now, I need to obtain DNA from our potential suspects and compare their DNA to the dried blood on the crossbow."

"Ah, what crossbow?" Luis asked.

"We found what we believe to be the murder weapon. Dried blood was on the bowstring."

Cerissa crossed her arms. "The Mordida lab reported the sample as contaminated, didn't they? The blood wasn't mortal."

Tig drummed her fingers on the table. "Correct. I'll need your help to compare the DNA on the bowstring to the DNA of our suspects. Will cheek swabs work?"

"I've never compared anything except blood DNA for vampires. Cheek DNA should work, but now isn't the time to experiment, is it?"

"You're right." Relief flooded Tig, relaxing her chest. Finally, they were making progress. "While I can't let you do the tests directly, could Luis do them under your supervision? He has the background. That's why I asked him in here."

"Sure, I could show him how to run the comparison. The machine in my basement is programmed to analyze vampire DNA, so it's fairly easy to run the test."

"Luis, would you?"

"Yes. And I suggest a double-blind. Have Jayden do a chart. Label the collection tubes with a random number, and he writes the number on a chart next to the name and keeps it secret. I won't know which sample belongs to which vampire."

Impressive suggestion—Tig's respect for Luis increased a notch.

"Perfect. I'll tell Jayden." Tig looked at Cerissa. "Do you have your medical bag in your car? To collect blood samples?"

"We don't need a big donation. A finger prick would be enough. How many samples?"

"Plan on six. Henry will be one of them."

"I don't have enough collection kits here. I'll drive home to get them and be back in about twenty minutes. Luis can come with me."

"Do it. And take Luis's car. I have an errand for Henry."

Luis and Cerissa rushed to the parking lot. Tig asked Henry to drive to Rolf's and bring Anne-Louise back. She'd found him and Christine just outside the door, probably listening to the whole thing, because he didn't give her any pushback.

Done delegating, she headed through the lobby past the tall glass windows.

Jayden came running up before she got to the door of the council chambers. "Tig, I figured out how the blood got on the bowstring."

She pulled him to the side so no one would hear. "Brilliant. Go ahead."

"I found an internet article about crossbow accidents. Picture the crossbow. The bolt travels in a rail, supported by a stock, like a rifle. The bow is in front parallel to the ground, with a pulley at each end of it. The string runs over the pulley and is drawn back toward the archer, bending the bow, creating tension. When the trigger is released, the string snaps forward, launching the bolt along the rail on the stock."

"Yeah, so?"

"If you ignore the finger guard and grip your free hand too high on the crossbow—if you hold the stock like you'd hold a rifle—the string will slice through your thumb. Or if you let your fingers wrap around and creep up the other side, the string will slice through your fingers when triggered. Particularly the index finger." Jayden smirked. "I bet if we go back and sift the leaves under the bushes around the mayor's fence, we'll find Olivia's fingertip."

Tig laughed grimly at the image. "If she didn't take it with her."

"Either way, the blood on the string must be Olivia's."

Picturing the white finger bandage and the so-called sculpting accident, Tig gave a grim chuckle. "I won't take your bet. The circumstantial evidence is piling up. Now, let's get that blood sample and close the case."

CHAPTER 65

CORNERED

TOWN COUNCIL CHAMBERS—FIFTEEN MINUTES LATER

The public could be legally excluded from closed session meetings, and Tig glanced around to make sure the room was cleared. Only the council and those necessary to the deliberations were allowed in.

The councilmembers slowly dribbled back to take their seats on the dais, returning late from their break, with Marcus at his usual town attorney desk to the side of the dais.

The slow pace worked in her favor. Cerissa and Luis would join them soon.

"What are they doing here?" Rolf asked, waving the gavel at Henry, Christine, and Anne-Louise.

Tig stepped to the audience podium. "Mr. Mayor and members of the town council. I asked to meet with you in closed session because we've had a break in the case." She waved her hand in the audience's direction. "They are necessary to what I'm about to ask you."

The main doors opened. Cerissa and Luis barreled in. Luis headed straight to the dais, carrying a large black medical bag, and Cerissa sat down next to Henry.

"Due to the nature of the breakthrough," Tig continued, "I could not speak publicly. I've recovered a piece of crucial evidence and need a blood sample from each of you."

Liza's eyes got big. "Seriously?"

"What?" Olivia squawked.

"*Beurk*," Anne-Louise scoffed from behind her.

"The chief thinks each of us got motive," Carolyn said. "Liza, you said you'd run against Winston, and I walked out angry at him for what he did to Henry. Rolf wants to be mayor too. But what motive does Olivia and Anne-Louise got?"

Tig was surprised the analytical councilwoman hadn't figured it out. "I don't need to explore anyone's motive right now. I've asked Luis to take a blood sample from each of you, and he's agreed." She nodded in Luis's direction. "The evidence we're comparing against has already been documented and tested by the Mordida crime lab. The blood we found on the evidence wasn't mortal. Mordida's lab has confirmed it's vampire."

Tig didn't care if the council knew at this point—it was the rest of the community she didn't want to tell in case she was wrong about Olivia. The councilmembers were sworn to secrecy over what was said in closed session. If Olivia wasn't the killer, but flapped her lips, she'd be in a world of hurt, not the least of which was losing her position on the council.

Besides, peer pressure might help persuade the other councilmembers to go along, and if peer pressure didn't work, the warrants would—Marcus had already gotten the San Francisco judge to sign them. Tig wasn't going to be made to wait again. Thanks to her inspiration last night as she spoke to Jayden, this time she'd come prepared.

"Luis will take the blood sample now if you all will—"

"What are you going on about?" Olivia interrupted. "I thought vampire DNA couldn't be read by mortal machines. What will a blood sample of ours even do?"

"You're correct, most DNA analyzers report the sample as 'corrupted,' which Mordida's did. But Dr. Patel programmed her machine to analyze vampire DNA. We are going to use hers to do the comparison."

"Well, dearie, she's a suspect. You can't use her machine—"

Tig locked eyes with the mayor and talked right over Olivia. "And while we will employ Cerissa's machine, Luis will conduct the test under my supervision. We are testing the blood of six people: all vampires on the council, Henry, and Anne-Louise. The test will be done double-blind. Luis won't know which sample belongs to which person. Only Jayden will. He'll number the swabs randomly and keep a chart of which swab corresponds to which person."

"I don't care." Olivia shook her head so hard she looked like a bobblehead. "You can't have my blood. You could take it and plant it on something. I am not going to let you do that."

"We are only taking microsamples," Tig said. "A tiny dot on a small cotton swab, enough for a test, but not enough to plant on anything. The blood will be consumed in the test."

Olivia stood. "Well, I refuse."

Rolf banged his gavel. "Sit down, Olivia. I suspect the chief already has warrants for each of us. You have no choice."

"Well, I never. This is unfair. I didn't do anything wrong. Why do you need my blood?"

"Methinks the lady doth protest too much," Henry said loud enough for Tig to hear.

Anne-Louise laughed. "Normally, I'd object, but since you're making these buffoons submit, I'll go along."

Tig cleared her throat loudly to silence the peanut gallery. "After we take your sample, each of you is restricted to the Hill until all the samples are processed. I've already notified the guard gate."

"But I have to go to my warehouse," Olivia whined.

"I'm sorry, councilwoman. Whatever you need there will wait until the comparisons are completed. We'll start with Rolf."

Luis rose from his end seat and walked around the dais, carrying the black bag to where Rolf presided from the middle. Taking the mayor's index finger, Luis pricked the ball with a metal lancet and touched a cotton swab to the dot of blood pooling on Rolf's fingertip. He handed the swab to Jayden, who dropped it into an evidence container, sealed the container, and wrote a number on the outside, not letting anyone view his work.

Rolf waved off the bandage Luis offered him and licked his finger instead.

Luis repeated the same procedure on Carolyn and Liza. When he got to Olivia, she bared her fangs at him.

"Knock that shit off," Tig ordered her. "Hold out your hand."

Luis pricked Olivia's finger and took the sample. He then took samples from Henry and Anne-Louise.

Henry's maker smiled smugly. Tig noted the reaction but didn't ask why, although one twist had occurred to her: Anne-Louise would have been in a position to plant Henry's blood on the bowstring.

But Tig refused to get ahead of herself. The test results would direct her next course of action. Hard evidence, not political maneuvering, would determine the guilty party.

Henry and Cerissa's basement—Two hours later

Tig perched on a tall stool Henry had carried from the kitchen to the basement and watched as Luis ran each sample. Cerissa was banished to the far corner and told not to come any closer. She was only there in case Luis had questions, while Jayden video-recorded the whole thing.

Henry had been told to wait upstairs. Anne-Louise hadn't come with them, and instead arranged a ride back to Rolf's place.

Prior to leaving council chambers, Tig had pulled Rolf aside and asked him to keep the council in closed session for the next two hours.

"Without Luis?" he'd asked.

"Don't make any big decisions. Just keep them all busy."

Rolf gave a tight grin. "We have a thirty-page waste disposal contract to review. I'll have Marcus explain it line by line. That should keep us occupied for a while. Everyone loves talking trash."

She resisted the urge to laugh at his bad joke. "Don't let them leave until I text you."

"I'll try."

"Do better than try—keep them here." With those words, she then left for Cerissa's lab.

Lost in thought when the machine *dinged* and the printer shot out a page, Tig suddenly sat upright at the sounds.

"That's the last sample." Luis grabbed the printout, leaned over the lab bench, the one in the center of the room, and studied the reports. Finally, he slid a page across the tabletop to Tig. "We have a match."

She looked at the printout for sample number two-three-six, and then showed the report to Jayden. "Who is this number?"

Jayden's lips quirked up. "Who do you think? Olivia."

Tig tapped her fingers on the lab bench. What to do next? She had no way to prove the crossbow found in Cerissa's car trunk was the one that killed Winston. The bolts matched, they were one short of a full pack, and silver flakes lined the crossbow's channel, but all of that was circumstantial evidence.

Olivia would whine, claiming the blood on the string was planted there too.

Tig wanted unassailable evidence before charging a councilmember with murder, no matter how obnoxious the councilmember was.

"I want a way to tie the bolt to the crossbow. Can the Mordida forensics lab tell if the bolt we removed from the mayor was fired from the crossbow we have in evidence?"

"Hmm," Jayden said. "We may be able to hire an expert to give an opinion of whether the crossbow's track created the marks. And the lab can test the silver residue in the crossbow's track to see if they match—"

Cerissa nodded. "If there are impurities in the silver—metal is rarely one hundred percent pure—they might be able to tell you how close the match is between the particles in the track, and the silver on the bolt."

"All right. I'm asking you and Luis to keep this to yourself. Do not tell your mates, do not tell anyone. We have more evidence to evaluate before I decide what to do. Agreed?"

"Henry will understand." Cerissa stepped over to the equipment and started cleaning around the machine. "I've told him before I can't tell him about things covered by doctor-patient confidentiality, and he's accepted the edict."

"Abigale will be fine too," Luis said.

"Good. Send me the bill for Luis's time and your lab services. Jayden, please pack the evidence samples and reports. It's time to call Ari and Seaton."

"Wait!" Cerissa hurried back over to Tig. "Before you leave, would you please remove this?"

The scientist raised her leg, placing her foot on the rung of the stool, displaying the ankle monitor.

Jayden grabbed a pair of clippers from a tool rack on one of the lab benches and did the job before shoving the ankle monitor into his back pocket.

Cerissa gave a relieved exhale as she lowered her foot. "Thank you, Jayden."

Tig huffed. "Now, can we please leave? We have work to do."

Sierra Escondida Police Station—Twenty minutes later

Tig had barely settled into her chair in the squad room when Ari poked his head through the doorway. "Can I come in?"

She rose to her feet and gestured for him to enter. "Here's the problem."

"Wait, I brought Seaton. He needs to learn this stuff."

"Yes, both of you come in here." She was counting on them being together to lend an appearance of accountability.

Ari took the chair she offered him and nodded a hello to Jayden. "Okay, what's cookin'?"

"We discovered the mayor had a hidden microphone connected to his desktop computer"—she patted the beige box sitting on the table—"but we haven't found any audio recordings."

"I've tried searching for the file extensions assigned by the programs, but the search returned nothing," Jayden said, standing up from his seat at the keyboard and monitor. "Any ideas?"

"Okay." Ari pursed his lips, looking thoughtful for a moment. "If we assume the mayor made recordings, but didn't want anyone to find them, there are two easy ways to achieve his goal. One would be to change the file extension. When he wanted to play the recording, he'd change the extension back. That takes more work but is better at concealing the files than the second way, which would be to use hidden folders to hide the files."

Jayden scrunched his brow. "The mayor didn't strike me as tech savvy."

"Then let's start with the easy one. Seaton, come on, take the hot seat."

Gaea's foster looked disgruntled. "If I must."

"Dude, you're gonna need a career soon. Lose the 'tude and get with it."

Seaton slid into the chair Jayden had vacated. "Yeah, yeah. Now what?"

"We've done this lesson already, remember?"

"First I have to figure out how many hard drives, right?" Seaton double-clicked to open file explorer. "Looks like only one hard drive."

"It's also possible he used an external drive to store the audio files. We'll check after we look for hidden files."

Ari moved to stand over Seaton's shoulder. "Okay, do you remember how to reveal hidden files?"

Seaton clicked the "view" button and then clicked the "hidden items" box.

"Good job. Let's look at what we have. Ooh, this may be an easy one after all." He pointed at the screen. "Tig, see that folder entitled audio files? Could be what you're looking for."

Seaton clicked and opened the folder. A long list of audio files appeared, titled by date and a person's name.

Tig scanned the list, her ire growing as she saw how many times her name appeared in a file title. That bastard had recorded their confidential communications.

Surprisingly, there was no recording labeled "Anne-Louise." Somehow, Henry's maker had avoided the office hotseat.

Tig touched the screen, pointing to Olivia's name and the date she met with the mayor. "Play that one."

CHAPTER 66

LIAR

Mayor's office—Audio recording from six nights ago

Tig listened carefully for any audio clues to tell her what was happening in the room. The recording started with the sound of papers shuffling, followed by footsteps and a door opening.

"Olivia, please come in," the mayor said. "What's this about? Your message sounded urgent."

A chair scraped on the floor. "Well, dearie, I've just learned something I find quite disturbing."

"And that is?"

"Henry's mate is distributing dark wine to various Hill residents."

The mayor *harrumphed*. A reminder Tig would never hear the mayor's signature sound again in person.

"My understanding was that she's grown clones," Winston said. "Her clones aren't fully mortal, but they produce mortal blood."

"But I hold the *exclusive* franchise, dearie. Here"—the rustle of paper flapping and landing on a desk muffled the next few words—"what Cerissa is doing on Leopold's behalf violates that clause."

"Please be quiet and let me read this." A long pause followed. "I must disagree, Olivia. Your franchise is exclusive to the collection of expired donor blood from hospitals and the like, and donor blood you yourself collect using storefronts where mortals are paid to donate. What Cerissa is doing is neither of those things."

"But—"

"I'll have Marcus review the clause if you want, but I already know what he will say."

"Don't bother, dearie. When Leopold starts selling *clone blood*"—Olivia said those words in the snootiest tone possible—"I'll appeal to the whole council. His servant is giving the blood away for free now. But once they start charging, all bets are off. I'll make a right to-do about it."

"Have you considered buying into their business? Or offering to provide delivery services for her product, using the system you've already established?"

"Bollocks. I'm not sacrificing my profit margin to become a delivery boy for Leopold or his mortal."

"But really, you should feel little to no loss to your business. From what I understand, Cerissa's goal is to supplement the blood supply—not replace donor blood."

"Which brings me to my main concern: all this talk of turning thirteen more mortals and inviting unaffiliated vampires to live here. I'm barely able to keep up with the current needs of the community for donor blood. And my supply is growing tighter and tighter. Mortals are finding ways to use expired blood for other purposes. What you have planned will make us dependent on Leopold. It's a bloody terrible idea!"

"Now, Olivia—"

"Don't 'now, Olivia' me! I didn't fight in a bloomin' war to see it all come undone. We can't afford to expand our numbers. Overpopulation will kill us more certainly than any stake would. Is that not the very reason we fought that war?"

"You're overstating your case. Creating a dozen new homesteads, letting unaffiliated vampires join us—it won't cause a food supply problem, and it's the right thing to do."

She scoffed. "I'm not going to let our community become dependent on Leopold and his mortal lackey. Don't you realize the danger we're in? All it would take is another national dispute, and New York could starve us into submission. We shouldn't have to live with Leopold's boot on our necks."

A chair squeaked—Tig recognized that squeak all too well, could picture the mayor leaning back and clasping his hands over his belly. "We both know you can't stop progress. Whether it's here, or somewhere else, clone blood is coming. Why not use this new source of dark wine to expand our numbers and take care of our current problem with the unaffiliated vampires?"

"But it puts us at the mercy of that New York bastard!"

"Well, my dear, you can voice your concerns at the public hearing. Cerissa hasn't gotten the development plan approved yet. And then there's the construction time." The chair squeaked again. "You have at least a year, if not two, before you feel the competition from her clones. And like I said, you shouldn't feel any loss if you do your job properly. As far as Leopold's concerned, the biotech facility will be in our jurisdiction, giving us control over the production of blood, not Leopold. You're overstating the problem."

"*Overstating*?" Olivia screeched. "Are you going to vote to approve her plans?"

"Now, Olivia, you know better. I can't discuss how I'm going to vote prior to the meeting. I have to consider the development plans and listen to the community before I decide."

"You lily-livered, toad-sucking wanker. You *are* going to approve it."

"Olivia, please settle down. There's no reason—"

"No reason? Give me that back." The sound of papers flapping. She must have grabbed the franchise agreement from Winston. "Dearie, your re-election is coming up next year. I may just run against you."

"That won't solve your problem. You couldn't vote on this issue—it'd be a conflict of interest with your own franchise. And if you push the council too hard, well, when your franchise comes up for renewal, they could decide to award the whole thing to Cerissa and let her handle all the distribution."

Olivia growled. "We'll see about that, tosser."

The door slammed shut, and the mayor *harrumphed*. "Where is my mouse? There—"

And the recording ended.

Chapter 67

GUILTY

Sierra Escondida Police Department—Moments later

Tig let out a deep exhale. Finally, the killer's real motive. No way could Olivia explain away the lies she told when Tig questioned her originally.

"Yes." Ari grinned and gave Seaton a fist bump. "Got her."

Tig nodded. Between the recording and the blood evidence, Marcus could now make a good case against Olivia. Hopefully, when the Mordida lab completed the silver analysis, it would only strengthen the case.

Tig picked up a pen and paper to jot down her next steps, how best to spring the trap. Before she could make the first note, the truth pounced on her like a lion attack in the Serengeti brush.

If Olivia hadn't been so intent on pinning the blame on Cerissa, on leaving the crossbow in Cerissa's car, she might have gotten away with murder. It would have been a credibility war, and Tig couldn't say how the battle would have ended. Olivia was a good liar. And delusional too.

Did Olivia really think Cerissa's project would give Leopold leverage over the Hill? Leverage that he'd use to starve them out of spite? The recording certainly captured Olivia's blind belief that once someone was your enemy, they'd always be your enemy. But if living a long life had taught Tig anything, it was that alliances changed all the time.

And from what Olivia had said from the dais, the councilwoman resented the unaffiliated, especially those turned after the treaty was signed. A stance that was unsympathetic and simply unfair. It wasn't their fault their makers had chosen to live outside the treaty, which now put them under a death sentence if they couldn't pony up the money to join a community. That was a circumstance of their rebirth that they had no control over.

Or was that all a smoke screen to cover up Olivia's fear of losing her source of income?

From everything Tig had heard, the Hill would need both donor blood and clone blood. Olivia might feel competition from Cerissa's product, but competition wouldn't put her out of business. No, Tig would bet a hundred dollars that Olivia resented most the idea of inviting a dozen unaffiliated to join the community and qualify for low-income housing.

Olivia was a big snob, with her button nose high in the air. Sure, she worked hard to keep the donor blood business running, but luck played a factor too. Housing prices just happened to be much lower when Olivia bought into the community. A fact she conveniently ignored when noting that many of the unaffiliated faced being priced out of the market. Her arrogance preferred to assume she was more savvy or hardworking or innately extraordinary.

Tig snorted in disgust.

In any case, once Olivia was in custody, Tig would ask the hard questions, and maybe get some answers. Maybe.

But she wanted this airtight. "Jayden, would you please stay here with Ari and Seaton and keep searching, look for anything else related to the mayor's murder? You have the list of other suspects. Make sure there isn't anything implicating them, anything Olivia could use to wiggle out of the charge. I'm going to go arrest her."

Tig's phone rang, and she answered, "Yes, Nicholas, I'm in a hurry."

"It took me a while, but I finished reviewing the credit card statements."

"Olivia bought a crossbow?"

"Two sets, actually, both crossbows and bolts. And get this—she used her business account so she could deduct the weapons from her taxes."

"As what, contract negotiations for her franchise?" Tig said with a snort. "Wait. That means she's armed."

"Precisely why I wanted you aware of the facts. I've texted Marcus too, so he knows."

"Thanks. I'm on it. Bye."

Jayden raised an eyebrow. "Do you want me to call Zeke and tell him to meet you at Olivia's?"

"Yes, and advise the guard gate, too."

"Will do." Jayden squeezed her arm. "And wear your stab-proof vest. The bulletproof type won't protect you."

Tig headed for the closet. Jayden had an excellent point. The stab-proof vest would stop an arrow or bolt. She had no intention of winding up like the mayor.

The police radio in the corner came to life. "This is the gate. We have a situation. Shots fired."

Tig *whooshed* over, scooped up the microphone, stretching the coiled cord, and keyed the button. "Chief Anderson here. Report."

"Olivia Paquin left the community. We told her she couldn't leave. Officer Cannon tried to stop her, and she shot him with a crossbow."

Fuck! Tig rocked on her feet and stared at the security monitors. Zeke lay on the asphalt, gripping his chest and writhing. As Tig had listened to the audio of Olivia and the mayor, her back had been turned to the video feeds.

What the hell? Rolf was supposed to keep the council in closed session until she texted him. "Did the bolt go through Zeke's heart?"

"Don't know. He's on the ground, moaning." The guard paused. "I couldn't stop her; I couldn't even move when she reached into the guard shack and pushed the gate button. I don't know what happened."

Tig scrubbed her face. To an uninitiated mortal, none of this would make sense. "Ten-four. I'll contact emergency medical. You wait there and do nothing—don't try to remove the bolt from Zeke. I'm on my way."

To Jayden, she added as she started moving, "I've changed my mind. You're with me."

"What do you want us to do?" Ari asked.

"Keep searching for anything else on the mayor's computer that nails Olivia."

"Will do."

Tig grabbed her stab-proof vest from the closet and tossed Jayden his, then jogged to the exit door. "Once we're in the car, call Dr. Clarke, have him report to the gate to take care of Zeke. Then contact Liza. We'll need backup. This isn't going to be pretty—Olivia's got nothing left to lose."

Rancho Bautista del Murciélago—The same night

Cerissa stayed in the basement lab to clean after everyone left. With the council denying her development application, her project was down the drain, so she had nothing better to do. The last thing she felt like doing was calling Leopold to give him the bad news.

When her phone rang, she read the caller ID, relieved it wasn't Leopold, and immediately swiped accept. "Did something happen?"

"Hey, Ciss," Ari whispered. "We have a situation."

"Yeah? What now? And speak louder, I can barely hear you. There's a lot of echo where you are. Why don't you have your video on?"

"I'm calling from the restroom at the police station, so Seaton won't overhear. Olivia escaped. She's headed to the freeway. But I got her license plate from the video—"

"Video? What video?"

"The gate surveillance video. Never mind. The key point is, I'm tracking her car."

"Why tell me? Tell Tig and Jayden."

"Ah, I can't. The program is so far advanced—and illegal—that I'm not willing to risk it."

She snorted. "You? Afraid of taking a risk? Now I've heard everything."

"Do you want to help or don't ya?"

"I'm in the clear now. Tig knows I didn't kill the mayor. That's what's important. Let her solve the case from here."

But as soon as the words left her lips, her stomach lurched. Until the council convicted Olivia, Cerissa's good name wouldn't be restored—although fleeing made the councilwoman look guilty as hell.

Ari huffed. "Ciss, you're too nice. You let people walk all over you. You should be the one to bring the killer in."

"Ari, don't be ridiculous—"

"Tig won't be able to catch her. She knows the direction Olivia went thanks to the intersection cameras, but from what we can tell, Olivia shot Zeke, which gave her a fifteen-minute head start."

"Is Zeke okay?"

"Sounds like the bolt didn't go through his heart. Dr. Clarke is treating him."

Cerissa exhaled sharply, relief coursing through her. Zeke would live without her help. Since the bolt didn't penetrate his heart, Dr. Clarke was competent enough to remove it.

"Ari, Dr. Clarke can handle Zeke, and Tig can bring in a helicopter from Mordida. Jayden told me they signed a mutual assistance pact with the Mordida police. They used it when they searched for the Carlyle Cutter."

"I wish I was there to pound on your head in person. Tig can't make that call. Olivia has nothing left to lose. She'll kill any mortal who tries to stop her. She'll rip out throats and claw people to death. She'll reveal what vampires are. Tig won't be able to contain the damage."

"All Tig has to do is track the freeway cameras—"

"Wrong again. With a fifteen-minute head start, Olivia can take an unmonitored exit off the freeway, drive the back roads, and hide out in someone's vacation cabin."

Cerissa brushed her hair out of her face. Even if Olivia escaped tonight, Tig could monitor all police reports for bites within a five-hundred-mile radius. The first time Olivia went hunting, Tig would read the police report and narrow her search.

Except this was Olivia. She had access to plenty of blood—she probably loaded her car with a month's worth of bags and could stay hidden for a long time.

Ari had a point. And he couldn't take off to track Olivia—not with Seaton there.

"I can loop the video your lenses record," Ari continued. "The Protectors will never notice; they aren't watching as vigilantly anymore."

Yeah, the Protectors didn't like her using her Lux abilities to interfere in vampire conflicts. She had put her neck on the line when she saved Karen's life, and as punishment, the Protectors required her to wear her lenses and record everything—everything except her personal time with Henry.

She pursed her lips. If it was worth breaking the rules to save others, why not break them to protect herself? Why was that so much harder to do? It was why she hadn't played the public relations game as well as Olivia did. And look at the mess that landed her in.

It was time to stand up for herself.

A sense of resolution settled in her chest. She tore off her lab coat and ran upstairs. "Send me the app."

"Done. You can track her. Flash to her car, shoot out her tire, anything to slow her escape and give Tig a chance to catch her."

As Cerissa sprinted through the house to her bedroom, a solution blazed through her mind. With a satisfied smirk, she added, "I've got a better idea."

Chapter 68

GETAWAY

OLIVIA'S HOUSE—FORTY MINUTES EARLIER

Olivia slammed the door as she charged into her ranch-style home. Rolf had kept them in closed session, blathering on about rubbish collection contracts and legal advice for two hours.

Two hours! What a wanker.

As much as she wanted to slip out the minute Tig had, she didn't dare—Rolf would have been on her arse, reporting her to Tig.

Bollocks! How had this happened?

How had she never heard DNA tests worked on vampires? Wasn't that something the community had a right to know?

Thanks to Rolf and his lip flapping, the kitchen clock read ten minutes to one. Did she have time to pack? Given a choice between fighting her way out or starting over penniless, she'd be damned before she abandoned her hard-won earnings.

She tossed a bag on the bed, threw in her jewel case, added a few changes of clothes and knickers—she could easily replace her wardrobe once she found a new home—then raided the safe for her six false passports.

If her mum had taught her anything, it was *be prepared*. Currency could be devalued. Stock markets could fall. Property values could plummet. But gold bullion was a girl's best friend.

She moved the bed aside, lifted a section of the solid pecan baseboard, and rolled back the carpet and pad. Her topnotch woodworking skills meant those daft coppers never noticed the removable panel. The steel door underneath the carpet covered a large square hole in the concrete subfloor she'd carved out—her sculpting tools had come in handy, and no one the wiser.

Hooking her fingers into the recessed handle, she lifted the steel door. In the rectangular space between the exposed rebar lay her hoard of gold, along with an empty space where the crossbow originally rested.

The gold was already packed in easy-to-carry cases with handles, and she carted them out to the boot of her Mercedes sedan. It took her eighteen trips to the garage, but *whooshing* at vampire speed made a snap of the work. The suitcase with her clothes and jewels went into the back seat. The passports, credit cards in different names, and cash stash went into her Christian Louboutin tote with the red-on-black ombre logo motif.

While packing, she groused to herself. Why had she tried to pin the murder on Cerissa? Leaving the crossbow in the boot of Cerissa's car—that decision had royally cocked up an otherwise perfect plan, damn her eyes.

Well, nothing to be done about it now. Olivia gave the closet one last look, grabbed some expensive shoes—this year's models—and threw them into a bag.

She'd pull a Lord Lucan, she would.

After all, if a lord could commit murder and then disappear, never to be found again, why couldn't she?

She didn't even give the house a final nostalgic tour. Instead, she dumped the extra blood bags from the refrigerator into an ice chest, poured in ice cubes, and left. She could always add more ice at a hotel or during a minimart stop.

With six suspects, Olivia wasn't surprised—pleased, but not surprised—when she arrived home and learned Tig hadn't put a stakeout on her place. Rolf and Liza were the only other vampire coppers the chief had, and since they were under suspicion as well, Tig couldn't exactly task them to watch her. Which left only Zeke.

The big unknown—was he watching her house from Robles Road? Or would he be at the gate?

Didn't matter. In the garage, she tore open the drywall and took out the second crossbow she'd hidden, adding more silver-tipped bolts. If she had to, Zeke would go the way of the mayor.

When she drove onto Robles Road, no other cars were out and about. No sign of Zeke, and at the guard shack, only the mortal guard was visible through the window. She drove past the exit sensor, but the automatic gate didn't open, forcing her to stop. She stared at the mortal, tapping the horn, trying to look impatient rather than nervous, and cocked her head in the direction of the wrought-iron gate, hoping he'd get the message.

Instead, the door to the guard shack opened and Zeke stepped out, gun in hand, pointed to the ground. The door shut behind him. "Turn around, ma'am."

She couldn't fire the crossbow at him from inside the car. With the steering wheel in the way, the bow was too broad. She had to wait for an opportunity to get out without him noticing what she had on the front seat hidden under her jacket, so she lowered the driver's window instead. "There's an emergency at the warehouse, dearie. One of the refrigerators died, and I have to move all the stock to another one, or we're going to be short this week."

Zeke frowned but looked thoughtful. The glutton wouldn't want to starve. They all relied on her—let them see how rotten it'd get without her deliveries.

He unhooked his phone from his belt but had to use his gun hand to tap the screen. Just the opening she needed to *whoosh* out of the car and position herself in the archer's stance, her feet shoulder width apart, facing square to the target, and making sure she kept her bloody fingers below the rail this time.

Zeke dodged, but not soon enough. She pulled the trigger. The bolt lodged in his gut.

Bugger. Well, I suppose they can't all be brilliant kill shots.

She *whooshed* over and grabbed his gun.

"Hey, you," she called out to the guard. "Open the gate, dearie!"

The door to the guard shack stayed shut, but the guard peered out the window's bottom.

Bloody rotter. No matter. She *whooshed* to him and flung the door open.

"Wh-what are you doing?" he asked.

Like the tosser's never been mesmerized before.

Olivia froze him in place, then reached around the open door and pushed the entrance gate button—she'd seen the guards push that button near a thousand times, so she knew how to find it—and got into her car, backed up, and drove out the wrong way.

Zeke moaned as she rolled past him.

I've been serving this community for over fifty years, making sure no one starves, and this is the fine thanks I get for my dedication.

No matter. She had friends back in England, friends who'd help her get established in a community that would appreciate her organizational skills. It didn't matter who had the blood franchise there—she could replace them and do better.

Sierra Escondida Police Department—A few minutes later

Tig switched on the emergency lights and siren, and then sped out of the police station parking lot. Jayden rode shotgun—literally. He held the shotgun across his lap—the business end pointed up and away from her—as he called Dr. Clarke. Once the doctor was dispatched, he phoned Liza next, and she agreed to meet at the guard shack.

When Tig reached the gate, she slammed on the brakes, put the police car in park, and jumped out. *Whooshing* over to Zeke, she checked him first.

"I'm okay, ma'am. Mighty painful but nothing vital."

That was a relief to hear. "Was it Olivia?"

"Yup. She did shoot me for sure. You'll have my testimony."

Good. On both counts. "Any idea of where she went?"

He moaned. "Bogus story about the refrigerators being out at the warehouse. Her car was loaded to the gills. My bet is she did a runner."

Liza arrived and pulled over to the curb, and Dr. Clarke parked behind her. He took over Zeke's care, and Tig headed back to her car. She didn't want to be there when the doctor took the bolt out.

Her phone rang. Ari. "What?"

"Olivia is southbound on the I-5. We caught her high-speed turn from the intersection cameras. Confirmed the license plate number to make sure it was her."

Tig refused to bite—she wouldn't question how he got access to Olivia's license plate number. Right now, the "how" didn't matter. Only the lead did.

"We're going to try to chase her down," Tig replied. "If you get anything more, call me."

I-5 Freeway—Ten minutes earlier

By the time Olivia hit the freeway, swerving a bit as she took the curving on-ramp, the dashboard clock read half past one in the morning. The sun would rise at seven-eighteen, but due to the late moonset, she'd be awake another hour after dawn.

Traffic was light as she headed south on the I-5. The surge of adrenaline kept her mind ticking. She might even reach the outskirts of Los Angeles before the sun forced her indoors.

Hmm. If they managed to stay on her arse until then, she could slip away in a suburban area moments before sunrise, invade a home, and take an hour to drain the mortals then sleep for the day. Or maybe she'd leave one alive to snack on before she hit the road again at sunset.

She didn't have to play by the treaty's rules anymore. A farewell tour of this country meant staying alive at any cost.

Truth be known, Tig had no way to track her, even now. The Hill didn't own a helicopter, and by the time the chief called for assistance from neighboring Mordida, Olivia would be lost among the mortal drivers, no way to spot her from above.

Would Tig even risk calling in mortals? Or did she know Olivia would drain them all rather than be captured?

In truth, she was off scot-free. She laughed at the term. Back in the day, a scot was a tax, and the term fit her circumstances. She was now free from the town's attempt to tax her livelihood by letting Leopold horn in on her business.

What a load of codswallop. It ground her gut that they'd let the *enemy* have such control of the Hill. The nutters. Not to mention all those unaffiliated vampires who had no right to exist. She'd fought in the war to make sure no new vampires were created, and still they slunk in through a loophole.

Utter shite, that was.

About thirty-five minutes into her drive—being careful not to exceed the speed limit—she saw a turnoff for a twenty-four-hour service station. Her gas gauge was low, and it'd be the perfect place to get ice for the cooler. She'd pay in cash to make sure she wasn't traced.

She took the dark off-ramp, slowing down, when her headlights caught something ahead of her. A flash of feathers and a large bird landed on the road.

An exceptionally large bird.

Olivia slammed on the brakes. But the feathered thing wasn't a bird after all. A human-like shape spread its wings in the middle of the off-ramp. She veered to avoid hitting it, not wanting to bash in her bonnet, needing the bloody car in one piece to escape.

With the heavy load in her boot, the car fishtailed, and she swung the steering wheel around the other way, catching her front right tire on the raised asphalt curbing.

The last thing she remembered was the car flipping, rolling her ass over teakettle into the ditch, and the airbag firing with a bang.

Briefly stunned, she shook her head to clear her mind and realized the car had landed right side up.

A damn good piece of fortune. Maybe she could pull the car back up the slope and onto the road.

She was trying to open the crushed door—not hard with vampire strength—when the winged creature returned, hovering over her side window.

Two giant white wings beat, stirring up dust. A flowing halter dress and long white hair blew around the creature in the night breeze.

An angel?

The creature raised one hand and fired a bright flash at the door. Sparks flew on contact.

What in the flippin' hell is that? A lightning bolt?

Am I hallucinating?

She tried again, and the door wouldn't budge.

"Bugger off," Olivia yelled at the thing.

The angel pointed at her. Then pointed at the ground. It didn't take long for Olivia to figure out the meaning, and a frisson ran up her back. The angel wanted her to *stay here*. It then waved its hands at the sky—one of which held what looked like a phone—and, with a little jump, flew off.

CHAPTER 69

NOT SO FAST

FREEWAY OFF-RAMP—MOMENTS LATER

Cerissa pumped her wings, gaining altitude, the crisp scent of low clouds exhilarating her. Using her true form left her feeling empowered, but also a little wary. The sound of a distant siren could be Tig. Appearing to Olivia as Lux to stop the murderer was one thing. But after the whole cougar-in-a-box accident, revealing her true form to Tig would get her in a boatload of trouble with the Protectors.

One hallucination Tig would dismiss. But two? Tig's tenacity would kick in, and she wouldn't let go until she determined what the strange winged creature was.

The farther up Cerissa flew, the better her vantage became, giving her a clear view of the freeway in both directions as the six lanes ribboned through the flat agricultural landscapes. The siren hadn't been Tig's. A northbound car with flashing lights sped in the opposite direction from which Tig should be coming.

It must be a California Highway Patrol car after a late-night speeder.

At the height she hovered, the cold night air whispered over her naked arms, goosebumps forming in response, and she refocused her vision on the distant traffic coming from the direction of Sierra Escondida. Two southbound cars raced toward her, lights blazing, but far enough away not to spot her. She watched for a few moments, and then it hit her. How would Tig guess which off-ramp to take? Olivia's car was in a ditch, not visible from the freeway.

Cerissa flashed back to her lab in the Enclave. She needed something, anything, to pique Tig's interest, to get her to take the same exit Olivia had. She rummaged through the lab supplies, not knowing what she expected to find. It wasn't like she had road flares hidden away here—no reason to have one in her lab, and no time to flash somewhere to buy one.

A bright light was all she needed. Anything that would grab Tig's attention. Christine's comment about Cerissa being a witch flickered in her mind. If only she could snap her fingers and make a roadside flare magically appear.

Wait. Magic. She'd worked with flash powder before, back before safety laws put the special effect out of reach of most magicians. Using her neural link to the lab's computer, she searched and found the recipe, then grabbed the chemicals, strontium nitrate and magnesium. Careful to ground herself so a spark didn't prematurely light the compound, her hand shaking, racing against time, *whooshing* around as fast as a vampire, she mixed the chemicals and rolled the flash compound in aluminum foil for easier ignition, creating three of them, and returned to the off-ramp.

Good. Olivia remained in her car.

Cerissa carefully touched down on the freeway shoulder a little ahead of the exit lane, laid each packet a foot apart, and bounced back into the sky. Now, all she had to do was hover and wait. Then the E-beam would be all the ignitor she needed to signal Tig.

Freeway off-ramp—Moments before

Olivia glanced at her watch. Damn the angel's eyes. It was after two in the morning. Did the angel expect her to stay here until sunrise and die? What did it want with her, and where in the bloody world did it come from?

A police siren sounded in the distance. Had someone seen the accident? Were they on their way to pull her out of this bloody ditch?

Or was Tig coming to arrest her?

No. It can't be.

Olivia grabbed the steering wheel, tore off the remnants of the airbag, and punched the ignition button. No sound. She rattled the wheel back and forth angrily. How would she get away if the car wouldn't even start?

Only one way out now. Olivia shut her eyes and tried to transform into a bat. Nothing. She bore down, willing her body to change, but it'd been over a century since she'd last flown.

Bollocks!

Waiting around wouldn't do at all. She'd have to run for it.

She wormed her way around to find Zeke's revolver on the passenger-side floor, stretching until her fingers finally wrapped around the barrel. She checked the cylinder; the gun was fully loaded. She punched her fist through the glass, which fractured into small mosaic pieces, peeled the windscreen back, and then boosted herself through the hole. She'd just crawled onto the bonnet when a bright light blinded her, a flash of something hot heating the metal near her hands.

The angel hovered overhead and fired lightning again, this time aimed up at the freeway behind her. She turned to figure out what the angel shot at. A bright flash of light and smoke followed each pulse.

Blimey. Tig won't miss that.

Using both hands, she gripped the revolver and fired. The angel blipped out of sight, returning a few seconds later. She fired again, and again the angel disappeared, only to reappear, but this time, the angel shot lightning, blasting the gun from her hands and scorching her fingers.

Her throat tightened as panic filled her. Then the angel shot more lightning at the car's bonnet, so Olivia scrambled back into the car to escape. Just as she slid into the driver's seat, the angel landed on the bonnet of the car, reached through the busted windscreen, and touched Olivia's forehead. A feeling of deep peace flooded her.

When she woke, the angel was gone, and a police car, with red and blue strobe lights flashing, was stopped on the off-ramp above her. Suddenly, a piercing white light pointed at her, smoke from the freeway blowing across them with the night breeze.

"Do not move." Tig's voice came amplified over a loudspeaker.

In a burst of panic, Olivia crawled out the windscreen's hole, gun in hand—four bullets left—and, ignoring the glass cutting her hands and knees, slid across the car's bonnet, landing in the mud and brambles. Maybe she could still run for it.

She glanced up, and this time she saw Tig, Jayden, and Liza form an arc surrounding her from above, their guns aimed at her, and no doubt filled with silver.

"Freeze," Tig yelled. "Olivia Paquin, you're under arrest for the murder of Winston Mason. Drop your gun. Now."

Olivia tossed the revolver away and plopped onto a large rock. She couldn't die here—she had to live to tell them what happened.

The angel's image continued to float in her mind's eye, the hypnotic sense of its touch lingering.

What Olivia had done would seem a trifle if only she could convince them a greater danger existed. The lightning the creature wielded was a power that could burn a vampire to ashes from a distance. With those powerful wings, it could sneak up on them and destroy everyone.

The treaty communities had to do something before it was too late. They had to know. She had to tell them.

Angels were *real*.

CHAPTER 70

TOUCHDOWN

RANCHO BAUTISTA DEL MURCIÉLAGO—A SHORT TIME LATER

Cerissa circled above the house, watching for Christine, and, not seeing her, landed lightly on the balls of her feet, the balcony shaking ever so slightly. She took in a deep, cleansing breath. To lift her wings and embrace the night air had left her calmly centered.

She'd finally fought for herself. Over the past week and a half, she'd gone the extra mile for Christine and for Henry. But herself? She'd deserted herself.

Ari had been right. Until Tig captured Olivia, the cloud would always be there, hanging overhead.

Now, her own good name would be restored.

The realization snaked its way through her: she didn't need more time with Fidelia—she needed to stand up for herself more often.

Revealing her true self to Olivia, signaling that judgment was headed the killer's way, had fortified her self-esteem. Besides, no one would believe an angel descended to stop Olivia, and no one would connect Olivia's delusional rantings with Cerissa.

She slid the balcony door open and tiptoed inside her room.

"And just where did you go?"

"Unray," she sang, her Lux mouth unable to make the English sounds for Henry. She morphed, returning to human form. "Toss me a robe, please. The night's cold."

"I can tell." His eyes flashed at her, focusing on her chest. "But it's against my best interests to cover up your loveliness."

She smirked at him, and he reached into the closet, grabbing the terrycloth white robe, which was warmer than her silk one.

"Thank you." She slipped on the fluffy goodness, pulled the belt tight around her waist, and slid her phone into the deep pocket.

"And what is in your other hand?"

"Oh, this?" She eyeballed the ceiling, trying to project an air of innocence.

"Yes, that."

"You've seen one before. It's a Lux high-energy weapon—an E-beam four point one, to be precise." She opened the dresser drawer and placed the E-beam among her underwear.

"Before you tell me why you're carrying a forbidden weapon, please explain why you aren't wearing your engagement ring?" The gold circlet with three diamonds sparkled in the palm of his hand. "I found it on your dresser."

She accepted the ring and slipped it on. "I was afraid of losing it. My Lux fingers are thinner, and it threatened to fall right off."

"I see."

Besides, had she worn it, Olivia would have recognized the magnificent ring, exposing Cerissa's true identity.

She crossed her arms. "But what are you doing in my room? Where's Christine?"

"No need to worry. She's with Evelina. The band is rehearsing tonight, and Evelina invited my child to listen to them play."

"I'm glad she's making friends."

"I'm grateful for the support. Evelina seems to understand what Christine is going through. That kind of empathy will go a long way toward healing Christine's soul."

"Good." Cerissa flopped onto the bed, the fatigue of morphing and flying catching up with her. "Come cuddle with me, and I'll tell you what happened."

Henry kicked off his shoes and knelt on the bed next to her, leaning over to kiss her gently. "So, what did my *angelito* do?"

She smiled at the new nickname. "I...convinced Olivia to turn herself in."

That skeptical eyebrow of his rose. "Indeed?"

"So we are now in the clear."

He stretched out on his side next to her, propping his head on his elbow. "When Tig and Jayden left abruptly, I assumed I was no longer a suspect."

"Tig made us promise not to tell, but now with Olivia in custody, I don't see the harm. If the chief speaks to you later tonight, act surprised."

"I will do my best."

She then told him the full story, including how she used the weapon. "The E-beam does a nice job of creating the illusion of lightning, and it ignited the chemicals to signal Tig."

Henry *tsked*. "Really, *querida*, that is not a risk you should have taken."

"Olivia will never guess the lightning was caused by a Lux weapon."

"That is not what I mean, and you know it. Showing her your true form will start rumors, and—"

"No one will believe her. It'll just make Olivia sound crazy."

He touched her jaw, lightly stroking along her throat, and down to the V of the bathrobe, headed for her breasts.

"Not now." She playfully slapped his hand away, then sat up, crossing her legs. They'd been busy nonstop since the council meeting, and she let out a sad little sigh, a precursor warning of what was to come. "We need to talk about something serious. What are we going to do?"

"About what? If Olivia's in custody—"

"About the council's decision. Leopold said he would move the lab to the Midwest if the council voted against the project. I can't leave you, but I'm committed to the Lux to complete the project and supplement the blood supply for the treaty communities."

He cocked his head to the side. "You won't have to leave me. I'll come with you."

"Henry, I can't ask you to abandon your home. And what about the winery?"

He rose and faced her, crossing his legs, their knees touching. "*Cariña*, I love you. Where you go, I'll go."

She shook her head. "You say that now, but it's not fair to you. Besides, you let yourself be flogged rather than leave this place. You're not making sense."

"I took a whipping so I wouldn't be *forced* out. With you, it's about love, and I love you more than I love the Hill." He took her hand, pressing his lips lightly against the skin by her engagement ring. "You're mine, and I'm not losing you now. If that means I must move for a while, I will. Nothing says we can't return later."

She squeezed his hand. "Oh, Henry."

"And we shouldn't give up so quickly. Leopold may have threatened to relocate the project to the Midwest, but let me speak with him. A six-month delay here would be better than starting from scratch in a new location where it might take a year or two to obtain approval to build. I'm sure if I spoke to him, he'd see reason."

Yeah, right. Given their history, she would bet on the *Titanic* to crush the iceberg before she would on Henry budging Leopold. "If anyone is convincing him, I will. He's my business partner. Besides, you two only recently mended your rift. I won't risk you two battling again."

"But if anyone should battle on your behalf, it should be me."

"I do like it when you fight for me."

"Knight in shining armor"—he gave a little bow—"at your service."

"And such a handsome knight he is."

"A very patient knight."

She laughed. "Ah yes, we were remiss last night, weren't we?"

"We were. Tell me, is it still too soon?"

"Too soon?" Then the light went on. "Oh! *Oh*. You want to try the handcuffs on me?"

"If you are willing..."

She leaned over and captured his lips, tickling them with her tongue until he opened to her. Melting against him, she let out a small moan. The thought of being at his mercy shot heat to her core.

"Well, since it's your turn to choose..." she said with a big grin.

Chapter 71

REHEARSAL

Rancho Bautista del Murciélago—Ninety minutes earlier

Christine breathed a sigh of relief. Once Tig emerged from the basement and abruptly left, it meant the blood tests had cleared her clients, so she phoned Evelina. They talked for a while, then Evelina begged off. She had to leave for band practice.

"Hey, why doncha come watch us?"

"You're sure?" Christine replied. "My being there won't disturb your bandmates?"

"Nah, they're used to having an audience. I'll swing by and pick you up on the way."

At the community center, a huge oak dance floor filled the area in front of the stage, with round tables scattered throughout the remainder of the room, their plastic tops naked of linens. Christine took a seat at one near the stage, turning the chair so she faced the five performers.

Wolfie and Evelina traded off as lead singers. Her advisor—as Christine had begun to think of Evelina—sang with extraordinary range. Her voice could handle everything from melodic pop to gritty grunge. The set they practiced ran the gambit of danceable music from the past thirty years.

Christine relaxed, letting the wall of sound wash over her, enjoying the clarity, hearing notes she hadn't for a few years.

Anytime her brain went charging to unwanted territory, she broke out her phone and played a quick ten-minute game. She didn't understand why, but something about the hand-eye coordination needed to play the game broke the obsessive thinking. Trusting Wolfie's advice and following the scientific research had helped her.

A little over two hours into practice, Zeke strode through the open doors. He came right to her, leaned over, and whispered, "Tig captured Olivia."

"That's great news," Christine whispered. "So Cerissa and Henry are completely exonerated?"

"Yup."

"Any accomplices?"

"Don't look like it. And there's no doubt Olivia did it. I mean, the eff'n bitch shot me—pardon my French."

"I don't understand."

"I was guardin' the gate, and Olivia shot me with a crossbow."

"Are you okay?"

"Hurt like a son of a gun." He put a hand over his stomach. "But Dr. Clarke took out the bolt and gave me a vampire blood donation to drink—mostly fixed me up, and by tomorrow night I'll be right as rain."

Christine touched where Zeke had pointed. He flinched, and she pulled back quickly.

So, not completely healed.

"I'm glad you're mostly okay. No one else hurt?"

"Nah. And I wouldn't have been shot except she got the jump on me—I didn't know she owned another crossbow. Turns out she'd plastered the spare behind a panel in her garage."

The band abruptly finished the song they'd been practicing. "Ah, if you two need the room," Wolfie said from the stage, "we could take a break."

"I'm sorry." Christine's face warmed. "We didn't intend to disturb practice. But good news: Olivia has been arrested for the mayor's murder."

Evelina gave a dramatic pose, the back of her hand against her forehead. "Uff da. Maybe everyone will get back to normal now."

"I hope so," Christine replied.

Should she volunteer her skills to defend Olivia? Setting aside the conflict-of-interest issues, she was the only attorney available, unless they brought someone in from outside the community to serve as Olivia's defense counsel for the trial.

That was assuming they held a trial—Christine still wasn't clear on how the Hill dealt with these things.

Zeke straightened. "You folks go ahead and practice. We'll sit and listen. Unless Christine would like to dance?"

He held out his hand. Really? What about his injury?

Evelina gave a coy smile and leaned over to Wolfie and whispered something. In four beats, the band started a slow love song.

Yeah, Evelina was playing matchmaker.

Christine stood and went into Zeke's arms. A nice feeling. Solid. Confident. But gentle, too. And he was an expert dancer, showing off his moves, turning her and then bringing her back against his chest.

At a hundred and sixty years old, she wasn't surprised he danced well.

What will he be like in bed?

Heat crawled up her throat and cheeks at the thought.

When the music came to an end, she stepped back and eyed him. She still couldn't believe someone who looked as young as him would want her.

He slipped an arm around her waist and walked her to her chair. There, he bowed to her and kissed her hand. Then, looking into her eyes, he closed the distance and kissed her deeply.

Her heart melted.

For a moment, she forgot they had an audience. For a moment, she forgot about being vampire. And for a moment, she even forgot about the pain of killing her best friend.

When hoots and hollers rose from the stage, she remembered where she was.

The corners of Zeke's lips cocked up. "What say we leave this gin joint and go back to my place? I guarantee my bed is a lot more comfortable than the back of my truck."

Though his words sounded confident, his eyes conveyed vulnerability, like he was afraid she'd say no as he waited for her answer.

Christine glanced over at the stage, where her advisor stood. "Go ahead and run along," Evelina said. "You don't need to stay for the whole rehearsal."

Christine nodded and whispered to Zeke, "That sounds like an invitation I can't refuse."

Chapter 72

Honey Mead

Sierra Escondida Police Department—Later that night

Tig closed the jail door behind her. Olivia had given a full confession, taking sole credit for the mayor's murder. Tig had tried to get her to hold off until an attorney arrived to protect her rights, but Olivia would hear none of it.

She'd attempted to barter for a lighter sentence in exchange for what she said was highly valuable information. When Tig asked what could possibly affect her sentencing, Olivia without hesitation said an angel had appeared to her, and "by golly"—as Olivia put it—warning them about the danger the angel presented certainly called for a lighter sentence.

Ha! That wasn't happening.

Tig video-recorded the whole thing. It would be up to the council to decide what to do with Olivia. Because if Tig guessed right, Olivia showed signs of dementia, the hallucination a clue she was turning revenant early. Strange, though, as the condition usually didn't begin until a vampire had lived a full millennium.

Or was there another explanation? Had Olivia suffered brain trauma when her car rolled? Would she be healed after her day sleep and repudiate the entire confession?

They'd wait and see.

Tomorrow night, Tig would have Dr. Clarke do a workup on the prisoner's condition. If she was turning revenant early, they'd need to write up her condition for *Living from Dusk to Dawn*.

And the reminder slightly worried Tig. She'd had her own hallucination when she saw a cougar instead of Cerissa in the cell's coffin. Was she experiencing an early sign? How long between the first sign and full-blown revenant?

She made a note in her personal log but didn't say anything to Jayden. She didn't want to worry him. The cougar could be nothing, just a glitch caused by stress, and even if the hallucination was an early symptom, it could be a very long time before she succumbed to the condition.

Notwithstanding Olivia's mental state, they did get an answer to one question—how Olivia found out the mayor would be outdoors and vulnerable. She'd followed him home after her meeting with him was over—the meeting Winston recorded—and then staked out his place, watching his patterns for two nights. She witnessed when the delivery service dropped off the bulbs and figured he'd be gardening sometime soon.

And Tig even got an answer to how Olivia found out about Cerissa's overnight stay in jail. A search of Olivia's phone revealed a text from Florence, gossiping about the incarceration of Henry's mate.

Tig glared at Florence and issued a final warning before tasking her to watch Olivia. "If you ever tell confidential police information to anyone without my permission again, I'll haul you before the council. You'll be lucky to get off with less stripes than they gave Henry."

Florence sat at the jail desk and kept her eyes focused on the video monitor watching the inmate. "Yeah, sure."

"You're lucky I don't charge you as an accessory after the fact."

"Hey, I said I wouldn't do it again."

Tig shook her head and strode off to her office. Maybe some of the new unaffiliated vampires would have police or military background. She would have to send a message to Rolf with the request.

Her phone rang. *Anne-Louise*. Crap. She'd almost forgotten the New York vampire was still on the Hill. She swiped accept and raised the phone to her ear.

"May I leave now? I assume you've completed your tests and I've been cleared?"

Tig took in a long breath. "You're free to go. We may need you to testify, but you can do so by videoconference."

"Fine. Who did it?"

Tig paused. Should she answer the question? By tomorrow night, everyone would hear Zeke had been stabbed and Olivia tried to escape. "Olivia Paquin is in our jail and has confessed."

Raucous laughter followed. "If you need an executioner, do not ask me. Feel free, however, to use the Butcher."

The call terminated. So Anne-Louise was one to hold a grudge. Good to know.

The final piece fell into place a few minutes later. Ynez called with the results of the metal tests. The silver in the crossbow's track matched the silver on the bolt they took out of the mayor's body. With Olivia's confession, Tig didn't really need the confirmation, but it was nice to know.

Finished with the case, she escorted Jayden back home. Once he was asleep, she grabbed what she needed from her home office and walked to Jose's Cantina. Leaning against the bar, she asked the bartender, "Do you have any mead?"

"We don't get much call for that. Let me check."

He disappeared into the back room, came out a moment later, and handed her the bottle. "Will this do?"

"Perfect," she said.

Made from honey, mead was the only liquor the Maasai drank.

He opened the sealed bottle and started to pour into a glass.

"Wait." She set the cattle-horn cup on the polished bar. She'd made the ritual cup herself, cutting an eight-inch piece of horn from the broadest section where the horn curved slightly, eliminated the point, hollowed it out, fashioned a base, and carved symbols into the sides. It could hold a pint, more or less. "Use this."

He looked surprised but poured. Hers wasn't the first odd request he'd probably gotten over the years.

"Thanks." She picked up the cup. "Put it on my tab, with the usual tip."

"Sure thing, Tig."

She carried the cup and walked the mile to the Hill Chapel, crossing Robles Road to where the cemetery lay.

The Maasai believed burying a dead body polluted the earth. Burial was reserved for the chief—the king, that was, not police chiefs.

And Winston Mason was the closest thing they'd had to a chief for fifty years.

Her people didn't have funeral traditions, no service for the dead, aside from rubbing the dead body with fat and leaving the corpse out for predators and scavengers to eat. If the animals ate them on the first night, the deceased was considered a good person. But if they didn't eat them by the second night, then the deceased was presumed to be bad.

To avoid the bad luck and dishonor of a relative left untouched, the family sacrificed an animal to rebalance and reset their luck.

She found the mayor's gravesite easily. A headstone already marked the freshly turned earth. An old oak tree shaded the spot. A nice place to rest.

But according to Maasai tradition, they'd never find out if he was a good or bad person. From what Tig knew of him, he was a bit of both.

She stood there, thinking back to the deaths she'd attended as a mortal, including her husband's. As one of the widows, she'd prepared mead for sharing among his age set. But it was considered bad luck to mention his name after death.

She'd come far enough that the old beliefs didn't hold as much power over her anymore. She held up the horn cup. "Here's to you, Winston. May the angel of death deliver you to a verdant garden where you may happily putter your way through eternity."

She took a sip from the cup. The mead tasted much better when she was mortal.

"You may enjoy this more than me." She then poured the rest of the liquor on the freshly turned dirt, took one more look at the night sky, and strolled back to Jose's Cantina.

As Tig walked, she wiped a tear from the corner of her eye. She was going to miss the old, pompous fool more than she'd expected.

Chapter 73

Moving to the Midwest

Rancho Bautista del Murciélago—The next day

As Cerissa worked during the day, she couldn't stop reliving their lovemaking from last night. What a night—she still couldn't believe how *inventive* Henry could be in bed.

She spent the day packing away all the plans and other documents she'd left scattered in the dining room. When three o'clock in the afternoon rolled around, she called New York, where the sun had set already, and explained everything to Leopold, including the council's rejection of the project.

"How dare they," he said with a snarl. "This is an outrage. My dear, pack and be prepared to move. I've found a new location close to the Michigan clan. They have guaranteed me the city will approve our development in sixty days if we place the lab within ten miles of clan headquarters."

"I'm not sure we can get new architectural plans drawn so quickly. Not to mention negotiating for the purchase of a new location."

"Of course we can. I won't let the Hill insult us this way. But I don't care if it takes twice as long, three times as long—I won't stand for the snub."

She wanted to say, *If you'd just take some time to cool off*, but figured the comment would go over badly. "I'll start making plans to travel to the clan's location and take a look at the real estate available."

"Do that."

She ended the call. When Henry woke at dusk, she told him. "Would you like to fly us to Michigan and check out the area? On Leopold's dime?"

His eyes lit up. "I would be honored. Oh, and Marcus is coming over in a few hours. He sent me a text. The council is meeting right now, and he wanted to talk with us afterward. They are making an official announcement to the community as to your innocence."

"That would be welcomed."

"And he offered to take Christine to the office so they could discuss Olivia's trial. Marcus assumed Christine will defend her."

Cerissa gaped at him. "Doesn't she have a conflict of interest, considering she represented me in the same matter?"

"I'm sure they will work out a waiver."

At nine o'clock, Marcus arrived alone. They all settled into the drawing room, Cerissa and Henry on the couch, Christine perched on the loveseat, and Marcus in one of the carved armchairs.

"I have news," Marcus began. "The council reopened your project's hearing."

Cerissa couldn't believe what she'd just heard and gave him a puzzled look. "I don't understand. What do you mean, the project hearing was reopened?"

"The council met and determined Olivia's duplicity tainted the original decision, in particular, her attempt to frame you. They declared the matter void *ab initio*—void from the beginning—and held a new hearing."

"Why didn't they invite me to the hearing?" Her initial shock had turned to anger, and she refused to stifle her newfound ability to stand up for herself. "It's my project. I should have been there."

Henry placed a restraining hand on her leg, like he thought she might jump up and pummel Marcus.

He wasn't far from the truth.

"No, you don't understand," Marcus said. "It means you don't have to re-file in six months. They voted to approve the development."

Henry squeezed her leg. "That is excellent news, isn't it, Cerissa?"

Cerissa squelched her anger and took a deep breath. "When may we begin construction?"

"As soon as your contractor pulls building permits. It's an easy matter of filling out the forms and paying the fee."

"I guess that is wonderful news."

"Indeed," Henry said. "Please thank the council for us."

"I will pass along your thanks." Marcus tugged at his mustache. "They also made a decision to award the blood franchise to you."

They *what*? "But I didn't apply—"

Marcus waved his hand. "We cannot wait. The deliveries must continue. Nicholas and I will work on getting the contracts put into your company's name."

"I thought only a Hill vampire was eligible to hold the franchise."

"Not always. And to avoid the problem created by Olivia's greed, the council decided to combine both the donor blood collection and the clone blood distribution under one franchise."

"Thank you, I'm grateful, but I don't know anything about running a distribution business—"

Henry squeezed her thigh again. "*Cariña*, do not say no. Rolf and I will help you. The process is not much different from distributing wines. And I'm sure Luis and his crew will be happy to resume donor blood deliveries if they will be working for you, so the transition should go smoothly."

With project approval and the franchise in hand, Leopold would be an idiot to say no. She felt certain she could convince him. Breaking ground here in the next month would be better than starting from scratch in a new location.

And the franchise grant was the sort of sweetener that would mollify her offended business partner.

"Now," Marcus began, "both approvals are dependent upon you and Leopold agreeing not to sue the town for what Olivia did when she was a member of the council."

Marcus set a blue-backed document on the coffee table entitled "Settlement Agreement."

Cerissa forced down the laugh threatening to escape. "My attorney will have to review the agreement." She waved it in Christine's direction. Her attorney got up and took the document. "And I'll have to speak with Leopold first, but in principle, I don't see a problem."

"Good." Marcus held out a box to her.

"What is this?"

"Gaea asked me to deliver a peace offering to you. She feels terrible about what happened at the chapel, and she wants to make amends."

Cerissa opened the box. A pound of her favorite chocolates, along with the diamond-encrusted heart Gaea had loaned her to wear at the engagement party. Between the earthquake, the court battle, turning Christine, and all that followed—it felt like a century had passed since the party instead of four weeks.

Cerissa gave a lopsided grin. Diamonds and chocolates. Gaea must have guessed how sentimental Cerissa would feel over the necklace. She opened the card attached to the box, letting Henry read the missive over her shoulder.

Dear Cerissa,

> Please accept my humble apologies for my behavior at the memorial service. That I was grieving for my first child is my only excuse.

Your friend eternally,
Gaea

Relief flooded Cerissa. What happened at the chapel had really hurt. She would call Gaea later to thank her and work on mending the break in their friendship.

Marcus then placed a long, thin velvet-covered box on the table. "Nicholas took care of getting your bracelet fixed today. Jayden wanted to do it himself, but he was too busy. With Olivia's confession, we don't need it as evidence."

She scooped up the box and popped open the lid, and tears blurred her vision. *Over. This is truly over.*

She strapped on the bracelet, joy welling in her chest, happy to have Henry's gift where it belonged. "Please thank both of them for me."

The gesture from Nicholas and Jayden warmed her heart.

It's so nice to have such great friends.

Marcus started to rise.

"Before you go," Henry said, gesturing for him to stay seated, "did the council decide what to do with Olivia? Do you still need Christine's assistance?"

"Well, apparently Olivia is as mad as a hatter. After Tig arrested her, she kept babbling about an angel landing on the road and how she swerved to miss the creature."

Henry's eyebrows rose. "Really?"

"And according to Olivia, the angel shot lightning from her hands."

Cerissa did her best not to smirk. "How strange. I wonder what caused Olivia's break with reality?"

Yes, she was gaslighting Olivia. And she didn't even feel bad about it. *Progress.*

"Dr. Clarke has examined her and thinks the act of killing the mayor put her over the edge. It seems she's in the early stage of going revenant, perhaps." Marcus picked up his briefcase and stood. "In any case, Olivia gave a full confession. She cleared you completely."

Christine *tsked*. "You should have waited until I spoke with her before taking her confession."

Marcus pumped the air with one hand. "We couldn't stop her. She thought the information would lighten her sentence. Tig told her no deal, but she still felt compelled to warn us that angels existed, that they presented some sort of existential threat, and that she had to do it right away."

"But an angel?" Henry said. "She didn't strike me as religious."

"Who knows?" Cerissa glanced at Henry and batted her eyelashes innocently. "A little late, but maybe Olivia finally had her road to Damascus moment, even if she didn't understand it."

Rancho Bautista del Murciélago—Ten minutes later

Henry still couldn't believe how everything worked out. Marcus left with Christine in tow, Cerissa went to her bedroom to work on her laptop—yes, he really needed to clear out storage from the room next to his and create a home office for her—and he entered his own office and eased into the desk chair to answer email.

Cerissa was right. The last ten days had been chaos. He never wanted to repeat them. The memory of the flogging waned, but would flash through his mind occasionally, causing him to shudder. He knew not to focus on the experience, to let it go like releasing a captured bird so the pain and fear could fly to the heavens.

A glut of email filled his inbox, and two hours later he was halfway through them when he frowned. A message arrived from the delivery service the Hill used—the service specialized in transportation of large items. He hadn't ordered anything. Had the scheduler made a mistake?

Opening the email, he stared at the message, dumbstruck. Four full-sized beds, including mattresses with frames, were scheduled for delivery tomorrow evening. He hit print, grabbed the sheet, and stormed off to find Cerissa in her bedroom. He knocked a little too menacingly on the door when he arrived.

She jumped in her seat. "Henry!"

He strode over and shoved the printed email at her. "What is the meaning of this?"

She scanned the page. "Each day, you sleep in one of your six crypts. I ordered beds for four of them. Seemed like a good compromise. Those cots you have are terribly uncomfortable."

"I do not mind them."

"But I do."

He scowled. "You are not sleeping with me during the day."

She leaned back in her chair, her emerald eyes filled with mirth. "Not every day; our sleep patterns don't align well. But there are some mornings when you go to sleep at sunrise, and the early moonrise wakes you at noon. That timing would work for me. And if we get the daylight bracelet perfected, maybe we can adjust our sleeping hours to match more often."

"Cerissa, I told you already, it's not safe to sleep together."

She smirked at him. "You're having a short-term memory problem. Maybe you should make an appointment with Dr. Clarke."

"Cerissa," he said with a low growl.

"Nothing happened when I napped with you the afternoon of the earthquake aftershock, and nothing happened when you slept next to me in *my* bed while you were...injured." She pointed at the king-sized bed in the room.

"But I attacked you when you entered—"

He would never forget coming awake, *whooshing* her across the room, and plowing her into the bare cement blocks that formed his basement walls. A few weeks back, after the earthquake, she entered his crypt to leave him a note, and he'd felt her fear through the crystal and simply reacted.

"Hold up right there. You *tried* to attack me"—she wagged her index finger—"one time, when I was upset about Agathe's summons. You didn't hurt me. You stopped. The crystal protected both of us."

He refused to agree with her and pointed at the email. "Why didn't you speak with me first?"

She crossed her arms. "Just like you spoke with me before negotiating a deal to be flogged? You knew what the mayor planned and gave Rolf a fallback position without telling me. And don't say that was different."

But it was different. At least to him, it was. Still, he suspected he wasn't going to win that point. "Why four mattresses?"

"You like to choose your crypt at random. With Christine here, I figured we only need mattresses for four."

He scowled. "You will make arrangements to return them."

"Because you'd prefer king-sized ones, perhaps?" she asked, batting her lovely, long eyelashes at him.

No, flirting wouldn't work for her this time. "Because I prefer none."

"Henry, did you ever wonder why I went after Olivia?"

He tucked his chin back, puzzled by the change of topic. "What does Olivia have to do with—"

"I finally realized I don't stand up for myself enough. I can save other people, but when it comes to saving myself, I'm not as good at speaking up. And the only way I'm going to get better is through practice."

He pursed his lips. Now she was fighting unfairly. "So ordering four mattresses for my crypts—without asking me—is your way of standing up for yourself?"

"In a way, yes." She gracefully stood and faced him. "Maybe I should have mentioned the purchase to you first."

"Perhaps you should have."

"And I ordered the full-sized ones because your crypts aren't large enough for a queen-sized mattress. With your long legs a larger bed would be better, but the interior measurements, well, a bigger bed wouldn't fit."

"Very considerate of you."

"Quique—I love you. But contrary to your pronouncement the other day, you are not right *all* the time."

How could he resist those eyes? They saw into the depths of his dark soul, and she loved him anyway.

Sometimes, he had to resign himself gracefully to his fate. Having a mate, a fiancée as unique as her, meant letting the walls he'd erected crumble. She knew her limits and didn't need his fears to protect her. She could take care of herself quite admirably on her own, as she'd demonstrated on more than one occasion, even if she believed she needed more practice.

He captured her lips before she could say anything further, wrapping his arms around her and pulling her close. He sighed into the kiss as her lips parted, and he sought out her depths, losing himself to her.

When they broke, he planted a kiss on her forehead. "Fine. The beds may come."

Her golden smile was all the reward he needed.

A Note from Jenna

Thank you for reading *Dark Wine at the Grave*. I hope you enjoyed it! Cerissa and Henry's journey continues, along with the adventures of Tig and Jayden and all the residents of Sierra Escondida, in Book Eight of the Hill Vampire series, *Dark Wine at Halloween*.

Here's a quick tease:

> After Henry and Cerissa discover a two-day-old vampire in the last place they expect to find one—a Halloween funhouse—they have no choice but to hand him over to the town council, who will decide whether he lives or dies.
>
> With dead bodies stacking up in a neighboring city, Henry and Cerissa must pull together to help the teen accept his situation and recover his memory, so they can identify and stop the crazed vampire who turned the teen—before he or she kills another mortal.
>
> If they don't, the killer's actions might reveal to mortal police the wicked truth: *vampires really do exist...*

Want to be among the first to receive updates on new releases, along with special announcements, exclusive excerpts, and other free fun stuff? Join Jenna Barwin's VIP Readers at jennabarwin.com.

Hate newsletters? Then follow me on BookBub:
https://www.bookbub.com/authors/jenna-barwin

And subscribe to author alerts to receive a notice when *Halloween* is released. (BookBub won't send an alert unless you subscribe to "author alerts"—you may want to confirm you're subscribed.)
Happy reading!
Jenna Barwin

P.S. To an author, reviews are better than dark wine!

Acknowledgements and Dedications

To my husband Eric—thank you for all you do. I couldn't write as much as I do without you. Love you!

To my friend Bill Taylor, who, just like Patrick, asked whether the world needed another vampire novel—to which I strongly responded in the affirmative. He passed away last year. Bill, even if you didn't like vampires, you will be missed.

To Ellen Keigh, Sharon Bonin Pratt, and Caitlyn O'Leary—thank you for your gentle suggestions and encouragement. Always appreciated!

To my editing team—it takes a team to polish a story and ready it for readers. Katrina, Trenda, and Arran—you are all fantastic! You push me to make the story better, and I sincerely appreciate it. Any errors in grammar, clarity, or plot are mine, not theirs. Their full names are:

- Katrina Diaz-Arnold, Refine Editing, LLC
- Trenda K. Lundin, It's Your Story Content Editing
- Arran McNicol, Editing720

And thank you to my cover designer, Christian Bentulan with Covers by Christian, who took my rough draft ideas and picked a winner. As always, he did an outstanding job on the cover design.

There are many other wonderful people who have helped me improve my writing, and also advised me on tackling the business of being a writer. The generosity of other writers, who have freely shared their expertise, is greatly appreciated. Thank you everyone, for your support and guidance!

Made in United States
Orlando, FL
21 March 2024